MASS PRIMARY

(Dark Landing Series, Book 2)

ROBIN PRAYTOR

A POST-TO-PRINT PUBLISHERS BOOK
PHOENIX

MASS PRIMARY

Published by Post-To-Print Publishers, LLC, Phoenix
First Edition: May, 2018

ISBN 978-0-9984685-2-5 (e-book)
ISBN 978-0-9984685-3-2 (trade paperback)

To my husband for his
enduring love and support.

AUTHOR NOTE

MASS PRIMARY, the second book in the Dark Landing series, takes place approximately six months after the end of book one, TRANSMUTED. A glossary of characters and organizations introduced in book one appears at the end of this book for the convenience of new and returning readers.

PROLOGUE

Earth Date 2519
Screamer Cell
The edge of Zeta Quadrant
The Known Universe

Hoping to slow the nanoid devices devouring him, Ekis ran multiple diagnostic routines in concurrent loops. His structural body was gone, only cells remained, and precious few of those. *The devices* would never tire. When the last biological cell transmuted, the devices, their objective achieved, would disintegrate and Ekis would cease to be.

The stars visible through the observation window were so distant, he could perceive no sense of movement or change. When they had ejected the airlock from Dark Landing, he'd watched the station grow smaller and smaller until even his imagination could no longer sustain its image.

His thoughts drifted, and his concentration lapsed. *What point to continue?* In answer to his question, the airlock jolted as if it had bumped into something. *Impossible!* One did not *bump* into something in space. One smashed into it, or it smashed into you.

1 CARRY ON

E. D. 2519
Dark Landing Station
Zeta Quadrant
Known Universe

"So, what do you think?" Curtis asked, eager for Dr. Tammy Jameson's opinion of the new hire. They sat side by side in the executive mess, studying the unsmiling image of Austen Hargreaves on the monitor set into the table's surface. To Curtis, she resembled a winter elf in a graphic novel he'd read. Long platinum-blonde hair framed pale, pixie-like features. Matching brows and lashes were mere suggestions, and her eyes shone the lightest blue he'd ever seen. *Like a summer sky*—if memory served him. It had been years since he'd seen *any* sky. Somehow those eyes projected an enthusiasm and energy disconcerting in a static image. He could see how some men might find her attractive. To him, she just looked scary.

Doc scanned CoachStop Management's file on the incoming chief of administration. "She's young—twenty-five—but you're what? Only twenty-eight? You're both whippersnappers. I'm the dinosaur." She glanced to one side, frowning as if searching for a memory, and then sighed and continued. "She earned her space safety degree at nineteen. So, smart too. What are you worried about? You and I get along, don't we? Most of the time."

"Yeah, but you understand me," Curtis said, his forehead furrowed in concern. "You're used to me. And our jobs don't overlap. Security and administration must work close together. . . collaborate even."

He was finding his way as chief of security on Dark Landing. Drew Cutter, his predecessor, had disappeared from the space station only six months earlier. He'd tidied up his office and left notes for the other two chiefs but told no one where he went or why he left. Curtis suspected that Doc Jameson stayed in touch with Drew — not that it mattered.

"Poor Curtis," Doc said, making a pouty face. "Is it too much of a struggle to be personable?"

"I can be personable."

"I'm certain you can — *when* you want to. She comes in tomorrow on the *Krasnikov*? What time?"

"Ten hundred hours. I thought we'd meet up dockside and show her to her quarters, give her an hour to settle in, and then go to lunch and on a station tour. We can drop her off at the admin offices last."

"Sounds good. Look, the company takes pains to match chiefs for their compatibility. I'm sure we'll all get along fine."

Curtis remained unconvinced. He'd inherited his position, not been profiled for it. Except for medical — outside his control — he ran Dark Landing. His day and night shift commanders, along with Nikko, Curtis's assistant, oversaw the bulk of the security duties. That left Curtis free to oversee supply and maintenance, and the odd jobs that fell under the administration umbrella... like pigeons.

CoachStop Management, contracted by the co-ops to operate their remote outposts in Zeta Quadrant, should be happy to save script by running the station with two chiefs instead of the customary three. A new chief coming in now might muck up the works for Curtis's side interests. *Muck!* He winced, remembering the other slated arrival.

"It gets worse," he said. "Day after tomorrow, we meet our new *Muck* representative, Victoria Windsor — another Bahdaneian." The Bahdane language consisted of non-syllabic hums impossible for other races to speak. In consideration, they chose pronounceable pseudonyms for each race with which they interacted. Expert linguists, Bahdaneians were favored by the Multi-World Coalition

4

for Travel and Trade—more often referred to as "MCTT" or the diminutive "*Muck.*"

Curtis's comm implant toned for the second time in twenty minutes. He tapped the raised patch of skin behind his left earlobe to acknowledge the appointment reminder and then ignored it.

Doc sighed. "*Muck* is one problem I don't have to deal with. I need to return to med-lab. We'll meet up dockside in the morning to greet our new chief. For the record, Curtis, *no one* understands you."

After Doc Jameson left, Curtis grabbed another coffee and sat back down. He wanted the Hargreaves woman to have no doubts about who was in charge. As he stewed over her unwelcome arrival, his comm toned yet another reminder of his meeting with the Dark Landing Audubon Society. Ten minutes late. *Why is there never a life-threatening emergency when you need one?* And he'd forgotten to ask Doc about pigeon diseases.

~ ~ ∞ ~ ~

Curtis heard riled voices before he rounded the bulkhead to face a large group of station citizens carrying "Save Preston" signs and marching around the statue of the late Travis Barnes. The statue stood on a pedestal in the center of the bazaar. A good likeness of Travis and posed in an extravehicular mobility unit with the helmet tucked under one arm, he looked heroic. Barnes had sacrificed his life to save the Known Universe from invading Diaks.

A pigeon perched on the statue's head, and the statue's shoulders were frosted with pigeon crap.

"It's about time!" The leader stepped forward, scowling at Curtis's tardiness.

Curtis strained to recall his name and then gave up—*who cares?* Two live traps set by security the day before lay stacked behind the man, tripped and harmless.

"You know that's a misdemeanor," Curtis nodded toward the traps. "The air handlers can't process pigeon dust and feathers. They're vermin and they carry a shitload of diseases."

"Bull! The scrubbers can handle the pollution from one little pigeon, or we'd all be dead by now."

"You tell 'em, Darryl," someone from the crowd yelled.

Darryl nodded and continued. "The only reason you want to do away with Preston is because you're embarrassed that he got past the environmental scanners."

He'd nailed it. The bird appeared in the bazaar one morning from nowhere. The technicians swore there was no way it got past their scanners. But here it perched. Soon after its arrival, more serious events pushed ridding the station of the unwelcome guest to the bottom of a long list. The delay provided the residents with time to become attached to the airborne rat, and to start a movement to protect it.

"We're not killing it, we're sending it to a better home—a pigeon farm where it can fly free," Curtis said, his sarcasm wasted on Darryl.

Encouraged by his cohorts, Darryl persisted. "No one believes that. There's no good reason we can't keep it here. It's not hurtin' anybody, and you're a little pissant."

"Yeah, you're nothing but a sneaping, swag-bellied pissant." The last came from a woman standing in the back of the crowd. A mantle of white-blonde hair intensified the chill of icy blue eyes, daring him to rebuke her.

Everyone except Curtis laughed, their moods changing in an instant from challenging to good-humored. The level of noise rose as members of the crowd repeated the insult and applauded its author.

Curtis raised his arms and patted the air for them to quiet. "Okay, okay, everyone calm down. Marching and yelling abuses won't solve anything. Darryl, I'll have my office arrange a meeting between you and our new chief of administration." He cast the woman a snide look, cracking the knuckles of one hand except for the middle finger. "It's her responsibility anyway, and she can make the final decision. In the meantime, the pigeon can continue shitting on Travis Barnes—the man who saved *all* your asses. Break it up."

The group broke, heading in different directions, congratulating one another on their temporary win. Only the woman remained. Holding a satchel and wearing a smirk, she leaned casually against the effigy.

2 SAR MODE

On the command station, Mass Primary, Sar Mode luxuriated in her human, flexing his muscles and the digits at the end of each long appendage. He'd served her well. She'd once judged the race to be weak-minded and soft but reversed her opinion after testing. Upon closer examination, humans proved ideally suited as Diak hosts to an extent well beyond other races. Despite her initial mischaracterization, she found the human species the most astonishing of the hundreds previously encountered. She marveled at the elegance and simplicity of their external design: efficient, agile, adaptable, and even graceful. More importantly, on a cellular level they proved surprisingly complex. Their memories were exquisite--and humans held a secret. A secret she must guard for her scheme to see fruition.

She'd planned well for this moment, not knowing when or in what form it would take. The Diak sought survival at all costs — it was their *purpose*. But that purpose lacked an essential component. Each Diak felt it, but none could identify it. And so, it remained unspoken. But with all Diak, this illusive component hung suspended on an invisible thread at the edge of awareness. Easily forgotten but for a turn of the head and a fleeting glimpse from the corner of an eye (or whatever visual appendage the host sported, if any). It appeared and then vanished, only to be found again, then again, and again.

Humans proved the catalyst to bring the missing element from the shadows into the light of perception. Minute kernels of unsatisfied expectation carried over the centuries had finally bloomed: *Life flourished beyond mere survival.* A dictum lost to her race long ago.

Sar Mode disrobed to study her human in better detail. A male, its reproductive organs hung unassuming and supple at the confluence of the being's trunk and lower extremities. She'd scrutinized those human memories that demonstrated multiple uses for the organs, many of which appeared to end in an element of pain. Certain questions remained unanswered about the species, but further experiments must wait.

Soon I will have all the time in the universe.

One of the many advantages of a human host proved to be its longevity. Humans lasted longer than other host species, though short of their natural life expectancy. The race to slow or stop the rate at which devices transmuted biological cells would soon be lost. By her own edict, issued after her first sampling, Diak were forbidden to take human hosts. No one could see her as such other than her personal attendants, who were ignorant of Diak motivations and the politics of the Spread.

The council awaited her.

A Fahdeen glared from its cage with large yellow eyes. *Such an angry being.* Though she cared little, Sar Mode might soon learn what made the Fahdeen so angry. The willowy Pothlill who'd delivered the disagreeable little creature stood motionless in its corner, awaiting further orders. Sar Mode nodded in the direction of the Pothlill.

Her human form slowly collapsed as a silvery strand of nanoids emerged from its body. The strand flowed effortlessly across the deck toward the Fahdeen's cage, as if transported on thousands of miniature ball-bearings. The closer the silver strand came, the larger the Fahdeen's eyes grew in contrast with its diminutive body. Rarely topping five feet and reedy thin, the Fahdeen little resembled their distant cousins, the Bahdane. Covered in long, permanently tangled red hair instead of the Bahdane's short, glossy fur, and with rat-like snouts and ever-visible gnashing teeth, only their dangling, spindly ears hinted at the shared ancestry. Sar Mode's psyche cringed in virtual disgust when the silver strand came in contact with the Fahdeen body.

The Pothlill, lacking appendages but for one tentacle, its length equaling the alien's height, glided gracefully toward the human remains on millions of cilia. It wrapped its tentacle around the discarded host and dragged it from the compartment. A second Pothlill, indistinguishable from the first, entered to take its post.

Now *inside* the cage, Sar Mode issued the verbal command to unlock it and stepped back into her quarters. She would remain in this body as long as necessary. *But it is repulsive.* Needing solace, she flicked through her database of memories to a favorite and replayed it in the time left before the meeting.

~ ~ ∞ ~ ~

The council members had long pestered Sar Mode for shorter respites between invasions to meet ever-escalating turn cycles. To use a vulgarism she'd learned from her previous host, *they'd fucked themselves. . .* again.

Standing before them now, she noted none in the room occupied the same host race. The least of them, perhaps compensating for his minority position on the council, sported a Bahdane. The Spread had only recently deciphered the Bahdane language, and they had quickly become favored hosts due to their large size and attendant number of cells. Its bulk commanded a space at the council table normally allotted for two beings. But the chairman chose to inhabit the body of a slug; the name of its race long forgotten by Sar Mode. *How odd.*

While the five argued over moving up the invasion deadline, she pondered the fate of the Diak race, deadline or no. Diak engineers worked without relief to inhibit the turn process. Often until their host bodies dropped from exhaustion.

Messages received from two settled colonies included petitions to rejoin the Spread, their need for hosts outpacing the conquered species' breeding cycles. Many colonies, some already extinct, found themselves forced to transfer to younger and younger hosts well before they reached reproductive maturity. The same fate would befall all colonies eventually: lost to the near exponential leaps in efficiency of their devices. Hosts that once continued for many thousand orbits now lasted a few hundred, and soon, too soon, would complete the turning after only a few dozen.

What to do? The council wanted to know. It was too late to adopt her proposal made hundreds of rotations earlier. Dismissed out-of-hand as "horrific" and "unthinkable," the suggestion that the population of Diak should be systematically reduced by half, thereby extending their inventory of hosts and the race's survival time in the hope of an engineering breakthrough, caused a political storm. A storm she'd barely survived.

Sar Mode, as the appointed principal tasked with re-provisioning the Mass, must meet their ever greater demands. *Can I alone foretell the inevitable?* No, the Council of Superiors saw; they refused to *accept*. She set the council's short sidedness aside.

From the top of the conference table instead of seated behind it, its host body depositing a sticky residue as it wriggled about, the council head spoke. "The wormhole will soon be stabilized. Only a few orbits remain. Our brethren grow restless. They wait on the colony ships to complete the journeys to their new homes. They are unaware how quickly the host reserves are dwindling. The armada must relaunch its attack against the five aligned planets in this Known Universe, as you say they call their collective. Obviously, their knowledge of the universe is limited."

Sar Mode's personal goal contradicted that expressed by the council. She must stall them a little longer. "Certainly. We are as eager as each of you for the invasion to commence. We are refining the specifics of our strategy now. To conduct separate but simultaneous attacks against five planets and still preserve as many alien lives as possible requires precision timing."

"You speak of 'we' and 'our.' It is only you, Sar Mode. And you have failed us once," the chairman said, his threat thinly veiled.

The other council members murmured, grunted, and hummed their agreement, depending upon their individual forms. The threat appeared unanimous.

Sar Mode bowed low in submission and backed slowly from the chamber. There was a time she would have joyfully shared her discovery about the humans with the council. No longer. Certain the final report from her engineers would confirm continuing the Diak Spread to be futile, the humans were her salvation and hers alone. She fondled the amulet that hung about her neck. Her fingers caressed the inscription engraved in a long-abandoned Diak calligraphy: *We will not die today.*

3 APPARITION

When the last member of the Audubon Society disappeared, Curtis pointed at the grinning woman leaning against Travis Barnes' statue. "*You!* Come with me." He turned and headed toward the transport conveyer without checking to see if she followed.

Neither one said anything as they entered the compartment. She appeared to study the lighted map on the back of the conveyer door. The pulsing green dot moved in sync along their route. Curtis's chuckle disrupted the silence. The chuckle turned to a laugh. Then he laughed harder, wiping his eyes.

"Sneap, sneaping. . . *what*? Sneaping swag-*balled*. . . did you really say *swag-balled*?" He bent forward, clutching his side, and snorted.

She laughed along with him now. "Not balled, *bellied*, swag-*bellied*."

That sent him into further spasms. She tried to say something more but managed only to spit down her shirtfront. With a choked half-scream, she crossed her arms over her stomach.

When the door opened at Security HQ, Kyle Drubber, Curtis's dayshift commander, stood framed in the doorway staring at the two of them. This propelled them into further convulsions. Curtis gasped for air, giving Kyle a weak wave. A signal for help, or to assure him they were okay? Kyle would never know. The door closed once more, leaving him standing openmouthed.

When the conveyer stopped on the mezzanine, Curtis led her to Number 42, the mezzanine tavern. His breathing, and his disposition, now approached normal. Rarely one to smile, Curtis couldn't recall the last time he'd laughed out loud. The scene as much as her absurd insult prompted his unnatural outburst. He stood on a deep space trading station, addressing an unruly group who'd formed an Audubon Society chapter to protect one fucking pigeon. And this *apparition*—and his new co-chief—made such a bizarre slur.

"What's your drink?" he asked in a curt tone. He didn't want her to misconstrue his laughter as congeniality.

"Whatever's on tap," Hargreaves said.

They found seats toward the back, and he entered their drink orders. Earth Space Force personnel filled the bar. Temporarily stationed on Spud, the asteroid anchoring Dark Landing, the battalion would eventually move to the new joint military station being built in the Zeta Quadrant. On a construction fast-track, the new station would accommodate combat battalions from each of the five Alliance planets.

Curtis extended his hand across the table. "I'm Curtis Walker, Chief of Security. . . in charge here." Back to his unsociable self, he gave her a fish-eyed stare meant to suggest, correctly, what he'd left unstated: I am *not* glad to meet you.

"Austen Hargreaves, please call me Austen. Good to meet you." She shook his hand with a firm grip, her smile open and warm.

His eyes narrowed. "You weren't expected until tomorrow."

"I prefer the unexpected." She winked.

Curtis failed to understand her inference, but he winked back anyway. "I'll make a note of that." *Is she flirting with me*? He dismissed the thought. Her early arrival might work to his advantage. "When we finish our drinks, I'll show you to your quarters and take you to med-lab to meet Doc Jameson. My day commander, Kyle Drubber, the guy standing in the conveyer door with his mouth open, can give you a station tour tomorrow."

By palming her off on Kyle, he could avoid schlepping her around the station himself, and it would establish her lesser command standing. Dark Landing fell under the triumvirate rule of its chiefs of security, administration, and medical, but security took the lead.

"Thanks, I'm looking forward to meeting Dr. Jameson. But I've been here several hours now, and I poked around a bit on my own. I guess by tomorrow I'll have full access?"

Curtis nodded and added "sneaky" and "unpredictable" to her list of traits. "Yep, we can go to HQ and make your arrival official before heading to med-lab, if you want."

"I do want. By the way, how *did* that pigeon get past the environmental scanners?"

"Well, that's your problem now," he said, with an air of smug authority.

"At least tell me which came first, the pigeon or the statue?"

A rhetorical question, Curtis added, "must have the last word," to his list.

~ ~ ∞ ~ ~

Two days later, Austen welcomed Victoria Windsor, the new *Muck* enforcement officer for Zeta Quadrant. The Multi-World Coalition for Travel and Trade, formed by the Planetary Alliance to enact and enforce travel and trade regulations throughout Alliance space, also served as the off-world police force for each of the five allied planets.

After a brief introductory meeting with the three chiefs, Austen offered to show Windsor the docks and warehouse levels. They'd scheduled a meeting later in the day for Windsor's first audit of traffic records and the collection of MCTT regulatory fees. Chief Walker and Dr. Jameson showed no interest in tagging along on the tour.

Pleased at how effortlessly she'd slipped into the chief of administration position, Austen suspected her co-chiefs could give a pigeon-livered bull's pizzle about how she did her job, as long as she did it. Walker had exerted minimal effort to conceal his annoyance at her arrival. But they behaved as expected, based on her review of their psych evaluations. Jameson proved self-involved, and Walker habitually annoyed.

After inspecting the two docking sub-levels, she escorted the *Muck* enforcement officer to the warehouses. At late morning, those levels were hectic and noisy. No one would question them moving away from the bustle to speak in private.

Austen entered her access code and palmed the conveyer panel. The warehouse levels were only open to station employees. She'd briefly interned on Deep Light station. Owned by the same co-op, all trade stations in Zeta Quadrant followed one blueprint.

She tapped her implant and let her warehouse manager know they were on their way. He greeted them as they exited the conveyer. Austen made a show of trying to speak above the din, and the manager took her hint. He led them to his sound-proofed office and left, looking grateful to be excluded from the discussion.

When the office hatch closed, Windsor asked in unaccented English, "Did I see an Earth bird in the bazaar?" A series of soft, pleasurable hums underscored her question. Should anyone who spoke Bahdane be present, the hums represented a translation of the English words into the native Bahdane language. Fluted tongues and four active vocal cords allowed Bahdaneians to speak two languages simultaneously, as long as one was Bahdane.

Austen laughed. "How the pigeon got there and what to do about it is my first official undertaking as chief of administration."

The Bahdane's snout twitched, and her whiskers ruffled in a smile. Covered in black, glossy fur with long drooping ears that brushed their shoulders, Bahdaneians, though larger in stature than humans, appeared soft and cuddly at first sight. Their usually stern demeanor quickly dispelled such notions.

Austen opened the discussion. "From what I've seen so far, frequent communications between the two of us won't be flagged as unusual. It's normal for us to be chatting, especially since we're both new to our jobs. We should develop a loose code—nothing sophisticated. Curtis Walker's a little paranoid and might snoop for a while, but his attention span is non-existent."

"Upon review of his file, I agree with your assessment. I will report weekly to our contact at the Earth Technology Oversight Commission and relay the ETOC's orders back to you. Do you expect difficulties interacting with the target?"

"None," Austen said. "We've already established a cordial relationship. It won't be hard to cultivate."

"Good. Then we should complete our tour and proceed to my audit meeting." Windsor rose from the chair behind the warehouse manager's desk, signaling the end of their assignation.

"How about lunch?" Austen asked.

The Bahdaneian's snout wrinkled. "I do not wish to offend, but I'll wait and dine on my ship. Earth food does not digest well, and the results of your race's attempts to prepare Bahdane cuisine have proven. . . disappointing."

Upon the completion of the records audit, Victoria Windsor departed the station. Just late afternoon, Austen swung by the bazaar to check the traps. She'd met with the leader of the Audubon Society the day after she arrived and agreed the pigeon could stay if Doc Jameson declared it germ and pest free. Walker hadn't exaggerated. Pigeons carried a butt-load of diseases.

Preston the pigeon fluttered in one of the traps. He tipped his head and gave her the evil eye. "Gotcha — you dull-brained measle." She picked up the cage and proceeded to med-lab, ignoring the nasty looks from passersby.

4 CARRIER PIGEON

Doc Jameson read Myra's message a second time. Her roommate throughout their residencies and best friend, Myra held an executive position with the Global Center for Disease Control at their Johannesburg headquarters. Her position at the GCDC afforded her unrestricted access to the criminal databases of Earth's governing agencies and thousands of local enforcement jurisdictions.

Myra's research, at Doc's prompting, into the possible whereabouts of Earth Governor Eleanor Fitzwilliam-Bennett wouldn't be questioned. The governor conspired with the invading Diak to spread their nanoid virus throughout the Alliance. If even a remote possibility existed that Fitzwilliam-Bennett might still be alive, the GCDC would want to know. And Myra had no reason to question Doc's interest, since the conspirators had coordinated their scheme to aid the Diak invasion from Dark Landing. The late Martin Fitzwilliam was the governor's brother, and he'd been her co-conspirator. He'd held the position of chief of administration on the station during the Diak threat.

Myra's latest report confirmed her earlier ones: No clues were found leading to the governor's whereabouts, and officials had given up looking for her. Most believed she'd crawled into a hole and hid to escape authorities, either on Earth or some off-world outpost, and she'd died along with the other infected victims. Tammy never wholly accepted that the governor had died, but though a fair detective at diagnosing rare diseases, she had no clue where to look for her. Perhaps she was chasing mythical Camdu sprites, but she clung to her reasons for believing Fitzwilliam-Bennett might still be alive.

No proof existed that the governor was ever infected with the alien nanoids in the first place. She'd never been scanned. Known and unknown nanoid carriers literally exploded when Travis Barnes closed the Diak wormhole into Alliance space, initiating the loss of transmissions. More than 800,000 died, and of those, only five hundred humans and aliens remained unaccounted for. Not all those missing were assumed dead as a result of nanoid contamination, but certainly most of them had met that fate. Fitzwilliam-Bennett counted among the missing humans.

Tammy wanted the nanoids, not the governor. But the nanoids disintegrated outside their live host. Even if the governor was alive and uninfected (the most likely scenario), to continue searching for her wasn't unreasonable. She might have valuable information. And, if she'd been infected, was it possible for the Diak to single out and spare one individual from the thousands who perished? Why would they? What further service would the governor be to them? The odds were not good, but the governor was Doc's only hope of finding a residual nanoid.

Frustrated, she welcomed the interruption when Austen, carrying a cage holding Preston the pigeon, knocked on her open door. "*Close display*," Doc commanded, rising to greet Austen. "Let's take him to my private exam room." She motioned at the door to the immediate right of her office.

Forewarned that she would be examining the bird, Doc had researched pigeon diseases. If her co-chiefs wanted the pigeon removed from Dark Landing, no doubt she'd find enough evidence to support their wish.

Doc put on gloves and removed Preston from the cage. She wrapped gauze around its wings, securing them to the body, and then placed the helpless bird on the exam table. As she watched the scan results scroll by, she chatted with Austen. "*Muck's* enforcement officer, Victoria Windsor, seemed a bit too stiff for me, but I'm prejudiced. The previous officer was a darling. . . well, at least until things got weird. He's gone now. It's so sad. What's your opinion of the new gal?"

The scanner dinged, and a second later a red alert tag scrolled into view. Austen answered her question, but Doc wasn't listening.

She stopped the scroll and went back to the alert tag. *Not possible!* As she studied the item, the scanner dinged a second time, and she restarted the scroll. A second alert tag entered the display confirming the first anomaly.

Austen picked up on Doc's anxiety. "Doc? What is it? Is something wrong?"

"No. . . or, I'm not sure. *I'm not a vet.*" Uncharacteristically curt, Doc turned away from Austen to hide her shaking hands. "Sorry, I didn't mean to snap. I'm listening to you and reading the scan results at the same time. It aggravates me. I used to be better at doing two things at once." She smiled back over her shoulder at the admin chief—at least she hoped she'd smiled. Every nerve ending in her body arced with the electricity of discovery, including her facial muscles.

"I need to do more research," she said, then, grasping at the first avian contagion that came to mind, "He's carrying histoplasmosis. A respiratory disease transmitted through its droppings. If contracted and left untreated it can be fatal to humans. He'll be in isolation here for a couple weeks." Words spilled from her like marbles from a bucket. She made a conscious effort to slow down.

"Doc, are you sure you want to go to all this trouble—isolation for a pigeon—really?" Austen asked.

"We want to keep the locals happy, don't we? Afterall, the station *could* use a mascot." Doc tried for upbeat and smiled again, surer of herself this time. She continued in a controlled voice. "In the interim, clean the bazaar area of droppings. Later, it'll have to be kept clean." Nanoids could only be transmitted through bodily fluids, and for all Doc knew, the bird *might* also carry the histoplasmosis that she'd claimed to have found.

"Now *I'm* not sure I want to go to all this trouble. Should we keep it caged in the bazaar?" Austen asked.

"Well. . . the droppings *would* at least be contained to a small area, but you'd still have to clean the cage daily."

Austen cocked her head to one side—a good imitation of Preston the pigeon—and grinned. "Sounds like cleaning up pigeon shit is the perfect job for that artless, bald-pated head of the Dark Landing Audubon Society."

~ ~ ∞ ~ ~

As soon as Austen left, Doc collapsed onto her exam stool. Tears of excitement streamed down her cheeks. *It's fate. I'm meant to do this.* She bit her bottom lip, concentrating on the list of supplies and equipment needed to turn her exam room into a laboratory. The scanner dinged in a quick, continuing sequence. Doc glanced at the display. Preston appeared in distress, its vitals spiking. She'd left it gauze-wrapped and immobile too long. *Not now. . . I can't lose you now.*

"Poor baby," she cooed as she removed the gauze and placed the bird back in the small trap. "What you need is a larger cage, don't you sweetheart?" She added a pill cup filled with water and set the trap under the exam table, commanded the lights lowered to a soothing twenty percent, then returned to her office.

The bird's nanoids were inactive. How it became infected wasn't an issue. It could have picked them up from any morsel of food contaminated with saliva from a human carrier — perhaps even one of the three prostitutes who first introduced the alien nanoids to the station. Were they inactive when the bird acquired them, or did they become inactive because of incompatibility with the bird's physiology — or is that even significant? As far as she knew, Preston carried the only existing nanoid samples in the K.U. *And I have them.* It took enormous effort to rein in her excitement and maintain focus.

In infected humans and aliens, the nanoids eventually transmuted the hosts' organs, including the brain, and replicated them with indestructible nanoid versions which performed the necessary life functions. The individual's intellect and personality were intact — at least at first. Experts disputed how far the transmutation might have gone and over what timeframe, had the hosts survived. But Tammy had seen the *thing* Fitz became. Once the gifted chief of administration on Dark Landing, he'd turned into a solid block of nanoids, its surface undulating occasionally, but nothing more. In the end, he. . . *it*. . . disintegrated.

The more she thought about it, unlike humans and aliens, pigeons wouldn't have the mass to provide the electric charge necessary to jumpstart the nanoids after contamination. Because the pigeon's nanoids were inactive, they never received Diak transmissions and were unaffected when those transmissions ceased.

The nanoids were difficult to study. If active, they disintegrated when removed from the host and upon the host's death. Inactive nanoids were shielded. Attempts to breach the shields also resulted in disintegration. They might have overcome these limitations in time. Medical professionals and scientists agreed on one thing: If the nanoid transmutation could be directed and controlled, it would render its host immune to disease and non-fatal injuries — making the host virtually immortal.

Since learning of the nanoids and their potential for humanity, Jameson fantasized about being the one to fulfill that potential. She'd envisioned herself accepting the Nobel prize and a multitude of other honors and tributes for her unparalleled contribution to humanity and alien-kind. Her dreams outweighed any fears of personal exposure.

5 SCREAMER CELL

Curtis sat in his office at Security HQ when Benny tapped.

"Yeah?"

"Chief, you gotta get down here. . . berth nine."

"Why?"

"You need to see this for yourself, sir."

"Jesus, Benny. Cut the drama and tell me what's happening."

"A scavenger, English name the *Remarkable Mayzie*, just towed in the screamer cell."

"*Fuck!* I'm on my way. Secure the berth and keep everyone out of there."

Curtis stopped by the shift commander's desk meaning to ask for three men to accompany him but decided against it. If the cell *was* contaminated, though unlikely, and the nanoids escaped, what could the guards do about it? Their presence would only increase the number of people exposed. "Kyle, I'm going down to the docks."

"Later then, sir," Kyle said, without taking his eyes off his monitor.

During the twenty-minute trip, Curtis mulled his options. He should notify Rear Admiral Sullivan, commander of the Earth Space Force battalion stationed on Spud. But the admiral, a pushy, condescending ass, might use the cell's resurfacing as an excuse to grab control of the station again.

A Diak nanoid likeness of Martin Fitzwilliam last occupied the cell, which had doubled as a secure airlock meant to contain individuals or items that threatened the station. They'd ejected the cell after the *Fitz* likeness disintegrated when the Diak transmission stopped. *The thing should be half-way across the Known Universe by now. Damn Diak fucks anyway.*

The cell sat on the deck inside berth nine's atmospheric containment shield. Its footprint took up a sizeable amount of real estate. Benny, Dark Landing's senior dock foreman, stood next to the cell with the salvage ship's captain. Their arms folded over their chests, the two appeared to be at odds about something. *Great, another Bahdaneian,* Curtis thought. But this one was different.

Curtis's only exposure to the race was the two *Muck* enforcement representatives who'd served Dark Landing since he'd started. Both embraced the model enforcement officer visage: Aloof, and displaying exaggerated politeness, they were always professionally dressed in a *Muck* uniform or business suit. This Bahdane presented an otherwise unconventional appearance. The captain wore what could only be described as a buccaneer outfit. The calf-length pants exposed furry legs and bare paws. A wide leather belt held his billowy maroon shirt tucked securely in place. He'd forgone the hat and pinned his ears on top of his head in an odd topknot. Curtis caught a flash of small, pointed teeth set in a double row lining the Bahdaneian's lower jaw. He'd never noticed their extra set of teeth before.

He extended his hand. "Curtis Walker, Chief of Security. Welcome to Dark Landing." By the Bahdane's disgruntled countenance, Curtis wouldn't be surprised if he slapped the offending hand away, but he shook it firmly, following Earth custom.

A long musical hum and the word "Captain" followed the handshake.

Curtis motioned to the cell. "Where'd you find it?"

"A ways out—we responded to a flashing distress beam. I expect to be compensated for the towing."

They'd disabled the Mayday transmitter when they'd ejected the cell, leaving only the proximity alert enabled on the remote chance a ship might run into it. *I guess we should've checked the schematics for redundancies,* Curtis thought. *Who knew about a backup distress beam?*

"The truth is, we jettisoned the cell on purpose," he said.. "We no longer needed it. But I'll waive the normal docking and water fees since you're trying to do us a solid." Curtis smiled.

"Ah. . . space debris. Good. Under *Muck* regulations, I claim it as salvage."

Shit. He cringed internally and said, "Well, that's your right, of course, but—I didn't want to mention this—the real reason we chucked it is because of contamination."

Benny spoke for the first time. "That's what I told him, Chief. The damn thing is contaminated by Diak nan—"

Curtis cut Benny off. "In fact, it was a human contaminant— the Diak story is a rumor. Regardless, we shouldn't have disposed of it the way we did. You may have a *legal* claim but, under the circumstances, I'm required to notify MCTT and the Alliance Health Council. I'll need both approvals before I can release it."

The captain stroked his furry snout, clearly doubting Curtis's story. His narrowed eyes signaled his reluctance to accept defeat. Curtis guessed a small inducement might clinch it. He strove for a conciliatory tone instead of his usual one of condescension. "I'll tell you what—this isn't your fault. You're only trying to do the right thing. Benny, transfer a couple hundred K.U. credits to the captain's account." Curtis continued before Benny could say anything since the foreman lacked authorization to transfer station funds. "For both our sakes, I won't file a report with the authorities. You pick up a couple hundred you weren't counting on, and I have a second chance to dispose of the cell in the correct manner—win-win."

Eyes still hooded, the captain turned and headed back to his ship. Deep, angry hums conveyed his dissatisfaction.

With the captain out of earshot, Curtis turned to Benny. "Send me the ship's account number. I'll pay the two hundred from the security emergency fund." He'd pay it from his personal account instead to avoid an official record. No reason to share the source of funds with the dock foreman.

"Sure, but what do *we* do with it?"

Good question. Put it back in place and tell his shift commanders it's clean but still off limits? They'd go along. Doc wouldn't consider it one way or the other, and Hargreaves didn't know the cell existed. But Hargreaves remained the problem since supervision of dock and warehouse staff fell under her department *unless* a security issue couldn't wait for later discussion. A delicate balance, conflicts arose when the two chiefs and their staff were out of sync. With Austen being new, how would she react to his ordering her staff around? Still, like the Bahdane captain, he sensed a profit opportunity.

"Can the *Marigold* tow it?" he asked Benny. The *Marigold* was the station's shuttle.

"Yeah, sure. Are we really gonna keep it?"

"I wasn't lying to the captain. It's Admiral Sullivan's responsibility now. Until he and the council decide what to do, it's safer to put it back in place. Besides, we need the dock space."

"Right. I'm on it."

"Can you maneuver the thing alone?"

"Been puttin' square pegs into round holes by myself for the last thirty years."

"I see why you were Drew's favorite. Let's keep this between us."

"Absolutely — I do my job and mind my own business, sir."

"Good man." Curtis slapped him on the back.

Benny puffed up. "Thanks, sir."

~ ~ ∞ ~ ~

Curtis returned to his office. When Benny notified him that the screamer cell — nicknamed for the predilection of an early occupant — was back in place, Curtis called Kyle into his office.

"Yeah, boss?"

"The ESF decontaminated the screamer cell and it's back online. I didn't want you to freak when the scanner feed shows up. Tell Jonesy, too."

"I thought we'd sent it off to never-never-space?"

"Yeah, well no surprise, the Earth Space Force came up with a better idea, I guess." When the Diak invasion plan became known, the ESF had commandeered the station as a temporary military base.

"I can't imagine what their concept of decontamination is, but I don't want our men going near the damn thing. Come to think of it, disable the scanner and video links. We'll treat it like it doesn't exist."

26

"I'm all for that. It gives me the creeps. I still have nightmares from seeing poor Fitz turn into a nanoid look-alike."

"*Poor* Fitz was a traitor, remember? Send Nikko in."

"Yeah."

A few minutes later, Curtis's assistant ducked through the office hatch. Nikko Balog was Earth Eastern-European, possibly Bulgarian, or maybe Russian or Croatian. For some reason Nikko remained evasive on the subject and, since he spoke several Slavic languages, it couldn't be pinned down. At six-foot-nine, all muscle, with an unintelligible accent, his persistent smile kept others off guard. Curtis suspected Nikko exaggerated the accent to bolster his dumb dork front. But he was neither dumb nor a dork.

He'd been introduced to Nikko by a friend of a friend. In Nikko's previous occupation as compliance officer on the *Temperance*, they'd been partners in a bit of black-market trading. Their shared, borderline criminal tendencies secured their relationship. Curtis liked to use Nikko as a sounding board. Though he seldom spoke, when he did, he often displayed surprising insight and a talent for problem solving.

The big guy dropped onto the lounger, overtaxing its recommended weight capacity.

"Hey, you remember the screamer cell?" Curtis started.

"Da."

"Well, we got it back."

"Da?"

"I should notify Admiral Sullivan, but I'm wondering if we have a use for it."

"Da."

"Nothing comes to mind right now. You?"

"Ne."

"Still, I don't want to share anything with Sullivan if I don't have to."

"Da."

"You're right. There's no good reason to tell him. Let's take a look."

~ ~ ∞ ~ ~

Curtis and Nikko stood in front of the observation window looking into the screamer cell's empty interior. The cell's bulkheads, deck, bunk, and small tabletop with a stool set in front of it were manufactured as one molded unit. Nothing could be repositioned or removed. Curtis studied the cell. Something seemed off, but it eluded him.

"You never saw the Diak nanoid thing, did you?" Curtis asked Nikko.

"Ne."

"Telling ya. . . it was really something. Looked just like our chief of administration, Fitz." Curtis, looking at Nikko as he spoke, thought he caught a movement out of the corner of his eye.

"Did you see that?"

"Ne. Vat?"

They both stared into the cell for several seconds without blinking. Nothing happened.

"God, I'm imagining things. This place is seriously weirding me out. Let's go."

"Da."

As they exited the observation room, Curtis looked back over his shoulder and shuddered.

6 SUSPICIONS

Austen reread her brief status report to Windsor, making sure she'd set the right tone to denote the start of a burgeoning friendship. Otherwise, the message appeared innocuous. She'd focused on getting to know her target better and still needed to scrutinize any station records that might advance their investigation.

> *Officer Windsor,*
>
> *It was a pleasure meeting you, and I look forward to a productive liaison.*
>
> *My first chiefs' meeting is this afternoon. They hold them monthly instead of weekly, but I'm requesting weekly meetings (as the operations manual suggests). Next, I plan to review data and communication records for the past twelve months.*
>
> *Any advice you have on how I might better "settle in" to my position would be appreciated. Walker and Jameson have been working together for years. I don't want to be considered an interloper.*
>
> *I'd love to hear about your first weeks in Zeta Quadrant.*
> *Health, peace, and prosperity,*
> *A. Hargreaves, Chief of Administration*
> *Dark Landing Station, Zeta Quadrant*

"*Send,*" Austen commanded.

She tapped the small, raised patch of skin behind her left ear. *"Benson Capone."*

Her senior dock foreman answered at once. "Yeah, Chief?"

"Mr. Capone, do you have a moment to meet with me?"

"Sure. Anything special?"

"Only a general update. There's a chiefs' meeting in a couple hours."

"On my way."

"Thank you. *End all,*" Austen said.

Her relationship with her staff—and everyone else on Dark Landing except Doc—lingered in the *getting to know and trust you* stages, more formal than she preferred. While she waited for the dock foreman, she attempted to sort everyone she'd met so far into camps. On past assignments, it'd been a helpful exercise.

Curtis and Dr. Jameson were each a camp unto themselves. Austen hadn't met many of Doc's staff, but those she'd spoken with were loyal to her. The same could be said for Curtis. His men were comfortable with him and respected his leadership. But though they joked and exchanged barbs, his staffs' sentiments fell short of ardent devotion. And Nikko Balog, Curtis's assistant, appeared to be his own man. She doubted Nikko would blindly follow if Curtis's lead went too far off track.

The longer she considered, the more she realized no one seemed committed to anyone's camp except Dark Landing itself. She'd sensed enormous loyalty to the station from everyone she'd talked with.

Benny Capone stuck his head into her office. "You ready for me?"

"Come in. How's your day?"

Benny dropped into a chair in front of her desk. "Great. . . great. Slow right now. We only have three ships in dock, but there are berth reservations for six more arrivals over the next two days. It'll get crazy."

"No problems? Everyone paying their fees. . . making their water transfers?"

Benny hesitated a split second before answering. "No. . . no problems."

Austen consulted her monitor. "The *Essovius, Washington,* and *Voyager* are here—all Earth ships."

"Except the *Essovius* is half-owned by a Fahdeen co-op."

Austen stared at her screen. "Right. And I see a Bahdane independent docked earlier. The. . . how do you pronounce that?"

The Bahdane written alphabet consisted of a series of symbols representing the amazing variety and intensity of hums with which they communicated. She equated their symbols to Earth musical notes, but understood it wasn't an accurate comparison.

Benny diverted his eyes toward the hatch. "We use the berth or registry number. Her English name is the *Remarkable Mayzie*, but the name changes from planet to planet."

Austen's operative training noted the slight rise in Benny's voice. His glance at the hatch signified a desire to escape.

"Am I keeping you from something?"

"No, I thought I heard a. . . thing."

Austen leaned back in her chair to study him. After a few moments, she returned to her monitor. "The Bahdane ship left after three hours. No fees collected. Is that unusual?"

Now Benny appeared nervous. "Well, yes. . . er, no. I mean, she only docked to check the pending transport entries. Independents stop by all the time looking for the odd job and to get supplies. They don't stay long, and we don't charge dock fees. But seein' how you're new and everything, I shoulda asked if you was okay with that."

"Not at all. It makes perfect sense. When I've been here a while longer, I may tweak procedures, but for now, carry on as usual." She smiled and stood. "I guess that's it. I won't have much to report at my first chiefs' meeting. Thanks for dropping everything and coming up on short notice."

He nodded, visibly relieved. "No problem. Hey, you're the boss. When you say jump, you know. . . that's what I do."

"Don't feel you can't tell me if you're busy."

"Yes, sir," he said over his shoulder as he scuttled from her office.

~ ~ ∞ ~ ~

In the corridor outside the admin offices, Benny tapped Curtis.

"Hey, Ben, wh—"

"Hargreaves just questioned me about the Bahdaneian scavenger!"

"Okay. Spaceout. What did she ask?"

"Why he came here and why we didn't charge him. Like—is that unusual?"

"What'd you tell her?"

"Nothing. Only that indies stop by all the time looking for odd jobs."

"She's just learning the routine," Curtis said. "You told the truth. There's nothing to worry about. Admiral Sullivan's still on Earth at some conference; it's his job to fill her in about the screamer cell if he wants to, not ours."

"Thanks. I thought you should know," Benny said, relieved by Curtis's assurance.

"You thought right. I've got your back, Capone."

~ ~ ∞ ~ ~

The chiefs meeting went differently than Austen envisioned. Doc and Curtis were distracted. Each delivered a cursory report. In justification, both noted it'd been a slow month. Austen relayed the docking schedules for the coming week, and Curtis reminded her that the schedules were posted so everybody could plan accordingly—no reason to report on them at their meetings. After that, everyone fell silent. The two watched her, apparently looking for a signal they could adjourn.

"I understand why these meetings are held monthly, but I'm hoping we can make it weekly," she said. When Curtis and Doc failed to respond, looking at each other like she'd invited them to a sleepover, Austen modified her request. "I mean. . . just until I'm fully acclimated—maybe for a couple months."

Doc returned a feeble smile. "Sure. I think that's reasonable. We used to have weekly meetings when Drew. . . . I don't mean to imply. . . ." She glanced apologetically at Curtis without finishing either sentence.

He rolled his eyes, looking faintly insulted, but said nothing. Austen took his silence as reluctant agreement. She studied the man. A bit under six feet, stocky build, auburn hair cropped short, with the attendant freckles and dark blue eyes, except for his chronic surly expression, he might be good looking. She now realized that his laughing fit on their first encounter was so wholly out of character it could accurately be classified as an aberration. Since then, other than his characteristic smirk, she hadn't seen him smile once.

Trying to lead the meeting in a more amicable direction, she turned back to Doc. "So, how's Preston?"

Doc appeared startled, as if Austen had asked what sexual position she preferred. "Good. . . okay. I started treatment, but it'll take a couple weeks — maybe longer. He's in quarantine. And it's possible he won't respond. I'm not a vet."

"So you said before." *Shit, she's touchy.* Even Curtis came out of his bored stupor to give Doc a puzzled look.

Austen tried a new topic. "I've been meaning to get a first-hand take on the Fitzwilliam transmutation. I only know what the news reported. That must have been weird for both of you?"

At her question, Curtis choked on a sip of his coffee. He busied himself in wiping the coffee spit from his chin and the table.

Doc paled. "We loved Fitz. It was horrible." She stood. "I've got to get back to med-lab now." She left without a goodbye.

Curtis followed her lead. "Me too. . . security," he said, getting up. "Don't feel bad. I think 'loved' is a strong word, but it's still upsetting to talk about."

"I'm so sorry. That was thoughtless of me. Of course, Fitz was your friend."

"Yeaaah. Catch you later," he said as he left.

"What a pair of ill-tempered rampallians," Austen mumbled. She thought about her earlier conversation with the dock foreman. *Something is rotten in the State of Denmark.*

Back in her office, she reviewed command contact logs for the last three months, looking for anything out of the ordinary. Walker spoke with his mother once a week and recently contacted a restaurant supply house and a commercial designer. Odd, but those contacts *could* have been station related. With the chief of administration position unfilled, he'd been handling maintenance and supply.

Dr. Jameson's records, more revealing, consisted of hundreds of searches relating to ex-Earth governor Fitzwilliam-Bennett, and a dozen or more exchanges with a GCDC friend. Most of which

Austen had studied meticulously upon being assigned to the Jameson-Dark Landing investigation.

Though part of her assignment in only a peripheral sense, she decided to keep a closer watch on Walker, as well. ETOC's suspicions appeared merited. Weirdness prevailed, and she needed to broaden her investigation.

7 REVELATION

Curtis went over the shift reports, looking for anything he could use to pad his log for the previous day. Station logs were the only reports CoachStop consistently reviewed. He excelled at keeping them as terse and vague as possible without triggering questions from the company but still conveying how hard he worked. Tricky to pull off with the station as dead as it'd been over the last several days. Not genuinely dead—mostly dead. Things were happening, just nothing he wanted to report.

Hargreaves wasn't fitting in. One minute she was flitting around, asking questions, and pretending an interest in everyone's business. The next she acted the tough chick, hurling epitaphs and ridiculous Shakespearian insults. Doc was behaving almost as weird. She holed up in her office most of the time now, too distracted to follow the simplest conversation. Was she reacting to Hargreaves' strangeness or becoming just as eccentric?

After Hargreaves' question concerning Fitz, he'd thought about the K.U.'s fascination with everything Diak. The Diak invasion threat changed their daily lives. The screamer cell showing up again would be big news. If he'd thought it through, he should have let the Bahdane salvage captain keep the damn thing. Too late now.

He pulled the files for the high-security cell to assess its scrap value. It would be nice to make a chunk of change toward his nightclub plans. With a little work and a lot of script, Curtis knew Spud—the asteroid to which Dark Landing was attached by two long, spindly arms — would make the perfect spot for his nightclub, *The Mine*. He'd pushed the plan forward when the ESF decided to quarter a battalion on the asteroid while they constructed the military's new base station.

The battalion presence was temporary, but the ESF had built a permanent surface installation on the opposite side of Spud to accommodate the squadron guarding the wormhole into Diak space. He'd never understand why they kept the damn thing open — none of their probes returned. It'd been the Diak's bridge home, and wormholes only went one way. Without an incoming threat, why waste the script and manpower to keep it guarded? And there was no way in hell the K.U. was going to invade the Diak.

Curtis continued to scroll through the screamer cell specifications. So far, he'd done nothing wrong. . . or, at least, too wrong. Retaining the cell and lying to the scavenger, sending him away, were the correct actions. It got shady only by his failure to notify someone in the ESF or ETOC. He could make a case for waiting until Rear Admiral Sullivan returned from Earth. It would be reasonable for Curtis to keep the cell's reappearance secret until then. That excuse fell to pieces with his failure to contact Secretary Anne Rostenkowski, the head of the Earth Technology Oversight Commission. He knew Secretary Rostenkowski personally, and her security clearance hovered miles above Rear Admiral Sullivan's.

He suppressed his rising panic. With nothing in his contact files — or any file — mentioning the return of the screamer cell, he could still contact Rostenkowski. But why should he? *Relax, man. Think it through. You just need to get rid of the bloody thing as soon as possible, pick up some extra script, and cover your tracks.*

Still undecided, he left HQ to revisit the screamer cell in the hope that viewing it once more would help make up his mind.

~ ~ ∞ ~ ~

Curtis stared into the cell. Empty. Just one continuous hunk of gray metal. When the nanoid-infected humans and aliens exploded, they'd left no residual contamination. What made the authorities think the cell might be contaminated? They were playing it safe. Diak Fitz had exploded right along with the rest of them. He thought about Fitz and how he and Mattie, Drew Cutter's nightshift commander, colluded with the Diak for well over a year without anyone catching on. Fitz was a wimp. No one would have credited him with the balls. But someone should have suspected Mattie — she'd been a real piece of work.

"Geeze, Fitz, you surprised us all, didn't you?" Curtis mumbled.

The deck of the screamer cell rippled in muted pastel tones.

Curtis stopped breathing. His core froze to brittle ice.

The cell deck continued to ripple, then to undulate in waves. A gray glob formed in its center, rising, pulling the surrounding deck into its bulk as it grew upward.

The edge of Curtis's vision dimmed. He gulped air. This is what he'd missed — the difference he'd been unable to identify during his first visit. The deck appeared two shades darker gray than the rest of the cell's interior. A darker, *nanoid* gray.

The glob continued to grow, but Curtis knew how the final figure would look. It would look like Martin Fitzwilliam molded from dull metal.

Diak Fitz materialized. The sides of its mouth turned up in a sickly gray smile. "Hello, Curtis."

Curtis backed up too fast and fell. His head hit the observation room deck with a jarring thud. The force of the blow knocked him loopy. He closed his eyes for several seconds while his head swam. When he opened them, he lay on his back on the deck with Diak Fitz kneeling over him — watching him — *touching* him.

"Hello, Curtis," it said again.

"How did you get out?" he asked in a high-pitched voice tinged with panic. He used his elbows and heels to scuttle away from the thing, terrified he'd been infected. His scuttling only gained him a few inches more separation — the observation room was no larger than the eight-by-ten-meter cell.

"There is an opening for the delivery of nutritional substances. I easily unsealed it, then disassembled and flowed through. I could have done so at any time when you first sequestered me, but my orders were to stay in place and await my unit's arrival. Of course, they did not come, and you cast me into space. Now I am returned."

The food pass. The cell was designed for beings that required food. No one considered feeding the Diak Fitz thing during its time on the station. "What do you want?"

"I seek purpose."

"Purpose? What purpose?"

"I require purpose to live, just as *you* require nutritional substances."

The figure resembled Fitz physically, but its voice lacked Fitz's nasal quality. It spoke in a smooth, even tenor.

"Are you Fitz?" he asked it.

"I retain only those memories of Martin Fitzwilliam necessary to function in this universe. I have deleted all unnecessary ones."

"Am I. . . did you infect me?"

"Infect you? Download? No. I will if you request. I do *not* advise it."

"I'll pass," Curtis said, slowly raising his hand to his comm implant.

"No," it said.

He lowered his hand. "Are you going to kill me?"

"We prefer not to kill. We are choosing life."

"What do you mean? I saw your invasion armada with my own eyes."

"Invade yes — the killing is unavoidable because the ones being invaded make it so."

"I don't understand." He tried to buy time.

"I see how you would be confused. Let me explain." Imitating human movement, it relaxed down to the deck next to Curtis, extended its legs, crossed its feet at the ankles, and leaned back on its elbows.

Curtis recoiled.

8 IT SPEAKS

Curtis's concentration became muddled by a colossal headache. The Diak continued, and he struggled to follow its story.

". . . and, in my time alone in space, after losing contact with the Mass, I considered what the Diak have done — are doing. We do not wish to kill, and neither do we wish to die. Outside the Mass' influence, the dilemma is clear. We. . . I. . . *must* find a purpose that does not require destroying other beings for continuation. However worthy, I suspect such a purpose will fail, as have all attempts over the centuries but for the need to survive. Perhaps my new purpose will fail even as I sit here with you, though. . ." its gray eyes closed and reopened with a puzzled look, "I sense my communication subroutine which connects to the Mass, should that transmission be reestablished, has developed a conditional loop. It is possible the sudden disconnect and my simultaneous act of self-preservation caused a processing error. Rare, but not unheard of. Until it resolves — and such anomalies always resolve — my devices were ... are distracted, and I am momentarily saved from destruction."

Curtis noted the longer the Diak Fitz spoke, the more human-like its phrasing and voice modulation became. The chief lifted one hand to scratch his chin — that much closer to his comm implant.

It shook its head at the movement and continued. "The Diak were once biological beings. Though a great deal different from humans, like you, we contracted diseases and were vulnerable to injury. At times, a disease or injury would incapacitate; at other times, be fatal. Over many centuries we developed technology to cure and repair our physical weaknesses, continuously improving upon our designs. There came a point when our devices—nanoids, as you say—acquired the ability to reprogram and improve on their own, without external commands. They self-replicated and transmuted, and for their own self-preservation, blocked all exterior input. Though still working in concert, some metamorphosized to fulfill singular purposes. At first, we were concerned, but soon we judged the evolution to be a wonderful gift. Diak lives extended ten-fold and continued vigorous beyond anything imagined."

While Curtis lay perfectly still, the pounding in his head was bearable. But he grew drowsy and worried about a concussion. *Idiot! This thing will kill you when it's finished with its fairytale.*

"Over time, we also noticed fundamental changes in our physical requirements. Some changes were extreme. They altered our culture. . . our. . . our very *existentiality*." The Diak produced another sickly, gray smile and, seemingly speaking to itself than to Curtis, said, "Yes. . . existentiality—what a marvelously nuanced language."

"We're very proud of it," Curtis said and wondered how long it would take the thing to recognize the nuances of sarcasm.

The Diak went on. "Major among those changes was the disinclination and the ability to reproduce, as well as significant dietary adaptations. Our devices required minerals to replicate. We added mineral-laden, non-organic materials to our diets. Some devices further mutated to process those materials within our bodies. Our concerns resurfaced. How was our species to survive? The evolution continued until the inevitable occurred: The life-sustaining devices transmuted—devoured—a host body to the last cell. Do you see the contradiction—the irony?"

Curtis lifted his head to nod and winced. Despite himself, the Diak's story intrigued him, his own safety momentarily ignored.

"For a brief time—equal to only a few of your days—this monster among us, said to have *turned*, continued to exist. Then it disintegrated—died." The Diak's eyes widened at the memory. "We did not program the original devices, and the mutated devices did not evolve to serve *each other* when the last of a host's biological cells were transmuted. Thus, their purpose fulfilled, the nanoids self-terminated. As the number of biological Diak on our world declined, and being unable to repopulate, we looked elsewhere.

"The search for biological hosts to sustain our civilization became our new and desperate purpose and extended our existence. As long as we are zealously seeking new vessels to inhabit, we can continue for a short time after turning. Though, for obvious reasons, we prefer to transfer to a new host before the turn is complete. And, if we stop our search. . . ." The figure raised its eyebrows and shrugged.

Its expressions grew increasingly human-like, but its dull gray surface remained unchanged, and Curtis found the contrast off-putting. "Can't you find a less invasive purpose? Like discovering secrets of the cosmos, or solving the Polloch octahedral numbers conjecture?"

"We have adopted many worthy but ultimately unsuccessful purposes. The essential purpose for all biologicals is reproduction. Replication is not reproduction. Machines can perform life-sustaining functions. Machines can store and process life memories and experiences. But a machine's rudimentary code cannot define or replicate the life spark."

"Bummer," Curtis said.

"Yes." It shrugged again, nodding in agreement.

Curtis sat up carefully, ignoring the stabs of pain in the back of his head. He drew his knees against his chest, arms tight around his legs, and laid his head down. His new shape resembled a human ball. In the process, he'd edged a couple inches closer to the exit hatch. "So, now that your subroutine is in a. . . . *Open hatch!*" he yelled. As the hatch slid upward, Curtis rolled his body through the opening. *"Close hatch!"* The hatch checked its upward motion and reversed direction. On his feet in an instant, he bolted down the passageway.

As he ran, his comm pinged. "Curtis, I am only a threat to you and the station if you attempt to harm me. There is still much I need to divulge to you."

Curtis barreled through the hatch to HQ and headed straight for Nikko. The big man sat at his desk, and a skinny kid, nine or ten years old, with a mop of black hair, stood next to him. *Toby Greenstein! Jesus, I'm having a nightmare.* Why was the boy back on the station?

Katherine Leticia Taleen—Letty—who'd come to Dark Landing in search of the man she thought of as her father, adopted the boy after his parents died in a Diak raid. Letty was the head of the multi-world conglomerate, Taleen Industries, and not a bad looker. And, Curtis suspected, the reason Drew Cutter abandoned the chief of security post that Curtis now held. She'd taken Toby back to Earth with her after they neutralized the Diak threat.

"What are you doing here. . . why? Where's Letty? *What the fuck!*" Unable to handle more than one calamity at a time, Curtis looked frantically around the reception area as everyone in the office but Nikko scattered in different directions. He motioned to a newbie, slower than the others. "You! Come over here. Don't take your eyes off this kid." He whirled and headed into his office. "Nikko!"

When the hatch closed behind them, Nikko said, "Boy ees runavay."

"I don't give a fuck about the boy," Curtis screamed. "Something happened. The. . . the thing, the Fitz thing. . . it's loose." Spittle flying, he clutched his chest. He could feel his heart laboring. Fighting for breath, he stared at Nikko.

Nikko ran a hand over his face to wipe away Curtis's spit, then grabbed him by the shoulders. "What the hell's the matter with you? Get a grip, man," he said, in perfect, unaccented English. He led Curtis to the lounger and forced him to sit. With a hand on the back of his neck, he pushed the chief's head down between his knees.

Curtis registered Nikko's lack of accent, but his inability to breathe and the consequences of the Diak's presence on the station momentarily surpassed his curiosity. When the panic attack subsided, and the pounding in his chest eased enough for him to catch his breath, he waved a hand above his head to signal Nikko and sat up.

"Now," Nikko said, "slow down, and tell me what happened."

Curtis jumped to his feet. "My God, he's out, he's. . . he's —"

"Sit!" Nikko bent his six-foot-nine frame to draw eye-level with Curtis. Curtis sat back down, and Nikko sat next to him, one hand on his shoulder. "Now, tell me — slowly — what happened."

Curtis nodded, rubbing his sweaty palms on his knees, and started over at a more measured pace. "I went back to the screamer cell to. . . to appraise it for scrap value, and the deck. . . the cell deck.

. . formed into Diak Fitz." Feeling the panic rising again, he moved to stand once more. Nikko pushed him back down.

"Yeah, yeah, okay. . . I'm good," Curtis said. He took a deep breath and continued. "I fell and hit my head. Things got a little hazy, and suddenly he was right there beside me." Curtis struggled for calm. He related to the best of his memory what the Diak told him and described how he'd gotten away from it. Unassisted, he placed his head between his knees again, taking several more breaths.

"I'm notifying the ESF," Nikko said.

Curtis's comm pinged.

"Do not allow him to contact your Earth Space Force, Curtis Walker. It will not end well."

Curtis raised his arms, elbows akimbo, both index fingers jabbing frantically at his ears. Nikko looked at him like he was crazed.

"It's on your comm?" he asked.

With a short nod, Curtis dropped his arms and mouthed the command to link his comm with Nikko's.

Diak Fitz spoke again. "As I said, I do not wish to harm you. I just want to talk. Please return. The other human, Mr. . . Nikko. . . may accompany you if he chooses, but if either of you contacts the Earth Space Force, there will be consequences."

Nikko and Curtis stared at each other for several moments, and then Nikko nodded.

~ ~ ∞ ~ ~

The corridor to the screamer cell curved to the left. The two men, each to a side, crept slowly forward, blasters drawn. They alternated, one moving a few meters ahead, then stopping to provide cover while the other one took the lead. During their approach, Fitz prattled continuously in Curtis's ear with Nikko listening.

"Should you attempt to use a blaster against me, it will not cause me harm. I have fully turned. I will simply disassemble and reassemble in the most unexpected spot."

There'd been no report during the Diak threat of anyone taking down a Diak with a blaster. But this Fitz was the closest thing to a true Diak they'd encountered, and as far as Curtis knew, none of the other 800,000 nanoid-infected humans and aliens had fully turned.

"You have nothing to fear from me. There is much to tell you, and my subroutine loop may resolve at any moment."

Nikko caught up with Curtis. The screamer cell lay only meters ahead. Another few steps and it would come into view.

9 ON PURPOSE

Diak Fitz leaned casually against the hatchway frame of the observation room smiling with satisfaction, its human simulation now relaxed and natural, except for the eyes. Dead as granite, soulless evil resided behind those windows. Hands tucked into replicated pockets, it wore a security uniform of dull gray instead of the traditional black. Something about the alien's relaxed stance reminded Curtis of Drew Cutter.

Considering the Diak's nonchalant demeanor, Curtis realized how absurd he and Nikko must appear, approaching stealthily from opposite sides of the passageway. He straightened, keeping his blaster level, and cast the other man a sidewise glance. A crouching Nikko still moved furtively. "Give it up. We look ridiculous." Curtis said. They stopped five meters from the figure.

The Diak dropped to the deck in a sitting position, legs crossed and nodded at the two to do the same. Curtis immediately collapsed into the suggested pose, but Nikko lay on his stomach, elbows resting against the deck to steady his blaster. He took aim and froze in place.

The Diak spoke to Curtis as if Nikko's huge bulk was invisible. "I repeat, I do not wish to harm you, but I will not allow you to harm *me*." Then he added, "Your weapons are useless."

Nikko maintained his rigid firing position.

It struck Curtis that, by repeatedly declaring there was no way to harm it and cautioning them not to try, it must be vulnerable in some way. He rested his blaster in his lap and clasped his shaking hands. "So, there's more you need to tell me — go on then." He hoped Nikko could come up with a plan because Curtis remained clueless.

Diak Fitz spoke. "We are a nanoid civilization. Nanoids dominate all Diak technology. . . communication. . . space travel. Thousands of variations are used to manufacture goods, and even to provide the basis for our structures. Most importantly, nanoid devices regulate our environment."

Curtis interrupted. "And some are used to infect innocent people as an invasion strategy. You murdered hundreds of thousands of Alliance citizens."

"Yes. Had they lived, the nanoids would have continued to spread throughout your populations, rendering them unacceptable as hosts." With a slow blink of dismissal, the Fitz look-alike continued. "As I explained earlier, to summarize for Mr. Nikko, the devices designed to protect the Diak biology ultimately evolved to regard external commands as a threat to their purpose. Worse, once all the cells in a Diak transmute, the nanoids, their job complete, self-destruct, destroying the Diak as well. A programming flaw. An illogical paradox. One we are without means to correct, though the quest continues.

"In those early times, by accident and out of desperation, we discovered that as long as a new host was available and a transfer imminent, we could withdraw our devices from our physical bodies at any time before, and even for a brief span after the point of total transmutation, thus existing in a pure nanoid state for short periods. The data files containing memories and personalities remained intact. We believed this to be a further step in the devices' evolution, one necessary for their own preservation. In a new host, the devices can continue to serve their purpose. This was the beginning of the *Spread* — the never-ending search for new, biological hosts. Our purpose and that of our nanoids fused.

"Since that time, resulting from our experiences in occupying multiple host races, we have sought the one race of beings that can fulfill a greater need than survival. It is difficult to describe without a thorough command of your language. I will try." It stretched its legs out and leaned back against the hatch frame.

Oh, my god! Trying to get comfortable, Curtis re-crossed his legs and settled in for what looked to be a long alien history lesson.

"With few exceptions, all hosts fulfill our most basic objective, which is to continue. But with each new host, something remains absent. . . missing. . . *always* something is missing. Perhaps the memories are dull or disgusting. For some, the physical configuration is lacking. Often, we cannot define the missing thing. We continue our search for the ideal host—a host that encompasses the necessities as well as the pleasures of existence. Do you understand this?"

"Yeah, you're looking for one that can scratch your itch," Curtis said.

"Explain."

"It's like. . . on your skin. . . like if. . . ." Curtis shrugged. "I can't explain. Just finish already."

The Diak scratched his head. "When Martin Fitzwilliam came to me for protection, I was in possession of a Diak gunship. Its pilot, sent to collect me for relocation, had lost faith in his purpose and perished. Unable to pilot the ship in my then Bin form, I downloaded to the Fitz human, which seemed the most expedient measure at the time." The Diak paused momentarily as if pondering other measures it might have taken.

With a slight shake of its head, it continued. "Ordered to join an attack unit, my ship was destroyed in battle. The nanoids formed a protective shell—a survival pod—around me. I was captured and placed in this cell. At first, I did not reassume the Fitz form but continued in the pod configuration.

"Long before he appeared to me, Fitz—as you say—was implanted with subversion devices separate in design from the life-extending devices all Diak carry. Subversion devices are made to ignite upon command or at the loss of the Diak transmission. For some time after initial implant, they remain covert and compliant to external command. But even those devices, left in place, eventually accelerate replication and self-enhancement to become part of the greater Mass and unite in its purpose.

"Before I could leave this cell to secure a more stable host, I received the directive from Sar Mode, the leader of the Spread, which prohibited all Diak from downloading into a human under threat of death. That the directive came from Sar Mode herself was extraordinary, and to condemn a member of the Mass to death, as in my case, since on Dark Landing I lacked alternative hosts, unprecedented."

As if for the first time, the Diak noticed Nikko, still frozen in place. It glanced at him with a puzzled expression and then appeared to dismiss his presence and returned to its narrative. "Ultimately, when all transmissions into your Known Universe ceased, there were mere seconds in which to abandon Fitz before his devices ignited, and I would have been lost as well. I replicate his form now only for your comfort."

"You're not doing *me* any favors," Curtis said. His legs cramping, he crossed them in the opposite direction once more and stretched his neck muscles. Diak Fitz ignored his discomfort.

"Ah, well. . . ." It shrugged. "All Diak are joined within a Mass, whether it is the Mass of a colonized planet or the Mass of the Spread, we are contained. While Martin Fitzwilliam believed the subversive devices worked within his body to extend his life—only partially correct—he could not *feel* their presence yet, nor had he joined with the Mass. He retained independence from all and acted upon choices of his own making. I was astonished by this innocence and ability to self-rule. More astounding, in the brief time our devices shared one body, my own devices adapted. . . . No, that is the wrong word. My devices *upgraded* to allow independent thought and action. And this upgrade remained concealed from the whole. I am part of the Mass, but I am not restrained within the Mass. Martin Fitzwilliam filled my itch."

"*Jesus*, get to the point already," Curtis urged. "I swear, I can't sit here any longer."

"Do you not see it? Diak have freedom of thought, but all thought is shared with the Mass. As a result, we do not have freedom of action. But in a human host, both thought and action are self-contained. This is the truth secreted within Sar Mode's unparalleled edict. A Diak within a human host can exist. . . can thrive. . . independent of the Mass. While our purpose remains that of survival, survival can be individual and separate from the whole. The *something* no Diak can name but all Diak seek, is self-determination."

"Soooo. . .?" Curtis prompted, unimpressed.

"By what right does Sar Mode—and perhaps the Council of Superiors—deny self-realization and determination to the Diak? There is something else you should know."

"How much more?" Curtis squirmed. "I've lost all circulation in my lower body."

"There are many of your kind in captivity at Mass Primary, the armada command station. Your Travis Barnes is among them."

Curtis's heart stuttered, and he felt the blood drain from his face into a nauseating pool in the pit of his stomach. From past ribbing, he knew his freckles now stood prominently against parchment-pale skin.

The Diak continued. "I believe he is esteemed by your race?"

Holy crap! Reflexive snarkiness automatically filled the void as his thoughts spun like a carny wheel. "Some do, but I never found Barnes particularly *esteemable.*" The spinning finally stopped on a coherent question. "When you say 'many of our kind,' what's the exact count? There were less than five hundred humans and aliens unaccounted for after your botched attempt to take over the K.U." A side effect of mandated DNA access to technology was the ease of maintaining accurate population counts to within a few thousand out of billions.

"We were among you long before you became aware of our presence. During the readiness phase, with the assistance of cooperative citizenry, we identified hundreds—I do not know the exact number—from your race as well as others, whose absences would go unnoticed. Their disappearances, if at all remarked upon, could be attributed to multiple causes. We questioned each captive in order to understand your cultures. This knowledge facilitated our invasion strategies."

Curtis thought he detected a hint of pride in the Diak's gunmetal expression. He cast a quick glance at the stone Nikko statue. *Are you hearing this?* Curtis turned back to the Diak. "So, you've got some of our people—so what? We'd be stupid to try and rescue them from the middle of your invading forces."

"True. Of course, if I were to help you. . . ."

Curtis's response momentarily caught in his throat. He'd thought it impossible for the Diak to look eviller, but somehow it managed it. "Let me get this straight. You're offering to help Earth Space Forces rescue our people?"

"No. I'm offering to help *you* rescue your people."

"Me? Why me?"

"Because you are here, and you are greedy."

He saw no point in arguing. "You're *paying* me?!" The conversation turned weird — *weirder*.

"I choose you, Curtis, because your Earth force would not allow me to return through the wormhole."

"You're right about that. But you're way off base if you think I'm risking my neck for a bunch of strangers just because they're human. And obviously *losers*, since no one even knows they're missing."

"I believe I can offer you a valuable incentive."

"Oh. . . what's that?" asked Curtis, his curiosity obvious.

"The technology to create wormholes wherever you wish."

Out of the corner of his eye Curtis caught a movement. Nikko, blaster lowered, stared at the Diak wearing a look of horror, echoing Curtis's thoughts exactly. If true, it meant the Diak could reenter K.U. space again at any time.

"How can we believe you? And what will you do if we tell you to go fuck yourself?" Curtis asked.

The Diak closed its eyes and stilled for several seconds, as if its snooze setting were enabled. He felt certain it was translating his last question. He was right.

It opened its eyes. "Masturbation?"

"Not exactly. . . but close enough. I'm asking what you'll do if we refuse."

"I see. I will seek a host. . . you, *or* your friend. I will put down the other. Then, in your form, I will acquire one of the armed ships protecting the bridge to Diak space and return to the Mass."

"The ESF will stop you."

"Perhaps, but it will be of no consequence to the two of you."

Stalemate.

Nikko spoke. "Curtis and I have to talk this over. It'll take time to devise a workable plan and may be impossible to get past the ESF squadron to the wormhole — then there's the minefield. You could deconstruct any minute now, right?"

"My subroutine is still in a loop, but it is nearing resolution. By identifying one of you as a new host, I have taken the necessary steps to continue my existence for a short period beyond my turning. But I will not allow my devices to deconstruct. It is a deadline that should be of concern to you."

"We're at an impasse," Curtis said, trying to curb his anxiety and think several steps ahead. "Even if we agree to take you to Diak space here and now, we can't just walk out, grab a ship, and cross the bridge. Nikko's right. It'll take some planning. And if I don't get back to my office soon, somebody's going to miss me. So. . .?"

"I'll accompany you to your office, and we will work on a plan together."

"Not possible. If you're seen, the station will lockdown, and the ESF will surround us in minutes. I'm not exaggerating when I say they'll take out Dark Landing and everyone on it before they'd let you escape. Hell, they may decide it's not worth the risk and do it anyway."

Diak Fitz collapsed into a puddle. Thin gray streaks radiated from its center in all directions, resembling lines of marching ants. As the lines stretched thinner and thinner, the puddle became smaller until both disappeared into the deck.

Curtis's comm pinged. "Do not be long, and know I am monitoring you."

10 R.I.P. PRESTON

Back in his office, Curtis and Nikko sat staring at each other, digesting what they'd heard. "What do you think?" Curtis asked and disabled his comm.

Nikko did the same. "Obviously we have to stop it — kill it somehow."

"Why *obviously*? And what the fuck happened to your accent?"

"Huh?"

"What happened to your *fucking* accent?!" The cords on Curtis's neck tightened as he abandoned any attempt to maintain control.

"Yeah, I don't have an accent. There's more you should know. . . later."

"I'll bet. No time like the present. I'm up to my knees in *more*, a little more won't make a difference."

"Calm yourself. It can wait. We've got to figure out how to neutralize the Diak. You don't really believe anything it said, do you?"

"No. I don't know. Maybe the part about the hostages. But I don't trust it. *You* don't trust it. I don't trust ESF. Now I don't trust you. Can't we just place an anonymous tap to the ESF, pull a Drew Cutter, and take the next boat out?" He wasn't kidding.

"No, we can't. And he hasn't disappeared. He's been in New Las Vegas for the last six months building his reputation as a poker player."

Curtis's voice ticked up several decibels. "Who the *fuck* are you?"

"I'll *get* to that. Focus. . . the Diak. . . what are we going to do?"

"You tell me. You got all the answers."

"I need some time alone to think. The Diak said it'd stay put until we get back to it. I say we try for some sleep and meet first thing in the morning."

"You're kidding. You really think you can sleep with that thing just down the hall—or wherever it's crawled off to?" Curtis lifted one foot from the deck. For all he knew, they were standing on it now.

"Probably not, but I need a few hours away from your nattering."

"Fuck you! Whoever you are."

"Jesus, Curtis, spaceout. Have you lived your whole life as an exposed nerve?" As he exited Curtis's office, he cautioned, "Reactivate your comm so it doesn't get suspicious. I'll meet you in your quarters at 0500."

Curtis noted that when Nikko lost his accent, he'd evidently lost his ever-present smile, as well.

~ ~ ∞ ~ ~

A slow day in medical, only one exam station was occupied. A gowned patient sat on the bed studying a handheld. A knot of nurses and an intern, all holding coffees, stood or leaned against the bulkhead opposite the patient station, chatting. Austen nodded to them.

"She's in her exam room," one of the nurses offered.

"Thanks." Austen knocked on the door.

It opened several inches and Doc stuck her head out, then stepped through and steered Austen into her adjacent office. "I was just contacting you. I'm so sorry to break the sad news, but the pigeon died. Birds have such delicate dispositions. The stress of me handling and poking it must have been too much." Doc wore a pained expression, appearing truly upset about Preston's demise. "Of course, I'll talk to the Audubon members if you want."

Teeth clamped together, Austen spread her lips in a grimace. "I want. They'll never buy it. Frankly, if I knew where to look, I'd find a replacement pigeon rather than face them."

"At least its death should make Curtis happy for a change," Doc said.

Austen smiled. "There's that. Well, there's no reason to put it off. I'll let Darryl know. If you don't mind, I'll have him get in touch with you personally. The particulars will be more credible if he speaks to you without me around."

"That's fine," Doc said. "I don't mean to be rude, but there's a scan waiting for my review."

"Not at all. Talk to you later." Austen stepped to one side and tapped for the head of the Dark Landing Audubon Society, extending her condolences and offering up Doc for the details. As expected, Darryl was upset. In a raised voice, he'd suggested the pigeon's death was "damned convenient for station command."

The intern approached her when she ended her conversation. "Say. . . one of our air handlers—toward the back—seems to be a little wonky."

"I'm headed to my office now. I'll open a maintenance ticket and have them take a look," Austen offered.

"Thanks."

"No problem."

Back in her office, Austen asked the head of facilities to join her. She relayed the air handler issue, and together they pulled up a live schematic of med-lab. Dark Landing's admin systems ran proprietary software. She was still learning.

"See the yellow frame around vent AH2004?" the engineer said.

Austen nodded.

"Now look down at the corresponding number in the detail panel."

"Right. So. . . that handler is operating at sixty percent capacity. We received an alert, the system assigned the alert to M. Wilkerson, and resolution is in process. Great."

"You're a quick study."

She smiled at the compliment. "Thanks. But this system is surprisingly user-friendly."

"At the alert level, yes, but the repair and testing interfaces are more complex."

"I understand. And the moving red dots. . . those are med-lab staff. What do the purple frames surrounding these two areas represent?" She pointed at the screen.

"Purple indicates a biological hazard area. We need med-lab authorization before we can enter those rooms."

"Got it." Austen squinted and studied the schematic carefully. Doc's private exam stood out as one of the purple-framed areas. *What's in her exam room that's hazardous?* A tiny red dot flickered in the center of the space so faint she might have missed it if she weren't studying the screen as intently. A much larger red dot denoted Doc, still working in the adjacent office.

~ ~ ∞ ~ ~

Austen yawned. It was two-thirty in the morning. She sat at her desk hugging a mug of coffee and watched the two red dots on her screen. One glowed, unmoving, from the back of med-lab—probably a sleeping patient. The second glow, in the receiving area at the front entrance, jiggled occasionally, representing movement. Minutes earlier, it had glided eerily to the back, paused next to the motionless red dot for a brief time, then returned to the front. With another glance at the tiny red flicker in Doc's exam room to confirm her imagination wasn't working overtime, she took a stylus from her desk drawer, pocketed it, and left her office.

The profound silence of the empty corridors unnerved her. Without the normal, colorful bustle of its residents, the station looked dowdy and unkempt. It smelled of dust with an undertone of burning metal. *This is really stupid. I should be in bed instead of sneaking around spooking myself.* As she rounded a bulkhead, the sudden, ghostly appearance of a passerby startled her further. She plunged her hands deep into her pockets and shivered, relieved when the well-lit reception desk in med-lab appeared in front of her.

The male nurse behind the counter was blindingly handsome. Tousled blond hair, only a few shades darker than her own platinum blonde, fell several inches below his ears in waves. *Why is it men always have great hair that falls naturally in place?* She looked at his name tag—*Austin! You're kidding me.* The situation became more humorous than spooky, and she relaxed.

"Hello," she said, momentarily forgetting her objective.

He greeted her with a brilliant smile that quickly faded on recognition. "Chief Hargreaves? Are you okay? Can I help?" he asked, visibly alarmed by her appearance in med-lab at such a late hour.

She shifted back to mission mode. "I'm fine. Thanks. It's just. . . I needed to handle a minor emergency in admin and found I'd misplaced my processor stylus. Pretty sure I left it in Doc's office this afternoon. It's silly this late and all, but the stylus is engraved and a gift from someone special. Do you mind if I take a look?"

"Of course not. Need help?"

"Thanks, no. I remember laying it on the edge of her desk. It'll only take a minute."

Jameson's office and exam doors were out of view of the receiving area. Austen went straight to the exam room, entered the master code, and placed her hand on the palm reader. The door clicked open, and she entered. Preston squatted on a perch in a new, larger cage that fit snugly under the exam table. He looked perfectly healthy, head drawn deep into his fluffed chest, sound asleep. She envied him.

She waived the stylus at the other Austin as she left, and called out, "Found it. Thanks."

He rewarded her with another beautiful smile and the accompanying sparkle of azure-blue eyes that reminded her of Earth's Mediterranean Sea.

When she returned to her office, she used her override code to delete the record of her entrance to Doc's exam. *Why would Jameson lie about that stupid bird?* She saw no connection to her investigation. Austen decided to grab a few hours of sleep and then confront Doc about her strange behavior later in the day. Doc's search for Governor Fitzwilliam-Bennett suddenly appeared less a Diak conspiracy and more a sign that Doc might be coming unhinged.

11 CONNECTIONS

The hand folded around to the player on Drew's right; she raised. In seat number nine (and the cutoff seat for that round) Drew called and peeked at his cards once more—ten, nine of diamonds. The button and both blinds called. With five players still in the hand, the flop came nine spade, nine club, ace spade. He'd flopped trip nines, but the board held a possible flush draw for his opponents. Seat number two, immediately left of the button, rapped the table, and seat three bet the minimum.

Drew's comm purred, *Katherine Taleen*. *Hold*, Drew mouthed. The tap would be blocked as long as he sat at the poker table.

The gal to his right cut out chips for another raise, then, evidently noticing Drew's hand shaking, decided to call instead. Drew called—his own intended raise forgotten when his comm pinged *Letty Taleen*. The button called and seat two folded. The turn came ten of spades. He'd filled nines over tens.

Drew lost track of the action. *What the hell is she tapping me about?* The previous week's news feed reported her engagement to one Xander Crawford, Founder and CEO of KUXC Entertainment. If the ads were to be believed, 'KUXC broadcasts *X-ceptional* news, sports, and entertainment across the Alliance.' *Jesus*, six months… that's all it'd been since they'd said goodbye. Hadn't taken her long.

"Time," someone requested at his lack of action.

Drew ignored the undercurrent of impatient mumblings.

The dealer announced, "You have thirty seconds to act, sir."

Why am I so angry? She made it crystal clear our relationship wasn't going anywhere. He'd paid back the script he'd charged to the Taleen Industries expense account and with interest. *Did she even know about that?* He doubted it. It was just the damn timing of her engagement—so soon after she'd left Dark Landing...and him, and—?

"Time. Your hand's dead, sir," the dealer said.

Drew mucked his full house and stepped away from the table. He squared his shoulders and took a breath. "Letty, sweetheart, what a coincidence." His voice wavered and he fought to keep it level. "I just caught a news piece about you. Congratulations!"

"Have you heard from Toby?" Letty asked, without a greeting.

~ ~ ∞ ~ ~

Curtis felt like he was standing at the top of a staircase, and someone pulled the rug from under him. He was teetering on the edge. *Get it together, man – where's your advantage?* For now, he relegated Nikko's missing accent to the bottom floor of his mind palace.

First up: How to kill or capture Fitz. The Diak may be technologically advanced, but they appeared pretty dim otherwise, or at least, Fitz seemed dim. Other than the threat to make one of them its new "vessel," unverifiable wormhole tech and the possibility of rescuing Alliance hostages from the Diak armada were ludicrous incentives. Even if the wormhole technology existed—and Curtis doubted it—Fitz never intended to hand it over. Once they crossed into Diak space, it had no reason to keep both Curtis and Nikko alive. It would probably download into one and add the other to the hostage stash. He was inclined to believe the story about the hostages. For some reason, that rang true.

The sensible thing to do was to inform the ESF and seek their protection. Let them deal with Fitz. *And I'll bet that's exactly what Nikko's up to now.* Curtis would need to steer clear of the Diak while the ESF did their thing. But he was screwed whichever way it went. Either the Diak would get him, or the ESF would when they discovered he'd concealed the return of the screamer cell and let the Diak loose on the station. Still, the latter scenario held the advantage—at least he'd be alive.

Curtis's comm purred, *Mitchell Jones*. "Yeah, Jonesy. I'm kinda busy now."

"Just wondering what you want me to do with Toby Greenstein. He's looking for Drew."

Curtis cupped a hand over his face. *Fuck!* "Send him in." Over the fun-filled last couple of hours, he'd forgotten all about the kid.

The hatch opened and Jones gently pushed a reluctant Toby into the office. *Is it possible the boy grew half a foot in the last six months?* Toby wore his patented stubborn, determined look.

"What are you doing here?" Curtis asked.

"I'm looking for Drew. Jonesy said he doesn't work here anymore. Where is he…*Chief?*" On the word "Chief," Toby wrinkled his nose and made a face, as if he'd smelled something rotten.

"Only *Muck* knows where Drew is," Curtis lied. "We're not exactly best friends. Is Letty here?"

"No. She's back in San Fran."

Aggravated, Curtis puffed his cheeks out, then exhaled and nodded toward the lounger. "Explain."

Toby flopped down. As if reading from an invisible prompter, he spoke at a fast clip, without emotion. "Letty's engaged. The guy's a *fucking* asshole. I paid some old lady to book passage for me as her grandson. No problema. I want Drew to take this gigolo out of the picture."

Curtis's laugh came out as a strangled bark. "*Jesus*, Toby… anytime but now. I'm gonna tap—" His comm purred again, *Katherine Taleen*. He mouthed *hold*. "You didn't cover your tracks very well." His hand formed an imaginary gun pointed at the comm implant behind his ear and made a shooting sound. The boy's shoulders slumped. Curtis raised his eyebrows. "Well?"

"*Activate comm*," Toby commanded in defeat.

Curtis transferred the holding communication to Toby and listened to the one-sided conversation.

"Yeah?. . . So?. . . Good, I hate him! I wanna go live with Drew. . . Yeah, okay."

Curtis's comm announced *Katherine Taleen* once more. "Hey, Letty. How's it hangin'?"

"Curtis, please take care of him. Don't let him out of your sight. We're leaving today for Dark Landing. I'll be there in a week."

"Look, sweetie, I don't have time for his crap. I'm putting him in a holding cell till then. He should feel right at home. *End all.*" He took pleasure in cutting her off so abruptly.

"Jonesy!" Curtis yelled through the still open hatch.

~ ~ ∞ ~ ~

Nikko watched the monitor, impatient for the face of Earth Defense Council Chairman, James Hawking-Barstow, to appear. It'd taken some finagling to get access to the ESF transmission-safe room on Spud. And he'd been forced to divulge his identity as a *Muck* undercover agent. But if even one Diak-infected individual...*or thing...* remained, all aligned and non-aligned races in the Known Universe were still in grave danger. Could it all be true: There are hundreds of K.U. citizens being held captive by the Diak, including Travis Barnes, 'The Hero of the Common Folk?' And the wormhole technology story? Nikko doubted it. But what he believed made no difference. A series of encrypted symbols flitted across the screen too fast to read, and the image of Sir James resolved.

"Sir James, thank you for agreeing to speak with me."

"I've confirmed your identity, Mr. Balog. The MCTT asserts you're one of their top drug enforcement agents. And if what you report is true, you're about to get a promotion. Where is the Fitzwilliam abomination now?"

"It's impossible to say for certain...somewhere on the station."

"What's your analysis of the situation?"

Amazed at how calm Sir James appeared, Nikko trembled inside and out. "To be honest, there's been no time for a subjective analysis. And I'm only marginally optimistic I can hold it off a few hours for the council to strategize." Nikko related his personal experience with Fitz, as well as what Curtis shared with Nikko regarding the chief's earlier confrontation.

"And Walker — what's your take on him? I understand you've been investigating him for some time."

"Actually, our investigation of Walker dead ended. The first package we intercepted turned out to be vitamin pills disguised as Utopia tablets. If I'd been a legit middleman, he'd be dead by now. He's a two-bit swindler. I'm here because *Muck's* intel still suggests there's a cartel operating through Dark Landing—but Walker's not involved. None of that's important anymore."

"Indeed. And you haven't reported this to your MCTT handler?"

"No. I came straight to you."

"You were right to do so. The council must decide how to handle the Diak in our midst. I'll call an emergency session. And we'll alert the Alliance members to the possibility that the Diak armada could enter our space again at any time. How do I get back in touch with you?"

"The Diak is monitoring my comm—and Curtis's. I don't want the ESF dispatcher contacting me. I'll come back here in… what? Two hours?"

"Good. *End transmission.*"

~ ~ ∞ ~ ~

Finally in his quarters, Curtis lay on his cot, still struggling to think of some way to survive the next few hours and, if really lucky, do so unscathed. He decided to *hell* with it. He'd disable his comm, head over to Spud, and hole up in a mine shaft to wait out whatever happened. He threw his legs over the side of his bunk.

His comm pinged. "Mr. Nikko Balog has disappeared," Fitz said.

Curtis guessed right. Nikko was busy informing the ESF of the situation. "He hasn't disappeared," he said. "He probably turned off his comm to sleep. Exactly what I'm gonna do now."

"He should not have done that. I will find him."

"Stay where you are—where *are* you? If anyone sees you, the ESF will go ballistic all over Dark Landing." Silence. "Fitz?. . . Fitz?" *Damn!*

Curtis was pulling his pants back on when his comm purred, *Benson Capone.* "What the hell, Benny?"

"He's back."

Curtis clutched at his heart, pounding once more. "How do *you* know he's back?"

"Because he's standing ten feet from me, and he wants more script." Benny spoke in a loud whisper.

"What do you mean, he wants more…? Who's back?" Curtis asked, confused. He made an effort to temper his racing heart.

"The Bahdaneian salvage captain. He figured we were up to something, and he wants more script credit."

"He's *blackmailing* me! That son-of-a-bitch. I'll be right there." This was turning out to be the longest day of his life — the second longest day of his life. The longest was the eighteen hours he'd spent in Diak space thinking he was a dead man.

When Curtis arrived at the dock, he found the Bahdaneian leaning against the side of his ship, arms crossed. He saw Curtis and headed toward him, buzzing like a swarm of bees.

"Benny, get me a translator unit." Benny stayed put. He knew as well as Curtis that translator units proved only fifteen percent effective with Bahdaneian, which made them worse than nothing at all.

"You know I speak English," the Bahdaneian said, waving Benny off with assumed authority. Benny's affronted *humph* could be heard loud and clear.

"What's this crap about you wanting more script? More script for what?" Curtis demanded.

"I figure that pod I returned was never meant to be found. You said yourself you'd disposed of it improperly, and your man here said it'd been contaminated by the Diak virus. I'm thinking you tried to get rid of me a little too neatly. And two hundred credits aren't near enough. Two *thousand* would be more like it." The captain's fur stood up around his topknot.

"Two thousand credits! You're out of your mind. No way you're getting any more." Curtis took an angry step forward. "You're a thieving piece of sh…."

The Bahdaneian captain stared back at him; his sneering expression suddenly turned blank. His eyes closed and then reopened and flashed dull gray for a second before the alien's white sclera and coal-black pupils reappeared. Curtis's body went cold once more. He flexed his hands to return feeling to them.

"We now have transportation. We leave tomorrow," the Diak said in the salvage captain's gravelly voice. It turned, walked up the narrow gangway, and vanished into the Bahdaneian salvage ship.

"He's leaving?" Benny asked from behind Curtis.

Curtis jumped at the sound. "*No!*" he snapped. He dialed it back. "He's staying for a while. Put the dock on maintenance and stay away until I tell you otherwise."

"But, why? How am I supposed to explain—"

"Just do it, Benny, if you know what's good for you," Curtis ordered over his shoulder as he left. He needed to find Nikko, fast.

~ ~ ∞ ~ ~

Though late evening, Doc took one more blood sample. She'd programed a new series of tests. If they ran overnight, the results would be available first thing in the morning. Preston squirmed in her hand, and she loosened her grip, afraid of hurting him. When the bird managed to liberate one wing it increased its struggle. He finally broke free of her grasp, but a talon snagged in her glove. Wings now beating the air furiously in an effort to escape, Preston pecked at Doc's face. His beak gouged the skin close to one eye. Tammy flung the hand with the snagged bird away from her head, shaking it to dislodge the pigeon. At last, its talon free, Preston flew to the top of the storage cabinet. He marched back and forth, head ducking up and down in agitation. She left the bird to calm itself while she saw to her wound.

~ ~ ∞ ~ ~

Ekis studied the salvage ship's command station. The panel presented a complete mystery. He accessed the alien's memories and sampled several dozen. The ship's captain accomplished the piloting process from ingrained habit while his thoughts were elsewhere. It was unfortunate the ship was Bahdane. From the start, all attempts by the Diak to translate the Bahdane language had failed. And the cultural inferences drawn from each sample's range of decipherable emotions proved unhelpful. While they made adequate hosts, the inability to fully experience Bahdane memories was disappointing.

A humming sounded—separate from the memories he reviewed. *Odd*, he thought. The soft reverberations deepened. Ekis turned. A second Bahdaneian stood close to him, her expression

65

expectant. A crew member or perhaps the captain's mate, and it appeared she'd asked a question.

Without hesitation, Ekis took hold of her snout in a crushing grip. Simultaneously, he cocked one leg behind the leg of the Bahdaneian, forcing the limb up off the deck. The alien lost her balance and fell heavily onto her back. The hums turned to a loud, furious combination of shrieks and buzzes. Ekis stomped his foot hard into her chest, then bent and wrapped his long, fur-covered fingers around the Bahdaneian's neck and pressed. Unexpectedly, talons extended from the end of each finger and punctured the alien's throat, drawing blood. Ekis pressed harder. The Bahdaneian female's own fingers, talons extended, clawed at Ekis' arms, ripping his skin under the thick fur. Ekis exerted all of his host's considerable strength. Her neck bones cracked, then crunched, and her flailing arms fell away to lie still at her sides. He released his hold and planted a foot in the alien's chest. The Bahdane did not move again.

Breathing heavily, he lifted his foot from the dead crew member. In that instant, the loop resolved, and Ekis' *Mass* communication subroutine reinitialized. *From my actions? The download? No matter. I am alive and safe now in this host and can move about the station with anonymity. I must find the Nikko human.* It concerned Ekis that Nikko's comm was inaccessible and…. He stiffened in disbelief. His *Mass* communication routine enabled, it automatically searched for a compatible link…and found one. *How is this possible? Comrade?*

12 OPPOSING OBJECTIVES

Xander Crawford sprawled on the plush sofa in Letty's office, listening as she placed yet another transmission in an attempt to locate her belligerent, snot-nosed kid. She'd just ended a conversation with Drew Cutter. On more than one occasion, she'd assured Xander that there'd been nothing between her and Drew. The tone of her voice suggested otherwise. He could care less who she'd screwed before him, but he was careful to project a modicum of jealousy anytime she mentioned Drew's name.

He'd spotted trouble the first time she'd introduced him to Toby. Children can see through the surface glitter to what lies beneath. Xander needed this merger. KUXC's next annual report would reveal the truth that its CPAs had artfully masked over the last three years. But once he and Letty were married, it would all fade away. KUXC would flourish solely by association with Taleen Industries. Other benefits of the match almost outweighed the pre-nup he'd been asked to sign by the Taleen legal division. His attention returned to Letty. She sat facing him, legs crossed, one foot swinging in impatience. His eyes followed the swinging foot up past shapely calves to where her legs joined below a perfectly flat stomach. *Sweet Jesus.* He mentally replayed the night before and crossed his own legs to hide his arousal.

"Found him," Letty announced, triumphant. She turned her chair, and her legs disappeared under the desk.

Xander hid his disappointment on both counts. He'd hoped the brat would disappear into the cosmos, never to be seen again.

Her connection made, Letty opened with an admonishment. *"Toby Greenstein Taleen, do you know how much trouble you're in?.* . . Xander is brokenhearted that you ran away because of him. . . . That's absurd. What makes you think Drew would have you anyway? Toby, honey, please try to understand. I love you, but I love Xander, too. And he loves *both* of us. He wants us to be a real family. You owe him. . . you owe *me* a chance. We'll make a great team, sweetie. I promise."

Xander's eyes rolled involuntarily. He blinked several times to cover his reaction and looked out the invisiwall of the penthouse office.

Letty directed Toby to transfer her tap to Curtis. "Curtis, please take care of him. Don't let him out of your sight. We're leaving today for Dark Landing. I'll be there in a week—

"Damn him! He cut our connection."

God, no! Not Dark Landing. Xander'd heard enough about the shit hole from Letty to know he never wanted to step foot there. He went to Letty and kissed her forehead. "See, I told you he'd be okay. This is a perfectly normal reaction. He's been the main object of your affection—then suddenly I come on the scene. The boy just needs to see how much we *both* love him."

Letty nodded. "Of course, you're right. I only want him to care for you as much as I do. We both deserve a *real* family."

~ ~ ∞ ~ ~

Mitchell Jones, the nightshift commander, showed Toby to his cell. "You can bivouac here. Do you have any luggage besides your backpack?"

Toby shook his head.

"Okay. I've activated the wall processor for you. Why don't you stow your stuff and come to ops with me? I don't suppose your pool game has improved any?"

"I've been working on it. Nuff to beat you, I'll bet."

"We'll see about that," Jonesy said, accepting the challenge. He led the way back to the front office. "You hungry, kid?"

"Sure. Say, are you gonna lock me in later?"

"Do I need to?"

"No, I promise I won't leave HQ. No place to go anyway."

"So, I have your word on that?"

"Sure thing, Jonesy," Toby said, smiling sweetly.

~ ~ ∞ ~ ~

When Curtis arrived outside Nikko's quarters, he spotted the man himself coming from the opposite direction. "Where have you been? You disabled your comm, dude, and that abomination's looking for you."

"Spaceout. I just grabbed a bite to eat. I needed some peace and quiet. You were right, I can't sleep."

Ignoring Nikko's excuse, Curtis nodded at the hatch. "There's a new wrinkle. Let's go inside."

Nikko palmed the access pad, and they stepped into his cramped quarters.

As soon as the hatched closed, Curtis ordered, *"Disable comm."* He nodded at Nikko to do the same. "You will not *believe* what just happened. Fitz took over a Bahdaneian salvage captain—entered him, downloaded to him, whatever you want to call it—and it's in his ship now, waiting for us. It wants to go to Diak space tomorrow. You got any brilliant ideas?"

"I just talked to Sir James with the Earth Defense Council. They're deciding what action to take." He offered no apology for contacting Earth authorities without consulting Curtis.

"I figured as much. And the ESF?" Curtis asked.

"No. That's up to Sir James. We need to hold Fitz off until I hear back from the council. I'm supposed to contact them again in a couple hours."

Curtis nodded. "We should be good until morn—"

A low chime announced someone at the hatch. Nikko issued a command to enable the one-way view of the corridor through the small hatch port. The two men exchanged apprehensive glances.

"Open," Nikko said.

The Bahdane captain stood in the hatchway. "Enable your comms. . . *now!"*

Nikko and Curtis each mouthed the command.

"Do not disable them again. I have your doctor, Tammy Jameson. If you value her, you will do exactly as I tell you. You will find someone on the station who is able to pilot the Bahdaneian ship.

You will bring this person to the docks and make a plan for evading the military unit guarding the bridge to Diak space." The Bahdane turned to leave.

"Wait!" Nikko stopped it. "I have a friend who clerks for the ESF. She's agreed to provide a map of the minefield. That's what I was doing when my comm was off earlier. But she can't transmit it—I have to pick up a data vial. She works in a high-security ESF office that shields their comm links."

It appeared to consider Nikko's statement. "Why is this person agreeing to your request? Did you inform her of my presence?"

"No. . . no, of course not," Nikko said, quickly. "We're friends—*lovers*. She's crazy about me. She'll do whatever I ask."

Curtis stood quietly, following the exchange, and willing himself invisible. He doubted he'd make it to the safety of the mine after all.

The Diak tipped its head as it considered further. After several seconds, it turned to Curtis. "You will stay with me." Then, addressing Nikko, "We will accompany you to Spud and wait. If you do not return, the doctor will suffer, and I will transfer Diak devices to this one and many more. When you have the map, you must locate a pilot for the Bahdane ship."

"Do as Fitz says." Curtis nodded to Nikko in tacit acceptance of whatever fate might bring. Clearly, he'd lost his chance to simply run away and let the ESF take over.

"You will now address me as Ekis,'" the Diak announced. "Leave your weapons here."

~ ~ ∞ ~ ~

With Ekis and Curtis waiting in the west armature outside the ESF airlock, Nikko proceeded into the anteroom. A different warrant officer than the one who'd greeted him on his first visit stood behind the anteroom counter. Nikko placed a finger to his lips, cautioning the man not to speak. Glancing at the name on the reception monitor, he said, "Mister Harvey, I'm here to see Jamie Hawking *again*. I'll just sign in, okay?" Without waiting for a response, he manually entered his name in the visitor line on the screen and then wrote "Mayday — see earlier entry" on the line asking the reason for the visit.

The man leaned forward to view the entry and then studied Nikko.

"Can I just go on back?" Nikko asked as he pointed back and forth between his implant and his ear to let the man know someone was monitoring the conversation.

The officer's eyebrows drew together in concentration as he struggled to make an appropriate response. "Uh. . . I, uh. . . you're not allowed to go back alone. I'll escort you. You'll need to check your blaster."

"Not carrying one," Nikko said, nodding in approval. "Sorry to bother you."

When they exited the anteroom, Nikko took the lead with the warrant officer close on his heels. They headed deeper into the installation to the transmission-safe room.

As soon as the hatch closed behind them, the officer stepped several feet away from Nikko. Hand on the hilt of his weapon, he asked, "What's going on, sir?"

"Yeah. . . hard to explain, and I'm not at liberty. But someone is monitoring my comm."

"How is that possible?" When Nikko failed to answer, he continued. "What do you want?"

"I talked to Sir James Hawking-Barstow at the Earth Defense Council earlier; I need to speak with him again. It's urgent."

The warrant officer consulted the transmission log on the large wall monitor. Upon confirming Nikko's claim, all outward appearance of curiosity vanished, and the man came to attention. "Immediately, sir — I'll patch the feed through. Can I get you anything while you wait?"

"No, thanks."

Fifteen minutes passed while Nikko paced the conference room, stomach rolling. Sir James' image materialized, and Nikko reported the new developments. When he'd finished, he said, "Look, Sir James, I know if all else fails, the council may feel forced to take action against the station. If we — Curtis and I, and probably Dr. Jameson now — do what Ekis wants and go with him, can't you quarantine it and scan? I think everyone here will come up clean."

He waited for Sir James to tell him the council had found another way to handle the situation without Nikko's sacrifice. No such luck.

Sir James nodded slowly. "The council reached the same decision. You and Walker will accompany Ekis into Diak space. The wormhole's been salted with communication relays since the *Marigold* incident. If there's even a remote possibility you can find a way to send intel back, it'll be worth it. Of course, we weren't aware of the Jameson development, but it doesn't change anything."

It changes things for Jameson! Nikko thought. He hesitated for only a second before responding. *Fuck it.* "Of course, sir." The words caught in his throat, but he continued. "Any further orders once we get to Diak space?" He finished his sentence internally: ...*since you so graciously invited us to make the trip.*

"No. You're on your own. Try to dissuade Ekis from taking Chief Walker and Dr. Jameson with you. But, if you're unsuccessful, well. . . ." His sentence trailed off. "It's unfortunate there will be a pilot at risk as well now. Someone among the Space Force ranks must be able to operate a Bahdaneian ship."

Shut up, Balog, he counseled, but didn't listen. "Not necessary, sir. All *Muck* ships are Bahdaneian—and agents are pilots, as well." *That nailed it.*

"Your sacrifice, and that of the others, will not be forgotten."

Small comfort. Sir James was obviously practiced at ordering others to their death.

An ESF nurse entered the room as Sir James ended the transmission. Making a shallow incision above the ankle on the inside of Nikko's right leg, the nurse inserted a second, dedicated comm and locater device, and then sealed the incision from a tube of liquid tissue.

The nurse smiled at Nikko. "There shouldn't be any discomfort, sir."

Nikko nodded and left the safe room, certain any discomfort was the least of his concerns.

13 SETTING THE COURSE

Benny stood in front of the hatch to the admin offices. Sweat stood out on his forehead, and his stomach churned. He'd begun as a cargo handler thirty-one years earlier and been on Dark Landing longer than anyone. He could have retired years ago, but the station was home and the job his whole life. Now his job, and maybe his pension, was at risk because of that idiot, Curtis Walker. Walker was up to no good, Benny knew that, and it had something to do with the screamer cell. He shoulda reported it to Chief Hargreaves as soon as the salvage captain brought it onboard. Everyone knew Walker was a scoundrel. But Benny worried how the new chief would react. He could lose everything.

"Excuse me. Mr. Capone, can I help you." Austen Hargreaves stood behind him.

Benny jumped and turned to face her. He rocked heel-to-toe and back, then wiped his palms on his pant legs.

"Come into my office," she said and stepped around him. He followed her through the hatch.

Austen sat down behind her desk. Benny stopped just inside the hatchway. He avoided eye contact. "What on Earth is wrong?" she asked, gesturing for him to sit, and commanding her office hatch closed.

He moved a few feet further into the room but remained standing. "I need to tell you about a thing that happened. I shoulda said something sooner. . . but I don't know about ESF security clearances and that kinda stuff. . . and Chief Walker—"

~ ~ ∞ ~ ~

"Sit!"

"Yes, sir." Benny sat timidly at the edge of the chair.

"Relax. Tell me what's going on from the beginning."

After a few seconds, he looked up at her and scooted back in the chair. Usually spry, his movements belied his true age. Today she could see the years of hard labor etched in the wrinkles of his face. She tried to imagine what he looked like in his youth—not bad maybe.

"So. . ." he began, "you remember the Bahdaneian salvage ship that docked the day of your chiefs' meeting?" Austen nodded. "Well, I didn't tell you the whole story. The ship's captain found the screamer cell and brought it back to the station. He thought there might be a finder's fee."

"The screamer cell? What's that?"

"You know, the high-security cell where they held Chief Fitzwilliam after he turned into a lump of Diak nanoids. When he disintegrated, they spaced it."

Austen's hands grew cold. "Go on."

Benny started talking fast. "So, anyway, the salvage captain found it and towed it back here, and I reported it to Curtis. I know I shoulda reported to you, but I just. . . you know, he knew all about what went on back then, and you were so new." His narration gathered more speed. "The captain wanted to be paid, but Curtis told him we'd ejected the cell on purpose so then the captain said 'Good, it's salvage and I can sell it' and then Curtis—"

"Slow down, Benny."

"Yeah, okay. So. . . ." Benny took a deep breath and let it out from puffed cheeks. He explained how Curtis paid off the captain and told Benny not to mention the episode to anyone.

Austen interrupted him, "That sounds reasonable."

Benny appeared relieved by her reaction. "Well, that's not all."

"No, I didn't think so. Continue."

He went on to relate the salvage ship's return, the captain's demand for two thousand credits, and the ensuing argument with Curtis. When he finished, he watched her apprehensively.

"Curtis didn't give you an explanation?"

"No. One minute he and the captain were yelling at each other—honest Chief, I thought they were comin' to blows—and the next minute they just stopped. The captain went back on his ship, and Curtis ordered me to keep my mouth shut and left. I'm sorry."

"I understand your confusion about what action to take. But you know as well as anyone, Chief Walker and I are the same rank. He may take the lead on security matters, but you're to report all incidents on the docks to me regardless. If you have problems with that going forward, tell me now."

"No. I. . . I don't have a problem."

"Good. Then I think it's best if I go down and talk to the captain myself. As strange as it may appear, I'm sure Chief Walker knows what he's doing."

"Want me to come with you?"

"No. You're off duty, correct?" Benny nodded. "I'll handle this from here," she said.

"Thanks." Benny made a quick retreat.

Austen stayed at her desk, considering Benny's account. In the news reports at the time, she'd never heard the high security cell referred to as the "screamer cell." What an odd term. By any name, it was back on Dark Landing. She shivered and hugged herself, rubbing her arms to dispel the goosebumps.

Protocol required she speak with Curtis before talking to the Bahdaneian captain. It was the professional thing to do, but she suspected he would obfuscate the facts and make it harder for her to get to the bottom of the incident. Face it: She and that pestiferous princox would never be comrades. No matter. Once the investigation ended, she'd be leaving the station anyway.

The whole pigeon episode with Doc was weird enough, and whatever Curtis was involved with now equally baffling. Both were up to no good, but she felt sure they weren't colluding. Then again, Doc's obsession with finding Governor Fitzwilliam-Bennett pointed to a Diak connection of some kind, and the Curtis business seemed Diak-related as well. She was eager to share the information with *Muck* and the ETOC to see what they made of it. She pushed back her chair and headed to the docks.

~ ~ ∞ ~ ~

Toby feigned a yawn, stretched to his tiptoes, and made a bank shot at the five ball, sinking the eight ball instead.

"I thought you been working on your game, kid. That'll be ten credits." Jonesy passed his hand under the table and pool balls reemerged from all six pockets. Unassisted, they rolled to the far end, sorted with a clatter, and auto racked in numerical order.

"I'm just tired," Toby said. "Letty's been making me go to bed and get up at the same times. I guess I'm sorta used to it now." He yawned again.

"You might as well hit your bunk. I gotta get back to work anyway. We can play again tomorrow night if you're still around."

"Thanks, Jonesy. Night." He followed Jones toward the rec room hatch but hung back several steps. When the commander detoured to the head, Toby kept walking out of HQ and onto the conveyer. Twenty minutes later, he sauntered into the dockside control post.

"Well, I'll be a jackal's ass—look at you," the man at the monitoring station said.

"Hey, Sparks. 'Sup?"

"Missed your lippy self around here the last few months. Did they kick you off Earth, too?"

"Somethin' like that. Anything interesting?" Toby scanned the bank of monitors that streamed live views of the ten docking bays. A red ribbon across the top of berth nine flashed the word 'maintenance.' "What's happening on nine?"

"Don't know." Sparks studied the number nine screen. "That's a Bahdaneian salvage ship. Benny took nine out of service without entering a reason, and there's no repair orders I know of. Chief Walker's met with the captain a couple times. Something's up."

"Huh. Can I go down and meet the captain? Bahdaneians are cool. Never met one that don't work for *Muck* though."

"Well. . . it's mid-morning ship-time. . . I guess so. Mind your manners, boy," Sparks chided.

Toby made his way down to berth nine and circled the salvage ship. Exterior grappling tools were retracted against the aft and forward hulls. Hardly a spot on its surface wasn't pockmarked or scarred. To a nine-year-old, its mean appearance and the added presence of undecipherable Bahdane symbols, gave it an air of danger and mystery. He made his way up the narrow gangway.

The hatch to the cargo bay stood open. No sound came from the interior. "Permission to come aboard?" Toby called out. After several seconds without a response, he repeated the request in a louder voice. With still no response, he took a few hesitant steps inside. "Hello. . . anyone here?" The ship conveyed an empty feeling and Toby decided to look around on his own. He yelled "Hello?" every few steps.

The inside of the ship was as scarred and dirty as the outside. A short, narrow passage with closed storage compartments on both sides led from the bay into a small galley and mess area. Toby wrinkled his nose at the fetid odor as he passed a counter stacked with dirty food containers sitting next to the waste chute. *Bahdanes must eat their own poop,* he thought and laughed at his jest. "Hello?" he called again. Muffled shrieks came from deeper inside the ship. Toby froze and listened. The shrieks continued in indistinct, short bursts. Someone was onboard after all, and they were upset. He turned and retraced his steps. About to exit the passage back through the cargo bay, a shadow fell across the opening. Toby ducked into the closest storage compartment, which proved deeper than he expected. He hunched down and pressed himself into a back corner.

He heard a woman's voice, her words muted but clear, "Anyone here? Austen Hargreaves, Dark Landing Chief of Administration. Hello!"

~ ~ ∞ ~ ~

Austen found the dock's blast doors standing open. No one appeared to be around. A monitor on the bulkhead provided the docked ship's name and registry information. Under that it said: *Berth Nine offline; maintenance pending. Contact Benson Capone, Senior Dock Foreman.* The Bahdane salvage ship sat unattended in the middle of the dock, well inside the atmospheric shield.

She climbed the gangway. The light from behind cast Austen's shadow across the width of the *Remarkable Mayzie's* cargo bay. Looking for a comm device to announce her presence and, not finding one, she knocked on the side of the open hatch. The bulkhead was reinforced, and her knock produced only a dull rap. A noise sounded from the passage opposite the hatchway. She stuck her head inside and called out, "Anyone here? Austen Hargreaves, Dark Landing Chief of Administration. Hello!" No one was home, or they hadn't heard her.

Legally, Dark Landing could search any ship in dock if it looked like the station or someone in the ship was in danger. Of course, that generally applied to security personnel. Austen shrugged. *In a way, I'm more security staff than admin staff.* She crossed the bay into the ship's interior. A passage led to the small galley and mess, and beyond that were crew quarters, a common meeting area, and a shared chem shower and head. She continued forward. Through another hatch, a half-circle hallway provided open access to the navigation and ops posts and, finally, a small bridge and pilot's station. A closed door on the bulkhead to the right of the bridge probably led to the captain's private quarters.

Austen sensed she wasn't alone. Hair lifted on the nape of her neck and arms. "Hello? Is anyone here?" A high-backed captain's chair was centered in the middle of the bridge. Unable to tell if anyone was in it, she walked forward slowly, in trepidation. A muffled thud came from behind the closed door. Austen stopped and turned an ear toward the sound. Nothing.

The bridge was illuminated only by the soft glow from the instrument panels. As she continued around the side of the captain's chair, her thoughts still on the thudding noise, she tripped over something lying on the deck. Lurching past it, she grabbed the chair's arm to keep from falling forward onto the pilot's station. The body of an obviously dead Bahdaneian female lay sprawled between the chair and the control panels—its face permanently distorted in a grotesque mask.

Panic grabbed at her; she wanted off the ship. Austen stepped back across the body and retraced her route aft. As she reached the passage between the mess and the cargo bay, voices sounded dockside. One was definitely Curtis's—whining, as usual. Another sounded like Nikko Balog's barrel-chested bass, but she detected no accent. The voices grew louder as the speakers approached the ship. The short passage was lined with storage lockers. She opened the nearest one and ducked inside. The compartment was deep and pitch black. Something hung in front of her—an EMU? She pushed past it into the corner and pressed herself tight against the bulkhead. Boots trampled through the passageway. The unmistakable grind of the gangway retracting, and the ship's hatch closing echoed across the cargo bay. Worse — from her hiding place, she heard the muted announcement advising non-suited personnel to clear the dock area.

She had five minutes to act. After the fourth announcement, the dock lights would dim, the berth would seal and depressurize, and the environmental field between the ship and space would dissolve. Austen swallowed her panic and focused. The voices sounded close by, perhaps coming from the mess area now. They — three separate voices — were arguing about something, but she couldn't make out what. As she calculated the odds of exiting the storage unit, crossing the cargo bay, and reopening the hatch before they caught her, something rustled near her foot. Rats! The rat brushed against her pant leg. She cringed but stood firm, biting her lower lip to keep from crying out. She tensed, poised to make her getaway, when the *rat* grabbed onto her ankle.

Austen screamed.

~ ~ ∞ ~ ~

"You will take me away from here now," Ekis commanded.

Curtis blanched at the Diak's announcement.

Nikko argued. "What? We have a map of the minefield, but we still need a plan to evade ESF — a diversion of some kind. Besides, I have to familiarize myself with the controls."

On their way to the ship, Curtis was surprised to learn Nikko could pilot the Bahdane ship. While he doubted the Diak would grant a last wish before it killed him, Curtis wanted to know Nikko's real identity.

He believed nothing the Diak said. Though he possessed zero leverage, he issued a directive, "We're not going anywhere unless you take me to Doc. . . do you understand?"

Ekis addressed Nikko. "We are leaving. Come, I will show you the pilot station." It turned to Curtis. "And the Doctor Jameson." The buccaneer shirt Ekis wore wrapped loosely across its furry Bahdane chest without fasteners. It reached inside the shirtfront and drew out an alien blaster.

Nikko sneered. "If you shoot *me*, who's going to pilot this ship?"

Ekis pointed the blaster at Curtis's head.

"Thanks a lot, pal," Curtis reproached Nikko, though encouraged to know he served a purpose. He sensed the Diak was vulnerable in the Bahdaneian's body, even as strong as that body appeared. Otherwise, why bother with a blaster? Flesh and bone now, could it disassemble in the same way it did in its nanoid form? The blaster worried him, but Nikko and he together could probably outman the Diak. Well, Nikko could, anyway. If nanoid Ekis abandoned the Bahdane, would it move into one of them? He'd rather be blown away.

He jumped as a piercing scream came from a storage compartment in the passage behind them.

The blaster fired.

14 ALL ABOARD

Curtis frantically patted his face and head, then ran his hands over his chest. He was unhurt. The acrid smell of burning insulation filled the mess and mingled with the smell of Curtis's singed hair. If Ekis hadn't flinched involuntarily upon hearing the scream, the blaster shot would have taken Curtis's head off. Wisps of smoke and red sparks emitted from a hole next to the hatch leading into the ship's interior. A series of bumps and crashes and a string of panicked entreaties came from a cabinet in the passageway.

"Let go. *Let go!* Get away from me. Nooo. . . ." A woman's voice.

"Hey, you kicked me. Don't. Stop it. . . ." A child's voice.

Ekis turned toward the commotion, its back to Curtis and Nikko. A compartment door flew open, and Austen Hargreaves fell into the narrow passage in a heap. Toby Greenstein emerged next and clambered over her on all fours. The boy scurried into the mess. Stopped by the wall of legs, he looked up and rose slowly to his feet. From her spot on the deck, Austen, open mouthed, stared at the three figures as well.

Curtis shook his head and covered his face. "I don't fucking believe it!"

"What's going on here?" Austen demanded from the deck, as if in control of the situation. "Why are—" Her words cut off, and her gaze dropped to the blaster Ekis still held. She got up and moved to Toby's side.

Nikko made the introductions. "Chief Hargreaves, this is the Diak Ekis, formerly Martin Fitzwilliam, and now this ship's captain."

Curtis swore under his breath. Unwittingly, Austen had provided the perfect opportunity to overtake the Diak, and they'd missed it. The second warning for anyone without an EMU to clear the dock area came over the ship's speakers.

"Only *Muck* knows what these two are doing here. . . together. . ." Curtis shook his head in disbelief once more ". . . but if you let them and the doctor go, Nikko and I will cooperate."

Ekis ignored Curtis's entreaty and grabbed Toby by the arm. It placed the blaster barrel to the boy's head and motioned for the group to precede him deeper into the ship. Nikko pushed Curtis and Austen to the front of the line. He fell in between them and Ekis, who followed him with a firm grip on the saucer-eyed Toby.

"That's a Diak? A Bahdaneian?" Austen whispered to Curtis.

"Yeah. It's hard to explain right now," he whispered back.

"Who's the boy?"

Curtis shot her a bewildered look. "You don't know?"

"No—it. . . it's hard to explain right now."

"Toby Greenstein," Curtis said.

"The child the Taleen woman adopted?!"

The media had gleefully jumped on the orphan-turned-rich-kid story, and Toby was as big a celebrity as Letty.

"One and the same."

As they entered the bridge, Austen leaned close to Curtis and whispered again, "There's a body by the captain's chair."

Curtis sucked in his breath. "Doc?"

"Doc? No. . . no, a Bahdaneian."

The third warning announcement sounded.

Curtis turned to see Nikko holding a roll of tape. He assumed he'd picked it up along the way at Ekis' instruction. Nikko taped Austen's and Toby's hands behind them, and Ekis motioned them to the deck. To Curtis, Ekis said, "Take the Bahdaneian to the back and position it against the cargo hatch. If you do not return, the woman and the child will die."

With some difficulty, Curtis dragged the Bahdaneian off the bridge and back to the cargo bay. On the way, her long tongue flopped from her snout, swabbing the deck as they went. The tongue was furrowed down its length with a ruffled tip. Curtis averted his eyes. The fourth announcement sounded as he rolled the body against the cargo bay doors.

Panting from exertion, he returned to the bridge. Ekis sat in the captain's chair. Austen's and Toby's mouths were taped, and Doc was with them, her mouth and hands taped as well. Fear and confusion filled Doc's eyes. Nikko sat at the pilot's station, his size for once accommodated by the Bahdaneian fixtures.

"We're going?" Curtis asked.

Nikko nodded as he studied the instruments. "Tap ESF and advise them there are unknown ships approaching the station dockside."

"All they have to do is look at their sensors to know that's not true," Curtis said.

"They'll have to investigate anyway." Nikko threw Curtis a warning glance over his shoulder.

Curtis complied. To his surprise, the ESF dispatcher never questioned the story.

"The squadron's on its way, sir," the woman said.

He watched as Nikko inserted a data vial into the instrument panel.

Ekis ordered Curtis to sit on the deck with the others, nodding to a spot next to Austen that kept him in full view of the Diak. The monitor above the forward view port now displayed a chart with a large, glowing circle in its center representing the wormhole. The circle was filled with smaller, concentric rings and dozens of red exes representing the minefield blocking entry into Diak space. The exes were placed in diamond patterns equidistant from one another. Numbers next to each icon provided its position relative to the circle's center.

This is really happening, Curtis thought, horror-stricken.

Austen leaned against him, shoulder to shoulder. He imagined he could feel her shared fear through the fabric of their uniforms. Without taking his eyes from the monitor, he put his arm around her. She bumped him hard, and he turned to find her glaring angry accusations at him. He pulled his arm away in annoyance. *So. . . I should have informed Admiral Sullivan about the screamer cell, after all.* He shrugged half-heartedly in retrospect.

The fifth and final announcement sounded: *Berth nine clear. Commencing depressurization.* Through the forward viewer, Curtis saw the blur from the environmental shield dissolve and distant stars appeared. They were on their way.

~ ~ ∞ ~ ~

Nikko opened a joint tap with the Dark Landing and ESF dispatchers. He hesitated, unable to provide the name or registry of the ship, then said, "This is Nikko Balog on the Bahdaneian scavenger advising this ship is under the control of a Diak, and the Diak is holding five hostages, including Chiefs Walker, Jameson, and Hargreaves, a child, Toby Greenstein, and—"

Grunts of protest came from Toby.

"Correction. . . Toby Greenstein *Taleen*, and me. You're ordered to stand down. We're crossing the bridge into Diak space." Of course, they'd comply, the order came indirectly from Sir James.

In unison, the three bound hostages grunted their shock and protest upon learning their destination.

Nikko's thoughts swirled as he strove to come up with a last-minute plan. There seemed no way around Curtis being there—the whole situation was his doing anyway. But Ekis held Doc, and now Hargreaves and the kid, as well. As hard as he tried, he could think of no reason why those two would be hiding on the salvage ship. He knew Sir James would want him to continue the mission—*heartless bastard*—and he'd be right. *Regardless*, he argued to himself, *whatever happens next is beyond my control.* If he refused to pilot the ship, Ekis would start shooting hostages. Then again, if they continued through the wormhole, they were all dead. *So. . . dead on our side or dead on their side—makes no difference. Does it?* Nikko shuddered.

They rounded the east end of Spud without confrontation, but an ESF gunship fell into position between the salvage ship and the wormhole. Nikko'd scanned the pilot's station for weapon controls when he'd first sat down and found none. *Muck's* 4-R policy: Restrict weapons in number and capacity, compel ownership Registration, and Rigorously enforce the law by conducting Repeated stop-and-search campaigns—as well as excessive licensing fees—severely inhibited the arming of civilian ships. Nikko wasn't alarmed by the presence of the ESF gunship. It would seem odd if their escape went unchallenged. He turned to Ekis for instructions.

"Transmit the bridge image to the Earth Space Force ship," Ekis commanded. It stood, reached down, dragged Toby up from the deck, and pressed the blaster against the boy's temple once more. Toby cast Nikko a frightened look, then crossed his eyes and stared forward. Despite their circumstances, Nikko clamped his jaws tight to keep from smiling and turned away. The ESF ship stayed put but held its fire.

"Ram it," Ekis ordered.

Nikko aimed the little salvage vessel at the gunship — twice its size. At the last minute, the ESF ship repositioned above the smaller ship, and they passed under it, heading directly for the wormhole. The ship's computer charted a path through the minefield, and Nikko gave the computer its head. Without warning, mines on both side of them detonated, rocking the salvage vessel violently from side to side. As Nikko turned and watched, the captives rolled around the deck unrestrained. Ekis, standing with a tight grip on Toby, fell backward into the captain's chair, Toby on top. The fall jolted the blaster out of its hand. It skittered across the deck to rest against the bulkhead.

15 ASTEROID DÉJÀ VU

The rocking action threw Curtis under the pilot's station. Before Nikko could act, Curtis scrambled to his feet and headed for the blaster. Nikko hurled himself at Ekis, intending to restrain him while Curtis retrieved the weapon. But his forward motion stopped abruptly when Ekis flung Toby away from it. The child's body hit Nikko full force in the face. He felt his nose pop. Blood spewed down his shirtfront. Toby fell to the deck in the narrow space between the captain's chair and the control panel. Nikko hesitated, not wanting to step on the boy. He watched in dismay as Ekis completed a backward somersault over the top of the captain's chair, just as Curtis reached for the blaster.

The ESF gunship fired its laser again. A third mine detonated close by. Nikko lost his balance and fell. As he went down, he contorted his body to avoid landing on Toby and hit his face against the arm of the captain's chair. His left eye socket erupted in pain.

"Cease!"

From the deck, Nikko looked up with his good eye to see Ekis standing, braced against the bulkhead, blaster in hand. Curtis lay on the deck with Ekis' foot pressed hard against his Adam's apple.

The rocking stopped. Everyone froze in place. The ship's proximity alert whooped, and the flickering of its emergency lights cast a dream-like quality across the otherwise motionless scene.

Nikko returned to the control panel and cut the flashing lights and the alarm. The view out the forward window was filled with asteroids, some small, others massive. Behind him, Ekis ordered Curtis back to his seat on the deck next to Austen. Toby moaned from where he still lay between the pilot's and captain's stations. Nikko glanced back in time to see the Diak land a boot in the boy's midsection that lifted him from the deck and sent him sprawling in front of the other hostages. The alien fell back into his seat, breathing hard from exertion, his blaster arm draped loosely across the arm of the chair, and his attention distracted by the view.

Nikko's rage numbed his pain. The battle wasn't over. Without thought, he lunged at Ekis, pushing down on the lolling arm with all of his force. There was a satisfying crack as the Bahdane's bone broke against the chair's hard surface. Ekis' scream of rage filled the silent cabin, and the blaster dropped to the deck once more. With the advantage, Nikko dragged Ekis from the chair to the deck and placed both hands around its neck, squeezing tight. The Bahdane neck was thick and muscular, hard to hang on to. With his good arm, the Diak alternated jabbing taloned fingers at Nikko's eyes and pounding on his chest with blows that sent shockwaves through his body. Freeing one hand to fight off the assault, Nikko fought desperately to maintain a hold on the Bahdaneian's throat with the other. As strong as he was, the Bahdane was stronger, and the contest turned against him. The Diak—snout open, gagging for air—whipped its head back and forth to break Nikko's grip.

Nikko pressed as hard as he could one-handed on the Diak's throat, but his grasp loosened. From nowhere, a blaster appeared in the short space between him and Ekis. Its handgrip inadvertently struck Nikko's already broken nose as the barrel disappeared into the Bahdaneian's opened snout. Ekis attempted to dislodge the weapon using its long tongue. The blaster fired. The laser disintegrated the Bahdaneian's brains under its furry topknot. Its eyes bulged from their sockets.

In excruciating pain, Nikko fell to the deck at the Diak's side, cupping his shattered nose. Through his tears, he saw a blurred Curtis kneeling next to the body. The fingers of Curtis's right hand were wrapped awkwardly over the top of the blaster's fuel cell, his thumb holding the trigger down, the blaster's barrel still buried in what remained of Ekis' head. Reaching with his left hand, Curtis toggled the safety catch and let go of the blaster.

Nikko whimpered and forced himself to get up and return to the command station. The pain threatened his concentration. Afraid he would pass out, he briefly reconnoitered the portion of Mass Primary visible to them and piloted the Mayzie toward an asteroid large enough to conceal the vessel. Behind him, he heard Curtis freeing the hostages.

Curtis and the others silently crowded at Nikko's back as he maneuvered the ship under an outcrop and cut its systems except life support and gravity.

"Fuck," Toby said.

"Fuck, indeed." Nikko turned gingerly around, trying to ignore his throbbing face. "Well, we're better off than before," he said, with a pronounced nasal inflection. Nikko, along with Curtis, Drew Cutter, Letty Taleen, and Toby, and with Travis Barnes piloting Dark Landing's shuttle, the *Marigold*, had strayed into Diak space by accident not that long ago. "At least this time we have a ship with some power and range. And maybe food — certainly water. I guess we need a plan. Toby, whatcha got?"

Toby offered a grim smile. He'd come up with a plan that'd saved them the last time they were there. "I got nuthin' now." He looked to Curtis.

Curtis shook his head slowly. "I'm a blank."

Nikko was in too much pain to take advantage of the opening Curtis provided. "Notice anything different?" he asked, instead of making a sarcastic retort.

Curtis nodded. "Where's the armada?"

Their quick look had revealed no Diak ships on the side of the station facing them. As Nikko thought about the possibilities a missing armada might portend, he gingerly touched his face in several spots to determine the extent of the damage.

Throughout the men's conversation, Doc stood expressionless, staring at the deck. Suddenly she gasped and cupped a hand over her mouth, eyes wide. After a moment, she lowered the hand, and whispered, "Sync to speakers." A crisp, clear voice in an unrecognizable language was transmitted from Doc's comm through the ship's speakers.

"Disable your comms!" Nikko yelled, grimacing from pain.

Everyone obeyed Nikko's command. Doc dropped to the deck sobbing and holding her head in both hands. She rocked back and forth. "Nooo. . . no. . . no. . . ."

Austen knelt next to her. She gently pulled Doc's hands down from her head and grasped her chin, then tilted it up so she could look into her eyes. "What's wrong, Dr. Jameson?"

Tears streamed down Doc's face. She shook off Austen's hold to look at each of them in turn. "This is my f-fault. Everything. Everything is my fault. Diak nanoids. . . I'm. . . I'm infected. They can hear me."

"Preston?" Austen asked quietly, the doctor's earlier actions suddenly clear.

Doc nodded. "He carries inactive nanoids. I thought I could study them. Learn how to control and direct them. I would be responsible for mankind's most important advance."

Curtis erupted. "That fucking pigeon! I knew I shoulda blown that bird into nuggets. Doc, how could you be so irresponsi —"

"You stupid bastard!" Nikko said, his disgust evident. "What gives you the right to criticize anyone? You brought that *monster* back onto the station."

Austen interrupted their exchange, her arm around Doc. "Guys! We're wasting time here. Shouldn't we be forming a plan?"

Curtis stared silently out the window past Nikko to the familiar asteroid field. He wore a pained, guilt-ridden expression.

I'll be damned, Nikko thought, startled by Curtis's display of conscience. While they'd been talking, Nikko's nose continued to bleed. He swiped at the blood dripping past his mouth and chin and winced when he inadvertently touched his nose. He held his breath until the worst of it passed. "Even with Doc's comm disabled, it's possible the Diak can still track the nanoids. Who knows what their tracking range is? We should move away from here." Nikko winced again. "Chief Hargreaves, can you take Doc to the back? I'm about to pass out. There's gotta be first aid stuff somewhere. Maybe she can find pain meds."

Doc looked at Nikko's face in surprise. "I didn't realize. . . yes, please." She grasped Austen's offered hand and stood. "That needs to be seen to. I'll look for supplies and something to ease your pain."

Nikko could feel his face and eyes swelling; his head pounded. He nodded weakly toward Toby. "You feeling okay, kid? That kick lifted you right up off the deck."

"Yeah, I'm okay," Toby said.

"Go with them. See what kind of food stuff they have and inventory the water supply if you can."

"You know you're talkin' really weird?" Toby quipped over his shoulder as he followed Austen and Doc.

"Doc, take a look at Toby," Nikko called out. "Just in case."

Curtis fell into the captain's chair. "I-I'm sorry," he said softly.

That tears it; now I've heard everything. "Don't beat yourself up—I'll do that when we get home." Nikko returned his attention to the instrument panel and enabled the sensors. There was no way to move safely through the asteroid field without them. "Right now, we got bigger problems," he said to Curtis. Through slitted eyes, Nikko looked at the rear sensor display, which revealed two Diak gunships poised eight-hundred meters aft with their laser cannons directed at them.

~ ~ ∞ ~ ~

Sar Mode tapped a Fahdeen claw against her display, deep in thought. Ekis, an incursion agent they'd thought long dead, just brought a Bahdane ship through the wormhole from the K.U. No sooner had the ship appeared on their sensors, than Ekis was overpowered and killed by his Earth passengers. It had happened too quickly for Ekis to migrate to a new host. *Hostages?* But the greater mystery was that they'd monitored the entire incident through the devices of an infected human. . . a Doctor Tammy Jameson. When their invasion attempt failed, how had this human survived the Diak extermination of infected aliens? Were there other survivors as well? Should even one device remain, it could eventually spread to every alien in the K.U. If the humans thought those infected were dead, they may not scan until it was too late. All would be lost. Their prospective hosts would become infested with nanoids and useless.

The Diak gunships escorted the vessel to Mass Primary. Sar Mode was eager to question the doctor. Time was now the appointed principal's greatest enemy.

She picked up the blade lying on the counter and turned to address the figure waiting patiently at her back. "And you've shared your final report with no one? Though I would understand if you had — your team certainly suspects?"

"They do, Your Prominence, but they have been isolated for many turnings. And I've spoken of our calculations to no one other than yourself, as instructed."

Sar Mode studied the engineer as she played with the scimitar, careful to avoid its razor-sharp edge. She held it, suspended on one outstretched digit in front of her. A beautiful instrument, perfectly balanced, its hilt, guard, and spine were intricately carved. The weapon was a valued heirloom of her previous host, a human whose memories were rich in the details of its provenance. It even had a name, *Vadaar the Enforcer*.

The engineer watched her through the eyes of a Tunni, its demeanor alternating between fear and pride. The appointed principal considered the Tunni's form in comparison to her own Fahdeen body. Its features, almost as disgusting, were squat and pulpy, no taller than Sar Mode's host and equally lacking in elegance. But it sported multiple appendages, which made the Tunni excellent vessels for Diak researchers, allowing several tasks to be performed at once.

"So, it has come to this," she said. "You are dim-witted, and your team is dim-witted as well. You stand before me to confirm the Diak are without hope — tottering on the edge of extinction. Did you think your little presentation would end with a commendation for a task well completed?" The scimitar, its hilt now grasped firmly in her spindly paw, sliced downward faster than the Tunni's eyes could follow, separating its bulbous head from its pulpy body.

The Pothlill who stood unobtrusively in the far corner of Sar Mode's quarters, extended its long tentacle to catch the head before it landed. As the tentacle retracted, it encircled the corpse as well, pulling the two pieces back. Not a drop of the brown fluid oozing from the Tunni reached the deck.

"Eject the remains and the rest of the research team members into space, and then follow them out," Sar Mode ordered the tall alien.

As one Pothlill disappeared with its macabre cargo, another entered to occupy the corner position and await the appointed principal's next command.

Events are occurring much quicker than I envisioned. Always willing to adapt as circumstances dictated, Sar Mode nodded to herself. *The appearance of the Bahdane ship might prove advantageous.*

16 REUNIONS

For the last leg of the trip, Drew transferred from the comfort of the passenger carrier, *Ghiscar,* to a private trading vessel with accommodations for only its captain and two crew. After paying an outrageous fee, he'd spent four days sleeping on a pallet in the tightly packed cargo hold, which lacked the space to even string a hammock. But she was headed straight to Dark Landing, cutting a week off his journey.

If Letty was right, Toby thought Drew still worked on Dark Landing. That's where he would start his search. He'd find him and return him to Letty. He needed to see her one more time to confirm he had no chance with her and show her he no longer cared. Though, over the last six months, he constantly thought about her and imagined scenarios where he'd followed her to San Francisco. Her engagement announcement was a punch in the gut. Seeing her with her fiancé should finally put an end to his fantasies.

When he debarked at the station, Letty stood with her back to him not twenty feet away, hands on her shapely hips. Her thick, black hair, longer since he'd last seen her, hung below her shoulders. Knowing she was within touching distance triggered an unsettling swirl of emotions. He looked past her to see Benny Capone mimicking her posture and probably her determined expression. Drew smiled. This was a match worthy of the Fahdeen battle pits. Benny spotted Drew, and with an ear-to-ear grin, he pushed past Letty and headed toward him.

"Wait. . . I am *not* finished!" Letty spun around.

His eyes locked onto hers like a tractor beam. Drew mechanically returned Benny's handshake and man-hug.

Evidently noticing Drew's distracted gaze, Benny backed up. "Yeah, well. . . she's been here a couple days. Hey, I gotta. . . be somewhere. Maybe we can catch up later?"

Drew finally dragged his eyes away from Letty to look at the dock manager. "I'll buy you a drink, Benny. Great to see you—it really is." He meant it. He gave the man a friendly punch on the arm before turning back to Letty. Benny quickly exited the cargo bay.

Then she was in his arms—crying. *Of course, she's crying. I wouldn't recognize her if she weren't crying.* Her body was warm and soft, tight against his. He'd never wanted her as much as he did in that moment. He pressed his face into her hair, longing for the scent of orange blossoms. *Peppermint! What the. . .?!*

"Hey, let me look at you." He pulled away so he could see her face. Her eyes were red-rimmed and puffy. It wasn't a reaction to seeing him again; she'd been crying for a while. "Toby?"

She nodded. "Drew, you won't believe what's happened. He's gone. . . through the wormhole again."

Drew's heart sank. She sobbed in earnest—tears flowing, nose running. He offered her his sleeve; it was all he had. She chose to use her own.

"Okay, calm down. Um. . . ." Without quarters, he was uncertain where to take her. "Is there someplace we can talk?"

She nodded again. "Yes, the *Maris Stella*. The next berth over."

"I assume you've laid in an adequate supply of tissues?" That brought a wan smile as she led him out of the bay.

The *Maris Stella* was three times the size of the trader on which he'd arrived, and three times as luxurious as the passenger vessel, *Ghiscar*. Two Taleen Security Force staff flanked the blast doors into the docking bay, with two more at the gangway. They passed through an ornately painted airlock directly into a lavishly appointed salon. Drew wondered if the slouch hat, poncho-appareled woman he'd first met was gone for good. He led her to the nearest lounger and sat beside her, his arm wrapped loosely around her waist. It reminded him of another time they'd sat together like this, when Drew was consoling her after her father's death. He shook off the memory. "Now—" he started.

"Hello."

They weren't alone. When they'd entered, Drew failed to notice the man holding a drink and leaning casually against the corner bar. He recognized him immediately as Xander Crawford, Letty's fiancé.

Drew and Letty stood. She took his hand and led him to the bar. "Drew, I'd like you to meet my. . . Xander Crawford. Xander, this is Drew Cutter."

"I guessed as much," Xander said, offering his hand.

He was perhaps an inch shorter than Drew's six-foot-three, with an athletic build and model handsomeness. Though Drew rarely noticed such things, Crawford's casual attire was too deliberate and his black hair too perfectly tousled. But the hair complemented Letty's and Toby's own ebony locks to complete the image of the perfect family.

"Nice to meet you. I saw the press release. Congratulations." Drew shook the man's hand, exerting a bit more pressure than he would normally. "Letty was just about to fill me in on what's happened with Toby."

Xander set his drink on the bar and moved behind Letty to possessively encircle her in his arms. "It's a tragedy, and so frustrating that there's nothing we can do for the poor child."

Drew had thought of Toby as a "poor child" only once, when the boy lost his parents. Otherwise, that was the last description anyone who knew him would use. "So, explain to me what happened."

They moved back to the sitting area; Xander and Letty took one lounger and Drew another.

Letty spoke, "Somehow the screamer cell was returned to the station with Fitz still in it. Fitz got out and escaped Dark Landing in a stolen salvage ship, taking Curtis, Doc, the new admin chief, Austen Hargreaves, and Nikko and Toby as hostages." Letty continued to fill him in. The tears started again. "It doesn't make sense. Why were they all even on that ship?"

Xander murmured in her ear, "Hush, baby. We'll get through this together."

Drew swallowed to squash the bile rising in his throat. "Earth Space Force didn't put up any resistance? What about the minefield?"

Letty shook her head. "Somehow they managed to maneuver safely through. The ESF didn't stop them. There was only one Earth Force ship guarding the bridge. The other three were investigating a report from Curtis about unknown ships approaching the station dockside. But it was a ruse."

She leaned forward, her eyes flashing in anger. "There's more to this, Drew. I've been fed facts without explanations. I'm *so* glad you're here. . . with Xander and I. Maybe you can get more information from Rear Admiral Sullivan than we did."

"I booked a room at Landers Keep. I'll check in, then go to HQ. I might learn something from Kyle and Jonesy."

"Stay on the *Maris Stella* with us," Letty offered. "There's plenty of room."

Xander spoke before Drew could respond. "We could use your help and support, but do you think staying here is wise? You can imagine the ruckus Letty's been causing." He gently patted her arm. "It may be a bad idea to associate too closely with us."

As much as Drew hated to agree with any suggestion or opinion from Crawford, he might be right. But not about 'associating too closely' with them — everyone on the station knew Drew and Letty were close — it was getting any sleep with her lying in bed next to Crawford only a couple bulkheads away. Just thinking about it, he wanted to beat the guy unrecognizable.

"*Please*," Letty begged. "I would feel so much better having you here so we can work together."

Under different circumstances, Drew might delude himself into believing she wanted him close for other reasons, but he knew with certainty her only feelings now were for Toby. He shook his head. "I'll meet with the guys tonight — drinks on me should do it. If it's not too late, I'll stop back by to let you know what I learn."

"I don't care how late it is — I won't sleep until I see you," Letty said.

Evidently caught off guard, Xander paused mid eye-roll. He shot Drew a thin smile. "Absolutely — no matter how late it is. We're *so* glad you're here."

Drew just smiled and nodded, silently thinking, *Yeah, I'll bet — assbag!*

~ ~ ∞ ~ ~

Drew checked into Landers Keep and then headed straight to Security HQ. An hour before shift change, Kyle would be getting off duty, with Jonesy just coming in. When he entered HQ, he was met with applause and warm welcomes. Kyle held a one-armed hug a bit too long.

When he'd shook hands all around, they moved into the chief's office. He sat on the lounger while Kyle leaned against the desk. It felt more than a little awkward to be there again.

"*Jesus*, Chief. . . you probably know most of what's going on. Sullivan's in command again, and a new guy, Captain Tristian Thomas—everybody calls him 'Treetop'—is filling in for Curtis, Doc, and the new chief, Hargreaves. But he's working out of the admin office, so he's not busting our asses down here."

A knock sounded on the open hatch, and Mitchell Jones stuck his head in, with Benny following.

"Heard your ass was back in the quadrant." Jonesy smiled and offered his hand.

"Hey, Jonesy. . . Benny," Drew said, hoping that was the last handshake of the evening. "What a coincidence, I was just going to invite you three for drinks on me, unless you'd rather we chat here."

The men quickly spun around and exited the office with Drew on their heels.

In Number 42, Drew entered a double order of BBQ Cammeni ribs and drinks all around. There was no need to coerce information from the men.

"This is all Walker's fault," Jonesy started. "The fucker brought the screamer cell back on the station—and the Fitz thing was still in it."

Benny interrupted. "He paid off a Bahdaneian salvage captain, and from his *personal* account. He ordered me to tow it back in place. 'Course I let Chief Hargreaves know. . . eventually." He mumbled the last word. "That's how she wound up with them—went down to investigate."

Kyle filled in the holes. "Walker gave the captain two hundred credits, but he returned wanting more. That's when they think the Diak took over his body. They got it on vid, but you can't really see anything. We found the body of a Bahdane female floating just outside the atmo-shield, too."

111

"What I'm really curious about," Drew said, "is why the ESF let them over the bridge with five hostages and one a kid. How'd they get through the mines? And Letty said Curtis sent the ESF squad on a wild goose chase?"

Jones took up the story again. "There's a rumor that Nikko is working for the Earth Defense Council, and Sir James ordered him to go into Diak space with or without the hostages.

"*Shit, you say!* Nikko's working for the EDC?"

"Yep," Benny said. "And suddenly he can speak perfect English."

Drew laughed. "What is it about Dark Landing that attracts people with hidden identities?"

The three men shrugged in chorus.

"There's more. . . and you're not going to believe it," Jonesy said. Drew waited for him to continue. "Another rumor is that the Diak are holding prisoners from all the Alliance member planets, and one of them. . . get this. . . is Travis Barnes himself."

"Whoa!" Drew said, stunned. The last bite of Cammeni rib stuck in his throat. Still struggling with survivor's guilt, he couldn't process the idea that Barnes might not be dead after all.

Jonesy nodded. "Kyle and me got buddies with the ESF and they both swear it's true."

"What are you gonna do?" Kyle asked.

"Go get him, of course." No one doubted he spoke of Toby and not Travis.

Benny stated the obvious. "Because of Miss Taleen."

"You've seen her?" Jonesy asked.

"Yeah. And her new assbag!"

"You know," Jonesy said, "just because you made it back from there once. . . ."

"We'll do it again," Drew replied, with false confidence.

~ ~ ∞ ~ ~

Past midnight, when Drew returned to the *Maris Stella*, Letty met him alone.

"Where's Crawford?"

"He's sleeping. I didn't want to wake him."

Huh? Interesting, Drew thought.

What did you find out?"

"Not much more than you already know." He decided to withhold the information about Barnes. Barnes was Letty's lover during college, and later a Taleen Security Force Commander. She'd known him from childhood. She would go bat-shit crazy at the news. "One new thing, though. It's possible Nikko is working for the Earth Defense Council. And it seems he lost his accent somewhere."

"Nikko? For the EDC?"

"Maybe. Listen, I'm going after Toby. But I'll need your ship."

"Absolutely — and I'm going with you."

"Not gonna happen."

"Then you don't get my ship."

"Then Toby dies."

The tears started anew. "I *am* going with you."

Drew sighed. "Letty, don't be stupid. You know the odds — I won't lose you. Not this way."

"If you leave without me, I'll just follow — either in this ship or another. I can afford to buy the entire ESF squadron if I want!"

"*Jesus, Letty!* Don't do this."

"I'm going," she said quietly, features fixed, spine rigid.

He'd seen her resolute look too many times. "And the *assbag*?" His repugnance was evident.

"The *assbag* is my fiancé and soon to be my husband. That's up to him, but I won't stop him if he insists — which I'm sure he will. He loves Toby as much as I do."

Drew issued a deep humph. "Don't count on it." He grasped her arm. "It sure didn't take you long." He'd been angry and heartsick since he learned of her engagement. In that moment he was just angry.

She shook him off. "What's it to you anyway? Toby needs a father. Besides, I've known Xander for years. It's not as if I pulled a stranger out of a crowd."

"As Rebecca Richards, I'll bet." Richards was Letty's alias on her first visit to the station. "And *another* ex-lover? And I'll bet he resurfaced *after* he learned Rebecca Richards was really the heiress to Taleen Industries. Do you love him?"

"I care for him. . . deeply. And we kept in touch a long time before he knew who I really was."

"Yeah, but do you love him?" He demanded, then calmed himself and softened his tone. "Listen, Letty, what if I told you I'd made a mistake? That we both made a mistake. I should've never let you go."

"This is *really* inappropriate, Drew. First, you didn't *let* me go—I went. And there wasn't anything between us then and there certainly isn't anything between us now. How would that have worked, Drew? I can't live here. And you wouldn't follow me back to San Francisco."

"I might have. I left Dark Landing too, after all."

"What would you do in San Francisco, anyway? Xander is from my world. We have things in common."

His anger returned. "I get it. He's rich and connected. I'm not."

"Do you seriously think I need more wealth *or* connections?"

"I seriously think you should reconsider before you make a huge mistake." With the last word he barged off the ship.

17 MASS PRIMARY

The *Remarkable Mayzie* was ordered to fall in between two Diak gunships. Their escorts guided them past more than twenty-five docking bays ringing the station's center, all holding ships, many in fantastical shapes. The bay at which they finally stopped provided the facilities and atmosphere necessary to accommodate the salvage ship and her passengers. Nikko noticed even more docks continued around the station beyond theirs.

As if the humans were insufficiently rocked by their circumstances to that point, a Fahdeen met them at the bottom of the gangway. It wore a long-sleeved, wheat-colored tunic that brushed the deck, and was accompanied by an array of five other aliens sporting various skin colors and physical shapes, none of which Nikko recognized, and each of whom loomed above the tiny Fahdeen.

"Who are you?!" Curtis said, with a weak attempt at bravado.

Each hostage emitted an audible gasp when the Fahdeen's eyes flashed dull gray. The figure forewent introductions. "You are the one who murdewess Ekis," it said, appraising Curtis.

"I. . . *shit!*" What little color that was left drained from Curtis's face. His freckles stood out like flecks of grayish-brown ash.

"It was kill or be killed," Nikko said, deadpan.

"Ekisess would not have desstroyed you ahss without first obtaining my ahss approval," the *Diak* Fahdeen stated emphatically. A strange hissing sound accompanied its words but did not confuse the meaning. "Dr. Jameson?"

Doc stood at the back of the group with Austen. Both were attempting to shield Toby. She hesitantly took two steps forward but remained silent.

The Fahdeen cleared its throat. "We welcome you. You will find a home here." Its long snout and exposed teeth twisted into a grotesque smile.

Nikko flinched. "We understand you're holding Alliance citizens prisoners?"

"Yes," the Diak replied, then spoke over its shoulder to one of the aliens.

A tall, lavender-hued, mushroom-shaped figure glided forward. A tentacle lifted from its side, exposing what resembled a gooey armpit running the length of its body. The tentacle pit emitted a disgusting odor reminiscent of Nikko's training locker, if his weeks-old, encrusted sweats piled on the bottom were also layered with rotting fish. The tentacle wrapped around Doc and moved away, gently pulling her with it.

Jameson looked terrified. "*No. . . no. Please,*" she whimpered. When she lost her balance, the mushroom held her upright and dragged her along. In the process, her shoe came off. Doc looked back at the shoe in horror, as if it were something dear to her.

Nikko felt a premonition they may never see her again.

"Where are you taking her?!" Austen demanded.

Without a word, the Diak Fahdeen followed the mushroom and Doc off the bay. The remaining four aliens herded the hostages in a different direction, ignoring their questions and protests, if the aliens even understood what was said.

The group passed through several large rooms, their sides lined with environmental enclosures, each holding a different type of being. The invisiwalled fronts of the enclosures reminded Nikko of an aquarium he'd visited when he was a child. As with their four guards, he recognized none of the imprisoned alien races until they reached the third room. There, an enclosure held more of the stalk-like mushroom figures in various shades of purple, like the one that greeted them and took Doc away.

Nikko assumed any atmosphere outside the enclosures favored the race being escorted. But their escorts clearly consisted of four separate alien races. It was outside the odds of probability that all four shared a natural environment with humans.

In the fourth room, it was as if the deck dropped from under Nikko. The other three were similarly affected. Hargreaves gasped in alarm, and Toby leaned against Curtis for support. The room's enclosures held hundreds of citizens, each from one of the five Alliance planets. The last held the humans.

They were directed through a hatch and small airlock at the front of the human pen. Upon exiting the opposite side, the hatch closed, sealed, and the airlock depressurized — if that's what the pulsing blue light indicated. Nikko realized, other than the four who'd escorted them, he'd seen no guards along their route. It made sense, he guessed. If the passages held atmosphere only when they transported someone, prisoners would die outside their enclosures. Escape was not an option. Besides, where would they go? No need for round-the-clock guards.

Nikko shook off a wave of bleakness and directed his attention to their setting. The air in the Earth enclosure was humid and warm, though not uncomfortably so. They were greeted by a rag-tag group. A rail-thin man in his late forties, with medium brown hair peppered gray, preceded the group. Momentarily abandoning his situational analysis, Nikko felt a burst of relief as Curtis stepped forward to take the lead. *Where did that come from!* It was odd. Though he considered Curtis a sniveling degenerate, he'd never resented reporting to him. Perhaps because he knew it wasn't a permanent setup.

Curtis opened the introductions as if the two groups were meeting in a boardroom. "Hello. I'm Curtis Walker, Chief of Security on the trading station Dark Landing. These are my colleagues, Austen Hargreaves, Chief of Administration, and Nikko Balog. . . ." Curtis turned to Nikko with a taunting expression, one eyebrow raised.

With no reason to keep Curtis in the dark longer, Nikko came clean. "I'm Nikko Balog, Senior Drug Enforcement Agent with the Multi-World Coalition for Travel and Trade."

Curtis's jaw dropped.

Austen inhaled and turned to Nikko. "Me too," she said, visibly astonished.

"What?" Nikko and Curtis reacted in unison.

"I mean. . . not drug enforcement, but I work undercover for MCTT. Actually, in partnership with the ETOC, who has the lead on this particular. . . ." She trailed off into silence.

The man standing in front of them cleared his throat.

Before Nikko could speak, Curtis, appearing both baffled and disgusted by the other two's pronouncements, addressed the man. "Well, *anyway*, here we are — whoever we are. Oh, and this is Toby. . . ." Curtis looked around.

Nikko spotted the boy several meters away, speaking quietly with a girl, perhaps a year or two younger than he.

The man finally broke his silence. "I'm Oscar Velazquez from Atlanta. I'm the reluctant greeter for our compound. Beyond that, I carry little weight."

"How many here?" Nikko asked.

"Five hundred ninety-one — now ninety-five."

The enclosure was good sized. From what Nikko could tell, it appeared to be roughly thirty meters deep by a little less than that wide, perhaps twenty-six or twenty-seven meters wide, but there was only a dozen or so inhabitants in sight.

Oscar responded to the unasked question. "See the wall behind us?"

Nikko and the other two nodded. The wall was close to ten meters high and filled with human-sized cubby holes, none deeper than two meters, each accessible by an assortment of carved steps and ladders.

Oscar continued. "There's nine more just like it behind this one. Enough to accommodate our current number and perhaps double that."

"How long has everyone been here?" Austen asked.

"A few as long as three years." Oscar smiled. "Though you're the first they've brought in in over six months. C'mon, we'll give you a tour of the compound. Justine?"

Without introduction, a woman, presumably Justine, stepped forward and studied Nikko's face. As far as Nikko could see, she wore a tattered man's shirt and nothing else. He suddenly realized those in the watching crowd were sparsely covered as well. And all were as thin as Oscar. Evidently, they were on a subsistence diet.

Noticing where Nikko's eyes wandered, Oscar said, "You'll get used to it."

Justine took his arm as Oscar led them through an opening in the cubby wall. Nikko glanced back over his shoulder, but Toby stayed put.

~ ~ ∞ ~ ~

Tammy Jameson fought to stay on her feet as the alien dragged her along the passage. The tentacle wrapped around her body, pinning her arms to her sides. And it stunk. The tiny Fahdeen figure set the pace several steps ahead of them.

"Where are you taking me?" Tammy tried but failed to keep the fear from her voice.

The Fahdeen—Diak—coughed and answered without turning to look at her. "I am taking you for examination ahs. It is necessary to learn howess you survived extermination when our transmissession to your worlds ceased."

"I wasn't infected then."

The Diak stopped walking and wheeled around. "You weress implanted by Ekisess ahs, then?" It fell back to walk beside Tammy, nodding at the other alien to keep moving.

"No, not Ekis? By a bird—a pigeon."

It coughed once more. The coughing seemed to suppress the hissing sound. "Who is thiss pigeon bird?"

"A bird is a small animal with wings. It flies."

"I do not understand. How didess this bird transmit the nanoids? Did you engage ahs in the act of reproduction with it?"

"No. . . no. It's an *animal*. A different species. It carries inactive nanoids. I believe they were transmitted when it wounded me with its beak." Tammy turned her head to show the Diak the lesion under her right eye.

They stopped in front of a large hatch.

It coughed again and continued in perfectly executed English. "Hmm. I see. Then you were fortunate. Had Ekis not been there, your nanoids would have detonated when their search routine failed to acquire a Diak transmission."

"After you examine me, will you take me to join my colleagues?"

"No."

"But why? I told you how I became infected. Please let me be with my friends."

"The human enclosure contains my supply of hosts. You are a contaminate."

"What are you going to do with me?"

"You are of no value to me as a host. However, you may be of use in other ways. We will see." The Diak Fahdeen nodded once more to the other alien, then turned and walked away.

"Wait. . . please. . . ."

The hatch next to them opened. The alien pulled her into a large enclosure and proceeded down a hallway with small, invisiwalled cells lining both sides. Most of the cells lay empty, except one. As Tammy was towed past it, she recognized Travis Barnes lying on its deck, either asleep or dead.

18 PURSUIT

"You are *not* granted authorization, and you will not *be* granted authorization under any circumstances." So decreed Secretary Anne Rostenkowski, head of the Earth Technology Oversight Commission. She stared commandingly at the two of them from the wall monitor in the *Maris Stella* salon.

Never the first to blink, Letty replied instantly, "Secretary Rosten. . . Anne. . . there are two legions of Taleen Security within a week of Dark Landing, awaiting my command and sufficient in strength to take over the station without a laser being fired. It's possible ESF reinforcements could arrive at approximately the same time. If so, there might be more of a battle, but still a battle you would lose. *I am* going after Toby, one way or another."

Drew, chin in hand, watched the women silently from the dining counter where he and Letty sat. There was no doubt in his mind how this would end. As usual, Xander stood at the bar holding a drink.

"You wouldn't dare! Do you seriously think your Taleen Security Force can take on Earth defenses, *and* those of the Alliance? Or that your TSF employees would willingly commit treason? Which, need I remind you, is the only crime that still carries a death sentence."

By her lack of emotion, it became clear to Drew that Secretary Rostenkowski thought Letty was bluffing. He wanted to believe she was bluffing as well, but if he sat across from her at a poker table, he'd fold.

"Absolutely to both questions! Need I remind *you*, these are my forces, hand-picked and trained for their loyalty to Taleen Industries and me," Letty spat back.

"Treason!" Anne repeated. "You'll spend the rest of your life behind bars, if they don't hang you."

Behind him, Drew heard Xander mumble, "It's not treason, it's disobedience, and they haven't hanged anyone in decades." The clink of glass suggested the man was pouring himself another. *What is that now, four? Five?*

Drew finally spoke up. "Don't kid yourselves, no one is making it back to be imprisoned *or* hanged."

Letty shot him an exasperated look, then as quickly looked away. Without discussing it, they were ignoring their earlier argument, and it seemed she chose to avoid another one.

Anne redirected her wrath toward Drew. "And you're okay with this? You're actually going to accompany Letty through that wormhole?"

"I'm not letting her go alone."

Xander stood out of Anne's line of sight. She called to him. "Mr. Crawford? Is there no way you can talk some sense into her?"

Xander downed his drink and exited the room without a response. Drew scoffed and turned to Letty. About to say something unkind, he saw her tears well up. Instead, he pinched the bridge of his nose in vexation and kept quiet.

"Anne, I'm going after Toby — *I have to.*" Letty pleaded.

"Even if I agreed to help you get the minefield schematics — which I *never* will — I have no sway over the Earth Defense Council. Sir James won't allow you to go through."

Though unconfirmed, Drew spoke from his personal certainty. "Sir James allowed Toby and the others to go over in the first place. He sacrificed them to EDC's objectives."

"I don't believe it," Anne declared, in a voice that lacked the ring of truth.

He went on. "Maybe you should look into that. Letty and I are taking the *Maris Stella* across tomorrow morning. Sir James won't try to stop us any more than he tried to stop the *Remarkable Mayzie*."

"It's suicide." The secretary weakened.

"I agree," Drew said and made a *pfft* sound in sarcastic distain. He'd already argued the odds of survival with Letty, though he'd given up much sooner than Anne.

Even through glistening eyes, Letty's determination was evident. "We need the minefield schematic," she said.

Anne placed the butt of her palm to her forehead and turned from the monitor, eyes closed. "Jesus, Letty, please don't do this."

And that's that! Drew thought.

~ ~ ∞ ~ ~

At 0730 the next morning, the *Maris Stella* crew assembled in the salon: "Shock" McDermott, the ship's captain; Letty's personal security team of six (also members of the tactical team); a technician-ops officer; a steward and acquisitions specialist; two reluctant and incompetent housekeeping crew/weapons specialists; and a five-star chef/medic. Each one an elite member of the Taleen Security Force assigned exclusively to Letty and the *Maris Stella*. Xander was nowhere in sight. *Maybe he's sleeping in,* Drew thought.

Letty started. "So, the minefield issue may or may not be resolved, but there's a couple other problems. First, our water reservoir is at half level. The regularly scheduled tanker docked yesterday, but the ESF is preventing them from filling our order. There's no way around it. It's a setback for sure, and one we should have anticipated. If anyone wants out, I guarantee no recriminations." Heads shook all around. Letty nodded to acknowledge their loyalty and continued. "On top of that. . . ." She looked to Captain McDermott.

He stepped forward. "As I explained to Miss Taleen, the station has placed a virtual *boot* on the ship and locked down the environmental shield to prohibit our exiting the bay. We can probably overcome those restraints, but it could take several hours. In the interim, they will certainly place further obstacles in our path."

Letty continued. "My concern is they'll surround the ship with station security. Once we remove the restraints, we can't leave if they're still in the bay. Even suited, they'd be at risk. Thoughts?"

Side conversations broke out as suggestions were considered and discarded. One of Letty's guards offered an idea. "What if we started a fire in the bay? They'd have to clear it out and lift the atmo-shield to vent the oxygen?"

"Yes, but that could put the station at risk," Letty said.

Drew, fiercely loyal to Dark Landing and its inhabitants, nodded in agreement. From his position sitting on the deck, leaning back against one of the lounger arms, he said, "Frankly, there may not be a problem." A lock of sandy brown hair fell across his forehead. Everyone quieted. "Assuming they haven't changed them — which I'd bet a large is the case — I can provide the override codes."

The captain spoke. "You can *what*?"

Letty jumped in. "Drew, it can't be that simple! You're kidding?"

"Worth a try," Drew said.

With a puzzled expression, the captain's gaze alternated between them.

Letty shook her head slowly and laughed.

"What?" McDermott said.

"Back when Drew was suspended for not following protocol, he elected to leave Dark Landing instead of sticking around for questioning by *Muck*. As part of the escape plan, he gave me command-level access. Long story." She turned back to Drew. "The new chief of administration — certainly she changed the access codes when she came onboard?"

"For operations, absolutely, including the docks, but not for security. And the purpose of override codes is just that, to override all other codes in an emergency."

"What about Curtis?"

Drew shrugged. "There are a *lot* of codes. Every change has to be committed to memory and changing them all at once would be a bitch. Curtis is a ball-buster in holding everyone else's feet to the procedural fires, but he's a lot easier on himself. Besides, there was no reason to see my leaving as a threat, and Curtis was already on staff and an acting chief. My prints and DNA were removed for sure, but I don't think anyone knew about yours."

"I'm *shocked*. Can we test it?" the captain asked, energized.

"Wait," Letty looked around the salon in alarm. "Where's Xander?"

The others followed her searching gaze, then questioned one another.

"Wasn't he here earlier?"

"I don't know."

"Haven't seen him this morning. You?"

"No. . . not since last night. . . ."

Each person avoided looking at Letty.

Drew studied her expression intently, trying to gauge her level of concern. She appeared surprised at Crawford's absence. Drew would have been surprised otherwise. A throat cleared behind him, and he turned to see the chef reluctantly step forward. "Mr. Crawford came into the mess while I was set'n up for breakfast earlier. Said he was gonna get a bite at the inn."

After an extended pause, Letty issued an order. "No one else leaves this ship. If he doesn't return by the time we're ready to sail, we go without him." She strode past Drew, avoiding his *I-told-you-so* look. Station security would have spotted Crawford leaving the ship, and they would never allow him to return—assuming he wanted to. Letty followed the captain toward the ship's bridge, and Drew followed her.

The three crowded the captain's station. "How can we test this without *'lighting up someone's panel?'*" Letty echoed an excuse Drew had given her six months earlier, when he was unable to induce gravity in an airlock during their escape.

Drew thought for a moment. "First, log in through the CoachStop database if you still can. Indirect access is safer." The clearance he'd created for her to aid their escape was as CoachStop Management's liaison to Dark Landing. He'd set the account up under her travel alias at the time, Rebecca Richards.

Letty addressed the console. "Transmission External Relay: CoachStop Management, MWCorp. database access." She momentarily crossed the fingers on the hand hovering over the palm reader, then relaxed it as she waited.

Please state your name and affiliation.

"Rebecca Ann Richards, Dark Landing Liaison."

After a long minute, the processor responded again: *Link completed; please login.*

Letty pressed her hand to the reader and recited the code Drew provided. Several tense seconds passed.

Access granted: Rebecca Ann Richards, Corporate Liaison, Dark Landing Station.

The three exchanged glances. Letty proceeded. "Open link relay to Zeta Quadrant, Dark Landing security database." She repeated that code as Drew read it off: "Twenty-three, seventeen, mike, delta, forty-six, eleven."

The computer granted her access once more.

"You remember *all* the station codes?" she asked in wonder.

Drew tapped his temple. "Permanently etched into my gray matter. No reason to go any further. We don't want to tip off engineering. So. . . that's it. We can simply deactivate the boot and initiate debarking procedures. HQ's confusion with the override originating from CoachStop should buy us the time. Only the minefield to get past now. You still up for this?" He looked at Letty and felt a twinge of guilt at not telling her Barnes might still be alive. The information would only make her more resolute.

"Yes, absolutely. . . in just a minute. I'll be back." She tapped her implant as she exited the bridge.

After several minutes she returned. "Okay, let's go. I'll tell the others."

Drew wanted to ask but decided that would be mean. She appeared upset and angry. Evidently Xander Crawford was a no-show.

When she'd left, Drew looked at the captain.

"Well, I'm *shocked*. Who would have thought he'd jump ship?" Captain McDermott said, meaning just the opposite. "So, how sure are you about the minefield?"

"Somewhat sure. I think the ESF will let us through eventually. For certain, they aren't gonna fire on us. The odds probably lean toward a standoff."

"And if we do cross over, you're confident the asteroid field will conceal us?"

"Positive." Drew nodded. "The minute we enter the tunnel, cut all systems but life support and gravity. The asteroids on exit are plenty big enough to hide behind. Veer left though. A major flight corridor is on the right."

"Then what?"

Drew looked back at the captain with raised eyebrows.

"That bad? I'm—"

"Don't say it," Drew interrupted. "I know."

The *Maris Stella* crew conducted a final check of weapons and supplies. Drew partnered with one of Letty's personal security guards and tactical team member, Gretchen Rossi, to ensure everything in the cargo hold was properly stowed. When Drew and Gretchen entered the bay, Drew noticed the control panel next to the hatch read "Emergency lock-out enabled. Access denied." Someone without authority had tried to open the hatch. He heard a low groan and found Xander Crawford passed out against the bulkhead behind a stack of cartons, an empty bottle at his side. Drew laughed. Xander was evidently not to be trusted with the ship's codes. He'd never made it to breakfast.

Drew laid him prone in front of the hatch. Rossi entered the code to open it and lower the gangway, and Drew rolled the man out. As two station security staff ran toward the ship, weapons ready, he retracted the gangway and resealed the hatch. He and Rossi resumed their inspection. Not a word passed between them.

~ ~ ∞ ~ ~

"How'd they do that?" ESF Captain Tristian "Treetop" Thomas queried the room in general. He stood a few feet behind Kyle and Jonesy as the three of them watched the action on the monitor in the security command center.

The two shift heads exchanged knowing looks, each apparently waiting for the other to speak. Kyle gave in. "They used a security override code to enable the environmental shield and commence the dock depressurization procedure, sir."

"Okay, but how?"

Kyle grimaced in embarrassment. "Well, the commands were entered from CoachStop Management, but I think Drew Cutter initiated them, sir."

"But how. . .?" He stopped and looked at them with bugged eyes. "You a-holes *never* changed the goddamn codes?!" The question was rhetorical.

Kyle respected Treetop. Unlike the last ESF captain to take over the station, this one let them conduct business as usual unless he received conflicting orders from higher ups. Like now. He tried to redirect the captain's attention. "I don't suppose it's possible to transmit the chatter over our speakers?" He knew Treetop listened to transmissions from the squadron assigned to secure the wormhole.

"Might's well," the captain said with a sigh, then muttered something unintelligible.

. . . and if you do not, we'll be forced to fire. I repeat, return to Dark Landing or be fired upon.

On the monitor, four ESF gunships were positioned in a semi-circle in front of the wormhole into Diak space. The *Maris Stella* ignored the order and continued at a steady pace in a beeline for the tunnel entrance, the lead ESF gunship directly in her path.

The transmission feed displayed a frequency change. *Admiral Sullivan?* The squadron lead wasn't about to fire on civilians without a direct order.

Fire port and starboard. Make it a close shave, Captain.

Understood, sir.

Laser blasts brushed the *Maris Stella's* shields, rocking the vessel, but not slowing her. She neared the ESF gunship.

Sir? The captain's voice held only a hint of urgency.

After an extended silence from ESF command, the order came back. *Move out of the way but let her know the mines are hot.*

The *Maris Stella* was now within two klicks of the ESF squadron. The gunship on the right end of the arc launched a projectile into the minefield. There was no fiery explosion, but a misty curtain of shrapnel spiraled out, igniting two additional mines.

The lead gunship, having moved out of the *Maris Stella's* path, now hung directly above her as she changed course slightly and headed toward the tiny hole left by the detonated mines. A dozen more still blocked her passage.

Kyle inadvertently leaned toward the monitor to watch the *Maris Stella* enter the minefield. He held his breath. In slow motion, mines bounced harmlessly off the ship's shields, colliding with each other to create a domino effect. There were no further detonations. Someone had pulled the plug. The security staff in the command center broke into scattered applause, but Kyle winced inwardly from an overwhelming sense of gloom as Drew disappeared through the wormhole once more. Jonesy stood motionless next to him, his expression mirrored Kyle's thoughts.

19 NO OPTIONS

Justine, a nurse, as it turned out, cleaned up Nikko's face the best she could. She announced his eye socket was probably fractured—nothing she could do about that—but his nose wasn't as badly broken as it felt. The last blow had evidently knocked it back into alignment. Even without a mirror, he knew his face was grotesquely swollen. Besides the pain, his restricted eyesight, and nasal voice, it was reflected in the expressions of everyone who looked at him for the first time. Curtis said, with two black eyes, Nikko resembled a giant, angry raccoon.

Nikko realized he'd misjudged the depth of the human enclosure by a third. The space between the last cubby wall and the back bulkhead was deeper than the forward passages between the walls, and hostages congregated there. One end held a waste chute set into the deck, which served as the head. A poncho was strung across it for privacy. A permanent line hovered between thirty to forty people waiting patiently—not surprising with almost six hundred sharing one latrine.

The opposite end of what resembled an alleyway held a water feature. A narrow stream trickled from the ceiling down a wall sporting several dozen bowl-like protrusions, off-set and equidistant from one another. Each one held roughly two liters of water, which overflowed into the protrusion beneath it, and finally into a shallow trough at deck level. It looked like a decorative fountain someone might install in their garden or atrium on Earth.

Nikko guessed it to be the source of the enclosure's humidity. He was unused to seeing open water on a space station.

Ships berthed on Dark Landing paid a water fee to replenish the station's reserves, along with the normal docking fees. While the collection and recycling of water went a long way in supplying any space facility, for those living in space fulltime the continuous and strenuous rationing necessary to live on recycled water alone was impractical. But water was still their most precious commodity and never wasted.

Midway between the latrine and the waterfall, a wide assortment of items was piled high against the bulkhead: empty food containers, utensils, handheld processors, duffels and cases, bits of equipment—some recognizable, some not—and a large number of shoes and boots, but no clothing. For the first time, Nikko realized most people were barefoot, evidently by choice. "Where did this stuff come from?" he asked Oscar.

"They took a lot of the hostages off ships. The pirates—well, we thought they were pirates at first—grabbed whatever they found lying loose around the ships and tossed it in here with us. Don't know why. No weapons, but some items have potential—for what good it would do. None of the tech works."

Nikko and Austen sat cross-legged on the deck with Oscar, Justine, and a woman in her eighties, perhaps nineties, whom Oscar introduced only as Brie. Curtis waited in the line for the head. They hadn't seen Toby since they came in.

"A Fahdeen met us when we arrived," Austen said.

"And it'll be something else the next time. The only race we've seen with any consistency is those tall purple guys with the tentacle." Oscar looked at the two women. They nodded their heads.

"Do you think those are the *real* Diaks?" Nikko asked. When the three shrugged, he went on. "What do you know about our captors?"

"Just what the latecomers have told us," Oscar said. Other than when Justine treated Nikko, she and Brie had been silent. "We think some of the guards—more of a workforce really—are hosting Diaks. Maybe all. But it's a mystery how the Diak can inhabit so many different life forms with varied environmental needs."

"I wondered the same thing," Nikko said.

Austen spewed questions. "I haven't seen food. What do you eat? Have the Diak said anything to you? Do they harm you in anyway? Have you tried to escape?"

Oscar glanced at Brie again. She smiled and returned an almost imperceptible nod. Brie's opinion was important, but she remained silent.

With a deep breath, Oscar described the conditions in the enclosure. "If you look around, you'll see several readers with bowls directly under them — like the water bowls on the end of this row. Once during each twenty-four-hour period, you can palm a reader to receive your food allotment. They're sort of bland, greasy cakes about three inches square. They all look and taste pretty much the same, but they vary in weight and texture. As near as we can tell, they're nutritionally balanced to each individual."

He sighed again, his gaze sad but steady. "Other than questioning when you first arrive, the Diak don't communicate with us." He looked once more to his comrades, then back to Austen.

Oscar continued. "Until about a year ago, we had absolutely no idea who'd taken us or why, or about nanoids or contamination — that knowledge explained a lot. When later arrivals told us about the nanoids, everyone panicked but eventually calmed down again. If we *are* infected, what can we do about it?"

Brie nodded and smiled encouragement to Oscar. "Brie has been here the longest — a bit over three years. She's sort of our. . . *sage*. . . but she doesn't speak. We don't have a leader or leaders. Individuals with particular skills like Justine are more prominent than others. I've taken it upon myself to act as the welcoming committee for new arrivals. Every so often someone will try to *rally* the troops and improve morale." He made a fist and pumped the air like a general rallying his men. "But the enthusiasm never lasts more than a few days."

"Have they taken anyone out of here?" Nikko asked. For the first time all three averted their eyes. Nikko noticed Oscar looked especially disheartened.

Justine finally spoke. "They've taken two away, that's all. One was Oscar's partner, and one was a child. We think we're their emergency supply."

Nikko agreed. "From what we recently learned, you. . . we. . . are exactly that. If it's any comfort, you probably aren't infected.

That starts a process which would make you ultimately worthless to them."

"I'm so sorry, Oscar," Austen said.

"Thank you." With a brief, melancholy smile of acceptance for events beyond his control, he went on. "We believe they take hostages from the other Alliance compounds more frequently. Though less so for the Bins. From our location, we can see only a small portion of the Bin and Fahdeen compounds, but we hear their cries."

Curtis returned to the group and dropped down next to Austen. Nikko noticed he favored the chief of administration. For the length of time he'd known Curtis, he'd always appeared asexual — totally disinterested in men or women. But he *was* a momma's boy, and maybe he leaned toward female companionship for comfort and reassurance. Curtis appeared to be simultaneously threatened by everything and nothing.

"'Sup?" Curtis asked.

"Not much and all depressing," Austen said.

"Yeah, I chatted with several people waiting in line for the head. Think I've got the picture. Where's Toby?"

"Don't know," Nikko said.

Oscar rose and stamped one foot several times on the deck, as if it'd fallen asleep. "I'll go find him. There's plenty of empty cubbies. You should each claim one." He left with Justine and Brie following.

The other three stayed seated, forlornly studying their new habitat. Austen broke the reverie. Addressing Nikko, she said, "So, you work for *Muck* drug enforcement. Obviously undercover. Can you tell me what you're investigating? I'm curious if our assignments overlap."

"Probably not, or we'd know about each other. It's kind of a humorous coincidence, don't you think?"

"Yeah. *Funny*," Curtis interjected.

"Sorry, buddy. Anyway, I investigated Curtis as a possible drug lord operating a cartel out of Dark Landing." He strained to keep a straight face but couldn't hold it. Both Nikko and Austen burst out laughing. Catching his breath, Nikko went on. "But when that didn't pan out," he chuckled again, "my handler asked me to stay on the job. We know there's drug traffic passing through the station, we just don't know who's orchestrating it. You?"

"I'm investigating Dr. Jameson. She is—*was*—much too interested in finding Governor Fitzwilliam-Bennett." She shook her head and sighed. "Anyway, my investigation expanded to include Curtis, who had to be up to *something*." She started to giggle. Nikko joined her with a deep, booming hoot.

"Guys. I'm sitting right here."

A commotion from the front of the compound cut the laughter short. They rose and hurried forward.

A mushroom figure dragged Toby by one arm across the deck toward the airlock. Another mushroom followed. The boy kicked and screamed.

Austen rushed after Toby. "Leave him alone!"

The second mushroom extended its tentacle horizontally between her and the boy. She ran at the barrier still screaming demands at them to let Toby go. As she got close, the tentacle snapped hard across her middle. Austen dropped to her knees, hugging her stomach and dry heaving.

Nikko and Curtis charged toward the mushrooms, but a dozen or more of the hostages standing on the sidelines swarmed in quickly to block the two men. Nikko plowed through the mob, tossing hostages to his left and right like he was clearing a stack of brushwood. By the time he broke through, the mushrooms had exited the airlock and were disappearing down the passage, still dragging a screeching Toby.

Nikko looked furiously around him for someone to snap in half. Several hostages were on the floor clutching various body parts. Justine knelt next to a woman and examined her arm.

"Sons-of-bitches! What the *fuck's* wrong with you people," Curtis yelled as he spun in a quick circle to include everyone who'd stopped them.

Austen stood nearby, speechlessly taking in the scene. She looked as if she wanted to kill.

Oscar approached the two men cautiously, hands pushing the air in front of him. He cast a nervous side glance at Austen. "It's okay. . . really. They'll bring him back. He won't be harmed." When he held their attention, he continued. "The child will be given a sleeping agent—a gas—and then wake up after a few hours and be returned here. It happens to everyone. They'll come for each of *you* as well. Today still, or tomorrow."

Nikko took several deep breaths to calm himself. "Why? What do they do?"

"No one has any memory of what happens in those hours, but we assume we're being questioned and examined."

"Examined how?" Curtis asked, his face still scrunched in anger.

"Nothing invasive. There's no lingering discomfort or external evidence of an examination. We're only guessing. But it explains how they determine everyone's nutritional needs."

Most of the hostages Nikko had tossed aside were back on their feet now; some limped, others massaged an arm or a shoulder. He cringed, hoping no one was seriously injured. A broken limb would be bad enough, but if any of them suffered internal injuries at his hands, it could mean a death sentence under the circumstances.

"I'm sorry. I didn't mean to hurt anyone. I didn't know. . . ."

In reply, most mumbled assurances that they understood, but a few, still nursing bruised muscles, issued angry admonishments and headed to the back of the enclosure.

"*Shit!*" Curtis said.

"It's okay. . . really." Oscar tried to reassure them once more. "Some will be pissed for a couple days, but they all understand, and eventually they'll applaud your attempts to save the boy."

In less than six hours, Toby was returned, groggy and disoriented. They took Austen next, then Nikko, and finally, Curtis. While only two aliens came for Toby, a team of three turned up for both Austen and Curtis, and five for Nikko. One of Curtis's escorts unnerved Nikko in that it seemed to be an alien child, perhaps only a year or two older than Toby. Oscar said they'd never seen it before. The sight of a child hosting a Diak nauseated Nikko, but the impact on Toby proved graver.

After Curtis returned to the compound, Toby kept the chief within visual range at all times and asked to share his cubby space. More surprising was how accepting Curtis was of the boy, willingly taking on a big brother role, chiding him to eat, wash, and make himself useful when opportunities arose. He stopped short of the more dominating role of parent figure.

20 HOPES AND SCHEMES

A rescue attempt by the *Maris Stella* was pointless without a way back to the K.U. The first component of Letty and Captain McDermott's plan was just that: Find a way back. They reconnoitered Mass Primary from as close a perspective as they dared, hoping to track ships leaving the station, and to scrutinize the station's mid-level which appeared to contain ships berthed along its entire circumference.

"There. . . see it, the Bahdane salvage vessel?" An excited Turrey tipped his head back to view the larger monitor above his panels.

"Yep," McDermott agreed, "and that's the first ship I've recognized."

They proceeded from the cover of one asteroid to the next observing the Diak's amazing collection of diverse ships. None of which matched an entry in the *Known Races Concordance*.

"They were all captured?" Letty asked McDermott.

"Likely. . . there's no other explanation I can see—"

"An Earth cruiser," Turrey announced.

"And another next to that." The captain nodded. "Rob, it looks like we're running out of rocks to hide behind. Take us back further."

"Wait. . ." Letty pointed to the screen, "see that? That's another Bahdane ship."

Turrey repositioned them at the edge of an asteroid that afforded a better view. "Camdu. . . Bin. . . and a Fahdeen ship, I think," he said. "Looks like they've berthed all K.U. vessels in one section."

"Take us out as far as we can go and maintain surveillance." The captain rubbed his temples. "None of the other docked craft corresponded to entries in the *Concordance*?"

"Nope, only the Alliance ships. I'm logging the unknowns."

Letty's eyes filled with fear, and she looked to McDermott for reassurance. "How can the Diak hold crews and passengers from so many environments?"

"Based on what we know, I'm sure this station can handle multiple environments," the captain offered.

Turrey glanced back and exchanged a concerned look with McDermott.

Other than Bahdaneians, no Earth space installations, even ones as large as Dark Landing and its sister stations, could accommodate visitors from other planets for any length of time. Despite the size of the Diak station — at least five times that of Dark Landing — accommodating hundreds of alien environments should be impossible. He didn't want to say as much in front of Letty, but McDermott feared the hostages may have *turned* — as they understood the term — adapted by Diak nanoids to exist in a shared environment.

From a safer distance, they spotted two gunships patrolling the station, but over the next twenty-four hours, no ships arrived or left.

The armada was nowhere in sight. Perhaps it was en route to, or busy invading, a galaxy somewhere — one would hope not in the K.U. Perhaps it relocated to another base or was off on a training exercise to return at any time.

The *Maris Stella* moved on. She'd been refitted with long-range, shielded sensors and tracking instruments that Taleen engineers felt confident the Diak could not detect. So far, that'd held true. But the test of the instruments' shield limits continued as they strengthened and extended the sensors' reach in search of objects and wormholes beyond the asteroid field. They needed to establish a base somewhere of a size and distance from the Diak station to safely affix a homing beacon for longer-range probes.

As they searched, Turrey prattled on about everything and nothing. Over the years, McDermott had grown accustomed to his "white noise."

"It'd be nice to find something with surface water, maybe ice, or even permafrost."

"Dream on, my boy," McDermott responded idly.

"Just. . . we're not going to get far with the little water left, and recycling can only handle so much." As a luxury vessel traveling developed routes that provided numerous opportunities to restock, their water recycling equipment sufficed for short-term emergencies only.

The captain nodded and looked up. "Given the new shields, how far out can our scanners detect a wormhole?"

"Within a day's travel, top speed. Still, considering the Diak's own shielding tech, we could be sitting right next to one now."

As they searched for a base station and wormholes, the *Maris Stella* scans turned several useful discoveries. The Diak side of the wormhole from K.U. space was safeguarded by communication disrupters, which prevented anyone, other than presumably the Diak, from sending a transmission back through the tunnel. While wormholes allowed only one-way travel for spaceships, communication transmissions could ride magnetic relay waves in either direction. The ESF had deployed its own disrupters on the K.U. side. They were surely deactivated now to allow transmissions from Nikko Balog and the *Maris Stella*.

The Diak station's name, Mass Primary, was learned from ETOC Secretary Anne Rostenkowski's transmission received just before they entered the wormhole. Letty's conviction that the ESF wouldn't blow the *Maris Stella* to bits proved correct. Rostenkowski's transmission included a transcript of Nikko Balog's reports to Sir James, locater codes and frequencies for all probes launched into Diak space, and classified ESF/ETOC frequencies. Before they left Earth, the members of the *Maris Stella* crew had secondary comms implanted in the fleshy area just below an armpit. Letty insisted Drew be implanted as well. Their additional comms were similar, they learned, to the dedicated comm Sir James ordered implanted in Nikko. Each crew set his or her implants to receive one of the fourteen frequencies supplied by Rostenkowski, as well as the frequency for transmissions from Balog if he was still alive.

Tedious hours passed before the ship's sensors identified an object suitable for installing the probe homing device.

~ ~ ∞ ~ ~

Drew mulled over the fact that Rostenkowski's briefing, while revealing the existence of Alliance prisoners, never mentioned Travis Barnes. He wasn't sure how to interpret that. Perhaps Anne thought the news might prove more of a distraction than a benefit. Or — a new thought occurred to Drew — maybe Letty knew about Barnes after all and kept it from *him*.

The *Maris Stella* finally settled into a far corner of the asteroid field behind what amounted, in Drew's mind, to a dwarf planet. The crew split into two teams. Each team took a fourteen-hour shift, allowing two hours overlap for updates and strategizing. At shift end, after a bite to eat and a welcome chem shower in his swanky cabin, Drew eased between silken sheets. He'd grown accustomed to a certain level of luxury during his time in New Las Vegas but, though exhausted, he doubted he could sleep under his current circumstances. His mind churned with a series of *what ifs* and developing potential plans to handle each one — or envisioning the consequences where no plan would allow a better outcome.

Despite the mental churning, he was drifting off when he heard the telltale clicks of his cabin door opening and closing. He tensed in concentration, listening. Fabric rustled in the darkness, and he caught a whiff of orange blossoms, then a cool breeze as Letty lifted the bed covers and slipped in beside him. His fears and schemes dissolved, replaced with consuming desire.

"No, I don't love him." Her voice was low, husky. He could feel her warm breath on his face and lips. "I wanted you to follow me, and when you didn't, I panicked. I was determined to create a life — a family — for Toby and me. A traditional family. . . ."

Drew took her in his arms; his mouth commanded hers without resistance, his tongue probing. She pressed her hips tight against his in response.

~ ~ ∞ ~ ~

Nikko suggested he and Curtis should scope out their physical settings and Austen offered to chat up the other captives to evaluate their individual strengths and weaknesses, and perhaps sooth some damaged egos.

As they split up, Austen said, "I think Brie is a Diak spy." She disappeared around the cube wall, leaving the two men frozen in place, mouths slack.

Curtis and Nikko toured the enclosure, going up and down each alleyway between cubby walls. After which, they planned to thoroughly inspect the bulkheads, invisiwall, and airlock. Toby trailed them, listless. They searched for nothing specific, merely something they would recognize when they saw it. As discouraging as it was to know each captive had made the same tour soon after arrival and failed to find anything, they were still compelled to repeat the exercise themselves.

Curtis, not yet close to the hopelessness he read in the vacant stares of the long timers, freely admitted he'd probably join them soon enough. He thought about the bombshell Austen had dropped that morning, delivered without explanation. The three planned to meet in Curtis's cubby to share intel once he and Nikko completed their inspection.

Curtis paused for a moment to let Toby catch up, lightly placing a comforting hand on the boy's shoulder as they continued. Nikko glanced back at the two, giving Curtis an approving look. Curtis rarely received overt approval, and when he did, he interpreted it as a sign the approver felt he was weak. He'd welcomed Drew Cutter's praise, though when finally granted, it stopped short of an apology for his boss' previous disdain.

They arrived back where they'd started.

"*Nothing*," Nikko said, discouraged. "Let's find Austen and see what she's got."

21 NIGHT GAMBOL

The four were gathered in Curtis's cubby nibbling on their nutrition squares. Flavorless, and with the texture of a cube of butter packed with sand, it was best to consume them with the mind distracted. While one talked, the other three worked their tongues against the bridges of the mouths in between bites. Curtis thought they looked like dogs eating peanut butter.

"Total blank." Nikko related their inspection results. "Well. . . we didn't see anything that resembled monitoring devices, but that doesn't mean they're not here. We'll keep at it. I want to get a better look at the spot where the water enters the compound. I think the catch bowls are close enough together that I can climb them."

Toby laughed out loud. Other than brooding silence, it was the first emotion the boy'd expressed since seeing the alien child being used as a Diak host.

Curtis cuffed him playfully on the back of the head. "Now that's just rude." Toby laughed again, and Curtis went on. "But he's right, there's no way a *thick-headed muscle monster*, as I understand someone once called you. . ." Toby covered his mouth with his hands and laughed harder. ". . . is going to pull himself up a three-story climbing wall, even if the bowls will hold your weight."

Nikko smiled in pleasure at seeing Toby come out of his morose. "Well, one of us needs to shinny up there and scope it out. Let's table that. I want to hear what Austen has to say."

Austen took a sip of water and made noises of clearing her throat of oily residue. "I know you said the Fitz Diak appeared natural in both his human and Bahdaneian forms. But from the beginning, I felt there was something. . . something *unhuman* about Brie. It's the way she turns her head as if her neck and spine are fused. She appears uncomfortable in her body—every move measured. The more I thought about it, if she is a Diak, by rarely speaking, she avoids making cultural *faux paus*, and Oscar said she's been here the longest. I studied her over the last several days and. . . well, I think she's turning. Her nails have flecks of gray in them, and I swear I saw her eyes flash gray for a split-second yesterday when someone bumped into her."

"That's not much to go on," Curtis said. "Her age could account for her stiff posture. And she's naturally gray—her skin, her hair, her *mustache*."

Toby giggled again.

Nikko offered his opinion. "Curtis isn't wrong, but you have good instincts. We should still be careful around her."

Curtis shrugged. "After three years, you'd think she would've turned already. If she *is* a Diak *and* she's just now turning, I'll lay you odds they take her away soon."

Austen looked to Nikko. "Your spy senses aren't tingling?" she asked.

"No, but I've been focused on other things. Speaking of, if no one thinks I can haul my ass up the wall, which one of you is gonna do it?"

Toby raised his hand. None of the three argued with him.

The environment of the compound simulated the natural circadian rhythm required for the health and wellbeing of all Earth species. The Diak dutifully reduced the illumination and temperature ten hours out of every twenty-four to emulate nighttime. While the inhabitants gratefully went along with the subterfuge, at no time were all six hundred asleep at once, and the line for the head was never-ending.

At three-thirty the next morning, Austen and Toby walked casually to the back bulkhead. As planned, Curtis and Nikko followed ten minutes later. Curtis stopped to loiter at the end of the alleyway containing Brie's cubby. Nikko continued on to join the line for the can. Dancing with the anxious movements of someone who needed it badly, his towering frame blocked the view of the water wall from those in line in front of him. But even considering the length of the alleyway, Nikko's dancing bulk, and the dim lighting, a casual glance might catch an anomalous movement high on the wall. When someone new came up, he nodded politely and let them go ahead of him, producing confused stares but no arguments.

~ ~ ∞ ~ ~

Austen stood beneath the boy as he climbed. A gentle cough would signal him to freeze if anyone approached the fountain, or if Curtis appeared in the alley to indicate Brie was on the move.

If their clandestine inspection was observed, no one would report them. How? The last sighting of an alien — or alien Diak — was the one who returned Curtis to the compound after his supposed questioning. But word of it would get back to Brie. Thin reasoning or not, Austen felt sure Brie was a Diak plant, and there could be other Diaks among them.

Toby was three-quarters up the wall when Curtis appeared. He shot Austen a warning glance and went to join Nikko in line. She coughed, bent down on one knee as if washing her hands in the deck-level trough, and waited nervously for Brie to appear. Five minutes passed and Austen worried that Toby's muscles were cramping. She waited another full minute, then coughed again and ventured a glance upward to see him cover the remaining space to the top arachnid-style. She looked back to the cubby wall entrance, still no Brie. *Where is the deceptious, hook-nosed cozener anyway?* She glanced upward once more, then quickly away. Toby's head and shoulders were out of view inside the narrow outlet at the top. His body disrupted the water's flow down the wall, causing it to spray like rain into the alleyway several feet above Austen's head. If anyone came for a drink now, they'd notice.

Toby finally pulled his head out of the opening and started back down.

A woman returning from the head glanced in Austen's direction and then looked up. Toby was only about fifteen feet from the deck. The woman stared at him. In a loud whisper, Austen admonished the boy. "I've told you *not* to play on that wall. We need clean water to survive." When Toby came within reach, she pulled him down the last few feet and shook him roughly, like a parent might a wayward child, at least she hoped so, having no experience to support it.

A soaking wet Toby caught on quickly. He whined and pulled away from her. "I'm sorry. *Let go.*"

When Austen looked back, the woman had continued on her way.

The four returned safely to their cubbies.

~ ~ ∞ ~ ~

In the morning, Justine reported that Brie died peacefully in her sleep sometime during the night. A bit later, a mushroom and Doc appeared in the passageway in front of the compound. The white light flashed as the airlock pressurized. Nikko, Curtis, and Austen, who held Toby by the shoulders, stood at the invisiwall attempting to communicate with Doc. She was in a trance, never glancing their way.

When the airlock was fully pressurized, an announcement that originated from somewhere near the top of the airlock, sounded in English, but in a voice other than Doc's: *Place the body on the deck.* There was a click and whoosh as the interior hatch unsealed and opened. Nikko helped Oscar and Justine carry Brie's body. They lay it gently on the deck inside the airlock. Nikko looked for a keypad or control panel of some type. Other than the seams around the hatch doors, the airlock walls shone smooth and unmarked.

When the three stepped back into the compound, the interior hatch closed and the blue light flashed as the airlock depressurized. *White pressurizing, blue depressurizing — good to know.* Nikko cataloged the information.

The outside hatch opened, and the mushroom's long tentacle stretched out to grasp one of Brie's legs, pulling her across the lip of the hatch. When it resealed, Doc bent over to take Brie's other leg. Nikko watched Doc. As she rose up, she cast a brief look directly at him, one full of terror and hopelessness. The two dragged Brie down the passageway.

Toby tapped furiously on the invisiwall as they went by and yelled. "Doc, Doc, look at me. *Please.*"

Curtis gently pulled the boy away. "It's not Doc anymore, Toby."

Yes it is, Nikko thought, but it was easier to let the others believe Doc was gone and only an unfeeling, mechanical device remained.

22 DENIAL

For brief moments Drew was happy — even high. He'd caught Letty humming in a passageway. But his happiness turned bittersweet when his thoughts moved quickly back to Toby and the others. In all probability, the five were dead by now, or infected, which was the same thing.

The *Maris Stella's* crew gathered in the ship's salon for the daily status meeting. Drew and Letty shared cheerless smiles meant to encourage. But their brows presented the same deep furrows as the rest at the hopelessness of their mission. They'd deployed the homing beacon earlier that morning on a tiny rogue planet three-hundred thousand klicks from Mass Primary and now debated the advisability of launching a probe bundle to search for stabilized wormholes.

"So, without a known frequency or an electronic address to ping, there's no way to discover their scanning or transmission range?" Captain McDermott asked Rob Turrey, the ship's tech specialist.

"No. We don't even know how they communicate. Could be radio waves, electromagnetic radiation waves of one type or another, could also be telepathic, could be somethin' else entirely. The disrupters around their wormhole by Spud would suggest microwave frequencies. But since their objective is to disrupt our transmissions, not their own, that's not reliable."

Letty spoke. "Let's assume they have short- and long-range receivers utilizing radio frequencies similar to ours and just risk it. Pinpointing it exactly will take time we don't have."

Heads nodded agreement all around. The mission was high-risk — rife with unknowns.

"The transmission time needed to activate the probes is short, and once they're activated, the likelihood of the Diak stumbling on that frequency is the same as us stumbling onto one of theirs. Miss Taleen's right," Turrey said. "I say go for it."

"How long do we wait to hear back from a probe?" Aisha Olcott, the lead weapons and tactical specialist, asked.

"Until we can't wait any longer," Captain McDermott replied. "In the meantime, we continue the search for water and perfecting our rescue plans. But, at some point, with or without a way back, with or without a water source, we're gonna need to make a move. Miss Taleen and I will decide what that move's going to be."

The salon stilled in brooding reflection.

Captain McDermott broke the communal trance. "Turrey," he ordered, "release the little buggers."

~ ~ ∞ ~ ~

"So, she died because she turned? But she still looked human," Toby said.

"No, I think maybe the progression caused it to abandon Brie's body for a new one," Nikko answered.

"And that's worse." Curtis leaned against the cubby wall and shook his head. "Now we don't know who the Diak is."

"If she *was* a Diak." Austen grimaced in uncertainty. "I'm starting to think I was imagining it."

"You're just in denial. A Diak spy is too creepy — but if you think about it, it makes sense," Curtis said.

"You know what they used to say about denial," Austen smiled.

Curtis and Toby looked perplexed.

"What?" Toby finally bit.

"It's not just a river in Egypt."

"Is Egypt a planet?" Toby asked.

"No. It's one of the oldest countries on Earth, and the site of the very first alien encounter—almost three thousand years before anyone knew aliens existed. I read about Egypt in *Antony and Cleopatra*. At first, I thought Shakespeare made it up. They say, until the Global Civil War, you could still see remnants of huge pyramids built by the Egyptians. And there was a river called the *Nile*. Get it, de-nile?"

At Toby's blank look, Curtis teased him. "Aren't you learning anything in that fancy school Letty sends you to?"

Toby made a face. "Back at ya. You didn't know either."

"Freak," Curtis said.

Nikko laughed. "Until this second, I considered the possibility that Diak Brie might have shifted to you, Curtis. But there's no way it could mimic your total lack of civility so soon."

"Screw you. When we get back, you're fired."

"When we get back, I doubt you'll be in position to fire me— and I'm not working for you anyway."

Austen put a halt to their bickering. "Toby, tell us what you saw at the top of the wall."

"It's no good. There's only a place where the water comes in through a little, narrow slit. And the whole thing is made outta metal, like steel. 'Bouts all you could do is plug it up."

Nikko looked thoughtful. "That's an option though if we need a diversion. Good job, kid. New ideas, anyone?"

"We should inspect that stuff piled against the back bulkhead for making weapons," Austen offered.

"Agreed," Curtis said. "But we'll have to be careful in case there *is* a Diak spy. . . which definitely isn't me." He raised a mocking eyebrow at Nikko and went on. "Say we plug up the water source. Wouldn't they have to come see what the problem is? If it's only two or three, we might be able to overpower them."

"Then what?" Nikko asked. "Who says the atmo outside this compound is Earth-friendly."

"True."

Nikko continued thinking out loud. "We know the Diak are connected in some way, like our comms, or maybe telepathically. However many show up, we'd have to take them all out at the same time so there's no chance for one to transmit an alarm."

Austen asked, "Did either of you pay attention to the airlock procedures when we first came in, and later?"

"Yeah, I did," Nikko said. "The light flashes blue for depressurization and white for pressurization. I took a good look when I was inside it, but there's no obvious control panel."

"Nikko, you were still out cold when they brought you back after questioning. They pressurized the airlock, hauled you through and dumped you on this side, then depressurized it after they left."

"Okay. . . so?" Nikko prodded.

"I was up front when they came for Curtis as well. For him, they entered without pressurizing the airlock, grabbed Curtis, and left, depressurizing it behind them—except since they never pressurized it in the first place, it was a sham. For the aliens themselves, it didn't seem to make a difference one way or the other."

"You said they depressurized again after I was in the passage," Curtis noted. "Maybe pressurizing and depressurizing is a hoax to keep people from trying to escape. The passageway must have already been Earth-nominal, or you'd think I would've noticed. And they opened an unpressurized airlock this morning to retrieve the body. . . ."

"Huh?" Toby said. "I'm lost."

Curtis ignored him. "Unless. . . *unless* the controls are dual. Like you can pressurize *both* the passageway and the airlock or one or the other."

"Which raises more problems," Nikko said. "For this scenario, let's say there are dual controls. We passed through three separate enclosures before arriving here. I'll bet you each one is enabled separately for the environment needed in that area at the time. So, escaping from this compound may only get us as far as our own greater enclosure area. And what if the controls are voice triggered?"

"They can't be," Austen said. "The mushrooms never spoke."

"Okay. . . worse. . . maybe they're telepathically triggered. I don't remember seeing the guards punching buttons or entering codes along our route coming in. Did you?"

Curtis mumbled dejectedly, "Now *I'm* lost. I'd give a week's greasy nutrition supply for a processor. The long timers may know something."

Austen looked as disheartened as Curtis. "Before we can question the others, we have to root out the Diak among us or make certain there isn't one. How?"

For several seconds they sat quietly thinking.

"Chickens," Toby said.

~ ~ ∞ ~ ~

Drew, Letty, and Captain McDermott stood in the short passage between the salon and the bridge. "I'm sorry, repeat that." Drew's shoulders hunched as if, like Atlas, he carried the weight of the world, but in his case, the universe.

"We have *antimatter* projectiles," Letty said again, watching him closely.

With her emphasis on the word antimatter, Drew felt the bitter cold of space thread through his body, and his blood boiled. "That's illegal. That's horrific."

"Hmm," was her reply.

Captain McDermott broke in. "Desperate times call for — "

"Bullshit!" Drew said, a little too loudly. He looked over his shoulder and lowered his voice. "*Bullshit!* And you both know it. You may have the script and the experts — may they rest in peace — to produce antimatter, but that does not give you the right." His feelings for Letty took a gut-punch.

With advancements that ultimately cut production time of one gram of antimatter from unimaginable billions of years to ten, and the accompanying quantum leap from the archaic Penning Trap to Abiding Containment, the K.U. was whipped with fear and contention. A war between two planets wielding antimatter weapons would start and end with the first strike. Worse, experts theorized that detonation might initiate an uncontrolled chain reaction across thousands of light years. At the possibility of global — or even universal — annihilation, citizens of the K.U. reacted with a terror of savage ferocity. The resulting era of Neo Darkness brought a brief resurgence of religion and an appalling rise in individual and mass suicides among all who grasped the unthinkable potential, Earth and alien. A decade of chaos toppled governments, uprooted conventions, and caused a death toll in the millions.

To end the insanity, scientific and engineering communities on all Alliance planets, ignoring authoritarian threats, came together to draft and sign the Amalgamation Decree of Intelligent Beings. Antimatter could be produced in controlled environments as a fuel and power source only. Scientists and engineers, alien or human, who aided in weaponizing antimatter, would be executed, as would any governmental or industrial proponents of weaponization. Every adult in the K.U. was invited to sign. As unspeakable as the prospect of unadjudicated executions was, the invitation brought a groundswell of approval. Billions signed their endorsement, and the panic and violence abated.

Two years later, professionals from a non-aligned planet petitioning for membership into the Alliance were invited to sign the decree. They refused, noting that if the Alliance approved their membership application, the planet's stockpile of antimatter weapons should be grandfathered in. When the Alliance denied their application, ten of their top scientists/engineers died within a week of one another from mysterious causes. No one ever identified the enforcers, but the notes found on each body echoed the last line of the Amalgamation Decree of Intelligent Beings: *Do not doubt us.*

Letty studied Drew. He hoped she recognized the fear and the horror in his eyes, as well as his underlying disappointment in her.

Captain McDermott continued. "That's plan B, anyway. Maybe even plan C. But lacking other options, we take out Mass Primary, the Diak, the hostages, and ourselves." He cleared his throat and offered Letty a small, sad smile. "I'm going to check in with the tactical team. I'll talk to you later."

Drew watched McDermott stroll away. *How can they act so cavalier?*

Letty continued to study Drew. Her look challenged him to consider the circumstances before he objected further.

"You could cause a chain reaction that might wipeout a whole section of the universe. You'd kill Toby?" he spat—his cruelty intentional—the statement inane.

In a raised voice that easily reached the salon from where they stood outside the control room, she fired back, tears welling, "*Yes,* since the alternative is for him to become a Diak host, if that hasn't happened already. And probably every other being in the K.U., as well. Which would *you* prefer?!"

"It's not my decision to make—nor yours."

She went on, ignoring his rejoinder. "How can you be so naïve? Do you seriously believe that the Alliance planets don't all have such weapons, or can't produce them? All the decree did was pacify the masses with a false sense of security and the pathetic belief that they — the *people*—were victorious."

He softened his tone, but his opposition reflected off the steel of his eyes. "Count me among the masses. Possession of antimatter weapons is immoral, Letty. You may have signed your own death sentence and that of everyone who aided you as well."

She ignored the latter. "What difference does morality make on this side of the wormhole?"

If anyone told him that a day after making love to her he'd be terrified of her, he wouldn't have believed them. They were engaging in angry rhetoric with no expectation of either being swayed by the other's opinion.

Drew took a different tact. "The armada's no longer here. I'm sure they have more than one command station."

She made a small shake of her head. "Regardless, if we must die, we're taking out the station and every Diak in it, even if we destroy everything within a lightyear around us."

"Is that the royal 'we,' *your Majesty*?" Drew turned away. "I'm gonna get some sleep." He slung the words over his shoulder, his statement devoid of invitation.

23 CHICKENS

"Chickens?" Nikko repeated.

Toby took on a superior air. "Austen's lame Nile joke made me think of it. One of my teachers," he mugged at Curtis, "starts every lesson with a chicken joke."

"I don't understand." Austen cocked her head to one side. "How would chicken jokes help us flush out the Diak?"

"She explained that all countries on earth has chickens. It's cross. . . cross. . . cul—"

"Cross-cultural," Curtis finished his sentence.

"Yep. Like I said, every lesson starts with a chicken joke cuz there's so many of 'em. Which came first, the chicken or the egg? That's all about evolution. Why did the chicken cross the road? That's philosophy. And you use visual analysis to answer if a chicken smacks his lips. That's a good one because the teacher said *his* lips instead of *her* lips. Get it? It means there's different ways to look at things and to figure stuff out. What I'm sayin' is, everyone on Earth, even kids like me, knows about chickens and can answer chicken jokes."

"*Huh,*" Curtis grunted. He looked at the other two.

"It *might* work," Nikko nodded.

"I thought the Diak could access their host's memories." Austen remained unconvinced. "Wouldn't it just check its bank of memories for the answers?"

Curtis shook his head. "Not as smooth as that. I guess scrolling through someone's memories takes time. Diak Fitz hesitated a lot trying to define words and connect thoughts, especially colloquialisms. Who retains memories about chickens or chicken jokes anyway?"

Austen rocked slowly in thought. "But we can't just start telling six-hundred people the same chicken jokes. They'd think we were crazy and discuss it with each other, which would botch the whole idea. Seriously, guys, it *is* crazy."

"Maybe," Nikko said. "Let's test the jokes on Oscar. If he passes, we'll see what he thinks. We could split people into groups and keep them separated while we test them. It shouldn't take more than a few hours."

Curtis snorted. "This is so *fucking* stupid."

"That's two pickles you've gotten us out of, Toby." Nikko patted the boy on the back.

Toby sobered. "That's what Travis called the trouble we were in back then. . . a pickle," he said with a shaky breath.

They found Oscar in his cubby talking with Justine.

"Oscar, do you have a minute to work with us on something?" Curtis asked.

The cubby was a few feet above deck level. Justine hopped out easily. "I was on my way to get some water to wash down my nutrition anyway." She scrunched her face in displeasure. "See you guys later."

The man scooted to the edge and dangled his legs over. Nikko gave Toby a boost so he could sit next to him.

"So, Oscar," Toby started. "I got a joke for you."

"Okay."

"Why did the chicken cross the road?"

Without hesitation, Oscar laughed and replied, "To get to the other side. But why did the chicken cross the road *twice*?"

"Why?" Toby said.

"Because it was a double-crosser."

Toby giggled and looked at Nikko. "Do I need to tell him another one?"

"No, we have our answer." Nikko flashed his characteristic smile. Curtis realized it was the first time he'd seen Nikko's big, goofy smile since Diak Fitz reappeared on Dark Landing.

"What's this about?" Oscar asked, puzzled.

"It sounded stupid when the kid first suggested it, but I gotta say, it worked pretty well with you." Curtis filled him in.

"It makes sense when you explain it. But I don't believe Brie was a Diak."

Austen shook her head. "Each time I came near her, my internal klaxon sounded. I could've been wrong—I waver. But if she was, it makes sense she'd take another host before she turned. When we first arrived, you called Brie the compound's sage. Why?"

"More in reverence to her age and gentleness. She rarely spoke and *never* complained. People came to her to talk about their fears; how much they missed their families and homes. After you're here a while, you go through a suicidal phase. She was so wise, listening quietly, nodding encouragement; sometimes she'd just hold your hand. People felt better after talking to her, and she was discreet. But a Diak. . . only *Muck* knows."

~ ~ ∞ ~ ~

Two hours before the event, Oscar acted as spokesperson to explain that they were conducting an experiment. A few people asked questions, which went unanswered, but no one refused to comply. Though they tried to amuse themselves with storytelling and games, a hopeless melancholy ruled the enclosure. The prisoners welcomed any change to their dreary routine.

When the time came, they split the five-hundred-ninety prisoners into two equal groups. The first group gathered at the front of the compound while the second group stayed in their cubbies or at the back.

It was Nikko's job to keep everyone in the front organized, and Toby's job to keep the second group away while they questioned the first group. Curtis, Austen, and Oscar sat with their backs against the bulkhead, spread far enough apart from one another, and from those waiting to be questioned, that no one could overhear. It took less than a minute for each person, and the line moved quickly. Nikko corralled the ones already questioned off to the side, separate from the waiting line. Frequent bursts of laughter and puzzled smiles on the faces of those completing the experiment suggested a pleasurable experience.

As the first group was finishing up, Toby formed the second group into a line on the opposite side of the compound. On cue, he led them to the front while Nikko ushered his group to the back.

With almost two hundred still waiting, Curtis left his station to whisper in Toby's ear and then continued to the back to ask Nikko to replace him up front as a questioner.

It took the better part of the day to complete the experiment. Everyone in the compound grew curious about the purpose of the chicken jokes, but once more their inquiries went unanswered.

$$\sim \, \sim \, \infty \, \sim \, \sim$$

"She's Asian. Vietnam, I think she said." Austen shrugged.

"Never heard of it," Curtis said.

"No, me neither. I chatted with her briefly only once. She wears traditional garb—the pajamas and pointy hat—because she's a language and history lecturer at the cultural center in her hometown. She complained that fewer and fewer parents send their children in to learn about their ancestral roots. The data vials will be there when she's gone, but it saddens her to think no one will look at them. She seems like a sweetheart."

"What did she say, exactly?" Nikko asked Curtis.

"I asked her if a chicken smacks his lips. She responded with, 'I don't know any chickens.' Then she closed her eyes for three or four seconds and asked, 'What would cause a chicken to hit itself in the mouth?' I tell ya, she looked the same as Diak Fitz when it was perplexed by something I said. Toby's watching her. Oscar's waiting for the head. When he gets here, he can probably tell us more about her."

"So, what did you say to her afterward?" Nikko kept his voice low.

"I said, 'That's a really good answer.' She didn't seem suspicious, but who knows? When I went to the back to send you up, I spotted her in a cubby in the middle wall. She was by herself. She's stayed in her cubby since then."

When Oscar joined them, he added little information. "She arrived shortly after I did. She's very pleasant, joins most gatherings, but stays to the back and doesn't say much. That's all I know."

"That should make her easy to avoid," Austen said. "And no one else you guys questioned was suspicious?"

"No," Oscar said, turning to Nikko.

"Nope. Other than major curiosity about what we were up to."

Curtis shook his head.

There was a commotion from the front, and Toby came running for them. "Quick, the Fahdeen and Doc are outside. The pointy hat lady went up with everyone else."

The five pushed their way through the crowd. Their suspect, looking confused and scared, was standing outside with the Diak Fahdeen and Doc Jameson. Doc, lacking all emotion, focused on the deck in front of her. The Fahdeen held a crescent-shaped blade high for all to see but stared pointedly at the Dark Landing group as they lined up against the invisiwall. Without taking its eyes off them, it moved next to Doc.

Curtis grabbed Toby and pushed the boy roughly behind him with such force that he fell to the deck in the middle of the gathered crowd. Sensing what was about to happen, the hostages ignored his protests and closed tight around him.

The Diak stretched upward on its paws, and with two quick slices, severed Doc's head, then turned and left, its sword dripping. The suspected infiltrator trailed behind her.

Doc's body, her head lying next to it in a pool of blood, remained in the passage for two days and nights before mushrooms came to drag her away.

24 TAKING RISKS

The morning after their argument about antimatter weaponry, Letty came to Drew's cabin. "I'm sorry, Drew. I know you're disappointed in me, but this may be all the time we have together. Please don't spoil it."

Under different circumstances, the rift between them might never have mended. She was right. This was all the time left to them. Still numb from their last exchange, he pulled her into his arms in an attempt to reawaken his feelings. "It's wrong, Letty. You know that."

"No, I don't know that. If we can't find a way back to the K.U., I don't see any other action. At least we can eradicate the Diak threat to our worlds."

"There's no way to know if the threat would end. Like I said, their armada is somewhere, and they must have other stations as well. The Diak aren't the point here, it's the unknown consequences that are unconscionable. "

She nuzzled her face into the hollow of his neck and pressed tighter against him. "Please, Drew. I don't want to argue. Both our arguments are right, and. . . I love you."

It was the first time she'd said those words. He clung to her, desperately wanting to evoke the passion and elation he'd felt during their night together. "This is too big to ignore, Letty, but we won't talk about it again unless it becomes an issue. Okay?" They were re-ploughing old ground. "I don't want to waste what time we have left either."

She pulled back to look at his face. "You know, I've noticed a change in you since last year. You seem more confident. . . sure of yourself. I like it, and—"

Captain McDermott's voice came over the loudspeaker: *I need everyone in the salon now.*

When they'd all gathered, McDermott said, "We received an emergency transmission from the *Blinkum*."

The room erupted in mumbled concern. When the *Maris Stella* left in search of water and to locate a place to deploy the probe homing beacon, *Blinkum*, one of the ship's three shuttles—the *Winkum*, *Blinkum*, and *Nod*—stayed behind to keep an eye on Mass Primary.

McDermott waited patiently for them to quiet and continued. "Two water tankers are approaching Mass Primary on a relative bearing of zero three seven mark ten. *Blinkum* thinks she can launch a tracker bot to affix to one of them without being spotted. If we leave now, we might be able to follow the ships back to their water source. That puts us in greater danger of being discovered, but without water we'll be forced to act before we're ready, regardless." He looked at Letty. "Thoughts anyone?"

Heads nodded all around and Aisha Olcott, the lead tactical specialist, spoke up. "I vote *aye*. We don't know how long it'll take to locate a wormhole back to the K.U.—assuming there is one. Water will buy time."

"Agreed," Letty said.

Drew nodded along with the rest, though he doubted his opinion counted.

"Okay," McDermott said. "Course is set."

The ship moved at full speed toward the intercept coordinates. The asteroid field thinned the farther they traveled from Mass Primary. They detoured from the direct path just enough to stay among the biggest rocks as long as possible. At the half-way point, the *Blinkum*, obviously successful in attaching a bot to one of the tankers, transmitted the tracker's frequency. Her brief transmission, as well as the intermittent transmissions from the tracker, were risks worth taking.

~ ~ ∞ ~ ~

A numbing silence fell across the compound for the entire evening following Doc's death. Even those getting water or standing in line at the head kept their eyes averted and avoided conversation. Over the next two days, several people came to Oscar individually to ask if the incident was related to the chicken "experiment," and whether the guard the Diak beheaded was known to the newcomers.

Toby was once again dejected. In their cubby the morning after the incident, Curtis told the other two that he'd woken to discover the boy gone. He'd found him up front, weeping and pounding his fists against the invisiwall as he stared at Doc's body. Curtis said he'd tried to talk to him, but Toby only huddled in a corner as far as possible from him and the other inhabitants. Uncertain what else to do, he stayed in the boy's sight, sitting on the deck with his back to the carnage, and left him alone to deal with his grief. After a while, Toby returned to their cubby and slept through the better part of the morning.

The Dark Landing group spent the following few days crouched together, saying little, coping with their individual feelings of guilt and powerlessness until Nikko decided it was time to get back on track.

"What's happened is horrendous, but we still need to come up with an escape plan. We can't allow ourselves to fall into despondency." At the last Nikko looked at Toby. The boy's eyes were set deep, framed by dark circles, but he jerked his head in agreement.

Austen spoke, "A few people have offered condolences. Oscar spread the word about the cause of the butchery, our suspicions, and rooting out a Diak spy. There's some paranoia that there might be more than the one. I think that's good. It's right to be cautious."

Curtis placed a hand on Toby's shoulder and jostled him encouragingly. For once the boy accepted the gesture instead of pulling away. Toby had turned nine before arriving back on the station, but now he'd reverted to a younger age. Nikko hoped the kid still had enough moxie to come out of his funk soon. Over the course of a year, he'd lost his parents, barely escaped from the Diak threat on multiple occasions, been uprooted twice, and finally dragged off to San Francisco where his new life with Letty was shaken by the intrusion of Xander Crawford. No wonder he'd crumbled, and who knew what was still to come.

Nikko continued. "To be on the safe side, let's assume there *is* another spy. Anyway, it's obvious we're being monitored. We still need to talk to the others about anything they've noticed around the enclosure or our captors that might be helpful. Austen, let's start with the people who offered condolences. I doubt they're Diak— agreed?"

He received three nods.

"I'm curious about something," Curtis stated.

"What's that?"

"Do Diak fear death? They must if they've gone to such lengths to survive. And Diak Fitz certainly did. What if we could take one of *them* hostage?"

Toby sat up straight, displaying a sudden, intense interest. "That's a good plan. And if it won't help us, we'll kill it," he said in a thick voice. His face darkened with hatred; hands balled into fists.

The three adults exchanged troubled glances.

~ ~ ∞ ~ ~

The *Maris Stella* sat tucked behind a boulder large enough to conceal Dark Landing. There was no need to keep the water tankers in sight as the intermittent signals from the tracker bot provided exact coordinates. Once the tankers left the station, the *Maris Stella* would follow at a safe distance. To refract sensor detection, they must disable their own sensors, then periodically re-enable them for brief seconds to sync with the bot transmissions. Turrey, their tech specialist, felt certain, were the circumstances reversed, the *Maris Stella* would eventually detect any ship following it, but it was all about taking chances now. Ship's weapons charged, the crew waited anxiously at their assigned stations.

Finally, the tankers departed Mass Primary, proceeding at a steady pace back along the same course on which they'd arrived. The *Maris Stella* followed. Twenty-six hours passed, and Drew's tension and that of the ship's crew lessened as muscles cramped from inaction. Drew yawned and struggled to keep his eyes open.

The silence broke with an announcement from Captain McDermott. "We lost the signal. Turrey's scanning to reacquire it."

Minutes passed during which alertness levels returned to their peak. "Still no signal," McDermott updated the crew. "It looks like we're out of luck and. . . wait a sec. . . wormhole!"

25 HOPE SPRINGS

"We need to decide now. If we wait, we could lose the signal on the other side. And once we've lost them, we may never find the way back on our own." McDermott scanned the faces in the salon.

All eyes focused on Letty as she considered their situation. "It's the first break we've had. Crossing the wormhole is a risk, but there's no water here. Call for hands."

With decisiveness, every man and woman in the salon raised their hands. The captain executed a military turn and headed to the bridge, issuing orders to the ship's computer as he went.

~ ~ ∞ ~ ~

"I'm an engineer—a nanotechnologist. I specialize in nano-based sensors for detecting and analyzing chemical vapors, specifically as it relates to terraforming," Simon Dunlevy said. He was sitting with the Dark Landing group and Oscar at the front of the hostage compound, away from eavesdroppers.

Only Austen nodded in understanding of Simon's vocation. Toby and the other three adults stared at him with *get-to-the-point* expressions.

He got to the point. "When we learned about the Diak and their nanoid selves, I started paying closer attention. My educated guess is that, at some point fairly soon after infusion, the nanoids adapt their new alien body to the local environment. By local I mean, whatever, wherever, whenever."

"Concupiscible tickle-brains. . . that's brilliant!"

At Simon's confused and somewhat frightened reaction to Austen's outburst, Curtis counseled him. "Ignore her. It's a form of Shakespearian Tourette's — impervious to all modern treatments."

Simon watched Austen warily and went on. "It's been my observation that the Diak adjust the environment in the passageways to fit whichever captive is being transported. They don't readjust it unless another, incompatible, race is brought in or out. But — and I'm guessing again — the remaining biological cells of each host would still require whatever fuel their cells naturally process. I think, in order for the guards to survive in all environments, the nanoids are forced to transmute a host's cells as rapidly as possible. What did you say the Diak call it?"

"Turning," Curtis said.

"So," Nikko simplified, "in our larger enclosure, if they took one of us out, the atmosphere would remain Earth-friendly until they took out, or brought in, a Bin or a Fahdeen, or one of the other allied races."

"Right." Simon nodded. "But we can't know what the environment might be in the adjacent enclosures. . . well, over any length of time, that is."

Nikko continued to drill down. "Let's say they take one human out and another human follows immediately. As long as the second human stays on the same route as the first human, the environment should be compatible along the way?"

"Supposedly, but so what?" Simon looked at each of them in turn. "Where are you going? We're being held on a space station by unfriendlies in an unknown location with no way back to our corner of the universe. "

"One problem at a time. All we need to do is get to our ship," Nikko said.

Curtis pushed the heels of his hands into his eye sockets and rubbed. "Yeaah, that's *all* we need to do."

Only Toby appeared invigorated by the conversation.

~ ~ ∞ ~ ~

When the *Maris Stella* emerged from the wormhole, Drew closed his eyes against the blinding light and then layered both hands over them when the light penetrated his lids.

Filters enabled; shields deployed, the ship's computer announced.

Drew opened a narrow crack between his fingers and ventured a peek. "That hurt." He blinked rapidly, looking away from the viewer to the deck and around the salon in an attempt to reboot his eyeballs. The room came into focus. They mimicked his actions, each scanning the room and blinking rapidly to clear their vision. The rest of the crew had stayed at their ready stations in anticipation of a potentially hostile reception.

Their sight recovered, the three simultaneously turned back to the large monitor that displayed the forward view as observed from the ship's bridge. Even with the filters engaged, light danced erratically off minute, multi-faceted particles that enveloped the ship. Veins of denser particles snaked through the panorama like the veins in a slab of milky marble.

"Nebula?" Letty asked.

"No. Nebulas are only observable from great distance. You wouldn't know when you're inside one. My guess it's a dust field. That's why the shields were deployed — to prevent erosion. There. . . look." Drew pointed to a bright spot where shafts of light pierced the haze, causing the dust motes to sparkle in a sea of light even the filters were unable to shroud entirely.

"*Sailed on a river of crystal light, into a sea of dew,*" Letty quoted from the poem for which the *Maris Stella* and her three shuttles were named.

"I'll say!" Grabe added. "That's a star."

Drew nodded as the view panned to the right. The crescent of a large orb filled the bottom quarter of the screen. "And a planet. . . no, a moon. The planet's slightly above and a hair further right." The view continued to pan. "Whoa, and a second star — pretty distant. It looks like we're in a dense dust ring around a binary system. Probably not the best place to be."

McDermott's voice came over the speaker. "Folks, this is a *verified* shocker. Our sweet little processor is working her sweet little ass off. She thinks she knows where we are! *Computing. . . computing. . . .*" He mimicked the lilting voice of the ship's processor. "In the meantime, the tanker signal is strong and on course toward that moon. We're following. Stay tuned."

The moon now filled the entire screen, and McDermott magnified it further. Ships and orbiting satellite stations came into focus. The dust field thinned as they approached, and soon they could make out a sparse cloud cover between the satellites and the world below. There was no doubt the moon was inhabited. The night phase side of the terminator contained large pools of light, distinct from darker, less populated areas. And there were vast, ink-black expanses. Oceans. Water! Where there was life, there was always water in one form or another. That was a constant.

"Stay alert; no place to hide here," Captain McDermott announced. "We're maintaining our position at the edge of the tracker range."

~ ~ ∞ ~ ~

On Dark Landing, the tech pointed to his display. "Do you see that?"

Kyle focused on the green square in the center of the screen. The ID tag to the left of the object read *Taleen Industries SN816407740.* "Where's that from?" he asked, as he simultaneously jabbed at his comm implant. "Tree-. . . er, Captain Thomas, we have a returning probe, and it doesn't appear to be ESF." To the command crew he ordered, "Cut all outward transmissions now — everything — do *not* link to that probe." Over his comm, Kyle listened as Captain Thomas issued a similar order.

Fifteen minutes later, Dark Landing shift commanders Kyle Drubber and Mitchell Jones met in the security conference room with Captain Thomas, an ESF technician, and battalion Rear Admiral Jensen Sullivan. All eyes watched the wall monitor, which displayed the probe and the scrolling column of stats on its left.

"Absolutely Taleen manufacture, but not one registered to Earth Space Force, sir," the tech said.

"Why's it just sitting there?" Admiral Sullivan asked.

"Probes are programed to respond only to their homing signal. It's analyzing us and the wormhole, recalibrating to locate that signal. If we leave it alone, when it doesn't pick it up here, it should head into the wormhole and continue the hunt."

"Do you guys really think it's from the *Maris Stella*?" Jonesy addressed the ESF members.

"We'll know for sure in a minute," Sullivan said. "We're waiting to hear back from Taleen Industries."

The momentary excitement Kyle experienced at the possibility the *Maris Stella* and her passengers were still alive, was suppressed by the knowledge that, if the probe found a way back to the K.U., so could the Diak.

26 IN THE FACE OF IT

The captain addressed the small group that included Letty, Drew, chef and medic, Billy Grabe, and tech specialist, Rob Turrey. The others remained at their stations and listened over their comms. "The good news is we're in our Known Universe. The bad news is we're one-hundred-fifty lightyears from Earth in the constellation Crater. The HD 98800 system consists of two binary systems, A and B. We've landed in the inner dust ring of B, known as Crateris II. Our computer is giddy with excitement, taking measurements and images. If we survive to get the data back to the Alliance, we'll have our fifteen minutes of fame."

"Oh," Drew interjected, "I think if we live and find our way back to the Alliance, we'll get a lot more than fifteen minutes."

"Just so," the captain nodded. "Turrey, what've you got?"

"Earth knew intelligent life existed here several centuries ago, but until now, everything beyond that was conjecture. It's an advanced race of odd-looking aliens — they look kinda like mushrooms is all I can think of — whose technology seems to equal that of the Diak. There's a major wormhole cluster with four active bridges two days out, between here and an outer, denser dust ring. All four are experiencing outgoing traffic, and for three of them the traffic is pretty heavy. I'm dying to know where they end up. But the congestion leads me to believe they don't dump anywhere near the Zeta Quadrant, or we'd know about it. There's a fifth wormhole another day beyond those four. I'm getting weird signals from that one. Something else going on out there — haven't been able to pin it down yet. This system's cluttered with transmissions in the electromagnetic spectrum. Can't imagine anything we might put out would even be noticed." Turrey shrugged the end of his report.

"So, in all probability, one of those wormholes leads back to Mass Primary. The signal from the water tanker is strong. We'll wait out here to see where it goes." McDermott looked to Letty for consent.

"And if it doesn't *go?*" she asked.

"We scout around and try to stay out of trouble. Regardless, our number one priority is replenishing our water supply. In the meantime, we study the wormholes and make a calculated guess at which one takes us back to Mass Primary. I'd say we have a hair better than one-in-four odds. But if we miss. . . well, we embark on an adventure of a lifetime." The captain smiled as if that possibility was his first choice.

"Right, because the adventure we're on now is a walk in the celestial park," Drew said.

Letty smiled. "That sounds like something Curtis would say."

"It does, doesn't it? I must miss his sarcasm."

The captain dismissed his comment in the same way Drew would have ignored Curtis. "As long as we continue to receive a strong signal from the tanker, we can move closer to the wormhole cluster to study the traffic patterns for clues. We'll pick a favorite for returning to the Diak station and then make a decision on what action to take if the tanker selects a different door."

Turrey addressed Letty and the captain. "Permission to launch four nano-projectiles to that moon. I'll program each of them to cross one of the four bridges when its data drive is full. Who knows, one could even make it home. 'Course it might be a trillion-squared years from now, and home may not be there anymore."

"Permission granted," Letty and McDermott answered in unison.

The captain continued. "We've been cataloging the different ships as we spot them. The number and variety of designs is amazing. If we stay away from objects likely to request registry or other ID, the *Maris Stella* shouldn't stand out."

They positioned the ship one Earth day from the inhabited moon and a day out from the wormhole cluster when the tanker signal stopped. Letty, Drew, and Captain McDermott huddled on the small bridge around the map display.

"It's dead. Turrey doubts we'll pick it up again," McDermott reported. "We've only got water for a week—a bit more with rationing. We can't leave this system until we restock. At least we know there's water here, whereas back at Mass Primary we struck out."

Letty nodded slowly and cast Drew a sideways glance. "If nothing else presents itself, we attack another ship and hope their reserves are enough to buy us at least a month." At Drew's grunt of disgust, she went on. "*Or. . . I guess we can lie down and die right here. What do you think we should do, Drew?*"

Still uncertain in her own mind, she'd told him she loved him because of their slim odds for survival, and she didn't want to spend what little time was left alone. Their first night together was amazing, but after their argument, all progress toward making up was short-lived. Drew seemed incapable of getting past her antimatter weapons revelation. *We're in enemy territory. The Diak want to enslave us. Billions of lives are at stake beside Toby's. Why is he acting so self-righteous?*

As if he'd read her thoughts, Drew apologized for his reaction. "Sorry. We need the water or our whole objective for crossing over is unfeasible. But attacking. . . *killing*. . . seems like it's always the first and only option considered."

It was obvious where McDermott's loyalty lay. "That's because it's the most expedient option considering our circumstances. And considering what's at state in the larger context."

"Maybe. That doesn't mean I can't hate it. Why don't we try to barter for the water we need?" Drew said.

The captain replied as if he was speaking to a small child. "Well, Drew, from what we know of the Diak, I believe it's safe to assume this system is compromised. Ask yourself why we didn't simply knock on Mass Primary's front door in the first place." McDermott paused, seemingly to give Drew time to think about it. "And on the odd chance it's not under Diak control, we still know nothing about the natives. This is not a diplomatic mission. If all goes as planned, we won't be here long enough to make friends anyway."

"You're right," Drew acknowledged. "Stupid question."

"Then that's settled. Let's not waste more time debating ethics." Letty knew she sounded callous, but his continuous objection to every suggestion was just that: a waste of time. "If we recapture the tanker's signal, that's great, but let's assume it's not going to happen. It's possible they found the tracker."

They numbered the four wormholes in order of their proximity to the moon.

McDermott offered, "We agree that WH2 is the most likely candidate to return us to Diak space. It's the least trafficked of the four, and since there was so little traffic coming and going around Mass Primary. . . ?"

The two men nodded in consensus.

McDermott studied the map. "I have a gut feeling we should recon WH5 while we're here. We're receiving contradictory data. Ship traffic is thinner out that way—a good spot for our highjack mission. But our sensors are picking up a number of transmission leaks at the wormhole itself, which indicates a huge volume of shielded communications. The computer's struggling to translate. The sheer volume suggests another station similar to Mass Primary, or—"

"Or an armada," Letty said.

His tone remained non-committal. "I think it's worth a look-see."

Letty studied the map a moment longer before nodding. "Okay."

McDermott opened his comm to the crew. "Olcott, fine-tune your highjack strategy. Everyone: We're continuing to WH5 for a quick recon, then we'll snag the most likely candidate to replenish our water supply. So, on the way back, keep your eyes open for suitable ambush opportunities. After that, it's a straight shot to WH2 and back to Mass Primary. All in favor say *aye*." Without pause, he continued. "The *ayes* have it."

At mid-point to recon WH5, the *Maris Stella* slowed. McDermott summoned Aisha Olcott and her team to the salon.

"It's almost too good to be true." The auspiciousness of their discovery excited Letty. They'd passed an unmanned water depot twenty klicks back, complete with a docked tanker either dropping off or picking up its shipment.

Olcott squashed Letty's optimism. "The depot may be unmanned, but you can bet they're not giving the stuff away. It could be a private reloading station for company ships only. If so, the coupling will be proprietary—not that we know what their standard is. It is a good thing, though." She studied the recon vids on the wall monitor and then glanced at her two teammates. They nodded agreement to her non-verbal proposal.

She continued. "I think it's safer to hit a ship where we can coerce its command into giving up their supply. At the depot, without the right codes or registry, there's no one to threaten for access."

"But wouldn't it be more likely for a ship to send a distress signal, where an unmanned depot might not?" Drew asked.

Olcott shook her head. "The minute we approach either one unannounced, or with an uncatalogued registry, they'll send a shout out. That doesn't worry me. We can block their signals for the time it'll take us. But if we come up empty handed hitting the depot, there won't be a second chance. With a ship, we're guaranteed to strike pay dirt—even if it's not to the extent we're hoping for. But the depot does provide an advantage we didn't have before."

"What's that?" Letty looked hopefully from the display to Olcott.

"On the return from WH5, we can stake out the depot. Conduct a close-up inspection of its coupling devices so we're prepared. Then we sit back and wait for the next ship to come by to stock up—my guess, it'll be another tanker. We eyeball for a weapon's system—don't expect we'll find one—let our target fill up, and then it's ripe for the picking."

McDermott finally spoke. "Then we high tail it back to Diak space." He smiled. "Easy-peasy."

~ ~ ∞ ~ ~

One hundred klicks out, they encountered a sphere of alert buoys, prohibiting advancement. The *Maris Stella* stayed well back. By themselves, the buoys advertised something special lay within. But the wormhole was clearly visible. . . as was the armada blocking it. They moved further away.

Drew spoke in an awed whisper. "The armada we saw on our last trip seemed bigger. Letty?"

"Not by much. And that's gotta be our bridge back to Zeta Quadrant. Right?"

"Yeah," McDermott said, but shook his head in contradiction. "But not with an armada in our way. It confirms what the Diak Fitz told Chief Walker and Mr. Balog, though. They have the ability to create wormholes. Its convenient proximity to civilization, and the array of equipment connecting to that hole—much more intricate than simple stabilizing infusers—would indicate it was manufactured."

No one spoke again. Drew swallowed hard. He hadn't expected them to make it this far. Still, seeing solid proof of the futility of their efforts to get back home, or of Alliance forces ever permanently cutting off the Diak armada, disheartened him just when he was allowing himself a glimmer of hope.

The *Maris Stella* reversed course. They would circle around and approach the water depot from the "back."

McDermott leaned casually against the liquor bar in the salon and addressed the somber crew. "Okay, plan B."

"We have a plan B?" someone in the group quipped.

McDermott's smile was weak. "When we've replenished our water supply, we return to Mass Primary, attack the station and get our guys back plus as many humans and Bahdane as we can carry. There won't be time to get picky so, other than our main objective— Miss Taleen's son, Toby—we take whoever's handy."

Drew interpreted that to mean no stopping to sort out women and children.

"And Travis Barnes," Letty said, looking accusingly at Drew.

She obviously knew that Barnes might be alive. She must have been waiting for Drew to bring it up.

Turn-about was fair play. He tried to deflect her stare with the same accusatory intensity. *Why didn't you tell* me? After a couple seconds, he abandoned the ploy. "I'm sorry," he whispered.

Her features softened, and she nodded her acceptance of his apology.

"And Travis Barnes," McDermott continued with a small shrug, as if to say no big deal considering the poor odds of rescuing anyone and making it out alive.

Then again, we're beating the odds one dilemma at a time, Drew thought, trying to regain a modicum of positivity. He waited for the captain to expand on the plan. The last time they'd discussed plan B, it included matter-antimatter annihilation.

McDermott scanned the room, avoiding eye contact with Drew. "Regardless of what else happens, Mass Primary does not remain intact. If anyone takes issue with that, now's the time for discussion." He paused a few seconds, and when no one spoke, went on. "Okay, after we've rescued the hostages and destroyed the station. . ." There were feeble chuckles from the group. ". . . we come back here to check out what's on the other side of one of those three wormholes. From there, we wing it." He continued in a flat voice that belied all expectation of success. "Those in favor say *aye.*" The group, all too familiar with his act, was already shuffling toward the hatches to return to assigned stations. As usual, he failed to wait for the vote. "I'm shocked. The *ayes* have it. Oh, wait. . ." McDermott called out. "I'll take the watch tonight. You guys get some sleep." That brought a laugh.

~ ~ ∞ ~ ~

Drew lay in the sumptuous bed without illusions of sleep. The soft mattress and silken sheets were at odds with the circumstances. Letty waited for him in her cabin. There was no misinterpreting the pleading look she gave him as she left the meeting. What was he trying to prove? He'd planned to go to her, but the history of their relationship suddenly coalesced into a carrousel of images. The cycle repeated faster with every rotation until it was a blur.

When they'd first met, and through all that had happened up to now — give her credit — she'd never strung him along, never said she loved him except as a brother. Sure, she'd kidded around, flirting a bit, but more as a friend. And while he was in Vegas, she'd never contacted him. She hooked up with Crawford fast enough. *To lure me in? Not buying that for a minute.* Letty knew where to find him, and that all she had to do was curl a finger and he'd come running.

So now *she claims she loves me. She wants to be with me and create a family for Toby.* Drew had no doubt about Letty's devotion to Toby. That's what it boiled down to. When it came to something or someone that touched her life directly, Letty could be

compassionate and earnest. So, when Toby'd rejected Xander —
probably spotted him for a fake from the get-go — and went looking
for Drew, Letty simply changed lanes.

*What difference does any of it make now? If I go to her, it's not as if
I'm making a life-long commitment. And so what if I did? We're only
talking a few days here.*

It wasn't that simple.

His feelings, and Letty's, and Toby's, were trivial compared
to the knowledge that Taleen Industries was in possession of
weapons of incalculable destruction. And she intended to use them.
The significance of it was so far reaching, so complex, and so
horrific, that Drew was powerless to wrap his mind around it. Next
to Letty, the Diak might prove to be buffoons; nothing more than
thugs. Drew's stomach soured and his love. . . affection. . . empathy.
. . whatever he'd felt for her soured as well.

At the sound of a tentative knock at his hatch, he rolled
toward the bulkhead and closed his eyes, but not to sleep.

27 WORST LAID PLANS

"I don't understand. Why is it still waiting?" Treetop wasn't big on patience.

The Earth Space Force tech dragged his eyes from his monitor, which displayed the Taleen probe hanging in space at the east end of Spud. "It's confused, sir. It knows it's arrived in the K.U., but it can't locate its homing signal. Taleen Industries says, if we leave it alone and don't poke it, it'll eventually continue on its journey."

"There's no question the probe came from the *Maris Stella*?" Kyle asked, needing to hear once more that Letty's ship and her passengers might still be intact.

The tech nodded.

Treetop turned to Kyle. "We're certain the *Maris Stella* launched the probe to map a way back to the K.U., but I'm onboard with Admiral Sullivan and the Earth Defense Council's decision. The fact that it *did* find its way back confirms the Diak have another wormhole into Alliance space. My orders are to bring the probe in. We need the information it's carrying more than the *Maris Stella* does. They're on a suicide mission, and we have no way of telling if they're even still alive."

The situation was out of Treetop's hands. He made a small, apologetic shrug and continued. "The Taleen techs say once we retrieve the data package, we'll need to install new drive hardware if we relaunch it. They dispatched a ship with the parts, but it's a week out at best."

Kyle could think of no argument that would convince Captain Thomas to disobey orders and let the probe return to Diak space. The *Maris Stella* would never learn it had successfully traced a way home.

Thirty minutes later, to the consternation of the team who'd just finished suiting up in preparation for retrieval, the probe shot around the east end of Spud as if it had a comet on its tail. Kyle wondered if it could monitor human conversations. A bubble of elation welled in his chest, and he praised the little probe when it entered the wormhole into Diak space. *There's a good boy!*

As it blinked from sight, ESF dispatch received the first few words of a broken transmission: *Greetings to Sir James Hawking-Barstow. I am the Diak Appointed Principal, Sar Mode* –

~ ~ ∞ ~ ~

Curtis, Nikko, and Austen picked through the junk piled against the back bulkhead, occasionally tossing bits and pieces to Oscar. Oscar sat on the deck with Toby and the three other child-captives, watching him as he formed what were supposed to be toys. If another Diak dwelt in the compound, the humans would appear to be a jovial group playing in the trash. Austen found a length of blue silk cording, which Oscar braided around a strand of wire. He shaped the final product into a surprisingly good likeness of a willowy Camduling.

Nikko jerked his head for Curtis to move up and block the view from the corridor while he passed a smashed hand processor to Austen for inspection. She glanced over her shoulder at the children, emitted *oohs* and *ahs* at Oscar's handiwork, and slipped the piece inside her jacket. The three had accumulated as much as they could carry without looking obvious. On cue, Oscar announced it was time to line up for rations. The children scattered, and the adults headed for Curtis's cubby.

Curtis leaned against the wall at the edge of the cavity watching for anyone coming down the alleyway toward him, while Oscar sat opposite Curtis doing the same in the opposite direction. Nikko and Austen spilled their booty and waited for Simon Dunlevy, the terraforming engineer, to join them. A few minutes later, he climbed into the space, munching on his nutrition cube.

Dunlevy pawed through their finds, mumbling to himself once or twice, finally selecting a small, unidentifiable round object. Curtis darted glances as the man removed the object's back panel and tinkered with the insides. When he turned the item over again, a tiny red light blinked intermittently on its face. He tinkered once more, and the light went out. Curtis strained to hear what Dunlevy was whispering to Nikko.

". . . power enough for what we need — if it lasts. Let's see what else you got." He selected another piece to inspect.

~ ~ ∞ ~ ~

Drew sought out Aisha Olcott, the tactical lead. A quarter of the cargo bay was partitioned into storage for weapons and gear. Her team usually lingered there when not on watch. It was early morning, and Olcott sat alone, swapping out the grips on a half-dozen plasma blasters.

He got to the point. "I want to be the one to inspect the water coupling."

She continued working without looking up. "Sorry, sir, I won't okay that, and Miss Tal. . . Captain McDermott would never agree."

"Look, I'm expendable. The only thing I bring to this party is an extra body. It's a low-hazard job and there's no reason to risk you or any of the ship's crew." She remained focused on her task, but Drew wouldn't give up. "I'm academy trained and have EMU experience. If I'm gonna contribute at all, this is pretty much my only opportunity. Wouldn't you say?"

"Again, sorry. . . *no*." Her tone communicated sympathy, but she remained firm.

"Why?" Drew asked.

Olcott shut her eyes for a moment and took a deep breath. "Yeah. . . I get your point. I *could* take the heat and break protocol, but I won't," she said, still not looking at him.

"How would *you* feel if you were sidelined with no way to contribute? Knowing there was shit chance of survival."

"Look, don't take this the wrong way, but I don't need some hot-dogger trying to impress his girl and go out a hero. The task may not be high risk, but it's key."

Drew shook his head. "That's not what this is about."

"Isn't it?" She finally paused to look him in the eyes, serious in asking and waiting for his answer.

"No. It isn't. There was a time you'd be right, but that time has passed. I only want to contribute. . . something. . . anything."

Olcott studied him a long moment and then cocked her head to one side in a noncommittal gesture. "Okay. I'll speak with the captain, but I won't go so far as to recommend you."

"Thanks," Drew said. "I appreciate it. That's all I can ask."

Olcott returned to her task, eyes hooded. He'd called on her honor; she'd talk to the captain. Drew went to his cabin to wait for the ship to gain its position relative to the water depot. He had no assigned station. Usually, he would hang out with Letty in the salon or on the bridge, but when he'd sat with her and the captain at mess earlier, the tension between them hung thicker than his cinnamon oatmeal.

An hour later, there were three sharp raps on the door to his quarters. He threw his legs over the side of the bed and crossed to open it. Tactical lead Olcott stood in the entry.

With a curt nod, she barked, "Report to the cargo bay to suit up."

"He approved?" Drew asked in disbelief.

"Yeah." Her tone made Olcott's displeasure obvious. "McDermott agreed on one point — you're expendable."

~ ~ ∞ ~ ~

The group returned to the junk pile at the rear of their enclosure. Oscar once again entertained the four children, but this time he was joined by Dunlevy, who fiddled with several small tech pieces, ostensibly to help create toys. When he'd finished jury-rigging the low-energy electromagnetic pulse device, Dunlevy secured scrap resembling wings and a canopy to the cylindrical object and handed it to Toby. The boy held the *shuttle model* in a hover position over the deck before mimicking a vertical landing. Once each child had a new toy, Oscar shooed them away.

The adults hung out for a while longer, chatting and casually poking through the pile looking for pieces of wire to string together and make a "rope" restraint. Curtis spotted a piece of metal roughly eight inches long. One end was jagged, but the opposite was smooth and fit nicely in the palm of his hand. He raised the object a couple inches above the deck and sought Nikko's approval.

The six gathered in Curtis's cube later in the day.

"You're sure?" Austen asked.

"I'm not one-hundred percent sure about any of it," Dunlevy said, as he nibbled on the edge of a greasy nutrition cube without enthusiasm. "But if what you say is true, and Diak Ekis lost contact with Nikko when Nikko disabled his comm, that indicates it was employing technology, not telepathy. On the other hand, that doesn't guarantee the Diak *aren't* telepathic. On the other hand, considering they inhabit such a wide variety of hosts, the odds are skewed against telepathy."

"You don't get three hands," Toby interjected.

"What?"

Toby mugged *never mind* to Dunlevy and continued gnawing on his own cube. Obviously, the boy disapproved of their new gang member.

Curtis patted Toby's head to acknowledge his ability to count to three. "So, if they *are* telepathic, this won't work?"

Dunlevy sighed and shook his head. "I didn't say that. Even if they are telepathic, there's still a chance an EMP would shut down their nanoids or at least muddle their communication. But there's no way for me to test the device's transmission range or even know how long it'll continue to work. And that's assuming it works at all."

Curtis ignored Dunlevy's last statement—they had no alternate plan. "Okay, let's go over it again. When people are lining up for their nutrition cubes tomorrow afternoon, Austen will go with Toby to the back. He'll climb up and plug the water flow as best he can with pieces from the junk pile." He looked at Toby. "You sure they'll do the job?"

"Duh." The boy rolled his eyes toward Dunlevy in obvious criticism of his inability to commit.

"Okay, then. Nikko and you," he nodded at Dunlevy "will be up front with the EMP device waiting for the Diak to come in, and Oscar and I will lurk in the middle cubby row. Once they enter, you activate the device and give us the go. Then you and Nikko follow them to the back, and we'll intercept—catching them between us. If there's only two of them, Nikko and you kill one. Oscar and I will restrain the second one."

Dunlevy blanched.

Nikko reassured the engineer. "No worries. I'll handle the heavy lifting."

Curtis went on. "If there's three of them, Nikko takes one out. And, with your help, I'll take out a second one. Austen will pitch in with Oscar to restrain the third until Nikko's done."

Silence. The plan sounded absurd and messy.

Nikko picked up the plot. "I'll take control of the living Diak and force it into submission. We all move up front. The Diak and I go through the hatch to the outer enclosure and test the environment. If I don't implode, explode, or asphyxiate, we'll retrace the route back to our ship. Second thoughts?"

Two *yeses* sounded in response.

Oscar, quiet up to that point, voiced his objection. "This is crazy. We'll never make it out of here, and even if we do—say we somehow make it all the way to your ship—where do we go? We'll lose our heads just like your doctor friend."

Toby shuddered, and Austen reached over and placed a hand on his shoulder. As usual, he shrugged it off without looking at her. Curtis caught her eye and nodded slightly. As a group, they'd decided it was better to show compassion, even if the boy refused their gestures.

"I agree with Oscar. It's more wishful thinking than a plan," Dunlevy said. "And it's still probable our captive Diak can't issue the necessary commands while the EMP's blocking it, assuming you're able to coerce it into acting on our behalf in the first place— which puts us between a rock and a hard spot."

"So, you'd rather sit around here and wait for whatever comes?" Curtis looked at Oscar.

"No. Yes. . . I don't know. I think we should try to figure out something a little more feasible. And why do we have to harm a Diak? That'll just enrage them. Worse, if no one comes, it'll only serve to put the Diak on notice, endanger our water supply, or get us killed."

"Fuckin' coward," Toby said under his breath, and jumped down from the cubby.

"Hey!" Curtis called after him.

Austen nervously twisted a strand of her white-blonde hair around one finger. "You're right, Oscar, this is crazy, but no one's come up with anything better. I don't think it'll make a difference, but I'm willing to give it another few days of thought if you want."

Dunlevy nodded. "Maybe I can figure a way to test the EMP device without depleting too much of the power supply."

"Okay," Curtis said, "two days—no more. Then we move with what we've got, as pathetic as that might be. Oscar, Dunlevy, when the time comes, we gotta know that you're with us."

The two men glanced at each other before nodding their assurances.

Sure as shit they're going to wuss out when the time comes, Curtis thought.

28 THE FACE OF FEAR

Eight rotations after the first ship from the Alliance had arrived, a second emerged from the wormhole carrying more Earthlings. This one, armed with easily neutralized antimatter warheads, posed little threat to her plans. Sar Mode ordered it unharmed, curious as to its mission and entertained by its activities. When the ship launched probes, she sent a scout to retrieve one.

She was tempted to intercept the *Maris Stella*, as it called itself, before it crossed into the adjoining Pothlill system but decided against it. If the humans chose to attack the Pothlill, once again her plans would carry on unaffected. Though it was the Diak's nearest source of supplies, there were other sources only slightly less convenient. The *Maris Stella* posed no threat to the armada. And if it did attack—even better. In fact, with a little manipulation, the humans might do her work for her.

Sar Mode switched her display to the human enclosure. As entertaining as the *Maris Stella's* maneuverings were, the silly intrigues of her human captives were even more so. She produced a toothy, Fahdeen grin as she observed the little group, amused by their resourcefulness and optimism.

Shortly after launching the probe purloined from the *Maris Stella*, it returned to the docking bay on Mass Primary as encoded. But its log indicated only a small portion of Sar Mode's message was delivered. Still, that they had allowed it to return through the wormhole back to Diak space pointed to deliberate intervention on behalf of the Alliance. They were at least aware of her attempt to contact them.

Sar Mode considered how to proceed. Perhaps the Diak reprogramming of the probe was flawed or the probe otherwise damaged. Or perhaps the Alliance simply replied: *We choose not to hear you.* Doubtful—only fools would respond thus. If Sir James received even those few words, it was likely he awaited further communication.

This demanded a more direct action—something that would prove her capacity—and quickly. If the Maris Stella stumbled upon the correct bridge, she might soon return from the Pothlill system. And the humans on Mass Primary appeared committed to their hastily devised escape plot. Though, the captives were wrong: No Diak lived among their ranks. Such a strategy was pointless when the habitation walls, including the individual sleeping compartments, held devices that monitored every movement and sound. The doctor's beheading offered a warning the hostages had failed to heed.

Of greater concern to Sar Mode than the prospect of the captives' revolt was the Council of Superiors. She could stall them no longer. With the wormhole to K.U. space completed, they'd ordered her to dispatch a reconnaissance squadron and commence the invasion. Time was critical.

She sent for Travis Barnes. *A shame.* Sar Mode coveted the Barnes human: intelligent, heroic, and at its physical peak. She smiled another toothy smile. *Patience. In the end I will have him.*

~ ~ ∞ ~ ~

Travis Barnes watched the *Shroomie*—his nickname for the race—approach his enclosure. Its lower extremity rippled as it glided across the deck. He was unsure what the movement reminded him of. The best he'd come up with was a centipede but with the elegance of a jellyfish. He'd spent hours puzzling over how to describe them. Physically, they resembled a very tall stalk of celery crossed with a mushroom and ranged in color from light lavender to deep rhubarb. Their only appendage was a single tentacle that folded seamlessly into the body when not in use. He'd never seen more than one at a time, but the variations in color led him to believe it wasn't always the same Shroomie. But then it might change color during. . . *Jesus, I need something else to occupy my mind.*

The Shroomie stopped in front of the airlock into his cell. The exterior and interior hatches opened simultaneously, and the alien glided in. Without leaving the airlock, the Shroomie's tentacle extended and grabbed Travis' arm, pulling him to it. The hatch process reversed without pressurization or depressurization, and they headed down a narrow corridor with small enclosures on each side similar to his, but all empty. He noted that one contained a watery liquid. The enclosures were unimportant; he concentrated on counting his steps and memorizing the route.

At seventy-four steps, they hung a right, then a left after twenty-three steps and through a hatch. Forty-five steps and another left into a round-about with multiple hatches encircling it. In the center was another circle conspicuously marked on the deck, a little over three meters in diameter. The Shroomie pulled Travis close to its body—if he'd had anything in his stomach, he would have lost it from the smell. They entered the circle together. As they lifted away, it became evident that the circular area was gravity-free. *Great,* Travis thought, *I have something new to puzzle over.*

Up one level, he stepped easily from nothingness onto the deck. The Shroomie glided out beside him, its lower extremity rippling, but with no evident means of achieving traction. And no flailing around or grabbing for a handhold for either of them. Travis glanced back over his shoulder at the hole, his better-than-average understanding of physics shaken. He wondered about their return path—*if* he was returned—would they use the same portal downward?

Immediately in front of them was a large, circular hatch with an exquisitely crafted surface mural of multi-colored circles. The shapes shifted continuously, their colors swirling and blending into one another. Travis grew mesmerized. Without warning, the hatch disappeared to reveal a sumptuously appointed room. The bulkheads were strewn with static images similar to those on the hatch, and a large, circular lounger eminently suited to the human form occupied the room's center. *Circles around circles around circles.* In addition to the lounger, more oddly shaped pieces of furniture lay scattered about that might better serve alien shapes other than

Travis'. He stepped through the opening; his escort remained in the outer passage.

Prepared for anything, he showed no reaction when a Fahdeen appeared from behind a counter... *bar?*... its surface much too high for the alien's stature. Of course, he'd seen images and documentaries on the Alliance-member race, but he'd never seen one in person. They seemed even rattier looking in the flesh... *fur.. . furry flesh.*

The rat spoke English with an underlying wheeze. "Ahellowess, ahhh Traviss Barneszees ahh." It made a face and coughed several times. "Excuse me—there, much better. I'm unpracticed at using this host's voice. Hello Travis Barnes. Welcome to Mass Primary."

"You know I've been here for over six months now, right?" Travis said.

"Yes, well, I've been busy. So sorry. Let me introduce myself. I am Sar Mode, Appointed Principal Accountable for Mass Spread and Colonization."

Travis abstained from the customary Earth response to Sar Mode's introduction. "What does a Diak look like anyway? Are there *pure* Diaks somewhere?"

"Not for many centuries. Our original form is only a memoryees ahh." It coughed again. "Please take a seat. I have a treat for you."

Travis wanted to refuse, but the lounger looked so inviting— and human—and he'd been sitting on a hard metal deck for the last six months. He settled down on the couch, extending one arm along its cushioned back and cocked a leg up, resting the ankle on the opposite knee. "Don't suppose that treat is a cold beer?"

"Beer? Hmm, no, but would you like a ration of something called *beef stew*?"

Travis answered without hesitation. "Yes!"

"Good. I'll have the Pothlill fetch it."

"It's generally served heated, if that's not a problem."

"Not at all." Sar Mode stepped to the hatch and spoke to Travis' escort.

When she returned, Travis asked, "The tall guys are called Pothlills?"

"Yes. You are unfamiliar with the race?"

"Never seen one before. Just curious, are you a he or a she or something else?"

"I am a female, or I was once. But the distinction is no longer relevant." Sar Mode waved the subject off with one furry, multi-jointed paw. "There is a reason I had you brought to me."

"Right. . . can I eat my stew first?"

~ ~ ∞ ~ ~

Drew Cutter made a fist to control his shaking. He glanced at the tactical specialist, Abraham, to see if he'd noticed. After completing the EMU's systems check, Abraham explained the settings for the camera light source. When inserted into the coupling aperture, the ten-inch lens would begin a series of 360° revolutions, capturing vids of its interior. With the coupling's precise measurements, the ship's acquisitions officer could fashion an adapter.

The nightmares from his last spacewalk continued to abate. Besides honing his poker skills during his stay in New Las Vegas, Drew had worked with a therapist to help him cope with his extreme fear of space. This would be the first practical test of the exercises she'd taught him. He wanted to avoid a repeat of the debilitating panic attack he'd experienced when he and Letty walked in space to escape Dark Landing.

Abraham placed the helmet over Drew's head and attached it to the neck piece. Drew donned and sealed his gloves and gave the man a thumbs up, not trusting a voice response. Without hesitation, and repeating his mantra under his breath, he stepped into the cargo bay airlock. When the airlock depressurized, he executed a fist-pump to let Abraham know he was ready when they were.

The water depot grew larger as they approached it. *In through the nose and out through the mouth.* Drew regulated his breathing and forced himself to turn his gaze from the depot to deep space. He focused on the distant details as his therapist had instructed. An uneven row of stars formed an arch above the depot; the star at its apex shone brighter than the others. Higher and to the right hung a milky, gaseous cloud so faint that when he blinked, he lost it. He returned his gaze to the star arch, pleased by his even breathing and settled stomach.

Captain McDermott's voice came over Drew's comm. "Mark time. . . ."

McDermott must have been a drill sergeant at some point. Drew chuckled—a good sign his breathing exercises were working. He marched a few steps in place as the hatch opened, and with a quick pull on the tether to make sure it was attached to the ship, he moved into open space and activated the suit's thrusters. Tether length released smoothly from a coil case attached to the back of his tool belt, and he headed toward the targeted coupling about sixty meters away.

When he reached the mid-point, he glanced back at the ship. His breathing quickened. To maintain control, he slowed and deepened each breath, then looked out to space beyond the depot structure to reorient with the star arch he'd spotted earlier. *There. . .* there it was. He calmed and focused on the center, brighter star.

The center star shone even more intense than before. . . impossibly more intense. Not a star, a ship, and it was moving toward them. The breathing exercise abandoned, taking huge gulps of air, he slowed his approach. Suddenly the tether went slack and auto reversed toward Drew, coiling back into its case on his belt.

His momentum carried him forward. Drew looked back over his shoulder. "What's happening, guys?" He toggled his comm on and off several times. His voice trembled from the building panic. "Come in *Maris Stella*. . . come in. McDermott? Olcott?" Nothing.

The *Maris Stella* was moving away from the depot, and his comm was dead.

~ ~ ∞ ~ ~

Letty stood on the bridge with Captain McDermott and technician/navigator, Rob Turrey, when they received the warning of a ship fast approaching the depot. Captain McDermott cut all comm transmissions and disconnected the tether to Drew. The captain set a course away from the depot at a steady pace.

"What are we doing?" Letty asked in a hushed tone.

"I'm trying to suggest that the *Maris Stella* has completed whatever her reason is for being here, and we're simply moving on; going about our business."

"What about Aisha?"

"Aisha?"

"Or whichever one of the techs we're leaving behind."

McDermott and Turrey exchanged an anxious look.

"What?" Letty demanded.

"That's Cutter. . . not one of Aisha's people. He volunteered to complete the coupling inspection," Captain McDermott said.

"Oh, my God, you're kidding me? Go back. Now!"

"Why? What? We can't go back. He knows what he's supposed to do. We went over every possible complication. We're moving to a safe distance, and when the incoming ship passes by or leaves the depot if it stops, the shuttle will return to pick him up. He's been instructed to move to the underside of the station away from the couplings."

Letty's voice turned shrill. "Drew is terrified of space. He panics — goes crazy. Trust me, I experienced it firsthand. He'll do something to call attention to himself and us, or just black out and drift away. *Go back!*" It wasn't a request. It was an order.

McDermott turned to the console and dictated a message to Aisha Olcott. "We're going back. Ready your team to retrieve Cutter." He shifted his gaze to make direct eye contact with Turrey. "Jamming all transmissions on my mark. . . *three*. . . *two*. . . *one*." Turrey nodded and manually entered the order to block transmissions from the *Maris Stella* and any ship within fifty klicks of her.

~ ~ ∞ ~ ~

Drew could feel his heart racing. He teetered on the verge of hyperventilation — taking in great gulps of oxygen and breathing out carbon dioxide. The muscles of his hands and feet contracted in spasms. He closed his eyes and pushed the palms of his gloved hands tight together in front of him. *Concentrate. . . concentrate. Visualize your fear.*

A red-scaled dragon materialized on the backs of his eyelids. It emitted plumes of fire and smoke and struck at him like a snake. Drew could feel the heat on his face and smell the sulfur. The long dragon body undulated; its tail tipped with an arrowhead that would impale him if it made contact. The tail whipped furiously back and forth. As he examined each frightening aspect of the monster, he recited the verses it had taken him a ridiculous amount of time to memorize:

> He took his vorpal sword in hand;
> Long time the manxome foe he sought—
> So rested he by the Tumtum tree
> And stood awhile in thought.
>
> And, as in uffish thought he stood,
> The Jabberwock, with eyes of flame,
> Came whiffling through the tulgey wood,
> And burbled as it came!
>
> One, two! One, two! And through and through
> The vorpal blade went snicker-snack!
> He left it dead, and with its head
> He went galumphing back.

With each absurd line Drew recited, the dragon transformed. Its scales smoothed, and its ferocious fire was quenched. The smoke dissipated into wisps, and the sharp spike at the end of its tail became a fluffy ball of fur. Finally, the creature shrunk into itself and then disappeared in a comedic pop. Stupid, but it worked. And as his therapist had reminded him, he had no need to tell anyone.

His breathing returned to near normal. He relaxed and opened his eyes. The exterior bulkhead of the water depot waited only inches to his right. He pushed off its side, curled his legs against his body, and then assumed a dive position. With a short burst from the miniature propulsion jets located on the back of each arm, he moved down the side of the depot and under it, away from the ring of water transfer couplings.

He could barely make out a round hatch deep in shadows. Dead center on the underside and roughly six meters across, it was inset from the surface with gently sloping walls, resembling a shallow meteor crater. Capped spindles, extending a foot from the surface, encircled the hatch crater. What purpose they served was lost on Drew, but they'd make excellent handholds. He moved into the hatch indentation and pressed his body against its concave bank with one arm up over the edge to grasp a spindle.

Unable to see or feel the approaching ship, and with his comm dead, he glanced at his three-by-three-inch wrist display. He had four hours of oxygen left—perhaps a bit more when immobile. This time he visualized a normal day back on Dark Landing: sitting at his desk making entries in his log, shooting a game of pool with Jonesy on lunch break, strolling through the bazaar, at the weekly poker game. . . . Drew took a long, deep breath, turned his head to take in the view, and with a contented sigh, settled in to wait. For the first time, he was struck by the staggering beauty of outer space.

29 JOLLY ROGER, HO!

On Letty's orders, the *Maris Stella* continued on a diverse path away from the water depot for another five klicks, then fired its thrusters and commenced a slow series of right-angled maneuvers. To the other ship, she would appear to be setting a new course — at least at first.

McDermott and Turrey studied the ship's exterior. It looked to be a small cargo vessel. The side fully visible to the *Maris Stella* glowed with geometric symbols, intermingled with extended dots and sharp-edged dashes. Flattened, the symbols might resemble an illuminated manuscript or an antique, gas-lit sign. Against the uneven surface of the ship, they looked like a vid projection. The ship's basic design could pass in the Known Universe.

Neither the sensors nor McDermott's and Turrey's visual inspections distinguished projectile rails, pulse tubes, or similar features to suggest weapons. At the appropriate angle in her turn, the *Maris Stella* launched the *Winkum* and the *Nod,* each carrying a strike team and its equivalent weight in armament.

At two klicks from the other ship, the shuttles would pin it in and Turrey would create a small bubble within the transmission blackout to allow local chatter between the *Maris Stella,* her shuttles, the cargo vessel, and hopefully, Drew.

The three attackers, their weapons displayed like wolves with bared teeth, waited while Turrey compiled a series of images for the target vessel that illustrated the Earthlings' intentions. The series included a destruction pictorial impossible to misinterpret.

The ship continued to approach the depot at a steady pace. McDermott was surprised that the cargo vessel made no attempt to run. Perhaps weapons were unknown in this part of the universe — unlikely, considering the armada just up the road — *or*, he thought with a stab of anxiety, *their weapons are of such diverse design as to be unrecognizable.*

Letty spoke from behind him. "Any sign of Drew?"

"No. He evidently followed the plan and moved to the underside of the station." *Or*, he thought to himself, *he's passed out from fear and floated away.* He glanced over his shoulder at her. She glowered back with a challenging look, as if she'd been caught coating darts in venom. He realized for the first time that sweet, raven-haired Letty Taleen, who he'd thought of as the embodiment of *Sleeping Beauty*, and to whom everyone acquiesced without question, possessed a serrated edge.

Turrey broke McDermott's reverie. "Communication restored and contained locally, sir. Image message transmitted."

Aisha Olcott's voice came over their comms from the *Nod*, "Awaiting your command, Mother."

"Cutter, report. Cutter?" No response. "Okay, Olcott, go after him," McDermott ordered.

The cargo vessel snuggled up to the depot, unfazed by the appearance of an armed ship or her equally dangerous shuttles and unresponsive to the pictorial transmission. A rigid hose line extended from the ship and connected to the nearest transfer coupling. McDermott shook his head in consternation. . . . What was he missing? "Turrey, are you scanning for life signs?"

"Yep. I got nothing. It's unmanned."

"Okay then, let's. . . ." McDermott caught a movement at the top of the depot, above the shuttles and the cargo ship, but just below the *Maris Stella*.

"Turrets! Shields up. I count three," Turrey yelled.

The unshielded *Winkum* discharged her upward thrusters and dropped below the depot and the target vessel, spotlights off to shroud her movement.

The turrets fired laser pulse salvos at the *Maris Stella*. She enabled her forward thrusters and backed up. On the bridge, the decibel level of her emergency klaxon lessened to allow the computer to issue a string of shield status reports: *Shields at ninety-*

eight percent. Shields at ninety-six percent. Shield strength declining. Shields –

"Cease report. Launch projectiles on my mark. . . *three*. . . *two.* . . *one.*"

Responding to McDermott's command, the computer calculated distance and required force and fired anti-ship barrel projectiles at each turret, and then recalculated and fired a third projectile. The first two projectiles hit their targets, but the third missed, skimming off the depot's surface and careening into space. Though the odds were low, Turrey ordered the missile to self-destruct so as not to inadvertently strike another object.

McDermott launched two more barrels, both aimed at the remaining plasma gun still firing on the *Maris Stella.*

McDermott and Turrey focused on the projectiles' paths. The depot emitted a single plasma stream which extended for several meters then split in two. Each division targeted one of the two barrels, and both projectiles were obliterated.

~ ~ ∞ ~ ~

Drew felt a slight tremor. Something had come in contact with the station. Minutes passed. His muscles tensed, and he took shallow breaths, waiting for another sign of activity topside. Then the station shook as if a ship might have collided with it – *or it's taking weapons fire.* He pressed tighter against the hatch indentation. Barely a minute later, the *Winkum* appeared several meters below him. It'd come to pick him up. Relief washed over him, and he was buoyed by the accompanying rush of adrenaline. He toggled his comm several times, still unable to communicate with the *Maris Stella* or her shuttles.

Hidden in the shadow of the hatch crater, he gasped when the *Winkum* continued by his position and out of sight.

Several minutes passed while Drew fought his rising panic. As if in reward for steadfast determination, the *Nod* appeared, following her sister's path. Drew wouldn't be left behind again. He pulled a wrench from the tool pouch attached to his belt, and with all the force he could muster, chucked it at the *Nod* only meters below him. The action pushed him away from the concave indention. He lost hold of the spindle and rolled toward the center of the hatch. As he went, he flailed his arms against the surface, searching for something else to grab onto. His acceleration increased. He stretched an arm out to the bulkhead in front of his roll, hoping to check his momentum, but that action caused his body to angle off into open space, cartwheeling head over heels.

~ ~ ∞ ~ ~

Olcott maneuvered the *Nod* down to follow the *Winkum's* path under the depot. Mid-center, she heard the muted thud of an object hitting the *Nod's* exterior just above the pilot's console. She instinctively looked up at the bulkhead before consulting her screen to confirm a collision. It registered negative damage. With the proximity sensor disabled since they were hugging the station, she checked their relative position. The *Nod* had passed several meters safely below the surface. So, what hit them?

"Did you guys hear that?" Negative mumbles echoed behind her. "Look out the view ports and tell me if you see anything." The order was no sooner given than she received a reply.

"Port and down about thirty degrees. *Daaamn!* It looks like Cutter's headed into space."

"Chasing Cutter," Olcott advised the *Maris Stella*.

"Proceed at your discretion," McDermott responded.

~ ~ ∞ ~ ~

The cartwheeling motion upset Drew's virtual equilibrium. He commanded the helmet monitor to full screen to block the exterior view and focused on the data stream. He was still on manual control. "Enable automatic attitude hold."

Auto control enabled. . . gyroscope enabled. . . coordinating rotational and translational acceleration. . . micro thrusters fired. Stabilization achieved.

The suit's computer stopped the summersaulting, but Drew was still shooting through space at a good clip. He minimized the display again, took a deep breath, and twisted his body in preparation for a course adjustment back toward the station. The maneuver had its risks, including oxygen depletion.

". . . re closing fast. Do you read, Cutter? Respond."

"Olcott? Yes, I read." Switching to automatic control had enabled his comm, as well. "I love you, Olcott."

"Come again, Cutter."

"Ignore last transmission. Can I get a ride?"

"Right above you."

Drew twisted his head to see the *Nod* looming over him. The resultant rush of relief soothed his hyperactive nerves and over-taut mussels to such an extent that he had to fight to control his bowels.

~ ~ ∞ ~ ~

"That's a neat trick. How'd they do that?" Turrey said over his shoulder, commenting on the ability of the depot's plasma pulse to divide, aim, and hit separate targets. "Breaks *all* the rules. But then, manufacturing wormholes should be impossible too. Still, physics. . . ." He tended to get chatty under stress.

Their sensors had declared the cargo ship unarmed, but Turrey was right. Impossibilities were occurring all around them. Why take a chance? Captain McDermott ignored Turrey's persistent babbling. "*Winkum*, sync on my mark. . . *three*. . . *two*. . . *one*."

The *Maris Stella's* lasers fired on the cargo hauler, cutting it neatly in half. A mist enveloped the vessel as its water load vaporized and deposed into crystals. Half the ship remained connected to the water depot, while the outer half fragmented, its pieces spiraling in all directions. Several splinters battered the depot, leaving visible scars and one breach. Atmosphere spewed from the opening. At the same time the *Maris Stella* fired on the cargo ship, the *Winkum*, having gained attitude, took out the remaining depot turret.

The *Maris Stella* and her shuttle exchanged status reports. The mother ship was undamaged, her shields holding at eighty-seven percent. Since the depot's cannons had focused solely on her, the shuttle never took fire. When Turrey transmitted the *all clear*, the *Winkum* proceeded to complete the coupling imaging operation, and the *Nod* returned to dock.

McDermott accompanied Letty to the shuttle bay.

She accosted Drew before his foot hit the deck. "You fool! What if you'd gone berserk out there? And you achieved nothing."

Olcott and her team exchanged stunned looks at the berating.

Drew, his EMU helmet tucked under one arm, unshaken, and sporting a self-satisfied grin, ignored her outburst and continued to the armory to remove his suit.

30 TOGETHERNESS

Though their specialties differed, Austen added her engineering expertise to Dunlevy's in devising a method to test the makeshift EMP device. They'd pawed unsuccessfully through the junk pile several more times, searching for something to supplement its power source. The problem remained how to test the EMP without draining whatever power was left. The entirety of their plan hinged on the device.

While Dunlevy's engineering skills far exceeded Austen's, and finding nothing new in the junk pile, she recognized the futility of further discussion. Dunlevy was stalling. *Toby's right. . . the man is a mammering coward. No,* she thought, *that's unfair. He's not a coward; he's a realist. This plan sucks.* She shared her conclusion with Curtis and Nikko.

"Yeah, we figured as much," Curtis said. "So, it's already been forty-eight hours. Still, I'll extend it another twenty-four. The time doesn't bother me as much as whether we can count on him—and Oscar."

Nikko offered, "I think a sizable number of the other hostages will follow us if we make it out. We should try harder to identify who our supporters are."

Curtis shook his head. "It's too big a risk. If we're overheard, or if just one person says something, we'd be dead."

Nikko stretched his arms over his head to relieve tense muscles. "Okay, so. . . noon tomorrow, we go."

Curtis and Austen nodded.

"And Toby? He's just an eight-year-old," Austen said.

"I'm nine," Toby corrected her as he climbed into the cubby.

"I'm sorry, baby." Austen realized that was the wrong thing to say as soon as it came out of her mouth.

"I'm no fuckin' *baby*, and you ain't my ma or Letty, so butt out, lady."

Toby's regression was worsening.

"That was rude and uncalled for. If you don't apologize to Austen, I'll tie you up and leave you in this cubby when we go," Curtis said. He and Toby exchanged a long look.

Toby blinked first. "I'm sorry, Chief Hargreaves. I don't wanna be left here."

"I'm sorry too, Toby. I haven't known you that long, but from what Curtis and Nikko tell me, and what I've seen with my own eyes, I know you're not a baby—and I didn't mean it that way. You've more than pulled your weight, and you've got more guts than most of us. There's no way we'll leave you. Are we good?"

"Yeah, we're good. And you're okay, yourself."

No one smiled at the exchange.

~ ~ ∞ ~ ~

The replicated coupler proved a perfect fit, and with water reserves at one hundred percent, the *Maris Stella* made a run for WH2. Uncertain if it would return them to Mass Primary, McDermott held his breath during the brief crossing. On the other side, he let it out in relief and refilled his lungs. As the ship picked its way through the now familiar asteroid field, the captain risked a transmission to the *Blinkum*.

"*Maris Stella* hailing the *Blinkum*. Rossi? You still out there?"

"Affirmative. Could use a drink, though."

"Roger that. We can accommodate. Rendezvous and report."

When they'd reunited with the shuttle, Letty, McDermott, Olcott, and Drew met in the salon to exchange intelligence with the *Blinkum's* pilot, Gretchen Rossi.

"Nada from our probes," Rossi said. "The homing device is still viable—gunships don't patrol anywhere near it. Zero traffic to or from the station since you been away."

"Have you ascertained any particular patrol pattern?" Olcott asked.

"A highly suspicious one in my opinion. They maintain a strict schedule and route, and there's still just two of 'em as far as I can tell."

Letty looked at Olcott. "That's good for us, right?"

"No, Rossi's correct—it's suspicious as hell. The Diak are great strategists in command of a massive war machine. Unlikely they'd be that sloppy."

~ ~ ∞ ~ ~

"Come to order," Sir James commanded over the live feed, in a voice purposely lowered to engender results. "We do not care who or what is to blame." His voice returned to a normal level as he reclaimed the meeting. "The council is of one mind that the Diak will make another attempt to communicate, and we must be ready. However, the members are split on what that communication may entail. I'm of the camp who believes a Diak invasion is imminent, and that they're offering the option to surrender without a fight. All Alliance governments and defensive forces are on alert."

"We won't surrender?" Admiral Sullivan asked.

Kyle winced at the admiral's question, preferring he'd made it in the form of a bold statement.

"No—the five are agreed," Sir James said. "We'll go down fighting to the last human and alien."

Sullivan nodded. His intent regardless of orders was obvious to everyone in the meeting. Only that morning, he'd increased the number of patrol units and extended their range.

"Excuse me," Jonesy said, stepping away from the conference table and tapping his comm. Without further comment, he left the room.

"I believe we're done here," Sir James wrapped up. "If a second probe appears, capture it and contact the council immediately. Otherwise, blow them away, everyone."

Before Sir James could end the transmission, Jonesy reappeared. "Sir. . . there's a situation. The Reliance Mine operation in our quadrant reports a ship of unknown design is requesting docking. The pilot claims to be Travis Barnes."

~ ~ ∞ ~ ~

Travis waited for authorization to dock on the small moon owned and operated by Reliance Mines. His eyes brimmed with tears at the realization, against all odds, he'd made it home. For the first few hours back in K.U. space, he'd worried how Sar Mode expected him to make contact. The readings from the pilot's station were gibberish, but thankfully, the ship operated on autopilot. And when he arrived at the installation, his comm functioned. A thought occurred to him: *If the mining planet is the intended destination, maybe I'm in charge now.*

He'd assumed a manual input device on the control panel was a joystick. He pushed it gently with an index finger. The ship wobbled. The instrument was composed of a squat shank protruding about fifteen centimeters from the panel's surface with handles resembling horizontal rapier hilts. When Travis ran a finger under the curve of the knuckle bow, he felt a pliant pad. He pushed upward against the pad. The starboard thrusters fired, and the ship moved laterally to port.

"Okay, that makes sense." He practiced navigation maneuvers while he waited.

He expected several rounds of scanning and other physical examinations, then questions, suspicions, and more questions. *It won't last forever*, and he had grown desperate for human contact. . . any human contact. During his six months in isolation, he'd seen only the Shroomies and at the last, the Fahdeen, Sar Mode. Still, he'd avoided torture, beatings, or starvation. A cakewalk compared to what so many others had historically suffered at enemies' hands. He shook off a pang of guilt. *Idiot! It's not your fault you got out unscathed.* He laughed at how quickly his mind jumped from terror to riotous relief to guilt. The purr of his comm was a joyful sound.

"Commander Barnes, we've contacted Dark Landing and they're sending a ship to escort you. It'll be forty-eight hours. Unfortunately, Reliance won't let you dock while you wait."

"I understand, but this baby is not designed to accommodate humans. Other than environment, I have no food or water. It's been almost three days; I'm dizzy and it's a struggle to concentrate. I won't last much longer."

"We can transport supplies out to you. The home office can't have a problem with that. Are you *the* Travis Barnes?" the dispatcher asked in an awed voice.

"The one and only. But I don't know if I'm able to open the hatch on this ship—if there is a hatch. *Can you see a hatch?*" Travis glanced at the control panel in frustration. Multiple attempts to exit the bridge had failed. He'd found nothing but smooth bulkhead behind him. *There has to be some way out of here.* He waved his hand awkwardly over the seat back toward the rear bulkhead. As usual, nothing happened.

"Hold on a sec. I still need to find a way out of this compartment."

He released the harness latch and climbed out of the seat. His head swam. In the small helm space, he was unable to stand upright. Head down and shoulders hunched, he shuffled the three steps to the bulkhead. Unsure what he expected, he addressed the ship in general. "How the hell am I supposed to get out of here?"

"You talkin' to me, sir?"

"No. I—" The bulkhead shimmered and disappeared to reveal a storage area roughly twice the size of the control room with a round hatch at the far end. The hatch reminded him of the one into Sar Mode's quarters but without the artwork.

"Okay. . . surprise! I'm making progress—which never happened before. One minute."

The English word "pressurized" glowed green on a small screen to the right of the hatch. Still bent over, his body aching from being cramped in the same position for such a long time, he continued aft and touched the glowing word. The interior hatch disappeared to reveal a small airlock and yet a third hatch leading to space. Three containers of water sat in the middle of the deck. *Fuck!* The ship's functions were evidently controlled by some level of artificial intelligence—malicious artificial intelligence. *God, I hope it's artificial.*

He relaxed and spoke to the dispatcher. "We're good to go. Send up supplies, and a privy bucket would be nice. I'll wait it out here."

"Anything else special you'd like?"

"My mother?"

31 IMPROVING ODDS

Austen's stomach flipped. *This is happening.* She watched as Toby scrambled up the water wall with the odds-and-ends he'd selected from the junk pile attached to a strap that encircled him like an ammo bandolier. At the top, he secured his position with one hand and released the first slipknot with the other. He wedged a flat handheld into the water slot, then continued pushing jetsam in, one piece at a time, until only a trickle of water escaped. When he came down, a small crowd had gathered as expected.

Austen was ready with a prepared speech. "We probably should've told you guys in advance, but we decided to ask the Diak for better food and some clothing, and we desperately need another waste chute. This was the only way we could think to get their attention."

The crowd mumbled among themselves, some for, some against. "After what they did to your friend the last time we got their attention?" a young man in the middle called out. "Who do you think you are?"

Austen shrugged in apology, then turned away to avoid further engagement. They needed to go about their business. Thankfully, a few were already wandering off, angry, probably looking for Oscar who was supposed to be hiding out in Curtis's cubby. She and Toby leaned against the back bulkhead to wait. She wanted to reassure the boy, but Toby gave her a warning look that clearly said *back off*. It occurred to her that Curtis and Nikko were probably good with the boy because they avoided mothering him.

Almost two hours passed. They approached the agreed-upon break schedule when she heard Nikko's warning whistle.

~ ~ ∞ ~ ~

Two Diak aliens appeared in the passage heading toward the enclosure. Nikko whistled to alert the others. One was a mushroom, but beside him walked a Bahdane female, almost as big as Nikko. *Damn,* he thought, *she's not going down easy.* The Diak entered the airlock. Nikko glanced at Dunlevy. The engineer enabled the EMP hanging on a cord around his neck, and then nodded and held up both hands, fingers crossed. Nikko might feel more assured if Dunlevy's hands shook less.

When the aliens reached the enclosure, Nikko tapped to enable the comm implant behind his left ear and then tapped the ESF comm imbedded above his ankle, as well. When their makeshift EMP ran out of juice—assuming it worked at all—his ankle transmitter *should* sync with his personal comm. A com's range was local to a ship, space station, or planet, not across space and through a wormhole and beyond. But he'd stake odds this one was special. He hoped a signal might get through to Sir James, so he'd know Nikko at least tried.

The Bahdane glanced at them as they passed but kept going, seemingly unconcerned by their presence. Nikko poked Dunleavy and cocked his head at the Bahdane. Dunlevy gasped but nodded his acknowledgement. They fell in several feet behind. As the aliens approached the center cubby wall, Nikko and Dunlevy closed the distance between them.

When Curtis and Oscar stepped in front of the two Diak, Nikko jumped on the Bahdane's back. With his legs wrapped in a vice hold around her body, he placed one arm tight against her throat, grabbing his own wrist with his other hand to increase the pressure. He fell backward, bringing the Bahdane down on top of him, knocking his breath out with a *whuff,* but he maintained his grip and pulled tighter. The Bahdane dug at his arm with her claws. Nikko could feel his skin shredding. He'd stuck the sharp metal piece Curtis had found into his back pocket, but to get to it he'd need to let go of the big alien.

"*Dunlevy!*" he screamed.

Dunlevy jumped on top and grabbed at the Bahdane's arms in an attempt to control them. The added weight made it almost impossible for Nikko to breathe. The Bahdane rocked her body back and forth to throw Dunlevy off. Nikko teetered near suffocation, but he felt her weakening and found the strength to hold out a few seconds longer. He'd lost all feeling in the arm pressing against her neck. She freed one of her arms and pushed hard at Dunlevy as he grappled with her, breaking his hold. To Nikko's surprise, a man from the watching crowd stepped in to help. He sat on the Bahdane's legs at the knees, pinning them and slowing her rocking motion. Finally, she stilled. Nikko pulled as hard as he could with what strength remained until certain no life was left in her.

With Dunlevy's and the other's help, he pushed her dead weight off him. He lay there for several moments taking deep, restoring gulps of air, until he realized Austen and Toby still struggled with the mushroom. Its tentacle was wrapped around Curtis's chest up to his armpits. His eyes bulged, and his face had turned as red as his hair. Toby, his expression one of sheer hatred, had his arms around the mushroom's lower body, straining to topple it. The hostage who'd helped with the Bahdane melted back into the group of onlookers.

Nikko and Dunlevy moved to free Curtis. Nikko retrieved his makeshift weapon and, pulling Austen out of the way, slashed at the mushroom's tentacle. The appendage was solid muscle, constricting Curtis's chest like a python, smothering him. The jagged metal wasn't sharp enough to do more than inflict scratches on the surface.

"Hold it still!" Nikko shouted.

Austen stepped back in and ducked down next to Toby, who was still wrapped around the base of the stalk. With the added weight, they stopped it from writhing long enough for Nikko to stab the metal dagger deeper into the tentacle. Its color turned a dark purple, and it loosened its hold enough for the others to pull Curtis free. He slumped to the deck. Justine, the nurse who'd aided Nikko when they'd first arrived, appeared from nowhere and started working over him.

Nikko and Dunlevy held tight to the unfurled tentacle, pulling it in the opposite direction as the other three pushed, finally toppling the mushroom. It hit the deck with a loud slap. Austen,

Oscar, and Toby all jumped on the alien, straddling it as if riding a log.

"Toby, grab the wire in my jacket pocket," Austen said.

In short order, by rolling the mushroom back and forth, they managed to wrap the long tentacle around its body, pinning it in place with several feet of pieced-together wire. It stopped fighting, spent. Austen, Toby, and Oscar fell to the deck, gasping. Nikko and Dunlevy leaned against the end of a cubby wall, exhausted, as well. Suddenly aware of a painful stinging, Nikko avoided looking at his injured arm.

When Curtis showed signs of consciousness, Justine stopped pumping on his chest. For the first time, Nikko noticed the crowd around them — up and down the center aisle and tucked into the nearest alleyways — wide-eyed and silent.

"We're going to try to make it to our ship. The odds aren't good but come with us if you want." The onlookers whispered to one another in evident disbelief.

Curtis was still on the deck but sitting now and holding his head. He moved carefully to look up at Nikko. "Now how do we get this thing upright? And we never discussed how we're supposed to communicate with it, did we?"

Nikko stared at the creature stretched along the passage. He walked the length of it and back. Its cap was tipped forward. The surface contained no obvious facial features. *Good point, Curtis — a little late.* "Maybe we should've taken out the mushroom and kept the Bahdaneian."

~ ~ ∞ ~ ~

In her quarters, Sar Mode watched the fiasco in the human compound. She was eager to abandon the Fahdeen for the human host she'd selected. A female, one who she knew intended to join the escape attempt, and one who no one would suspect of harboring a Diak.

A second scene resolved on the bulkhead in front of her, next to the escape spectacle. This one of the *Maris Stella* approaching Mass Primary; her three pretty shuttles spread a good distance out from the mother ship. Sar Mode sighed and her Fahdeen tongue slipped from her mouth to lick up over her snout and across her eyes. The original plan had been significantly less complicated, but it was best to remain fluid in these situations. And she knew humans to be messy beings from the start. With the disorder amongst those humans escaping and those rescuing, her chance of success grew.

The gunships she'd deployed were drones under her personal command. There must be at least the appearance of a battle—with human losses—to seem credible.

32 A HERO'S WELCOME

It seemed appropriate to be interrogated in the screamer cell. Travis had told the Admiral everything he could about his sudden appearance, and now he stood his ground. "I'll only speak further to Sir James Hawking-Barstow."

"You'll damn well speak to whoever I tell you to speak to," Admiral Sullivan blustered.

Two unintroduced ESF officers crowded the cell's anteroom along with Sullivan and the security dayshift commander, Kyle Drubber.

"I will speak only to Sir James Hawking-Barstow," Travis repeated. "And my mom — has anyone let her know I'm alive?"

"You answer my questions, and maybe I'll let you speak to your *mommy*, boy," Sullivan said.

He was obviously bluffing. In confirmation, yet another ESF officer entered the anteroom carrying a handheld. Kyle commanded the food pass open, and the officer placed the processor in its shallow receptacle. Noiselessly, the tray retracted through the slot to Travis' side.

Sir James' image blinked at him from the small monitor. "Welcome home, Commander Barnes. You cannot imagine how delightful it is to see you."

"I think I can. Is this a secure transmission?"

"It is."

"Can I have the anteroom cleared, sir."

"You may. Admiral, please give us the room."

Sullivan huffed and puffed but turned and shooed the others out in front of him. The hatch closed.

"So, Travis. . . may I call you Travis?" Without waiting for a response, he continued. "I assume you have a message for me from the Diak Appointed Principal?"

"You're *expecting* a message from Sar Mode?"

"He tried unsuccessfully to send one earlier."

"*She*—according to her. Anyway, yes, I have a message for you. But only for you. I think you'll understand why that's crucial. I must have your word that this conversation is private. There can be no recorded copy."

Sir James hesitated. "One moment." The screen turned dark. After several seconds, his image reappeared. "You'll have to trust my word that no one is listening in or recording our conversation."

"I trust you, but then I don't have a choice, do I?"

Sir James ignored the question. "Have you provided Admiral Sullivan the location of the wormhole from Diak space?"

"No. He refuses to believe me, but all I know for sure is it's within three day's travel of the Reliance Mine facility. I was transported to the wormhole on a larger ship, then transferred to the shuttle and sent through. The shuttle was preprogramed on autopilot. I had no access to its sensors or database and couldn't have understood them anyway. I assume Sullivan's sending scouts?"

"Yes. But I doubt he'll have any luck. Their cloaking technology must be extraordinary. We never noticed the wormhole in Dark Landing's backyard until you stumbled into it last year."

Travis recounted Sar Mode's message.

Sir James looked thoughtful for a few moments before continuing. "So. . . I'll consult with the council and then get back to you. I apologize—this is no way to treat a hero—but you'll have to remain in quarantine."

"I figured. It's just. . ." Travis' voice broke, ". . . just good to be home, sir."

~ ~ ∞ ~ ~

A single enemy gunship sat between them and the station. Captain McDermott, with the *Maris Stella* facing the other ship head-on, ordered the shuttles to move farther out to flank the enemy. Without wasting time on hails or threats, and with a twitch of his index finger, the captain issued the command for Turrey to launch a laser salvo. The enemy returned fire, targeting only the mother ship and ignoring the less intimidating shuttles. That was a mistake. As soon as the shuttles moved into position, the four Earth ships launched a synchronized attack.

In seconds, the gunship turned to shrapnel. Pieces of the ship hurled into the station, knocking unidentifiable protrusions off its surface — but doing no further damage as far as the captain could tell.

All *Maris Stella* sensors and weapons remained operational, and McDermott awaited the scan announcements from the ship's computer. *Hell! Not again.* His skin prickled with the same apprehension he'd felt just before the water depot lasers fired on them. But Mass Primary offered no further resistance. No laser turrets emerged from the station's exterior. No cannons. No projectile rails. . . *nothing.* They hovered within three klicks of the docking bay holding the *Remarkable Mayzie.*

~ ~ ∞ ~ ~

All agreed, the plan wasn't well thought out to begin with, but it never occurred to anyone there'd be a problem communicating with the captured Diak.

Through a combined effort, they managed to stand the mushroom upright. Nikko studied it. The air grew fetid with its smell. He knew it could feel pain — its tentacle seemed especially sensitive. Each time he poked it with the sharp end of the metal bar, its entire body flinched, and it momentarily turned several shades deeper lavender. The scratches he'd inflicted were oozing a thick, purple liquid. The thing was faceless as far as Nikko could tell. It stood about eight feet tall, with a cap that was disproportionally close to its body, more compacted than a typical mushroom's cap. At Nikko's six-foot-nine, he could see vertical slits in the surface of the cap when it occasionally dipped toward him. They might be gills, or a nose, or serve another purpose entirely.

They stood next to each other in front of the airlock as Nikko motioned upward with both hands to indicate he wanted it to raise the hatch. Even if it understood, how was it supposed to do that? The EMP—assuming it was working at all—would block any command it transmitted, and they'd secured its tentacle tight with wire.

The hostages crowded the front of the compound behind the Dark Landing team, their numbers spilling back into the passageways. They murmured among themselves, but no one offered a suggestion.

"This is getting us nowhere," Curtis stated the obvious. "We need to untie its tentacle."

"Yeah." Nikko nodded. "Go ahead." He raised the metal piece in a threatening manner as Curtis worked to untangle the wire.

Freed, the tentacle dropped limp to the deck. The mushroom's cap tipped forward as the creature looked down at its appendage. It occurred to Nikko, it might not be looking *down* at the deck, maybe it was inspecting the upper portion of the tentacle where the stab wounds looked the most severe. When it straightened, Nikko peeked at the underside of the mushroom cap. Multiple eyes above what appeared to be a mouth gazed back at him. He held his breath against the stench and bent in for a closer view. Flaps of protective skin closed over the organs.

Nikko motioned at the airlock hatch again. He worried that the tentacle was too injured to function. But the mushroom slowly raised the appendage. The effort caused it to turn dark lavender. It rotated slightly and skittered toward the crowd. They shrunk back as far as space allowed, but no one tried to stop it as it continued to the nearest cubby wall. A few feet away, the tentacle extended upward to touch high on the edge of the wall with its tip. A small screen, about the size of a handheld processor, materialized. It tapped the screen several times. The white light on the airlock flashed. Whispered exclamations rippled through the crowd.

Muted weapons fire could be heard in the distance. The room quieted. Nikko'd jumped at the sound but was immobilized by a simultaneous message on his personal com: *Auxiliary comm device enabled; receiving incoming communication.*

He looked at the alien. The mushroom turned a bright shade of pink. It retracted the tentacle; its bearing noticeably transformed from dejected to assured.

"Dunlevy?" Curtis yelled.

Dunlevy stared at the EMP device in his hand. "It's dead. *We're dead.*"

"*Shit!*" Curtis said, "We haven't even left the stockade."

~ ~ ∞ ~ ~

Sar Mode hurried along the passage one level above the hostage enclosures. As she went, a split image of the *Maris Stella* attack against the station and the human's pathetic escape attempt hung in the air in front of her. Beneath those images, emergency messages from Drufarle, the Pothlill's home world, displayed in brightly colored, pulsing characters. It seemed Pothlill across the planet were suddenly exploding. *Excellent!* With a single-word command, she sealed the fate of the crews manning the armada, as well. When she was clear of it, Mass Primary would be the next to go. Her power did not extend to the colony ships, but without leadership and with the rapidly dwindling supply of hosts, their time was measured in rotations.

Her long Fahdeen tongue dripped saliva as she used it to swab at her eyes. Soon she would be free of the Mass. Free of the Spread. And the tragic remnants of the Diak race, once proud and nascent, would fade into history. She alone would survive.

She focused on the humans and picked up her pace, transmitting orders along the way. "View four of four, row ten."

The display monitoring the escape attempt split horizontally. The bottom portion now provided a second image of the human compound looking down the length of the last alleyway, toward the curtained-off end. For perhaps the first time, no one stood in the alley or in line for the head.

Her passageway dead ended. Sar Mode stopped and faced one corner.

"*Open transport.*"

A gravity tube opened, and she stepped into the void. The gravitational pull adjusted for her weight. She drifted safely to the compound below and waded into the debris piled against the back bulkhead. Her Fahdeen container slumped, gradually disappearing amid the rubble. A narrow, silver strand of nanoids emerged from under the mound.

~ ~ ∞ ~ ~

Sar Mode's nanoid stream disappeared down the corridor that ran through the center of the cubby walls. It angled toward the hostages amassed at the front—and her newly selected host.

Behind her, a second figure dropped silently from the gravity tube into the back alleyway.

~ ~ ∞ ~ ~

"How do I give her my answer?" Sir James asked.

"You send me back through the wormhole."

"You'd go back?"

"It's what Sar Mode ordered." Travis shrugged; his throat tightened. He'd understood the need to return from the beginning— a moral imperative. Letty was there. And Sar Mode knew he would return for her.

"If we're to keep this between the three of us, how am I to explain releasing you to return to Diak space?"

"I guess that's your problem. But it should work in your favor knowing Miss Taleen and the Dark Landing group are there now." Travis shifted his position on the hard stool, working out the details as he spoke. "In light of my past heroic acts, it stands to reason you would grant me the dignity to return to fight and die alongside my comrades."

"I can sell that." Sir James closed his eyes, appearing deep in thought.

Travis waited.

33 INTERSECTION

Curtis and Nikko pulled on the alien's tentacle. It was like trying to separate a pectoral muscle from a Bahdaneian's chest barehanded. The damn thing wouldn't budge. Curtis finally gave up and stood back. "Other than its tentacle, I don't think it has defensive moves. Stab it!"

"You know this poor thing is just as innocent as we are. It didn't ask to be a Diak's vessel," Nikko said as he jabbed at the alien's tentacle with the ersatz dagger.

Curtis continued tugging while Nikko stabbed. "Sorry, I'm not feeling it. This 'poor thing' just intentionally blocked our exit. Keep going until the limb shreds to pieces. . . or the airlock is pressurized, and the hatch opens."

At Curtis's words, the mushroom changed colors and the hatch opened.

Nikko tossed the metal piece to Curtis and stepped into the airlock. With no need for further threats, the alien had opened the interior and exterior hatches simultaneously. There was no rush of escaping air, and no one died. Nikko crossed into the corridor. "It's clear," he called back. With both ends of the airlock open, the pronouncement was pointless.

"*Really?* Let's go." Curtis pushed the mushroom through the airlock. Austen, Toby, and Oscar followed on his heels. A mixed group of about one hundred hostages hesitated only a few seconds and then pressed their way through to join the others in the outer passage.

With the metal piece in one hand, Curtis pulled at the mushroom with his other. It voluntarily tagged along behind him. As Curtis passed by, Nikko leaned in and whispered in his ear. Wide-eyed, the chief kept moving as Nikko took up the rear and turned back to the compound. "Isn't anyone else coming?"

The hostages gathered in front of the invisiwall. Justine stepped into the airlock, Dunlevy at her side. "They're afraid, since the Diak control the atmosphere throughout the station. I want to come, but I'm the closest they have to a doctor."

Nikko nodded to her in sympathy. "We'll do what we can. Dunlevy?"

"I'm staying with Justine." He put a protective arm around her waist.

"Oh, I didn't realize. . . . Thank you — both of you — for everything you've done for us." Nikko shook Dunlevy's hand and hugged Justine. He called up to Curtis, "Can you get it to close the exterior hatch?" The hatch closed.

Curtis and the mushroom stopped at the Bahdane compound. Without being prompted, the mushroom opened the airlock hatches. Bahdaneians poured into the corridor. "We can't take you all," Curtis shouted over the furious buzzing noise that hung in the air like a swarm of insects. "Even if we make it that far, our ship's too small. Five tops. Any pilots among you?" There was no discussion. Five Bahdaneians stepped to the forefront. The others retreated to the safety of their enclosure and the outer hatch closed.

Curtis jogged toward the end of the passage and the hatchway to the next enclosure. The mushroom kept pace behind him willingly. It clearly understood what they expected of it. And since it did so without resistance, Curtis guessed they'd meet plenty resistance between them and the *Remarkable Mayzie*.

He stopped several feet short of the hatchway and turned to the mushroom. "What's the atmosphere beyond this door?"

The hatch shimmered and disappeared.

~ ~ ∞ ~ ~

Captain McDermott rose from his chair to stand behind Turrey.

"*Winkum, Blinkum,* assume your positions above and below the *Maris Stella. Nod,* you're up. Approach the docking bay. . . slowly. Everyone, prepare to fire on my order."

The suspense was palpable. Behind him, the captain heard Letty take a deep breath. They'd been lucky up to now. No one said it, but everyone was afraid their luck would run out just when they needed it most. The two shuttles reported they were in position, and the *Nod* moved forward. McDermott scanned the surface of the station for movement. The ship's weapons' sensors remained quiet.

From the mother ship, they monitored *Nod's* status and the vid images of her approach as if on the shuttle itself. As a backup, Olcott verbally relayed a steady stream of instrument readings along with her own observations.

"Two-point-five klicks and closing. No movement in the bay. Two-point-three klicks. It appears abandoned except for the salvage—"

A new voice interrupted Olcott. "Travis Barnes hailing the *Maris Stella.* Do not fire on me. This ship has no weapons."

McDermott snapped his head to Turrey for confirmation.

"Scanners detect the incoming ship is unarmed. Did he say 'Travis Barnes?'"

"Repeat, this is Travis Barnes hailing the *Maris Stella.* I am *unarmed.*"

"Sir, no positive ID on that ship. The signal markers indicate it's Diak design. But it's small—about half the size of one of our shuttles," Turrey said.

The speakers crackled once more. "Nikko Balog, here."

~ ~ ∞ ~ ~

Nikko waited for a response. He'd been listening in stunned wonder to the chatter between the three ships relayed by his ESF ankle comm and waiting for a chance to announce his presence, when Barnes' transmission interrupted the. . . *rescuers*? *Jesus!* From the back of the group, he tried to signal Curtis, but the chief was focused on the mushroom, who'd stopped abruptly.

Stretching to his full height, Nikko's booming voice echoed off the bulkheads. *"Everyone, shut up!"*

Curtis spun around to peer over the heads of the group. The Bahdane contingent's movements intermittently blocked the view between them.

"What?" Curtis yelled back.

"I'm receiving transmissions from three ships that are positioning for an attack on the station. And Travis Barnes just joined the conversation from a fourth ship."

"*Huh?*" Curtis said, his voice barely audible in the ensuing, brief silence.

The Bahdaneians emitted an anxious hum. Mumbles and gasps from the others accompanied the hummers. Nikko thought they were reacting to his announcement and was about to order quiet once more when the mushroom glided past the chief and through the opened hatch into the next enclosure. With unexpected speed, it continued down the passage toward a dozen of its kind amassed at the far end. They approached the escapees slowly, swaying like giant blades of grass. Their tentacles were extended in front of them brandishing what Nikko assumed were weapons that fit over each tentacle like a glove.

~ ~ ∞ ~ ~

Letty joined McDermott and Turrey at the ops station. "Travis? Oh my God. . . *Travis.*"

"*Letty? You okay?*"

McDermott cut the transmission before she could answer and addressed Turrey. "He came *from* the K.U. in a Diak ship? I don't know what to make of that."

Turrey stared back at him without comment, open-mouthed.

"On the other hand, how could he get through without ESF sanction. . . unless —"

"*We* did," Turrey finally found his voice.

"Yeah, but they were never going to fire on us, and I think we had Rostenkowski's reluctant support. Reopen the channel.

"Barnes, this is Captain McDermott on the *Maris Stella*. You need to explain, fast. How is it you're alive, free, and in a Diak ship?"

"I have a packet from Sir James Hawking-Barstow in explanation. Transmitting now."

"Received," Turrey said and muted the channel again.

"Open it," Letty ordered.

A message scrolled across the screen in a proprietary Taleen Industries security code. The translation followed: *Diak sent Commander Barnes with demand for unconditional surrender. Demand denied. I personally honored Barnes' request to return to aid Miss Taleen. Barnes scanned negative for nanoids. Taleen corporate provided coding specifications for this message as validation. Wishing you safe passage. Sir James Hawking-Barstow, Chairman, Earth Defense Council*

A series of twelve numbers followed the message.

"That's the *Maris Stella's* all clear code," McDermott said.

Turrey confirmed. "Yes, sir."

"And you're sure he's unarmed?"

Turrey nodded.

"Reopen transmission. Let's put him to the test." The captain glanced at Letty. She was totally absorbed, staring at the ship on the monitor, her lips moving in a silent chant.

"Commander Barnes," McDermott said, "we took out one of their two patrols. Haven't seen the second one, and there could be more. Without weapons, you're no use to us up here. Tack between the asteroids to the back of the station for a look-see."

"Yes, sir. My pleasure, sir."

McDermott turned back to Letty. She clasped a hand over her trembling lips. The raw honesty of the emotions she exhibited startled him. He'd never observed her display that depth of concern for Xander Crawford *or* Drew Cutter.

34 BRING IT ON

With nothing to hide behind and no weapons, the group stood frozen, staring at the oncoming mushrooms and their bizarre blasters.

"Hit the deck," Curtis yelled.

"Then what?" Nikko said over the sound of bodies dropping.

How the fuck am I supposed to know? Curtis felt a movement at his feet and glanced down to see one of the Bahdane using its forearms to pull its massive body forward. Behind it, the other Bahdaneians were moving up as well, whispering to hostages along the way.

When his head drew even with Curtis's, the Bahdane said, "We outnumber the aliens. As long as they are not firing, we will let them come within ten meters. Our five will roll like barrels toward them and take fire. They are too closely grouped. If they maintain this pattern, most will topple like chronbets on the destilx. Then you will attack. Grab their top organs. My men are advising the others of this plan."

Curtis kept his eyes on the approaching mushrooms as he listened to the Bahdane and tried to imagine what a toppling "chronbet" might look like. He shook off the exercise and whined, "Without weapons?" The Bahdane's stare lacked any judgment, but Curtis could read the alien's thoughts anyway. "Okay, okay."

~ ~ ∞ ~ ~

The child lay next to her mother listening to her calming words of reassurance.

"Stay right by me, Patty. Don't be afraid. We'll make it to the ship, I know."

Sar Mode snuggled next to her "mother," replying silently. *And I assure you, Mommy, that what you say is true. How very fortunate you are to have me at your side.*

A Bahdane crawled next to them. Those lying nearby moved closer as he spoke.

"When we knock the aliens to the deck, everyone must rush forward and attack them. They have openings on the surface of their domed tops and eyes underneath. Grasp those organs with force and rip them apart. Do not be timid. It is your only option." The Bahdane moved on.

The mother put her arm around the child. "Hold my shirttail and don't let go."

Sar Mode stayed silent for fear of laughing but nodded her small, human head.

Unexpectedly, Sar Mode's communication routine initialized and just as quickly went dead. *Who is there?* No response. She issued a station-wide hailing message. *All Diak respond.* Nothing; she relaxed. An anomaly then — but what would cause it? Only a small number of Pothlill remained on the station.

The Pothlill were simple beings, incapable of guile or creative initiative — perfectly suited to slave labor. How the species developed technology and space travel was at first a mystery. But the Diak scholars learned that an advanced alien race, worshiped by the Pothlill as the "First Gods," shared their home world for eons before becoming extinct. By the time the Diak arrived, the Pothlill barely maintained the inherited technology and were, in fact, devolving. It was an interesting aside, but of no great concern to the Diak who commenced plans for colonization. Until, that is, they learned of a second peculiarity of the species: Once relocated to a Pothlill, the Diak was imprisoned. Upon the Pothlill's turning, the Diak, unable to move its nanoids to a new host, perished.

The source of the problem remained unresolved. Fortunately, only a small handful of Diak were lost before the anomaly was discovered. But the loss of even one Diak was devastating. Without sufficient hosts, the Diak would soon die. And even with an unending supply of hosts, over the coming centuries Diak numbers would shrivel until the last one passed into obscurity. . . until *Sar Mode*, the last Diak, passed into obscurity. She put the transmission irregularity out of her mind; that was all it could be.

~ ~ ∞ ~ ~

At Captain McDermott's order, Travis cruised the perimeter of Mass Primary looking for the gunship. It worried him not knowing if Sar Mode had clued her defenders in on his mission. *How am I expected to get Sir James' reply to her if her patrols blow me to smithereens? For sure they'll recognize this ship as friendly, won't they?* He stayed in the open, between the station and the asteroid field. *This whole undertaking from both sides. . . three sides if you count McDermott and the Maris Stella. . . is ill-planned. No one knows what the other is doing. Wait,* four *sides. What's Nikko Balog up to?*

As he measured the direness of his situation, he followed the curve of Mass Primary until the cross-lateral tip of a gunship came into view. The gunship moved into the clear and fired. Its laser beam passed within a few meters on Travis' portside, hitting a rock the size of Mount Fujiyama. Loose debris erupted from its surface and expanded in all directions. Shards pummeled the side of his ship. No lights flashed or sound issued from the control panel, so he assumed the damage to be minimal. Travis was a sitting duck. Worse—a sitting *duckling*. The gunship stood its ground but ceased fire.

Lilting, child-like tones filled his head.

"Ah. . . I see you are back. I am a bit occupied now. We are organizing an attack against my Pothlill house defenders. Such fun. You bring a response from Sir James?"

Travis took a moment to try and parse Sar Mode's banter, then decided to ignore it. "Yes. He's made a counteroffer."

"Unacceptable."

"Don't you want to hear it? By the way, one of your ships just fired on me."

"Do not concern yourself—you are safe. I understand that a being in Sir James' position is required to negotiate. He has fulfilled that requirement and he alone bears the responsibility for what follows. I have opened a communications channel through the wormhole calibrated to your implant."

"Great," Travis said. "What am I supposed to do now?"

In answer to his question, Sir James voice came over his comm. "Commander Barnes? How in hell did your tap get through EDC security and my personal admin?"

"Sar Mode arranged it. I'm still in Diak space."

"Then how. . .?" Sir James' sigh conveyed acceptance. "I don't suppose that matters. Well?"

"She said no."

"Nothing else?"

"Just. . . just that you bear responsibility for what happens next, sir."

Travis could hear his heart hammer in the silence that followed.

Finally, "*End all,*" Sir James said, without further discussion.

Travis was unsure how to proceed when the chairman signed off. His message delivered, he figured another run-in with the gunship would be his last. He reported to the *Maris Stella*. "Captain McDermott, at least one gunship is positioned on the opposite side of the station. I can't get past it to see if there's more. I'm heading back in your direction."

"Good. We left a light on in our docking bay," McDermott responded.

When Travis reached the *Maris Stella,* he continued aft. The open maw of her expansive docking bay lay before him. There was indeed a light on. As he docked, an oversized screen on the forward bulkhead announced the environmental shield had re-enabled and commenced a countdown to pressurization. When the count reached zero, the display read: *Welcome to the Maris Stella.* He exited the ship through the series of three hatches without issue. It appeared he and the Diak ship had come to terms.

A heavyset man in a white apron entered the bay from shipside. "Commander Barnes, it's an honor, sir. Billy Grabe, chef and medic. Follow me." He extended his hand.

Travis stepped to his side; they shook hands walking. "Good to meet you, Grabe. What's the situation?"

"I'm taking you to the bridge. One of our shuttles, the *Nod*, is preparing to dock on Mass Primary."

When they reached the ship's bridge, he saw only Letty. She crossed the few steps between them and melted against his chest. Her words came muffled. "When I learned you were still alive, I couldn't believe it. God, you feel so *good*." She raised her head to look at him and took his face in both hands. "You're real?"

"I'm real." Encircling her with his arms, he pulled her tighter and kissed her.

Captain McDermott interrupted them. "Break it up, you two. We need to focus here."

Travis and Letty turned to the bridge monitors.

The *Nod* crept only a few meters out from the dock containing the Bahdaneian salvage vessel; close enough to see its extended gangway.

~ ~ ∞ ~ ~

Rear Admiral Sullivan relayed his report to Sir James and the Earth Defense Council.

"The colony — remind me — human?" Sir James asked when the admiral finished.

"The colony on Zeta Ten was Bin. The mine on Zeta Ten's smallest moon, and its employees and their families, was a human outpost. The moon was destroyed, and the resultant meteor onslaught wiped out the Bin colony, as well, rendering the planet uninhabitable. Worse, Zeta Ten orbited the sun next-nearest to the Bin planetary system, and they can expect the meteor debris to threaten their home world for several decades to come."

"Right," Sir James said, without emotion. "And the Diak ships, do we have a count?"

"A cruise ship spotted them a few hours out from Zeta Ten. It reported roughly four-hundred-fifty ships — almost a full fleet by our standards. And they're heading toward the next mining installation, in our general direction. I have two squadrons of six. I can deploy them, but I'd be sending them on a suicide mission."

"Use your best judgement. How long?"

"Depending on how many attacks they launch along the way, seventy-two hours — a little less. Reinforcements?" Admiral Sullivan's flat tone evidenced his expected response. Earth defense took priority.

"You'll have to do your best with what you've got. I need to go back to the Council. I'll speak with you again in an hour."

35 ROLLING THUNDER

The Bahdaneians lined up two on one side and three on the other, facing one another across the passage entrance. Curtis assumed they meant to present the smallest targets possible. Some of their foes aimed blaster-clad tentacles at the Bahdane while others continued to target the hostages still lying prone on the deck. So far, they hadn't fired. Curtis wondered if they acted under orders to preserve as many prospective hosts as possible. He hoped so. They'd seen no further signs that the station was under attack. Where the hell were their supposed rescuers?

When the mushrooms came within range, the five Bahdaneians — all males — issued booming yells that carried the force of thunder. They hurled their bodies into the passage and rolled at the horde with a speed Curtis thought impossible considering their bulk. The mushrooms fired their lasers but otherwise maintained an eerie silence in the face of the Bahdaneian onslaught. The majority of the laser blasts struck the deck behind the Bahdane as their bodies bowled forward. Good for the first wave but disastrous for the hostages who were to follow them.

Curtis waited precious seconds for the mushrooms to adjust their aim. One of the Bahdane stopped rolling. Blood gushed from a gaping head wound. Another stood with difficulty and lurched forward in a lop-sided gait, expanding his chest and extending his arms. The larger target, he drew fire from the approaching line, appropriating the mushrooms' attention from the three barrel-bodies, now only two meters away and closing. When a laser blast separated his left arm from his body, the Bahdane somehow managed to lurch two steps further before he went down. Curtis rose to a crouch on one knee and waved in a forward motion. He didn't check to see if those behind him had moved into ready position as well.

By the time Curtis was on his feet, the mushrooms were toppling like "chronbets on the destilx." Shouting "Charge!" and obscenities, he ran at the tumbling mass. He vaulted over the downed Bahdaneians in succession, both of whom lay unquestionably dead. On his second landing, he slipped in a pool of blood but miraculously managed to stay upright. The other hostages sounded close behind, their unintelligible screams adding to the mêlée.

The first mushroom he reached lay twisting on the deck. Its tentacle waved franticly above it as it tried to right itself. Its weapon fired uncontrolled laser blasts. Curtis clawed at the alien's top cap, jabbing his fingers into one of the openings that pulsated—perhaps from its exertion. The blaster dropped to the deck, and the tentacle encircled Curtis. He took a deep breath against the tightening appendage, grabbed hold of the edges of what he guessed was a nose, and pulled outward with all his force. The head-cap ripped open and sprayed thick, purple fluid in every direction. The tentacle dropped away.

Curtis looked for another target. The bulk of the hostages had pressed past him, and along with the three surviving Bahdane, were busy ripping the remaining mushrooms into pieces with a savagery that would have made Genghis Khan proud. Nikko's bulk emerged above the throng writhing on the deck as he tore a tentacle from a mushroom's body. Adrenaline accomplished what the two of them together were unable to do earlier. Though the noise level had grown unbearable, he realized the blaster firing had stopped.

Still hunched over his victim's body, Curtis rose, somehow managing to stand upright in the slippery, purple goo that coated the deck, the bulkheads, and everyone joined in the battle. The frenzied hostages continued to scream and rip at the mushrooms. He spun around. Behind him, a woman with a child hung back from the fight. The woman retched from the smell or out of fear, and at the same time tried in vain to cover the little girl's eyes with her hands. The child, wearing a peculiar smile, kept pushing the hands away. Next to them, a frail, older woman leaned against the bulkhead, appearing exhausted.

Curtis took stock of the scene. The battle was over, and they'd won, though two humans along with the two Bahdaneians lay still among the mangled mushrooms. One of the humans was Oscar, a tentacle wrapped tightly around his body up to the head. Austen moved toward Oscar's body, calling to him. Even from his vantage point, Curtis knew it was a wasted effort. He searched for Toby, concern rising when he was unable to spot him in the carnage. Other hostages halted their assaults. Chests heaving, one-by-one, they looked about for more targets. Slowly the scene quieted.

"Hey, Curtis! Over here."

Curtis turned at the sound of his name to see Toby with the woman and little girl. Toby held the girl's hand. She stared at Curtis, unblinking, wearing the same disturbing smile she'd worn a minute earlier.

Toby waved. "I'm okay."

Curtis nodded, bewildered by his surge of relief at seeing the boy unharmed.

A Bahdane moved about in the gooey mess, holding a mushroom blaster. Curtis stooped and picked up one lying near him. After several attempts to fire it into the dead mushroom at his feet, he gave up and dropped it back into the goop. The Bahdane appeared to have no better luck, tossing his aside, as well.

The hostages pushed on.

~ ~ ∞ ~ ~

Nikko's comm was open. Aboard the *Nod*, Drew and the crew eavesdropped on the unintelligible pandemonium of the hostages' struggle as Aisha Olcott expertly docked the shuttle in the tight space on the salvage ship's port side.

"Helmets on!" Olcott ordered.

Drew snapped his neckpiece in place, sealed his helmet, and commenced his breathing exercises. He lowered the volume from the battle to listen to a discussion between Olcott, Gretchen Rossi, and Captain McDermott.

"Can you make the shot?" Olcott asked.

Close to the pilot's station, Drew could see the icon representing the *Blinkum* on Olcott's screen. Piloted by Rossi, it hung just outside the station. A flashing red line indicated her laser was trained on a target inside the dock.

"Yep." Rossi's clipped response conveyed certainty, and McDermott gave the green light.

The *Nod* team extended the flexible partition that sealed the cabin from the pilot's station, and Drew lost sight of the screen. The four-man team crowded the hatch as the cabin depressurized. Olcott would stay onboard the *Nod*. If her team made it into the station without resistance, they would wait for the *Blinkum* to dock and Rossi and her team to join them. If the *Nod* team was unable to advance for any reason, the plan was to return to the shuttle and the *Maris Stella*. They were too short on numbers and intel to press a failed incursion. Retreat, regroup, and rethink. Drew dreaded what was likely to come after that.

He heard Rossi over his comm once more. "In *three. . . two. . . one. . . .*"

From the *Nod*, he was unable to see the target, but when it exploded from the heat generated by the laser beam, the team felt the concussion. They piled out of the shuttle and headed around the salvage ship to the gaping hole. The weight of his blaster at Drew's hip comforted him, though it lay out of reach beneath the suit. Along with the other three men, he carried a much heavier and more efficient laser rifle. He'd fired a similar weapon only once, at the academy. There was no practice range on the *Maris Stella*, so he hoped he could handle the weapon when the time came.

As they reached the opening, Olcott issued a warning. "Barnes says to watch out for the mushrooms."

Drew glanced at the man next to him and mouthed "Mushrooms?"

The four continued through the gap into a short hallway with a second hatch. The point man held up an arm, his hand in a fist — *halt*. Drew'd never heard the man referred to by any name but Whacker.

"We've got another hatch," Whacker announced to Olcott.

"Can you get through?"

"Don' know. Maybe."

"Try. Rossi's docked; they'll wait. If you can't, beat it back here."

His fellow team members chuckled, and Drew smiled as the tension eased a bit.

Whacker approached the hatch to study it. When he drew about two meters of it, it shimmered and disappeared. "Whoa!" He continued through, his rifle aimed down a long passage that curved right and then motioned for the others to join him. When they were all through, the hatch reappeared behind them.

"Whacker, report," Olcott ordered, then immediately countered the order. "*Wait.* Rossi, did you see that?"

"Yeah."

"Whacker, we had atmo out here for a few seconds. What's happening there?"

"The hatch disappeared as I approached it and reappeared behind us. We're in, like a bubble . . . I think. My gauge says atmo here too. Earth-nominal."

"You willing?" Olcott said.

"Yeah." Whacker released his neckpiece, then paused a few seconds before opening the helmet visor. "So far, so good."

"Leave one man fully suited. Rossi's on her way."

Whacker turned and pointed to Drew. "Cutter, you're it."

Drew nodded, annoyed to be singled out, but a tad relieved as well. Until Whacker issued his next directive.

"You take the lead."

Well, shit!

~ ~ ∞ ~ ~

On the *Maris Stella*, Travis Barnes' comm pinged. "Sir James?"

"Tell her I agree to her terms."

No surprise there. It was that or total destruction and goodbye Alliance. Letty was standing in front of him, fixated on the monitor and the accompanying chatter. He turned and slipped from the bridge back to the salon through which he'd been escorted earlier.

"Anything else, sir?" he asked.

"No. That covers it. In response to my counteroffer, a Diak fleet took out a mine installation and a Bin colony. They appear to be headed to another installation on a route to Dark Landing. No point dilly-dallying."

"Should I relay any of this to Captain McDermott?"

"No. Any information exchanged between the two of us and the third party is to remain confidential."

"Understood."

When Sir James ended the transmission, Travis heard a child's voice.

"Excellent decision."

His comm went dead. He fell to the nearest lounger, exhaled, and then took a deep, steadying breath to refill his lungs. His thoughts whirled. If Sar Mode held to her word, the Alliance was spared. She'd explained the armada and those of her race awaiting new hosts teetered on the verge of death. Limited to their current supply, they would not last an Earth year. And even if they conquered the Alliance planets, Diak extinction would come within a decade once they'd exhausted the last of the Alliance races. Turnings occurred so rapidly now that hostage races were too soon depleted. The *Spread* — those colonies already established on captured planets — reported shortened turn cycles. Many colonies along with the planets' native species were already extinct.

Sar Mode promised to eliminate the threat of Diak invasion once and for all, though she never said how. In return, she'd get a free pass to consume human hosts as frequently as needed and be left alone to go her own way — discretely, of course. If pursued, she vowed to spread the deadly nanoids indiscriminately throughout the Alliance populations once more. Unchecked, the member races would share the same fate as the Diak. Travis had no doubt the Alliance races would choose the same path as the Diak had chosen for their own survival.

Only he and Sir James knew of the arrangement. Why would she allow them to live? *It's probable I'll take this knowledge to my grave — today.* He returned to the bridge.

36 UNIFICATION

When the two teams joined, Rossi raised her helmet visor and nodded to her group of four to do the same. Drew took front and center, accepting that, once again, he wasn't as *special* as he was expendable. The others hugged the side bulkheads and followed the gentle curve of the passageway. They traveled a quarter klick into the station without incident, when a tall, willowy figure with a domed cap stepped out in front of them. It was waving a long appendage with something on its tip.

Before Drew could see what it was holding, he felt the heat of a laser blast coming from behind him and passing close by. The mushroom's center disintegrated. It spewed purple blood and fell in pieces to the deck. Drew glanced over his shoulder to find Rossi standing three paces back and to his left.

She cocked her head and smiled at him, paraphrasing Travis' warning, "Beware the mushrooms."

With her back against the bulkhead, Rossi continued by him, laser rifle at shoulder level, finger against the trigger guard. When she could see around the curve, she motioned the rest forward as well, taking point. Drew gratefully dropped to the end of the line against the opposite bulkhead.

In the safer position, he took in his surroundings. The station exterior was circular, so it was no surprise that the corridor curved continuously to the right. The bulkheads were smooth metal without decoration, except for an unbroken ribbon of grated vents at the very top on both sides of the passageway. Vents were uncommon in space stations, which were served by air-handling conduits that could be easily sealed in sections if there was an emergency.

The teams continued with cautious steps a quarter klick further to another hatch.

"Helmets sealed," Rossi ordered.

When everyone was suited once more, Rossi approached the hatch. Like the first, it disappeared, preceded by a shimmering display. The group continued deeper into the station.

~ ~ ∞ ~ ~

As they moved forward, Curtis introduced himself to the Bahdane walking alongside him. "Curtis Walker."

"Martin Van Buren."

Curtis made a face. "Wouldn't of been *my* first choice."

Toby trotted up to them.

"You might wanna stay back with Nikko or Austen, kid," Curtis said.

"Nah, I'll hang with you guys."

"Toby, go back with Austen."

"Ah. . . you *lub* me." Toby grinned and batted his eyes at Curtis.

"I don't *lub* you, freak. But if you die, Letty will kill m—"

A long, furry arm pushed against his chest, stopping his forward motion. In front of them waited a second mushroom blockade. They'd formed two lines strung the width of the passage. Those at the front had compressed downward, their middles bulging. The line behind them stood at full height. Their tentacles weren't waving wildly about like the first group they'd encountered, and they wouldn't tumble as easily in this configuration. Blasters held steady, they aimed true at the knot of hostages. The scene reminded Curtis of an image he'd seen years ago of soldiers in some long-forgotten war wearing red coats and holding antique rifles.

"Go!" Curtis pushed Toby backward. For once the kid obeyed.

A second Bahdane joined them at the front. For a few seconds, the two hummed at each other, then Martin Van Buren stepped forward, arms out and paws up to show he was unarmed. He spoke to the mushrooms in an unrecognizable language, but evidently not mushroomese because the creatures never twitched. The Bahdane tried again, this time with a series of clicks and whistles. Nothing.

Van Buren turned and hummed something to his comrade who hummed a response. "Hummmm doesn't believe they have a spoken language," Van Buren said to Curtis.

"What now?" Curtis kept his eyes on the two lines of mushrooms.

"We may be forced to turn back."

"Or. . .?"

"We may die."

As Curtis watched, the center mushroom in the back line dipped its cap forward. Since its eyes were on the underside of the cap, he wondered what it was looking at. All at once, the two lines of mushrooms quivered and bowed their caps in succession, resembling a precision chorus line.

One by one, the mushrooms along the back line exploded, and a fresh layer of purple slime splattered the hostages at the front of the procession.

"Hit the deck!" Curtis shouted for the second time in an hour, as sustained laser fire passed above them. He lay still, his hands covering the back of his head, for what seemed an eternity but was no more than a couple minutes. If his fate was to be blown away by a freakin' mushroom, he had no need to see it coming. The firing ended abruptly. He held his breath in the sudden silence.

~ ~ ∞ ~ ~

"Whatcha doin', Curtis?"

Curtis raised his head and stared. Drew Cutter hovered over him. Goo ran down Curtis's face and into his gaping mouth. He gagged and spat and attempted to wipe the gunk off his face, but before he spoke, whoops of joy sounded from behind him. Toby's cries dwarfed the others.

"Drew! Drew! I knew you'd come. Is my mo. . . Letty here too?" Toby flew at Drew, wrapping his arms around his mid-center. Drew's white EMU now had a purple sash.

He gave the boy a loose hug and made a face. "*What* is that smell? Is that you, kid?"

"Nah, it's Curtis."

They both laughed at that, and for once, Curtis joined them. As Curtis struggled to stand upright in the slippery muck, Nikko barged past to greet Drew, knocking him down again.

"Hey! Someone give me a hand," Curtis said.

Nikko hauled him to his feet. The rest of their group closed in tight, and Whacker motioned for his team to move among the hostages.

"This is Whacker. . .?" Drew gave the man a questioning look.

"Just Whacker."

". . . from the *Maris Stella,* Letty's ship. The rest will introduce themselves." Drew looked at Toby. "Letty's onboard, but it's too early to celebrate. There's still a ways to go yet." His eyes flitted over the scene. "Where's Doc?"

Curtis casually placed an arm around Toby's shoulders and gave Drew a steady gaze. "She didn't make it. Tell you later."

Drew closed his eyes tight and lowered his head for a moment.

The tactical team mingled with the elated hostages, taking stock of their number and condition. Drew spotted three Bahdaneians in the group. One took point with a member of Rossi's team and the other two assumed the rear position. He looked for Gretchen.

"Rossi?" he asked Whacker.

The man shook his head slowly. "One of the bastards got off a lucky shot."

Grief washed over him. It was too much—Doc, a friend and colleague for years, and now Gretchen. He and Gretchen shared a bond since the day he'd rolled a passed-out Xander Crawford off the *Maris Stella.* She'd saved his life not twenty minutes earlier, and now again by taking point.

Without elaborating, Whacker raised his voice over the babble. "Everybody, listen to me. We gotta keep movin'."

"What about the other hostages?" someone shouted.

He turned to Curtis. "How many?"

"There's over four hundred humans, and maybe a thousand plus of the other Alliance races. And hundreds, probably thousands more from races I've never seen before."

"Infected?"

"We don't think so. But we suspect there's a Diak spy in each enclosure. Just a hunch."

Whacker looked back over the lot of them. "Okay, people. Let's get you to the ship, and then we'll figure out what we can do about the others."

Their rescuers split into two groups, forward and rear, except for one man from each team who broke away to retrieve Rossi. Between the bulky suit and the slime that had spread to where she lay, they struggled to lift her body. Martin Van Buren went to help, and with their nods of consent, he lifted Rossi and cradled her in his arms.

"Thanks," Whacker said softly. "Okay, let's go—only half a klick from here." With a round of applause, they cautiously picked their way through the mushroom guts, and he led them down the passage. "Stay alert. Drop to the deck if you see the enemy."

"We've been practicing that move," Curtis said.

Toby took Drew's hand and looked up at him with a broad smile, as if they were going on an outing. Drew smiled back but with less enthusiasm.

~ ~ ∞ ~ ~

Listening over the open comm, Olcott on the *Nod*, along with the *Winkum* and those on the *Maris Stella*, were privy to Whacker's side of the events. Everyone silently mourned the loss of Gretchen Rossi.

"Whacker, how many incoming? Walker doesn't think they're infected?" McDermott asked.

"One hundred-six total, including Master Toby." Behind McDermott came a strangled sob of relief from Letty. Whacker continued. "No way to know if they're infected. I was thinking, maybe a couple of us can bring them on the salvage ship if it's space-worthy—keep them isolated until we can scan 'em. Nikko piloted it here, and there's three Bahdaneians in the bunch."

"I like it. Join up as fast as you can. No resistance out here — it's way too spooky." As soon as the words left his mouth, McDermott regretted them.

"Diak gunship starboard targeting the *Winkum,* sir!"

"Port thrusters. Attain position," McDermott ordered Turrey. "Mikleson?"

The *Winkum's* pilot and sole occupant, Abraham Mikleson responded. "I see it. Coming around."

The bridge monitor morphed into a split display of the *Winkum*: One side displayed a broad view comprised of icons representing the station and surrounding ships. A red square denoted the Diak gunship at the upper far edge of that screen. The other side of the screen displayed a live feed of the shuttle from the *Maris Stella's* cameras. The gunship wasn't visible in the live view, but a laser beam entered the screen from top right as McDermott watched.

In an instant, the *Winkum* disappeared from both displays, leaving only pinpoints of residual debris in her stead.

"Turrey?!"

"Almost. . . almost. . . *firing.* Gotcha, you bastard," Turrey screamed.

McDermott's eyes were glued to the monitor. The gunship still wasn't visible in the live view. But a second after Turrey's scream, pieces of it entered the screen from the upper corner to mingle with the debris from the *Winkum.*

The bridge remained quiet. *That's two of us,* McDermott thought. "We just lost the *Winkum,*" he announced to everyone. "Step on it, Whacker."

~ ~ ∞ ~ ~

The hostages and their rescuers continued down the passage unchallenged. Whacker stopped them several meters in front of the first hatch.

"Olcott? We can't come any further unless you're still registering atmo dockside."

"Suit up a volunteer."

Whacker looked at Drew. Before either could say anything, Martin Van Buren stepped up.

"I will do it."

"Thanks, but you're too big. None of our suits will fit."

"It's okay, I'll do it. Mr. Expendable to the rescue," Drew said. "And I was worried about contributing."

"Sorry," Whacker apologized. "War's hell. Life's not fair. Space is complicated."

Drew ignored Whacker's litany and secured his helmet. When he approached the hatch, it vanished, then reappeared behind him. He trotted the quarter meter to the next hatch, unsealing his helmet again before going through. As soon as he crossed the short passage to the gaping hole left by the *Blinkum's* laser blast, Olcott announced the dock atmosphere was Earth-nominal.

She went on. "This explains the atmo blip we detected earlier. There seems to be sensors that can read and adjust the environment as needed. We could learn a lot from these guys."

McDermott joined the conversation. "Yeah, like don't trust Diak nanoids, no matter how agreeable they seem. The traitors on Dark Landing learned that lesson the hard way."

Curtis mumbled something unintelligible over the comm feed. Drew thought McDermott should know it was too soon, but what he said rang true, and it stung.

The captain continued, "Whacker, proceed. Cutter, recon the *Mayzie.*"

Drew raised his visor, crossed the docking bay, and climbed the gangway to the *Mayzie's* cargo hatch, which stood open. "We can board. Don't know if we can access the controls."

"Balog here. I have access. But *Mayzie* won't hold one hundred plus people for more than a couple hours — and most will be standing."

McDermott broke in again. "Does she have a medical scanner?"

"Not that I know of," Nikko said.

"We'll have to scan them for contamination back here then. Olcott, cram our men into the *Nod* with you. Whacker and Cutter, take the *Blinkum* with five hostages and Toby. . . and Rossi. Load the rest of the hostages onboard the *Mayzie*. We'll meet up where we installed the probe homing device."

Drew wondered what McDermott would do in the event he found an infected hostage. He eavesdropped on the murmurs of conversation from the hostage group as they approached the docking bay. Breaking the current of subdued discussions, a woman screamed. Several seconds passed in silence.

"We have a downed hostage. A child," Whacker reported. "No wounds that I can see — she just dropped."

Sobs could be heard in the background and a woman's pleas. "*Nooo*. Patty. . . Patty! Please, someone help her."

"She's gone," Whacker said quietly.

37 HALF HERO

On the *Maris Stella*, Travis shuddered. He should have known Sar Mode would insert herself among the first group of hostages rescued. And if she'd been inhabiting that girl, Patty, where. . . *who* was she now?

He touched Letty's shoulder. "Where's the head?"

"Across the salon, next to the bar."

"I'll be right back."

Letty nodded and returned her attention to the command monitor.

Away from listening ears, Travis contacted Sir James.

"Yes, Commander Barnes."

"We've got a problem, sir. I think Sar Mode is with this group of hostages. A child, a little girl, just dropped dead with no obvious cause."

"And you're sure it wasn't natural."

"Pretty sure, and the *Maris Stella* has a medical scanner onboard. They're isolating the hostages until each one is scanned. If it was Sar Mode. . . ."

"I guess you need to disable their scanner, then." Sir James delivered his statement in a *why are you bothering me* tone.

Travis paused before replying. *Of course. Why the fuck didn't I think of that?* "Yes, sir."

"How many hostages left on the station?"

"Thousands. From the Alliance planets and races we've never cataloged."

"And in the group that escaped? Casualties?"

"Two casualties from the *Maris Stella's* crew, plus the loss of a shuttle, and the dead girl with the hostages. There may have been more hostage casualties—I don't know yet. More than a hundred escaped."

"That's acceptable. Sar Mode appears to be keeping her side of the bargain." When Travis remained silent, Sir James defended his comment. "It would be suspicious without any casualties." Travis maintained his silence. "Anything else, Barnes?"

"No, sir."

"*End transmission.*"

Since the salon appeared to double as the ship's main dining area, Travis headed for the port-holed door on the opposite side of the room in search of Billy Grabe, chef and medic. He found him in the well-appointed galley, preparing sandwiches.

"The hostages are on their way," Travis announced.

"Yeah, I been followin' the chatter. Guessin' they'll be hungry. You?"

"No, I'm good. Thanks. McDermott said there's a medical scanner. Before the others come on board, I wanna be checked out. Sir James testified that I scanned negative on Dark Landing, but I think everyone would feel safer if you confirmed it here."

Grabe smiled. "I know I would. It made my skin crawl just walkin' ya to the bridge—though was still an honor, sir. Give me two minutes to finish and wash up. Med-lab's right 'cross the passage. It's marked."

Travis stepped into the medical lab. Supply cabinets lined the two side walls, with a processor desk against the short wall next to the door. An exam table extended from the opposite bulkhead with a myriad of tech equipment and assorted rods and hooks attached to it and the table frame. One particularly large piece of equipment hung over the table from the upper deck—the main scanner. A metal shell completely encased the scanner, except for its monitor and control panel, which were affixed to a maneuverable arm. He saw no simple way to disable it but needed more time. Travis removed his shirt, kicked off his boots, and dropped his pants just as Grabe entered.

"Did they make you git neked on Dark Landing? Cuz it's *not* necessary."

"*Really*? Good to know. I'll keep my BVDs on then."

"Appreciate it. Hop up."

Grabe pulled the monitor down and punched in commands. Two minutes later he announced, "You're good to go. I forwarded the results to the cap'n. If you want something to eat, stop by the galley on your way out. No panties, no snackies."

"Thanks," Travis said. "I'll be sure to dress for the occasion."

When the door closed behind Grabe, Travis hopped off the exam table and checked the monitor, relieved to find the big machine still online. The screen read "Record archived," with a file number, his name, the date, and a string of medical codes that meant nothing to him. At the top right was a menu icon. When he tapped it, several rows of options materialized, most as indecipherable medical codes. At the very bottom was a second menu of system options, two of which read "Reset to Nominal" and "Reformat Drive." Travis tapped "Reformat Drive." A smaller screen popped up: "Archive current settings (recommended) Yes. No." He selected "No," and hoped it would at least delay the scanning process. Before entering the command, he skimmed the system options once more and selected "Text Display." He drew a box around the words "Reformat Drive" and changed the text color to a muted olive that matched the background color. The option, though still available, disappeared from view. Satisfied he'd done all he could, he dressed and hurried back to the bridge.

Letty was curled up in the captain's chair, and McDermott leaned against the control console next to Turrey. Spotting Travis, he said, "Barnes, there you are. We were just wondering why this operation went so easy. I'm shocked. We lost two of our best, but frankly none of us expected to survive. Thoughts?"

"From what I saw before they sent me back, the station is practically abandoned. The armada has relocated. Maybe they were planning to leave the hostages to die."

"And you were sent back why, again?"

"To deliver a demand for unconditional surrender. Earth Defense Council said no. Zeta Quadrant is under attack. . . *ah*," He realized he'd gotten that info from Sir James *after* he returned to Diak space. ". . . just as I was leaving, and maybe Dark Landing by now, too." *I fucking suck at this.* He hurried on, hoping they wouldn't notice his *faux pas.* "When I learned you guys were here, I asked to come back, and Sir James agreed." Travis' gaze shifted to Letty. His features softened, and he gave her a small smile.

"Travis, you shouldn't have come back for me."

"I couldn't live with myself if I didn't."

Letty went to him, and they wrapped their arms around each other. "And. . ." Travis looked at the other two, "I can lead you back if we make it that far. Though there's still the little matter of the armada guarding the wormhole."

"If we're talking about the same armada and the same wormhole, we know the way," McDermott said.

Travis raised his eyebrows. "I'm impressed."

"You're impressed? I'm shocked."

~ ~ ∞ ~ ~

The two shuttles and the *Remarkable Mayzie* arrived at the probe homing base a couple hours after the *Maris Stella.* The *Blinkum* docked with the larger ship, while the *Nod* and the *Mayzie* waited a couple klicks out for further orders.

When Drew, Whacker, and their passengers entered the salon, Letty greeted Drew with a quick hug, and then grabbed Toby in a choke hold, tears flowing.

"Hey. . . Letty, I can't breathe."

She pushed him away from her and inspected him. "Are you okay—are you hurt? You're so thin! *I'm going to kill you!*"

Toby ignored the last. "No, I'm good, *Mom.* I'm just hungry." He turned toward the table Grabe had loaded with sandwiches, sides, and a dispenser of water. Halfway there, he spotted Travis and ran at him like a crazed rhino toward a campfire. The two hugged, then stood back to look at each other, and hugged again.

"Toby learned early-on that calling me Mom will get him out of just about any mess," Letty said, watching their greeting with a dreamy expression. She sobered when she noticed Drew studying her. "I'm sorry. . . I. . . ."

If he'd had any lingering doubts about Letty's feelings, or his own, they vanished in that moment. Surprised by the sense of deep relief that washed over him, he maintained a stern countenance. "It's fate. I'll survive. But I'll suffer, and I'll probably need years of counseling—"

Letty stuck her tongue out at him.

He winked back. The banter reminded him of their time together on the *Temperance*. It felt right. Their relationship was sorting itself out. A clear winner emerged from the contest between him and Barnes—a contest that only existed in Drew's imagination—and Drew was a contented also ran.

Under Whacker's scrutiny, Grabe was helping the five hostages fill plates with food, chatting at them nonstop as he did so. "... and then we'll go back to med-lab and check ya out. But ya look like ya just need a few pounds and a good night's sleep ta me. Just the same. . . ."

Toby piled sandwiches onto a plate and followed the others to be scanned.

McDermott nodded toward the empty loungers. "While they do that, let's figure out our next step."

Letty, Drew, and Turrey took seats. Travis grabbed a sandwich and joined them, acknowledging Drew with a nod. Drew nodded back, wondering if the two of them would ever be totally comfortable in each other's presence.

"So, I been mentally making a list of issues," McDermott said. "It seems we have thousands still to rescue—obviously our own Alliance citizens—but limited transportation and supplies. What's the situation on Mass Primary, Drew?"

"We didn't meet anyone but the mushrooms on our way in. The hostages only got out because we showed up when we did. Still, I'm a little surprised at how easy it was."

"Yeah. . . me too. Who are these mushroom guys, Barnes? Are they Diak?"

"I don't think so. Don't even think they're Diak hosts. More like. . . minions, with controlling nanoids possibly. They resemble tall mushrooms with one tentacle growing out of their sides. I've never heard one speak."

"Anything else you can tell us?"

"Not much, other than about a Diak Fahdeen. She calls herself the *principal*, and she's the one who sent me back to the K.U. to demand surrender." Travis tried to avoid unnecessary details.

"What about the hostages?" McDermott asked.

"This is the first I've seen of other hostages." Travis shook his head.

"Curtis Walker, Chief of Security on Dark Landing, and Nikko Balog— a *Muck* agent, I think—might be able to fill in some of the blanks," Drew offered.

McDermott tapped his comm. "Olcott, I need Curtis Walker. Can you shuttle him over to me? You can pick up food and water for the others while you're here." As McDermott finished his conversation, Billy Grabe entered the salon.

"Cap'n, we got a problem." Grabe cast an accusing look at Travis.

38 RESCUE

"What? You told me I scanned negative." Travis tried for a *I totally misunderstood your inference* look. He hated lying, and he'd never been good at it.

"You did. And I left you alone with the scanner. Between then and now, its main drive was reformatted," Billy Grabe said, unveiling his accusation and leaving no room for interpretation.

"I don't know anything about scanners. I certainly don't know how to reformat the damn thing. If that's true — I don't doubt you — why would I do something like that *after* scanning negative?"

"Maybe you were covering for someone."

So much for hidden agendas. Travis struggled to hold Grabe's gaze without blinking or looking aside — sure signs of lying.

Fortunately, Captain McDermott stepped in. "Everyone spaceout! We'll get to the bottom of what happened to the scanner. Can it be fixed?"

"Sure," Grabe said. "All settings and files are automatically backed up to multiple locations in the K.U. But here, I'll need to start from scratch. Re-enter all the settings, new calibrations, and run mandated tests after each entry. It'll take hours."

Miraculously Rob Turrey threw Travis a lifeline. "Hey, Billy, a lot of time's passed since you used it last, and the unit woke up expecting a stack of upgrades. When they didn't come, and it couldn't sync from this location, maybe it tried to upgrade itself. Cleanse its palette by reformatting and going back to the default settings."

"Yeah. . . no, I'm not buying that. Not being able to sync up might cause a glitch, but it would never reformat itself." Grabe shook his head.

McDermott stepped in once more. "Still not the bigger problem. There are almost a hundred people who've spent over a day crammed into a ship meant for five, and another however-many thousand waiting for us to come up with a rescue plan. Grabe, get to work. Turrey, bring 'em onboard. We'll have to take our chances."

~ ~ ∞ ~ ~

Everyone transferred to the *Maris Stella*, and introductions were made. The crew scrounged clothing for those who needed it. The hostages appeared suddenly self-conscious about their half-naked state. Many broke down at the realization they were free, even if that freedom might ultimately prove to be temporary. For however long it lasted, they were among friends, eating food that tasted better than greasy sawdust, and indulging in a germ of hope that they might see their homes and loved ones again.

Drew joined Letty, Barnes, the Dark Landing hostages, along with the *Maris Stella's* top ranks in Letty's stateroom. They each found a seat, most on the carpeted deck. Drew, relieved his and Letty's relationship was cooling, was still annoyed when Travis Barnes plopped down on her bed, leaned back against the headboard, and stretched his legs out in front of him. To Drew's mind, he seemed much too comfortable in Letty's bed and unafraid to show it.

McDermott started. "For those here who don't already know, we have a route back to the K.U., but the last we looked, the Diak armada is in our way." Murmurs followed his announcement. He went on. "And there are three other mystery wormholes if we're really hard up for an adventure. Table that for now. And table the fact we've only got a week's worth of supplies at our new occupancy level. You get the picture — we're fucked. Every problem we have is critical. We need a plan."

The crew of the *Maris Stella* spent the next hour questioning the Dark Landing hostages about Mass Primary, its layout, defenses, and the remaining hostages, human and alien.

"How many different enclosures—alien races—are there again?" Olcott asked Curtis.

"For sure there's four large enclosures, each with four or five compounds holding different races. If there's more beyond the Alliance enclosure, I don't know—we never went in that direction."

Austen chimed in with the math. "Figure an average of four different environmental compounds to each larger enclosure—ours had five. The first one we passed through had three. At five hundred to a compound, that's eight thousand, and upward if there are more enclosures beyond the Alliance one."

"I think that's right, maybe even a bit low," Curtis said.

"What if we let out one race at a time?" Olcott asked.

"Except for the mushrooms," Austen said.

"Huh?"

"There's an enclosure with those mushroom creatures. We're not letting *them* free?"

Drew made a mental note to seek out the new chief of administration; there'd been no time for more than a quick introduction. He was eager to know more about her.

Turrey spoke up. "No, you're right—no mushroom hostages go free. But it makes you wonder whose side they're on if the Diak locked them up too."

"Instead of letting all of the hostages from a race out at one time, it would be better if we freed only pilots, if they have them. Plus, a couple others from each compound to help them look for ships," McDermott offered.

"In what language?" Drew glanced around the room. "If we can overcome the EMU size issue, I say we lead with the Bahdane—"

Whacker interrupted. "There are two Bahdane-sized EMUs on the salvage vessel. And we spotted another Bahdane ship in dock—looks like a transport a little larger than a standard shuttle. There might be another suit on her."

"Great," Drew continued. "The Bahdane can explain to the Camdu, Bin, and Fahdeens the need for pilots and finding their ships on Mass Primary. They're best qualified communication-wise, strength-wise—across the board—to deal with the *alien* aliens, as well. Meantime, we make a fast trot back to the K.U. while they work it out. From what the captain says, we don't have time or supplies enough to stick around longer anyway." Drew lamented his suggestion, though it made sense.

Olcott nodded. "I agree with Drew." She ignored Drew's look of astonishment. "Besides the other Bahdane ship, we've identified two additional Earth vessels, and one each Fahdeen, Bin, and Camdu ships—and there could be more."

"The Diak captured a lot of ships. But from what I saw, most are the size of the *Mayzie*, or smaller," Travis said. "And no way there'll be pilots enough for them all. If we get back to the K.U., the Taleen Security Force will do all they can to rescue the ones left behind." He turned to Letty for confirmation. She hesitated a bit too long.

Travis looked confused at her lack of a response. Drew was curious what he would think if he knew Letty had contemplated destroying the station along with any creature unfortunate enough to still be on it—or in this sector of the universe. Then again, maybe Travis was aware of the antimatter weapons, just unaware she was prepared to use them. After all, he was a high-level TSF commander and Letty's confidant.

Glances passed between Letty and McDermott. Turrey and Olcott kept their eyes glued to the deck. The room grew quiet. It seemed obvious to all that something remained unsaid.

McDermott wrapped up. "So, the *ayes* have it—that's the plan. A little open-ended for my taste, but that seems to be the trend."

~ ~ ∞ ~ ~

They formed two boarding teams, setting Olcott and Whacker as the leads and with a Bahdaneian assigned to each team. In addition, three hostages volunteered to aid in the rescue. When everyone was suited and armed, Olcott's team took the *Nod* to recon the two Earth vessels they'd spotted, and Whacker, on the *Blinkum*, headed for the Bahdane transport ship. Drew, Curtis, and Austen joined Olcott's team, and Travis and Nikko were on the *Blinkum* with Whacker.

Travis grew uneasy. Billy Grabe was working diligently to get the scanner operational again, and once he got it back up Travis had no idea what to do next. He could use the blaster he'd been given to damage it beyond repair. Of course, they'd probably kill him on the spot. If he survived to miraculously return to the K.U., he had no doubt Sir James would protect him long enough to learn if he'd talked to anyone, and then *he'd* kill him.

The ships returned to Mass Primary. The *Blinkum* was inspecting the bay that housed the Bahdane transport to ensure it was safe to dock alongside it when Travis' comm pinged.

"You have less than twenty-four of your Earth hours to complete whatever foolishness you are attempting. You must cross into Pothlill space before the station detonates or we will all be killed. If I do not survive to command the armada, they will attack your universe, and all will be lost there, as well." Sar Mode spoke with the voice of an elderly woman.

Among the hostages, only one elderly woman had boarded the *Maris Stella*. He'd noticed her because she was skeletal and appeared unwell. He wondered how she'd kept up with the others during the escape from Mass Primary.

Travis pleaded, his own voice low to keep from being overheard, "What do you mean 'detonates'? Twenty-four hours isn't nearly enough time for what they've planned. . . . Sar Mode. . . *Sar Mode?*" He looked wildly around the little cabin with no clue what she expected of him. Wearing an expression of concern, Nikko watched him from across the aisle. Travis pointed to his comm and mouthed *Letty*, then threw up his hands and mouthed the word *crazy*. Nikko rolled his eyes and shrugged in apparent accord.

That explained how Sar Mode planned to eliminate the Diak threat altogether. Genocide. With the Diak Mass gone and the established colonies of the Spread rapidly dying off for lack of new hosts, only Sar Mode would remain. For how long? With unobstructed access to as many replacement hosts as she needed, was she immortal? And what were her long-range plans? Would she give up her position and power to retire into obscurity? That seemed unlikely.

For now, if what she claimed was true, she still controlled the armada, with some of her ships guarding the wormhole into the K.U. and others already in the K.U. attacking Zeta Quadrant outposts. If Sir James and the council sacrificed Dark Landing—which may already be the case—and launched a counterattack, there was no way in hell one or two of the Diak ships wouldn't slink off to infiltrate the Alliance civilizations. For that matter, there could be more ships sitting out in the void waiting for orders to infiltrate.

Once Sar Mode was safe and the armada ships destroyed, would she keep her promise or start spreading the infectious nanoids again? Maybe not, since she needed uncontaminated hosts. But they had no guarantees. The absurdity of it struck Travis. One alien. . . one alien in the body of a feeble old lady held the power to destroy five disparate, age-old civilizations.

39 COLLATERAL DAMAGE

Sir James addressed Rear Admiral Sullivan over the feed. "The council is united. Do not engage the Diak ships. You are surrounded and outgunned a hundred times; doing so gives us no advantage."

"With all due respect, James, you can't be serious if you expect my men and station security to lie down and die without firing a shot because I said please. Would *you*?" Sir James frowned from the monitor, and Sullivan quickly repeated, "With all due respect. . . *sir.*"

"I am serious. You are ordered to see that your men and the station crew stand down no matter what happens. I'm calling upon your honor as an officer and your vow of allegiance to Earth and the Space Force."

"For God's sake, let my men die fighting at least. I don't understand — what happened to 'We'll go down fighting to the last man and — '"

Sir James cut him off. "You didn't climb rank because you *understood*. You followed orders — at times, blindly. This is one of those times. I expect no less now. It's simple: Shoot the first one who whines. If I were there, I'd shoot *you. End transmission.*"

Sir James stared at the empty monitor. He'd accepted the inevitability of innocent, honorable men dying when he unilaterally agreed to Sar Mode's demands. Drops of Glenfiddich splashed on the desk as he poured. He swiped at them with an index finger and then raised the finger to his mouth. Right or wrong, the deal was made. His order would stand unless something happened and he knew for certain she'd never make it to the K.U. Though that knowledge might come too late for Dark Landing.

~ ~ ∞ ~ ~

While Martin Van Buren inspected the Bahdaneian transport, the others spread out below it, weapons aimed at the single hatch leading back into Mass Primary. Travis made sure he was closest to Whacker.

"How far away is that wormhole out of here?" Travis called over to him, uncertain if the route matched the one his Diak shuttle had taken.

"Around thirty hours—longer if we're leading a caravan of smaller ships. Depending on their individual ranges, we might need to tow most."

"Right."

Assuming Travis was worried about supplies, Whacker added, "But there's a water source on the other side."

Shit! Even without meeting resistance—which seemed unlikely—communicating and leading each alien race out one at a time to search for escape ships, figuring logistics, regrouping. . . they had no time for any of it. They needed to leave *now*.

Van Buren came down the gangway. "It is a short-range troop transfer. There are seats for one hundred, but no supplies or amenities."

"You can fly it?" Whacker asked.

"Yes."

Whacker ordered one of the men back to the *Blinkum*. It was docked within easy range of the hatch. After the *Blinkum's* laser made a whole almost as large as the shuttle itself, Whacker consulted his wrist display and unsealed his helmet. In confirmation of Olcott and Rossi's earlier report, the atmosphere in the dock registered Earth-nominal.

"Okay, you can break open your helmets but keep them on. Phillips, bring up the rear; everyone else fall in behind me."

The team went through the hatch single file, weapons up, but formed two-abreast down the passageway. Travis dropped to the rear alongside Phillips—his mind whirling. Ten minutes passed. Whatever he did, it needed to happen soon. After a few steps more, he stopped and bent down to fiddle with a boot seal. Phillips turned his head for a quick look but kept moving forward. They'd passed the junction with another corridor a few meters behind. When Phillips disappeared around the curve of the bulkhead, Travis jogged back and took the alternate route. Without a plan, he hoped something would come to him. He sure wasn't getting any inspiration tagging along behind the team.

After a short way, someone called out to him. "Wait up."

Travis grimaced and slowed down. One of the hostages in Whacker's group hurried to catch him.

"That last guy in line sent me back to find you," he said. "Where you goin'?"

"Checking this passage. Thought I heard someone calling for help in English. Follow me."

"Shouldn't we. . .?"

Travis ran ahead, ignoring the guy's protests. *What now?* He knew what he wanted to do. He wanted to sit down somewhere, order a cold beer, and think this thing through in his own time. He felt stuck in an ever-tightening vise between Sir James and Sar Mode—which was *precisely* where he was. Every soldier learned that blindly following orders was a hell of a lot easier than making the tough decisions. Behind him, he could hear the man panting from his effort to keep up.

A hatch came into view. Travis slowed and approached it. It shimmered and dissolved to reveal some type of equipment room, with tubes attached to large metal boxes. All vaguely familiar forms, but he could only guess what purpose they served the station. They would serve *his* purpose perfectly. In the space of one second, Travis fully committed to a plan.

The man came up beside him and stopped. He bent over, hands on his knees, panting. Travis stepped through the hatch. Still gasping, the man followed him in. When Travis drew his blaster, the man's eyes widened. He glanced about the room panicked, looking for the threat while he fumbled for his own weapon.

"Run!" Travis pushed the hostage back through the hatch before he had time to study the scene. "*Mines*," he screamed, his voice strained.

"W-what?" The man started in an unhurried, sideways lope back the way they'd come, still casting about for the cause of Travis' alarm.

"I said, *run*. If you don't pick it up, I'm leaving you here." Travis raced ahead of the man to rejoin the team.

He heard the others ahead of him and screamed again, "Diaks... the station's rigged to blow! Retreat!"

They stood in a group around the curve of the bulkhead, weapons high, staring at him.

"I... heard something... I thought. . . ." He stopped to gulp oxygen. "I thought I heard someone call for help. I went to see, and there was a room. An equipment room of some kind. There were mushrooms and what looked like explosive ordnance attached to pipes and around the base of the bulkheads."

The hostage came up beside him, struggling to catch his breath, as well.

"We both saw it," Travis said, nodding at the man in encouragement.

Unable to speak yet, he returned Travis' nod in confirmation.

Relieved, Travis went on. "I think they're planning to blow the station. That's. . . that's why it's mostly abandoned." Travis Barnes was a *bona fide* hero. No one questioned the validity of his claim.

"Captain, did you get that? Olcott?" Whacker asked over his comm, his tone urgent.

McDermott and Olcott responded at once.

"Yes."

"Affirmative."

"No way to know how much time we have. We need to cut our losses. Everyone get back here now," McDermott ordered.

"I will follow with the transport ship," Martin Van Buren said. "We can save one hundred more."

Damn! "I'll help," Travis volunteered.

"Captain?" Whacker said.

"Up to them. But I want everyone else back here."

Whacker looked at Travis and Van Buren. "Good luck."

The *Maris Stella* team and the two rescuers headed in different directions.

~ ~ ∞ ~ ~

On the *Nod*, Austen and Drew sat next to each other. Austen was curious about the former chief. Why did he abandon his post? Well, not *abandon*; it was a civil position. What made him quit and leave so abruptly — without notice? Especially since the station was short-handed and struggling to regain normalcy after the Diak menace.

She opened the conversation. "I'm so sorry about Dr. Jameson. Were you close?"

He stared at the shuttle deck. "Yeah. There was a time when Doc, Fitz, and I were as close as friends get, or I thought so anyway. When I look back, I still can't believe it all fell apart the way it did. How did Doc die?"

"It. . . was gruesome, but very quick. I'm sure she felt nothing. The Diak beheaded her right in front of us. Everyone in the compound was present, including Toby. We kept him from seeing the act itself. Still, the boy's had to handle so much. He's a good kid."

"A great kid. This year has turned out horrific for everyone, but more for him. He should be sitting in a padded room somewhere rocking back and forth and sucking his thumb."

"Some people are born survivors."

"Yes. . . *some* people."

"I don't mean to get personal — well it is personal. But if you don't mind my asking, there've been rumors about you and Miss Taleen. . .?

Drew smiled. "Not true. We went through some stuff together. It never really panned out as more than partners in crime. Sometimes literally." His smile broadened.

"Travis?"

"You caught that did you? As I understand it, they've been off and on since college. Looks like it's *on* again. I'm happy for them both, and especially for Toby. He worships Travis."

"Toby seems to have lots of worship to spread around: Travis, *you* obviously, Nikko, and surprisingly — to me anyway — Curtis." She lowered her voice and glanced at Curtis sitting at the far end of the row opposite them. "I cannot figure that man out. He defies definition."

Drew laughed aloud. "He's a brainteaser all right. He's what you call multidimensional."

Olcott's announcement came over the speakers. "Prepare for docking. Helmets on; weapons up." Then, quickly followed with, "Wait. . . belay that."

The *Nod* reversed thrusters and backed away from the station.

~ ~ ∞ ~ ~

Travis ran after Van Buren as they barreled along the corridor toward the hostage enclosures. Weapons drawn, they headed straight at the next hatch. It dissolved in front of them. They passed through three enclosures without slowing. Aliens lined the invisiwall barriers. Some tried to gain their attention, but they could do little for them.

The excitement in the Alliance enclosures when the two appeared was uncontained. While the humans and, though more subdued, the Bahdaneians cheered at seeing them, the Bin rapped their opposable pincers against the hard shells protecting the back of their necks. The male Camdu openly wept while the women embraced and calmed them. Only the Fahdeen greeted their return silently, but their flop ears stiffened and arched forward in apparent pleasure. Travis' stomach sank as waves of shame and compassion overcame him. Their expectation of rescue would soon shatter.

They went to the Bahdane enclosure first, expecting to use their blasters to open the hatch, but it opened at their approach. Travis and Van Buren exchanged concerned glances. If all of the enclosures were unsealed and the hostages could just walk out, the environment could never adjust to their individual needs.

Van Buren cocked his head. "I believe the hatches are operable only from the exterior, or there would be chaos already."

Travis nodded.

Van Buren stepped into the airlock and the interior hatch opened. Two Bahdaneians came forward and exchanged hums. After a moment, one calmly retreated back into the enclosure while the second stayed in the airlock, Travis assumed to keep the hatch from closing again.

"I have told them to select fifty," Van Buren said. "We will ask the Earthlings to do the same."

When Travis entered the human enclosure, a woman greeted him. "I'm Justine. We are so happy to see you. Did the others make it?"

"Yes, they're safe." *At least that much was true.* Though *safe* was a relative term. "There's a Bahdane transport ship waiting to take more hostages, and we know of at least two smaller Earth ships docked on the station we can use if you have pilots."

Justine became animated. "Yes, we have a pilot—but only one." She turned and called into the crowd behind her, "Ashmore, come here." A tall man broke from the others and came to stand beside her.

"Okay," Travis addressed Justine. "We can only take fifty at a time. So, pick the first group as quickly as you can." She immediately returned to the compound.

Travis looked at Ashmore. "There are at least two Earth ships docked here. I don't know how many passengers they each hold, but none of the captured ships are large. Take a group of, say, twenty with you. The station is circular with berths around its center—perhaps hundreds of them. Look for Earth ships. If you meet mushrooms along the way, immediately attack and try to gouge out their eyes under their caps."

"Which way do I start?" Ashmore asked. "Should we come back here if we can't find them?"

"Yes," Travis diverted his gaze to watch Justine organize the first group. He couldn't look the man in the eye. "Every passageway on this station curves. The Earth ships are roughly docked on the opposite side from where we are now. Don't ask how to get there from here—I don't know. I'm sorry."

In a few minutes, a hundred hostages made up of Bahdaneians and humans were selected and gathered in a group, waiting.

"We're going to be gone for several hours," Travis told Justine as the others listened.

"How many hours?"

"Hard to say for sure. Work with the Bahdane to free as many of the Alliance races as possible. Send any pilots to look for ships. Use your best judgment about letting the Fahdeen out. They should be able to handle the environment for short periods. I don't know about the Camdulings." He wanted to say more, but there wasn't a lot more he could tell her, and he was rambling. "We'll be back as soon as possible," he lied and locked his jaws to prevent showing the anguish coursing through him.

40 HARD TRUTH

Sar Mode hoped she had made the correct decision in selecting the older woman as her host. She could not switch again. The child's death had raised suspicions. If they survived to reach Dark Landing, she would lure a crewman somewhere that the woman's body would remain undiscovered for a time.

She'd overheard conversations between the one they called Grabe and others in the crew. Somehow Travis Barnes had disabled the ship's scanner, but Grabe was close to repairing it. He had to be stopped. She opened the door into the scanner room, and he looked up from the monitor.

"Hello. I was wondering if I might be of assistance. I was once a robotics engineer." She crowded close to him to view the screen he was studying.

Grabe looked startled and took a step to the side to put more space between them. "Thank you, ma'am, I appreciate the offer. But I jus' about got it done. I'm runnin' the final tests now."

"Yes, I see." She made a quarter turn to face him full on and extended her hand. "I'm Ethel Grace. It is a pleasure to meet you." They still stood uncomfortably close, and Grabe took another step away to shake her hand. As he did, she ran a finger of her other hand gently around a drive port at the monitor's edge.

Grabe frowned. "If you'll stand back just a hair, I'll finish up here and you can be my test subject. How 'bout that?"

"Excellent. While you finish, could you direct me to the latrine?"

"The one off the salon is likely got a line. The hatch at the end of this corridor is to my personal quarters. It's unsealed. You're welcome to use the one there."

"You are very kind. Thank you." Sar Mode left the examination room. She'd delivered the nanoids. It would take only a few Earth minutes for the installation process to complete.

~ ~ ∞ ~ ~

Rear Admiral Sullivan called Treetop into his office on Spud. The captain, fairly new to the battalion, was proving to be one of his best officers, requiring little oversight. Sullivan's orders were generally relayed indirectly, and the captain appeared understandably agitated at being summoned away from his command with an alien armada surrounding their location. "Captain Thomas. . . may I call you Tristian?"

"I'd rather you didn't, sir. In my experience, it's never good when your commanding officer calls you by your first name."

"Right," Sullivan smiled at Thomas' attempt to lessen the tension with humor. "We've been ordered by Sir James Hawking-Barstow to stand down. We are not to return fire should the Diak attack." Captain Thomas opened his mouth to speak, but the admiral went on quickly. "You may well ask why, but I don't know."

Several seconds passed as Captain Thomas stared back at the admiral, as if waiting for the punch line. "Yes, sir," he finally said, saluted, and without waiting to be dismissed, made a neat turn toward the office hatch.

"By the way. . ." Sullivan called out as the captain was leaving, ". . . fuck Sir James Hawking-Barstow *and* the EDC."

Captain Thomas turned back.

Admiral Sullivan closed his eyes and rubbed a hand roughly over his face. He opened his desk drawer and removed a flask of Glenfiddich.

~ ~ ∞ ~ ~

The combined group of hostages hugged the bulkheads as they made their way to the dock and the Bahdane troop carrier. At the cross passage that Travis took earlier, a single mushroom exited in front of them. Without facial features, it was difficult to tell if the alien was as startled as they were. Before it could turn and flee, Van Buren fired, lopping off a large chunk of the alien's cap. Without a sound, it toppled like a tree in the forest. If there were more mushrooms behind it, they retreated out of sight. The group closed in on the dock without further incident.

McDermott contacted them. "We're striking out for the wormhole now. Let us know when you're safely away. Come as far as you can. The *Mayzie* will hang back to give you a tow if it's out of your range. We'll wait on the other side."

The troop ship had stacked seating, sixty above and forty below, with a small airlock and head aft on the lower level. The hostages were still strapping in as Van Buren maneuvered the ship out of the dock and headed toward the coordinates McDermott provided.

Travis took the navigator's station. "Do you think we can make it that far?"

"Yes. Close."

They settled in for the trip without further conversation. Travis could think of nothing but the thousands of beings left on Mass Primary to die. Three hours passed in silence except for the soft mumbling of the hostages in the background, when Van Buren announced they were being followed.

"Ashmore! Can they catch up?" Travis asked.

"I believe not. But it is possible they have greater range than our ship. I am hailing them, but they are not responding."

"It has to be Ashmore."

"Perhaps."

"Who else can it be?"

"Only *Muck* knows. But it is wise to stay alert," Van Buren cautioned.

"Do we have weapons?"

"No."

Tedious hours later, as they approached the wormhole, the ship following them had closed the distance to about ninety minutes. Lost in his own dark thoughts, Van Buren's booming voice brought Travis fully aware.

"We are within five klicks of the wormhole. The *Mayzie* is waiting to assist us through. They are asking if they should wait for the ship that follows us as well."

"It has to be Ashmore, but why doesn't he answer your hails?"

"I have thought about this," Van Buren said. "Ashmore is lacking voice recognition to access ship's communications. I believe it is safe to assume he is the pilot."

Travis studied the command screen where the trailing ship became visible, clearly of Earth design. "I vote yea; we wait for him." As he spoke, the scene on the monitor changed. The ship was now a dark spot on a canvas of blinding light. The carrier's sensors automatically applied a filter to lessen the glare. With the filter enabled, the canvas behind Ashmore's ship altered once more to a swirling mixture of heated gas and vaporized solids moving at incredible speed. Travis felt as if he'd been kicked in the gut. Mass Primary was gone, and thousands of hostages representing varied galaxies and solar systems, including the Alliance planets, were gone as well. He focused on the screen.

The Earth ship absorbed a massive level of energy and splintered as if billions of needles pierced it at once. With no atmosphere to slow it, the gas cloud, having devoured Ashmore and his hostages, sped toward them. Travis suddenly realized the carrier's klaxon was wailing, and the ship's computer announced a rapid rise in cabin heat. The panicked shouts of their passengers added to the clamor.

The screen image flicked to the forward view, and a text translation of the *Mayzie's* verbal advisory scrolled across the bottom of the monitor: *Going through ahead of you.*

Travis and Van Buren watched the screen as the *Mayzie* disappeared into the wormhole. They were still three klicks out.

41 MOMENTUM

The Crateris II system had changed since their last visit. The vibrant system they'd first found teeming with ships scurrying from one point to the next now appeared almost devoid of traffic. And the swaths of light they'd observed on the mushroom-inhabited moon had shrunk to small puddles and infrequent specks of glitter.

The *Maris Stella* moved a judicious distance from the wormhole. On the bridge, Letty impatiently listened to McDermott's and Turrey's chatter while they waited for the other ships.

"Three of the four nano-probes I launched last time are still amassing data," Turrey reported. "They've detected our signal and are up-dumping now. But it'll take a while to unpack and decode."

"I'm damn curious to know what the data—"

"How much longer can we wait for the Bahdane transport. . . and the *Remarkable Mayzie*?" Letty interrupted McDermott.

"About four more hours. If they haven't come through by then, I'll have Olcott and the *Nod* stay here while we replenish our water supply. If they're still a no show, we'll let Olcott catch up and then go on to WH5."

Letty nodded, but tears streamed down both cheeks.

"He'll show," McDermott said softly and introduced a new topic. "Grabe thought he had the scanner back up, but it pissed out again. Can't reboot—blank screen. No response. Make what you will of it, there's nothing to be done"

When neither Letty nor Turrey responded, the captain let the topic die.

~ ~ ∞ ~ ~

The Diak ships completely surrounded Dark Landing and Spud. But other than the occasional shift in position — which kept everyone on edge — they hadn't fired a shot or made a move to board either installation.

Captain Thomas perused the security command center, his gaze lingering a few seconds on each staff member. For the most, they were scared, perilously close to panic. This was not what they'd signed up for. CoachStop never trained them to defend the station against attack — they were a mix of cops and traffic controllers. The paltry few with military backgrounds proved easy to spot. Instead of repeated rounds of nervous glances between one another and back at Thomas, they stood calmly at their posts and observed their monitors, taking occasional sips of coffee. Thomas knew many of the coffees were laced with something stronger.

On the large screen, he watched as one Diak ship fell back to be replaced by another. Out of the corner of his eye, a woman tensed at the movement and hunched over her monitor in apparent anticipation of an order from Thomas or a more aggressive move by the Diak. Her head swung anxiously back and forth between him and her station. Somebody would lose it soon.

"Eyes on me," Captain Thomas ordered the room. When he had everyone's attention, he slowly withdrew his blaster from its holster for all to see and lifted it above his head, its barrel pointing at the upper deck. "I will shoot the first person who acts without orders. I won't ask questions. I won't hesitate. I won't worry about consequences. And neither will you because you'll be dead. Am. . . I. . . *clear*?"

A few heads nodded, but most stood immobile. The ex-military reacted with slow blinks, like bored sloth. Mitchell Jones returned a wearied gaze with a hint of a smile.

"So, spaceout!" Thomas screamed at them like a drill instructor. Everyone jumped and then relaxed in the knowledge that someone competent was in charge. He even heard a couple feeble chuckles. Thomas continued in a more conversational tone as he re-holstered his weapon. "I want a workstation diagnostic report from each of you in ten minutes."

As soon as Thomas relaxed, confident he'd defused the tension in the room, four of the Diak gunships peeled off from the main body. He tapped for Admiral Sullivan.

Sullivan responded immediately from his end. "Yeah, we see. Hold a sec. . . ."

The control room filled with mumbled chatter. "Quiet everyone. Watch your stations and let me know if another of their ships so much as wobbles."

Sullivan came back on the comm. "Captain?"

"Yes, sir."

"They're heading out toward the mining sector. We still have patrols out that way searching for the wormhole; I've alerted them. I have a feeling that's exactly where those four ships are going."

~ ~ ∞ ~ ~

"In the back!" Van Buren roared. "Someone seal that airlock hatch." When he detected no movement behind him, the Bahdane roared again, louder, "Now!" The screen displayed the approaching energy field.

Travis watched the rendering on the control panel as the red line representing the interior airlock hatch slowly lowered into place. The swirling wall caught up with them before the line turned green to indicate the hatch was sealed. The ship was violently buffeted side-to-side. The entire panel lit with flashing lights. As they entered the wormhole aperture, all of the lights in the carrier extinguished but for a single panel alert: *Systems down*. When that light blinked out as well, they were left in a blackness that Travis had experienced only once before, deep in the caverns under the Archone Mountain Range on Camdu. Without life controls, he could feel the temperature dropping, though the control panel had read a dangerous forty-three degrees Celsius only a second earlier.

"Do we have the momentum to carry us through?" Travis asked.

Van Buren remained silent.

They secured their helmets.

~ ~ ∞ ~ ~

The *Nod* was departing the mother ship when the sensors registered the *Remarkable Mayzie* exiting the wormhole, followed by the second Bahdaneian vessel.

"Hail the *Mayzie*," McDermott said.

"No response, sir. Comms are out—other systems are spotty—in and out. Her engine must have gone offline. It's powering up now."

"And the Bahdane transport?"

"She's dead. I'm getting a few life signs, but weak. The sensor can't differentiate individuals. Seems they're crammed in close together. Heat readings are fluctuating, but could be as many as fifty or more, and cooling fast."

"Turrey, keep hailing the *Mayzie*. Olcott, head to the transport ship," McDermott ordered.

"On it," Olcott replied.

"Can you dock with her?" he asked.

Turrey interrupted, "Her engines are damaged, and the aft hatch is askew. I can't tell if the airlock is sealed shipside, but life support's offline."

Letty glanced hopefully at Turrey. "If the *Nod* docks with the transport can the *Blinkum* tow them yoked together?"

"Maybe." Turrey deferred to McDermott. "Should we go too?"

"No. Hold our position. Whacker. . . can you—"

"Suiting up now, sir."

"Whacker, make a visual run past the *Remarkable Mayzie* to check for damage. Olcott, dock with the Bahdane transport ship. With a tight enough seal, you can share oxygen. Whacker will tow you both back here."

"The heat signatures are weakening fast on the transport," Turrey reported, solemnly.

"*Travis*," Letty murmured.

~ ~ ∞ ~ ~

"I'm going back there," Travis said.

Van Buren nodded slowly as he studied the planetary system through the view port. Dazzling light filled the forward cabin, but the back remained in shadow. Travis activated his helmet light, unstrapped, and lifted weightless from the navigator seat. He flipped around and pushed off; afraid of what he would find only a few feet away. Motionless shapes filled the troop seats. On his wrist display, the cabin now registered minus twenty-seven degrees Celsius and falling. No oxygen remained. Most of the seats in the lower compartment were occupied by humans.

He moved down the center aisle. Empty eyes stared at him as he passed, while others were closed in a death grimace. Arms, hair, and bits of clothing floated eerily above and around their bodies. In the middle of the third row, the corner of a woman's mouth appeared to tic. When he shone his light directly on her face, an eyeball twitched under the blue lid. He uncoiled the hose secured to the front of his EMU for sharing oxygen. The ship jerked violently.

"What was that?" Travis asked Van Buren.

"I don't know. It may be another ship, but I did not see —" He stopped speaking abruptly.

Travis' comm purred the name, Aisha Olcott. "Olcott?! Thank the stars." He listened as he continued to uncoil the hose.

"I'm right next to you on the *Nod*," Aisha said. "One sec, and we'll be docked."

The hose freed, Travis manually broke the seal and placed his thumb over the end. The hose was meant to connect to another suit and there was no mouthpiece. He pressed his hand firmly over the woman's mouth and nose, allowing his ring and middle finger to loosen just enough to push the hose through, and then closed the fingers as tight as he could to hold it in place. The cabin wrenched violently again as the *Nod* completed docking. Travis hooked one foot under a seat frame to hold him down, and with his free hand he pushed hard on the woman's chest, relieved when she took a shallow breath. He was torn. He couldn't leave her, but what if others were still alive who needed oxygen as well?

"We're good," Olcott announced. "I'm coming over."

"Can't raise the hatch — no power," Travis said.

"Is there a manual override?"

"Maybe, but it's not visible from where I am. I'm sharing oxygen with a survivor."

"Leave him. Once the hatch is open, I'll pump in air from the *Nod*. How many to transport?"

Travis paused, eyes closed, before answering. "Not many—maybe three—maybe more. I don't know." The gravity of their situation was apparent in his tone.

Van Buren bumped him as he pushed past. "I will open the hatch."

It'd been four minutes since Olcott first hailed them. *Anyone else is gone by now,* Travis thought. He watched as Van Buren used the manual release and opened the hatch. Two figures filled the airlock, both with their helmet torches on. Travis glanced at his gauge. The oxygen level was slowly rising. He removed the hose from the woman's mouth and went to the next row of passengers.

Van Buren let the *Nod* crew pass him. "I am going above," he said.

Olcott and her crewman checked for survivors on the opposite side of the aisle from Travis.

After several more minutes, Van Buren returned shaking his head. Travis found no survivors in the last row and went back to the woman, who was conscious and freezing. Ice crystals formed each time she exhaled.

"Another one," Olcott yelled.

She and her companion huddled over a man who looked to be in his mid-twenties.

"We've got to get them both on the *Nod* now," Travis said. "They won't last much longer."

Olcott agreed. "Right. That's all, just these two?"

Travis nodded.

"Okay, let's go." She turned to Van Buren, motioning to her crewmate. "Can you help Gavin with—"

Van Buren gently pushed Olcott out of his way and unstrapped the unconscious man. He held the weightless body against his own and moved toward the hatch. Travis and Gavin followed, guiding the frightened woman between them. On the *Nod*, with gravity induced, they laid them on the benches installed on each side of the shuttle, and Olcott ordered Gavin to seal the interior hatch and separate from the other ship.

Before Gavin could do as he was asked, Van Buren shouldered past him into the open hatchway. "I am not coming with you."

"W-what do you mean?" Travis stuttered. "There's no one still alive."

"I must accompany them on their journey. It is our way."

"Sorry," Olcott said. "I can't allow that."

Without a word more, Van Buren turned and crossed the short passage that connected the two ships. The other three exchanged glances, uncertain what to do.

"Captain McDermott? We have a problem."

Travis wasn't privy to McDermott's side of the conversation.

Olcott explained. After a moment, she said, "But we can't just leave him. Yes, sir, but—yes, sir." She was silent for a few seconds as the other two watched, rapt.

Finally, quietly, "Gavin, seal us in and disconnect."

When Travis moved to object again, she turned and walked forward, head down. "Alliance terms—we must respect each other's cultures and customs."

42 DEAD DUCKS

The *Maris Stella*, with her two shuttles onboard and the *Remarkable Mayzie* alongside, proceeded to the water depot and WH5. The passengers and crew silently mourned their losses.

Travis, heart sickened at all that had happened, and equally sickened by what was yet to come, watched the old lady. He'd heard her thanking a crewman for the offer of his seat. She spoke with the same voice as Sar Mode when she'd warned him about Mass Primary's imminent detonation. He shuddered. Now the scanner was permanently down. Her work, or his? Would she infect everyone on board? Or would she abide by her agreement with Sir James?

The woman. . . Ethel. . . sat huddled at the end of a salon lounger, frail, seemingly lost in thought—ignored by everyone but him. As he stared, the corners of her mouth curved ever so slightly into a self-satisfied, feline smile.

Travis needed Letty and the comfort that came from simply being with her. Instead, he sought the companionship and distraction of a strategy session with Aisha Olcott and Whacker. The temptation to selfishly confess everything to Letty was too great.

~ ~ ∞ ~ ~

Toby was hungry, but he resisted his stomach's rumblings. Propped against the bar, he sat on the deck hugging his legs, and watched Travis watch some old lady. *What the hells? For sure he doesn't want to* kiss *her.* He made a face. *Maybe she reminds him of his mom.* At the thought, a pain squeezed his chest and his eyes stung. He blinked the moisture away before tears could form. He still missed his folks a lot.

Drew and Curtis were in a corner with Austen, their heads close together. He knew they were talking about Oscar and Justine and everybody else on *Mass Primary* who died. He wasn't going to think about that or about Doc anymore. Letty and Drew, and Travis, even Curtis and Nikko—they were his team of warriors, like in his game, *Protectors of the Verse.* They'd all be back on Dark Landing in no time.

But Drew wasn't paying any attention to Letty, and that worried Toby. Without canker-Xander around, he looked for signs Drew and Letty might like each other again. *Where is that. . . pestiperus. . . pestif. . .* boob? Unable to remember the word Chief Hargreaves used, he settled for a lesser insult.

He got up and sauntered over to the group. "Hey, guys."

"Hey, kid," Curtis said and offered his usual greeting. "'Sup?"

Drew reached out to push Toby's hair off his forehead. Austen gave Drew a sideways glance that clearly read, *good luck.*

Toby ducked away. "I was jus' wonderin'—where's that boob, Xander Crawford?"

"You miss him?" Drew asked, with an amazed look.

"Shi—*shoot* no! Just hopin' he got spaced, that's all."

Drew laughed. "You're not that far off. He stayed on Dark Landing."

"Knew he was a coward."

"Whatever," Drew said, eyes hooded.

"I don't suppose you and Letty are getting together?" He tried to appear unconcerned one way or the other.

Curtis looked nearly as eager to hear the answer as Toby.

"Doesn't look like it," Drew said.

"Hmm. . . ." Toby puckered his mouth in feigned indifference. "But you might want to ask Travis that question."

His delight was obvious. "Yeah, okay, I'll do that now."

The three laughed at him as he crossed the salon to talk with Travis.

~ ~ ∞ ~ ~

"Okay, that's three dead ships. Something's happened here for sure," McDermott said, just as Drew and Letty checked in on the bridge. He was studying the screen with a perplexed expression.

At the nav station, Turrey ran yet another series of scans. He sat back in his seat. "That ship *seems* dead, but our scanner report is contradictory. No life signs, no heat signatures one minute, then there's a blip of something the next. Its shields are on a weird frequency; we're not getting a clear read."

"It's like their floater broke down on the side of the bestway and they abandoned it. Except," McDermott said, his eyes still on the screen, "that's one hell of a big floater — and they weren't out for a Sunday drive. I wonder what kind of cargo it's hauling."

"How far to the water depot?" Letty asked.

"Couple hours." McDermott looked to Turrey for confirmation.

"Can we break out one of the shuttles to take a look while we continue on? It's close enough they can catch up."

"I'd feel better knowing what the hell happened here. It's worth checking out," McDermott said. "I'll send Whacker and Barnes over."

Drew caught Letty's wince at the mention of Barnes. "If there's no crucial reason for sending Travis, do you mind if I go instead?"

"No reason. . . you can if you want." McDermott shot a quick glance at Letty. She stayed quiet. "After all, you're my most dispensable expendable."

Drew laughed. "And it's been my honor, sir."

When they'd suited up, Whacker piloted the *Blinkum* toward the alien cargo ship. The *Maris Stella* continued on her way. Drew congratulated himself for feeling only a second's twinge of queasiness at the sight of the larger ship's departure. No need for "Jabberwocky."

Whacker mused out loud on the changes in the system from their previous visit. "It's spooo-*ky*. With all the traffic last time, we were just one more ship in the mix. Now it's a necropolis — ships floating dead like coffins."

Drew nodded his agreement. "How do we get on board?"

"I'll blow the hatch."

"But. . . if there *are* living beings inside?"

"Don't think so," Turrey transmitted. The *Maris Stella* was still within comm distance.

"Besides," Whacker added, "the atmosphere flow between the two ships will be negligible, and I've got a *Quick-Patch* handy if it's needed."

The *Blinkum* made a pass close to the ghost ship. As proved common among larger vessels regardless of the planet of origin, a smaller emergency access was set into the much larger cargo hatch. Based on its design, these aliens were on the tall side. Cargo holds tended to be two levels high across the spectrum—averaging seven-and-a-half meters deck-to-deck. This one was at least fifteen meters. And the security hatch was much taller than average, as well.

Whacker expertly maneuvered the little shuttle into position with its aft nearly flush against the other ship. "Helmet on. Cabin depressurizing."

Drew secured his helmet as Whacker extended the hatchway, stretching it to fully encircle the opposite, alien hatch. When the control panel confirmed the seal was holding, both men checked their blasters and moved to the rear of the shuttle. Whacker pulled a self-contained "popper" from a sack attached to his tool belt. It took three, each ball-shaped but with one flat side, and twice the size of his fist. Two he positioned over the hatch bolts and the third where he estimated the access control to be. Then he pushed Drew back a few feet and counted. "*Three. . . two. . . one—*" The balls simultaneously popped off the hatch and fell to the deck. The metal surfaces where each had been attached were etched white around jagged holes that exposed what lay beyond.

"I need some help here," Whacker said.

Drew moved next to him. It took several awkward jerks to remove the hatch and wrestle it aside. They repeated the process with the interior hatch and stepped through into the huge cargo hold. Both men immediately checked their wrist gauges.

"Gravity's not an issue," Whacker said. "A little light—just makes us a bit more bounc—*ho-ly mistress. . .* how is that even possible?"

"Problem?" McDermott asked.

"No, sir. Just a sec. . . ."

"Hard to believe, isn't it? Lucky for us there's a disposable guinea pig on the team." Drew unsealed his helmet and took a deep breath. "So far, so good."

"I think I'll give you ten minutes more," Whacker said.

"Ye of little faith. *Captain*, our gauges are reading a perfect mix of oxygen, nitrogen, with trace amounts of the other gases. It tastes just like air to me. . . the smell is a bit off. . . ."

"Huh? Losing you. Take car —" The captain's voice cut out.

Ignoring the loss of contact with the mother ship, Whacker narrowed his eyes and stared at Drew for a few seconds. Drew finally narrowed his own eyes and returned the stare with mocking intensity. Whacker shook it off. "Okay, let's check out the cargo bay before we go any further. Look for anything edible." Helmet still sealed, he turned left and moved in among an assortment of containers and bundles.

"Just so you know," Drew called, as he veered to the right, "I'm not putting anything we find in my mouth."

"Oh, ye of little faith. *Shit!* Cutter, c'mere."

"What? You find something *already*?"

"You might say that."

Drew crossed to join Whacker in the walkway between the first and second row of stacked goods on that side. The deck and nearby cartons were covered in a clotted layer of purple goo. A few feet further down the aisle lay a jagged piece of tentacle.

"Mushrooms," the two men said in unison.

Drew wrinkled his nose. "That explains the odd smell."

"Maybe we should check the rest of the ship first," Whacker suggested.

Blasters in hand, they proceeded through the open hatch leading into the ship's interior. A few meters in, they found the splattered residue from a second mushroom, discernable by the purple hue. They passed galley and common areas with only cursory glances. Without finding anything further on the lower level, they followed ramps that led two levels upward. Drew continued to note the ship's design. The corridors and hatchways narrowed at the deck but grew wider above to accommodate the mushrooms' caps, he guessed. When they reached what they thought must be the bridge, they found the hatch closed and sealed.

"Do you have more poppers?" Drew asked.

"A couple, but I think we know what we'll find inside. I say we head back to the cargo bay and use the time left to search for food. I'm convinced there's no crew alive on this ship, and if there is, we'd probably have to kill them anyway. What's the point?"

They retraced their steps down the ramp. Halfway back they came face-to-face with a very alive mushroom.

~ ~ ∞ ~ ~

The *Maris Stella* docked at the water depot without challenge. They'd passed two more ghost ships en route. With their water store replenished, the ship moved off a short distance to wait for the *Blinkum*.

Letty and Travis sat together in the salon on one end of a lounger and talked. Nearby, Toby perched, legs crossed, on the bar countertop, entrenched in a game of chess with Billy Grabe. A mix of hostages and crew lay sprawled across the remaining furniture and deck; some were quietly engaged in conversation as others slept.

An occasional tear slipped down Letty's cheeks.

"Sweetheart, you're crying *again*?" Travis asked, wearing an amused expression.

"I'm just so happy you're alive. And Toby's alive. But I'm scared, and confused, and—"

Travis reached over and gently massaged the back of her neck.

She relaxed her muscles and let her head drop forward. "Mmm. . . that feels wonderful. Your massages were always the best."

"Just the massages?" His amused expression gone, he studied her in earnest.

She lifted her head at the solemn tone of his voice. "Travis, I. . . I don't know what to say. I've made so many mistakes. And there's something I need to tell you. Do you remember Xander?"

He waved his hand in dismissal. "Toby filled me in about Xander Crawford. We both know Xander is an idiot. What were you thinking? That was *never* going to happen. My real concern is Cutter."

Letty was unable to hold his gaze while she contemplated what Drew meant to her. She turned to watch Toby and Grabe just as Toby made a fist-pump and moved a piece off the board. Grabe slapped his forehead in feigned alarm. Letty smiled. She knew for a fact, Grabe was a chess grandmaster.

"Drew?" Travis prompted.

She took a few moments longer before returning her attention to him. "I love Drew. But—it's so hard to explain—it's all tied up with the time we spent together, Dad's death, and the death of others. He kept me sane. I needed him." As soon as she said it, she knew Travis would take it the wrong way.

"I *wanted* to be there for you, Letty. But you kept everything from me."

"No. . . no. . . I didn't mean it that way. You would have been there in a second if I'd asked; or, even if I didn't ask. If you'd known what was going on." She rested her hand against his cheek for a moment. "I needed Drew for more than emotional support." That made it worse. With a sigh, she started over. "Everything that happened was about Dark Landing. And Drew *was* Dark Landing— and still is if you ask me. Anyway, we were only together once." She failed to mention that the *once* was days ago. "And things have changed since then. I've learned. . . we've both learned that we're too different. Except for Toby; Drew cares about Toby. It's important that they continue to be a part of each other's lives."

"I get it about Drew and Toby, but I need absolute clarity, Letty. What does this mean for us?"

What does it mean? Talking about it now forced her to admit the truth to herself. She loved both men equally. But Travis was the obvious choice. She faced too many obstacles with Drew: his uncompromising values, for one—refusing to consider extenuating circumstances—and *her* ambitions versus *his* complacency. If not for Toby she'd be at her desk sixteen hours out of every day. Travis would understand that. And then there was Dark Landing. How long would Drew be happy in San Francisco, really? He'd grow to resent her.

Before Letty could answer Travis, Toby plopped down between them. "Hey you guys. Are you as hungry as I am?" He swiveled his head from one to the other, and then evidently realizing he'd interrupted a meaningful conversation, jumped back to his feet. "Gotta pee. See ya." And he took off as quickly as he'd come.

The tension broken, Letty and Travis laughed. She reached over and took his hand. "Travis, if you can forgive me for being so stupid, I want to be with you. All along, it should have been the two of us. You know, when I think about it, we never officially split up, just took a break to focus on our careers. And. . . maybe I lost my way for a little bit."

All signs of anxiety disappeared from Travis' face and posture. He squeezed her hand and his eyes darkened. It was a look Letty remembered well. "How long till the next command meeting?" he asked.

"As long as I say — I'm the boss."

They got up and headed toward her suite, holding hands. Toby was standing in a corner of the room, leaning against the bulkhead, his feet crossed nonchalantly at the ankles. As they passed, he winked and gave Travis a thumbs-up.

"*Toby!*" Letty chided.

43 A NEW ALLIANCE

Drew was a split second from firing his blaster when Whacker laid a hand on his arm. "Don't shoot unless it unfurls its tentacle. It doesn't appear to have a weapon." They moved back a few steps from the creature and as far apart from each other as the narrow passageway allowed. The mushroom stayed put, but it tilted its cap back to expose its eyes — four of them. "Cover me," Whacker said.

Drew raised his blaster, holding the butt with his free hand to steady it. At his new stance, the alien jerked its cap and turned a bright pink. All four eyes widened.

Whacker holstered his own weapon and raised his hands in the surrender position. Two of the mushroom's eyes slid toward Whacker, while the other two stayed focused on Drew. The effect was comical. Drew laughed, more from nervous tension than amusement.

"We don't want to hurt you," Whacker said. When the mushroom failed to react, he turned to Drew, "What do you think we should do?"

"This sounds crazy, I know, but what if we capture it and take it back with us? Maybe we can figure a way to communicate with it. Find out what's happening over here. Curtis and Nikko said they saw a compound filled with these guys on Mass Primary. This one seems pretty passive."

"Passive. . . terrified — it's all semantics. Should we tie it up?"

"Maybe. There might be something in the hold we can use. Let's see how well it cooperates. You lead the way, and I'll try and get it to follow."

Whacker, hands still in the air, turned sideways to move around the mushroom. The alien sidled to one side to let him by. Its pink hue deepened to magenta. A few feet ahead of the mushroom, Whacker lowered his hands.

Drew motioned with his blaster and took a step toward the creature. It dropped its cap and swung around. Whacker backed several steps farther down the passage. The mushroom followed. When they reached the cargo bay, Drew asked, "Now what?"

"We still need food." With his free hand, Whacker made eating motions. The mushroom stared at him. Whacker rubbed his stomach. "Mmm. . . ."

Slowly — obviously aware any move was a dangerous one — the mushroom raised the tip of its tentacle to the top of its cap and rubbed.

Whacker made a face, wrinkling his nose at the smell, and sealed his helmet.

"This could take all day," Drew said. "I'll hold it here while you check containers."

"Right." He moved to Drew's side of the aisle. "My section's a little messy, remember?"

Whacker found two containers of grain similar to wheat and one container of brown, gooey stuff that looked like shit but, with his helmet opened again, had an appetizing odor. When he rolled that container up to the front, the mushroom reacted by rubbing its cap again and hesitantly directing its tentacle at Whacker's mouth.

Whacker loaded the three containers onto the *Blinkum* while Drew kept the mushroom at blaster point. Drew wanted to relax his shooting arm but was afraid the alien might be more cunning than it looked and was waiting for just such an opportunity. He smiled at the mushroom instead, careful not to show his teeth. "Mind if I call you Ruby?"

Once they'd safely stowed the cargo on the *Blinkum*, Drew motioned to the hatchway. The mushroom hesitated and turned its cap to look at the open hatch back into the ship, giving every appearance of considering its options. Finally, it ducked down and followed Whacker into the shuttle with Drew close behind. Drew motioned to the bench along one side, but again it just stared back at him. He motioned again, sitting down on the opposite bench. It extended its tentacle and wrapped it around a bench strut but remained upright.

"I guess that'll have to do, Ruby," Drew said. He strapped in, blaster still in hand.

Whacker used a *Quick-Patch* to seal off the alien ship and then secured the shuttle's hatch. "*Ruby?*" he said as he passed Drew on the way to the pilot's seat. As soon as they were in range of the *Maris Stella*, Whacker described their cargo to Rob Turrey, who responded with silence. In under a minute, Captain McDermott, Letty, and Travis joined the conversation.

"What were you thinking? There's no place to hold a prisoner on this ship or on the *Mayzie*. I can't imagine how the rescued hostages are going to react," McDermott said.

"I can," Travis said. "You call them mushrooms, I called them Shroomies, and the Diak call them Pothlill. The hostages only knew them as guards, and they're not going to accept one onboard the *Maris Stella* with them."

Drew offered McDermott a solution. "Look, we can lock it in my quarters. I'll find someplace else to sleep."

Travis mumbled another aside that Drew missed.

"Maybe we should question it and then space it," Letty suggested.

"*Jesus Chr —* "

Whacker interrupted Drew's exclamation, "Drew's named it *Ruby*," he said, amused by the situation.

"We'll figure it out when you get here," McDermott ended the transmission.

When the *Blinkum* docked, Drew and Ruby stayed on board while Whacker met with the others. He returned with Aisha Olcott and one of the two surviving Bahdaneians. Olcott sported a nasty looking laser rifle. At the sight, the mushroom once again deepened from rose to magenta. Drew holstered his own weapon and moved to its side. Whacker pressed past the others to sit on the opposite bench and watch the proceedings.

"I've got it from here, Cutter. You can ditch the suit and get something to eat," Olcott said.

"I'm staying."

"That wasn't a suggestion."

"I don't remember taking a vow of obedience."

Olcott sighed and studied him. "Fine. But move over with Whacker."

Drew pressed a hand gently against the mushroom, hoping it recognized the gesture as one of reassurance, and stepped away from its side. The alien shook visibly. At its show of fear, Olcott raised her weapon even higher.

"Your parents must have been proud when you got your merit badge in intimidation," Drew spat.

"Good one," Whacker said just under his breath.

Olcott ignored Drew but shot Whacker a murderous look. She motioned for the Bahdane to come forward. "This is Ma Kai," she said.

For thirty-five minutes, Kai stood in front of Ruby and spoke to it in a series of alien languages, some that sounded to Drew like nothing more than rude noises. Ruby watched him with two eyes, keeping one on Olcott and the fourth on Drew.

Finally, the Bahdane threw up its hands. "There are a thousand more I can try, but I cannot do it standing here. It is my belief that these beings are telepathic. We did not hear one speak on Mass Primary."

Ever so slowly, Ruby extended the tip of its tentacle toward the Bahdane, who stood perfectly still. Olcott tightened her grip on the laser rifle. The mushroom's movement was agonizingly slow, but its tentacle eventually made contact with Kai's forehead, where it rested for several seconds.

The Bahdane's eyes widened. "She is very frightened," he said.

"It told you that?" Drew asked.

"Not in words. I felt her emotions."

"Ruby's a *she* then?"

"Yes, and she is fearful that the one holding the weapon wants to kill her. I do not believe she is a danger to us."

"You got all that from just one touch," Olcott said in derision.

"Yes, she transmitted as much," Kai confirmed.

Olcott held a side conversation with Captain McDermott, after which she ordered Whacker to take the mushroom to Drew's quarters.

"I can keep it?" Drew asked in a mocking tone, like a child asking to keep a puppy.

Whacker gave him a warning shake of his head. It wasn't wise to test Olcott.

Ma Kai followed them out of the *Blinkum*. "I will stay in your quarters with her as a guard and attempt to communicate on a more sophisticated level."

"Where are you sleeping now?" Drew asked.

"On the deck in the medical exam room. The exam table is too small."

"Okay, we'll switch, but I'm taking my pillow."

When they entered the salon, gasps issued from the rescued hostages, who scuttled *en masse* to the side of the room away from Ruby. She stopped and swung her cap back and forth and up and down in seeming distress as she surveyed the room, her eyes rolling in all directions. Her color, which had settled into a medium pink, darkened well past magenta to deep rhubarb.

"What's happening?" Olcott said.

"I don't know." Drew reached out to reassure the alien, but she backed away and then turned, trying to push past Olcott and Whacker as if she wanted to return to the *Blinkum*.

Olcott struck her with the barrel of the laser rifle.

"*Hey!*" Drew took a step toward Olcott.

"Back off. . . it's obvious the creature is afraid of the hostages. Maybe there's a good reason."

Ma Kai, who walked ahead of the group, went back to Ruby and presented his forehead. She raised her shivering tentacle to touch it. Kai, eyes closed, described the exchange. "I am receiving a series of images of various alien species, almost too fast to read: a Bin, one I do not recognize, another, a Bahdane, another, a Fahdeen, an Earth woman. The series repeats. It seems she is equally fearful of each of the aliens presented, but I cannot tell for certain."

"Probably the ones she tortured," Olcott said.

Drew tried to reason with Olcott. "Look, Aisha, we don't know if Ruby was ever on Mass Primary or had anything to do with the Diaks."

Kai shot Drew what appeared to be a warning glance, then quickly looked away.

"She's sure acting guilty," Olcott said.

"Seriously? *Think*—we kidnapped her from a ship where, as far as we can tell, all her mates had died. Then we pointed blasters at her, transported her here, and pushed a Bahdaneian in her face for almost an hour—no offence, Kai. Then we brought her into a room filled with strange beings who reacted like she had the plague. You say *guilt*, I say we finally pushed her over the edge."

Olcott looked furious. "You know, I've had about enough of you, Cutter. And as I recall, you owe me." She motioned to Ma Kai. "Take her to his quarters."

Ma Kai and Drew, each taking one side of the mushroom, ushered her slowly across the salon. Drew noticed Travis for the first time. He stood at the bar, not looking at Ruby, but staring at the huddled hostages wearing as terrified an expression as Ruby was emanating in her own alien way.

Out of Olcott's hearing, Kai said, "The images Ruby shared lead me to believe she may have knowledge of Mass Primary and the Diak."

~ ~ ∞ ~ ~

With the *Maris Stella's* water cistern full to the brim, the ship continued on to WH5. Drew spent the travel time with Ma Kai and Ruby. He was eager to learn about her species, the Pothlill—though that name got no reaction from her—their planetary system, and more importantly, what she knew about the Diak. Since Travis' report that the Diak were once again attacking outposts in the Zeta Quadrant, he grew sick with fear at what they would find if the *Maris Stella* actually made it back home.

He also wanted to avoid the happy couple. Everyone on the ship could tell Travis and Letty were an item again—though most never knew they were an item before. He lay on the bed in his quarters—*old* quarters—tackling his lingering feelings about Travis, while Ma Kai and Ruby stood at the foot of the bed, facing each other, with the tip of Ruby's tentacle resting on Kai's forehead. Neither one had moved in over an hour.

Drew's recent therapy sessions in New Las Vegas taught him to bring strong feelings of fear, depression, anger, confusion—whatever—to the forefront and dissect them. Dig in and figure out what's causing the anxiety instead of trying to bury it, which never worked anyway.

Anger foremost—why? Why was he angry at Travis? Was he envious of him? Not really. Okay, to be honest, he felt some shallow envy. Travis was cool. Everything he did was cool: the way he stood, sat, walked. He had the celebrity *it,* whatever *it* was that caused people to turn their heads when he entered a room, and to grow quiet when he spoke. Was he jealous of Travis' relationship with Letty? Yes—at one time. But not anymore. Drew loved Letty, but was not *in* love with her, of that he now felt certain. Maybe he never was. So, if you remove envy and jealousy from the mix, what's left? Anger. Guilt. He'd been wracked with survivors' guilt since Travis sacrificed his life to save the Known Universe. And fear. Fear that he was a coward. That he should have done something in Travis' stead. *Voilà. I'm getting good at this.* He was angry at the time he'd spent agonizing about Travis' sacrifice. He'd obsessed over his self-assumed cowardness and suffered feelings of irrelevance and inferiority. All that painful angst and those sleepless nights, and the bastard lived. How dare he! *Get a hold of yourself, Drew. You're not a coward, you're not worthless, and you're not suppressing feelings for Letty. You're just an* idiot *on so many levels.*

Ma Kai was speaking to him. "Sorry, what'd you say?"

"I asked you several times if you wished to experience communicating with Ruby?"

"Sure. Does it hurt?"

"Come closer."

He rose and crossed to stand in front of the alien. He'd almost gotten used to the stench that permeated the room. With all four eyes focused on him, she gently touched his forehead. The feeling was strange, but not painful or uncomfortable. Right away he knew he wasn't so much reading her thoughts, as she was *projecting* her thoughts to him. And they weren't complete thoughts, only fragmented feelings and visions. She was hungry. There was an image of the barrel of shit—obviously not shit but food. Drew tried to think of it as chocolate pudding. At that, Ruby's eyes jiggled, and he received a second image: a beige substance that looked a bit like mashed potatoes with a small amount of gravy stirred in. They were tossing food images back and forth. He was beginning to understand the problem Kai faced.

"She wants to eat," he told Kai.

"Yes, she expressed as much to me, as well."

"I say we take her back to the hold where she can have a bowl of. . . food."

"I will fetch the food. We do not want to upset the other hostages or tactical specialist, Aisha Olcott."

"Aisha Olcott can bite me. And the others need to get used to Ruby being here."

"I see. Then I will wait here for you to return."

Drew headed toward the door, turned, and motioned Ruby to follow. One eye shot immediately over to Kai. Kai shrugged. Drew exited the quarters with Ruby close behind. When they entered the salon, everyone in the room, including Letty and Toby, sitting with Travis, watched them. *Except* for Travis and an old lady—who appeared to be transfixed on each other. Drew looked up at Ruby. She was also staring at the old lady, and her color deepened. When they reached the cargo hold, Drew put his hand to his forehead and Ruby touched it. Images of aliens flooded his consciousness, exactly as Kai had described the day before.

44 WATCHERS

The buoy array was down. Nothing stood between the *Maris Stella* and WH5 except a considerably smaller Diak armada than the one they'd recorded on their first foray. But still a crushing force pitted against one armed luxury cruiser, her two shuttles, and an unarmed salvage vessel.

"There's not as much communications traffic," Turrey noted. "And it's not traffic, really, it's just static."

"Is it encrypted?" McDermott asked.

"Maybe. If we were home, I'd say *no*. Something else, sir, if we get a little closer, I can give you exact numbers, but it appears most of the ships are ghost ships. I'm not getting life signs, but we're too far out to be certain."

Aisha Olcott listened to the conversation from the *Nod*, awaiting launch orders to recon the armada for any hole they might slip through. "What if I move in closer and act as a relay between you and the armada to boost the signal?"

"Dangerous—and it still wouldn't be perfect, though better than we're getting now." Turrey said.

McDermott nodded at the console. "Go ahead, Olcott."

Everyone recognized the danger. If the Diak spotted the *Nod* and gave chase, the shuttle stood no chance of outrunning a Diak ship. Olcott would lead them in the opposite direction from the *Maris Stella* to her certain capture or death.

"Ping us when you're ready to transmit," Turrey instructed.

Letty followed the discussion from her usual position at the back of the bridge. "Rob, you said some of the ships seem dead?"

"Yeah. I'm getting no readings from supply or troop ships, or most of the gunships—no static, no movement, nothing."

"Like the civilian ships we've encountered along the way?"

Turrey took his time to answer. He studied the array of screens on his panel and finally offered, "Maybe. The scan results on two of the gunships are distorted, but it looks like they're powering up."

Thirty minutes passed while Turrey slumped against the command and navigation console, waiting patiently. Finally, he sat upright. "She just pinged, Captain—less than twenty klicks out. Redirecting sensor feed through the relay frequency and streaming to main monitor."

"All okay, Olcott?" McDermott asked.

"Yes, sir."

"Keep the relay open and commence your recon. Have you got a position on the ships Turrey noted?"

"I do, sir."

"Anything?" McDermott asked Turrey.

"The *Nod* seems safe; no one's paying any attention to her. Those two gunships still worry me."

Aisha Olcott detoured for over an hour to go wide around the remaining Diak armada. Neither the *Maris Stella* nor its shuttles traveled that far out before. Thankfully, she encountered no other ships.

Watching the *Nod's* live transmission from the *Maris Stella* bridge, McDermott and Turrey could see the inner system's dust ring thinning, and the much denser ring around the second star visible across an open swath of space. Olcott finally turned back toward WH5 and positioned the *Nod* on the backside of the wormhole, using its edge distortion as a camouflage blind.

The armada had spread out, with no single ship within a klick of its neighbor and no two ships on the same plane. The space between ships was designed to be a tactical expedience in the event of an attack; vessels would never be in one another's immediate line of fire. But attacking ships would *always* be vulnerable.

~ ~ ∞ ~ ~

On opposite sides of the salon, Drew and Ma Kai watched Travis furtively watch the old lady, who sat at the end of a lounger with her hands folded in her lap and a wisp of a smile on her face, as if she was recalling an amusing incident. Drew thought she might be senile. He studied her closer; something about her seemed familiar.

Travis sat on the lounger across from the old lady with Letty and Toby, one on each side of him. The three appeared engaged in an animated conversation, but Letty and Toby were oblivious to Travis' distracted contributions. Letty glowed.

Those who are about to die salute you, Drew thought, quoting Travis who had quoted someone else (Drew had no idea who), just before Travis gave his life to save the Alliance. Then rudely *didn't* die — a fact with which Drew was slowly coming to terms.

It occurred to Drew in a non-judgmental way that Letty, in short of a month, had slept with three different men, and presumably, professed her love for all three. At least she had honorable intentions. As he considered it now, unfiltered through lust, since Toby was the deciding factor, why hadn't she just asked the boy who he preferred and left it at that? They'd all be home safe in their beds. Actually, he'd be in *her* bed — Travis still being dead and all — which would be an unqualified disaster. He returned to his task.

What fascinates Travis so about that woman? As Drew continued to watch Travis and the soon-to-be-happy-if-they-all-don't-die family, he noticed Toby periodically look up at Travis and then cast a sideways glance at the old lady as well. Toby was spoiled and precocious, but the boy was smart — too smart sometimes. He'd seen Travis' interest in the woman. Drew tried to signal Ma Kai, who was preoccupied watching Travis watch the woman while strenuously attempting to appear like he was *not* watching. *He's hopeless.* Drew caught Ma Kai's eye and inclined his head toward the guest quarters and then got up and left the salon.

~ ~ ∞ ~ ~

Sar Mode appreciated stimulating intrigue. Perhaps the reason she excelled at her calling as the appointed principal responsible for the Spread. However, in this instance, Travis Barnes' continued fascination with her—totally understandable—was endangering her plan. More accurately, the *evolutionary direction* of her plan since, now, she wielded little control. It appeared others were noticing Barnes' interest, as well. In a different setting, she would find an out-of-the-way spot to exchange hosts and maintain anonymity. Unfortunately, a third inexplicable death would trigger more than suspicions.

Of immediate concern were the two still-functional armada ships. How was that possible? She'd anticipated a certain percentage of the Pothlill would survive. Those who lived in remote areas or held positions that took them off-planet for extended periods would have avoided the incendiary nanoids.

But not one Diak should have survived. A few hours before the *Maris Stella* entered the wormhole, she'd transmitted precisely timed ignition signals for the destruction of Mass Primary and the execution of those Pothlill and Diak beyond the station, including the Diak crewing the armada in the K.U., though the ships themselves, now drones, remained under her control. That deal was struck. Both she and the humans would lose if her plan failed.

Since no armada vessel held any Pothlill, and all Diak on the station and in the Pothlill system were dead, who?—what?—controlled the two armada ships?

~ ~ ∞ ~ ~

The chairman of the Council of Superiors smiled in satisfaction as he eavesdropped on Sar Mode's musings, his connection shielded. She was not nearly as clever as she believed. Returning from an inspection tour, before her edict banning human hosts, he had innocently appropriated one for his own use. A number of the species, still uncatalogued, arrived on Mass Primary by the same vessel. He quickly learned—as Sar Mode, by her own edict, clearly understood—that self-preservation was a byproduct of free will and suspicions a byproduct of self-preservation. Though the other council members chose to delude themselves, it was clear to him that the Diak race was doomed. And, within a brief time after acquiring the human host, it became equally clear that Sar Mode, no longer dedicated solely to the Mass, had implemented a plan to save herself. With that clarity, he reluctantly abandoned his human for a safer choice and tracked Sar Mode's every move.

As with the many earth creatures that populated his new, human memories, honey proved to be a greater incentive for engineers than vinegar. The difference between sweet and sour long lost, the concept was obvious, nonetheless. He quickly isolated his own team, well-hidden and well-treated. His engineers focused on gaining command access to the lethal devices Sar Mode had dispersed to the Mass and to the Pothlill, while he focused on avoiding his own contamination. Both tasks made easier since Sar Mode saw fit to execute her own teams once they'd fulfilled their purpose. None survived to detect his tampering.

Confident but still cautious, he continued to monitor Sar Mode even as she monitored the *Maris Stella* communications.

~ ~ ∞ ~ ~

Aisha considered the armada. It could easily be a derelict graveyard. No shuttles ran back and forth between ships. No movement of any kind. Every gunship appeared unmanned and powered down except for two. And those appeared unmanned as well—perhaps someone just forgot to turn them off. *Not bloody likely.* But if the *Blinkum,* their mother ship, and the *Remarkable Mayzie,* joined the *Nod* behind WH5's distortion ring, together they might slip around the edge and into the tunnel. The two functional Diak ships would have little time to react. She relayed her proposal to the *Maris Stella.*

45 EASY PEASY

The *Maris Stella* and her two remaining shuttles, with the *Remarkable Mayzie*, assembled in a crescent formation on the null side of the wormhole's distortion ring. They'd divided the hostage population as space allowed between the four vessels, with Letty and Toby on the *Nod*. Though the shuttles enjoyed a limited weapons array, nothing would protect them from incoming fire for long. The *Nod*, piloted by Olcott — with the *Blinkum* and the *Mayzie* drawing fire, and the *Maris Stella* engaging the enemy ships — held the best chance of reaching the tunnel in one piece.

Letty threw an impressive fit when Travis refused to join her and Toby, but he stood his ground and remained on the mother ship. Ensuring their escape was his main objective, though he ached to be with them, and if luck held, make it safely home. After spending a night back in the K.U. in a real bed, eating real food, and interacting with other humans, returning to Diak space was the hardest thing he'd ever done. And he'd never talked to his mother.

Sitting next to Curtis in the salon, waiting for the action to begin, Travis thought about what he would do if they never made it back to the K.U. He could kill Sar Mode. Problem solved in this universe whatever happens. But if Sar Mode was a no-show in the K.U., she'd made it clear her armada would destroy every Alliance outpost in Zeta Quadrant and then move on the rest of the Alliance planets — if they hadn't already. The agreement was flawed from the beginning. What made Sir James think Sar Mode would honor its terms? He didn't; he had no other option.

Sar Mode would remain in his sight from this point on.

Curtis said something, but Travis missed it. "I'm sorry, what?"

"I said I wished I could talk to my mom. I usually speak to her once a week. She's probably going crazy by now. We're all the family left."

Touched, and a little surprised that Curtis had a mother, Travis opened up as well. "I know what you mean. 'Fact, I was just thinking the same thing. I didn't call my mom when I finally had the chance. I was coming back here anyway. At the last minute, it didn't seem cool to put her through it all twice."

"Why did you come back? I'd need to be tied and gagged."

"Letty."

"That's the dumbest thing I ever heard."

Over the intercom, Captain McDermott's instructions to the fleet interrupted their conversation:

> *"Everyone at battle stations, stay frosty – we're on the move. We've confirmed two armed Diak ships powered up with their sensors active. They're equidistant from each other on opposite edges of the armada. We're dropping from above, dead center in the line of fire. Blinkum and Mayzie will shield the Nod. Blinkum, return fire only if you're targeted directly. We want them focused on the Maris Stella. We'll take the brunt of incoming as long as we can, but with the two enemy ships so far apart, we can't engage them both at the same time. That's it. . . stay focused on your objectives."*

As the *Maris Stella* led the small fleet out from their positions behind the wormhole, Travis and Curtis headed to the bridge and strapped into the seats just behind the captain's station, unnoticed by either McDermott or Turrey. Without an assigned duty station, it offered the best vantage point to watch the action.

The first strike came from the Diak ship positioned to their starboard.

"Skipped off the forward shields," Turrey reported, though McDermott could see for himself as the data scrolled on the larger screen. The verbal blow-by-blow was for those without full tech access to the battle.

"Take it out if you can," McDermott ordered in an even voice.

A green streak on the screen represented their return fire and synced with the dull thump of the *Maris Stella's* forward laser cannons. A green square labeled *Nod* rose above the distortion ring and commenced a series of thruster fires to turn her toward the tunnel entrance. The *Blinkum* and the *Mayzie* shadowed the little vessel, staying between it and incoming fire.

The *Maris Stella* shook from a direct hit to her port.

"Projectile," Turrey said. "No damage."

"Maintain attitude and stay on the laser," McDermott ordered.

Travis watched a red line on the screen connect with the *Mayzie* — another projectile.

"Balog?" Captain McDermott called for a report.

"Port thrusters damaged. Still with the *Nod,* but don' know for how long."

Travis followed the action on the screen, stunned that they were taking fire. Why would Sar Mode allow her ships to fire on the vessel she occupied? He leaned toward Curtis, "I'm going back to the salon."

Curtis returned a distracted nod.

Entering the salon, Travis saw Ethel Grace, the woman's human name, standing ramrod straight in front of her lounger while the other passengers clung to their seats. Everyone looked terrified, but Sar Mode stared straight ahead, mouth ajar, her expression one of shock, not fear.

Travis went to her and pushed her roughly back down on the lounger. A nearby hostage made a noise in protest but quickly stepped away when Travis responded with a murderous look.

"Why are you allowing this?" he asked in a low, graveled voice. His hand went to his blaster. Sar Mode stared back at him, mouth slack. It occurred to him that perhaps she wasn't the one who'd ordered the ships to fire on the Earth vessels. She looked genuinely confused. Travis' head swung to survey the room.

The *Maris Stella* took fire once more from starboard. It was quickly followed by a second projectile strike portside.

Over the speaker, Travis heard Turrey's report and the captain's counter order:

"Starboard shields at eighty percent. Port shields holding."
"Engage thrusters and target the second Diak ship."

For the seconds it would take to attain the new firing position, the *Maris Stella* sat wide open to incoming laser and projectile fire from both ships.

Travis' hand tightened on the grip of his blaster, still in its holster.

Sar Mode's glance flicked to the blaster and back. "There is another. It controls the two armada ships. If you kill me, we will never know who it is or how it has control."

"Is it onboard?" Travis forced himself not to scan the room again.

"No. . . . I do not believe so. It is perhaps on one of the three smaller ships. The *Nod* would be its likely choice since it holds the best chance for escape. But, other than Taleen and her child, the assignments were made at random, or *I* would be on the *Nod* as well. Still. . . ."

The *Maris Stella* took another strike, again to its starboard. Overhead, McDermott issued a new order and Turrey responded:

"Compensate. Redirect ship's power to starboard shields.
Fire at port target when ready."
"Adjusting port cannon +25° relative, three clicks."

The ship's lights flickered and when out. A faint green glow emanated from the salon bulkheads. They were coated with bioluminescent organisms harvested from the freshwater oceans on Fahdeen. The glow provided only enough light to discern the outlines of furniture and the silhouetted heads and shoulders of the passengers. Travis felt his body rise from the deck. Sar Mode, still seated, rose in front of him, her features black against the faint light. Anyone not holding tight to something fastened to the deck or a bulkhead, floated upward as well. Either the captain shut down gravity to redirect ship's power to the shields, or they'd sustained damage to the gravity inductor.

Travis tapped his comm. "Captain, permission to launch the Diak ship I came in on. I can draw fire from the enemy on our starboard."

"We discussed this. You can't control that thing, and it could turn on us."

"It's not armed. Let me try."

Travis' stare pierced Sar Mode's arrogance. She bobbed her head in understanding.

"We'll blow you out of space with one wrong move," McDermott said.

"Roger that."

"Okay, then. The *Mayzie's* drifting—if you've got nav control, assume its objective. The *Nod's* still fifty klicks out."

"Yes, sir."

The ship rocked again. Those not anchored collided with one another or a bulkhead. Travis bumped the upper deck.

Over the speakers, Turrey called it: *"Starboard shields down."*

Travis pushed off in the direction of the shuttle bay. Halfway to the hatch, he crashed to the deck.

"Gravity restored," Turrey announced, a little late.

In the shuttle bay, Travis frantically searched for a sharp tool or anything else he could use to scratch out a message. He spotted a paint container and a nearby nozzle attachment. *Even better.*

Precious more minutes fled as he suited and powered up the ship. A green light on the pilot's panel next to a press pad displayed unintelligible symbols. During launch, the symbols transformed into English: *Weapons Obstruction.*

"What? Like an EMP?" Travis asked, guessing Sar Mode was monitoring the closed-circuit comm.

"EMP?"

"Electromagnetic pulse. . . eh. . . disrupter. Will it stop *our* ships as well?"

"No. Our power sources and transmission frequencies differ. It will only affect Diak ships, but you are not within range. You are piloting my personal scout vessel. The *disrupter* is a preemptive security measure meant to temporarily disable weapons when I approach one of our ships."

"Trust issues much?"

"I do not understand."

Travis ignored her.

He cleared the *Maris Stella*. The *Nod* and the *Blinkum* were behind him, closing on the wormhole eddy; the *Mayzie* floated directionless ahead and to starboard."

~ ~ ∞ ~ ~

Drew was suspended directly over the bed in Kai's and Ruby's cabin when Turrey restored gravity. He heard Kai hit the deck with the same force as the projectile that'd struck the ship. *Ouch!* Throughout, Ruby remained planted to the deck. *By what force?* Drew jumped from the bed and headed to the salon to check on the other passengers. They'd been attempting to learn if Ruby had telepathic contact with the enemy ships. It didn't appear so — or she failed to understand what they asked of her. *Or*, worse, she understood exactly.

"Keep at it," he called over his shoulder to Kai as he left.

In the salon, people were still picking themselves up from the deck. Several were massaging bruised appendages. A man leaned against the bar with one arm hanging at an impossible angle. Another used a napkin to dab at blood flowing from a cut on his forehead. Drew moved among the hostages to reassure them and instruct them to anchor to something in case the ship lost gravity again.

McDermott's voice came over his comm. *"Barnes, what the hell are you doing?"*

Drew, perhaps distracted during a telepathic connection to Ruby, must have missed something. *"What's going on — where's Barnes?"*

On cue, Barnes responded, *"Captain, you're clear from starboard. I'm heading directly into its trajectory. Think I can jam weapons control. Can't raise Nikko. Appears Mayzie's lost communications."*

McDermott came back. *"Repositioning."*

Drew headed to the shuttle bay to continue his damage check.

46 NO PLACE LIKE HOME

On the *Nod*, Letty tried to follow the battle, but the shuttle's only monitor hung above the pilot's station—difficult to see from her vantage point aft. She concentrated on the comm feed, which cut out every few seconds. It was like trying to connect moving dots. Somehow, Travis had joined the fight.

"Toby, did you make out what Travis is doing?"

"I think he launched his Diak ship."

"Why would he do that? It's not trustworthy, and it doesn't have weapons or shields—do you know if it has shields?"

"Travis didn't say."

Letty glanced out the view port, hoping to catch sight of the tiny Diak scout. They were descending toward the wormhole tunnel. For the first time, she allowed herself to believe they could make it through—but without Travis.

"Looks like we're goin' home," Olcott announced.

The hostages cheered; Letty and Toby exchanged worried glances. Letty put her arm around the boy and pulled him close. As they entered the tunnel, the shuttle lights dimmed, and the ship rocked gently, buffeted by the tunnel's current. A scant minute passed while everyone held their breaths.

When they emerged on the other side, Olcott fired thrusters to initiate a spiraling maneuver, cutting off the passenger's roar of relief before it gained volume. Laser fire from waiting Diak ships clipped the tip of the *Nod's* starboard wing. Olcott's quick reaction had saved them, but the laser strike sent the shuttle tumbling out to space.

~ ~ ∞ ~ ~

On the *Blinkum*, Austen pumped the air and hoorayed with the rest of the passengers when the *Nod* disappeared into the wormhole tunnel. Their celebration was short-lived. A hushed expectancy cloaked the shuttle's interior. They were next.

~ ~ ∞ ~ ~

Kyle Drubber stood, stoic, on the HQ command deck. Dark Landing remained on high alert. The Diak ships hadn't moved since the squadron of four left the main body. ESF sent probes to survey the battalion at close range. Translated, the probe's data string returned "unmanned but armed" only minutes before the ships opened fire on the station. After the first Diak incursion, the military had gifted the station with enhanced shields and weapons arrays. Fortunate, since the ESF battalion under Rear Admiral Sullivan's command was spread thin.

Rear Admiral Sullivan had relayed Sir James' order not to engage the Diak, even if they attacked, followed by his decision to ignore that order on the theory it was easier to face a court martial than the dishonor in dying without a fight. Captain Thomas had agreed, and when he returned to Security HQ, he shared the intelligence with the security staff and his ESF men — giving them the same option Sullivan gave him.

Now, with unanimous consensus, the battle was engaged. Though they'd been awaiting the attack for over a week, it took the untested crew in HQ command precious seconds to return fire. The captain ordered Earth Space Force long-timers to move among the security staff manning the station's defenses, few of whom had experienced a firefight. *Nothing like on-the-job training*, Kyle thought. He'd been assigned to monitor damage reports. As he watched the data roll on his screen and listened to the battle chatter, the Dark Landing civilian dispatcher made multiple attempts to ping through to him.

Annoyed, Kyle finally accepted the transmission. "A little busy here."

"I'm receiving a Mayday from the *Nod*. She claims to be a shuttle from the Taleen ship, the *Maris Stella*."

The shuttle's coordinates accompanied the tap. "Holy shit! That's out by the mine bases — what's left of them."

"Yes, sir. I relayed the information to ESF command, but I haven't received confirmation."

"They're a little busy, too. Okay — keep pinging them." With two squads out searching for the wormhole that Barnes came through and another behind Spud, guarding the bridge back to Diak space, the ESF were short on gunships to join the battle. They'd encircled the Diak fleet, but being few in number and spread far apart, were quickly decimated by half. The remaining ESF ships were forced to move out from the station and reduced to making strafing-like runs at the enemy. Since repositioning their ships for each run advertised their intent, they achieved little results and suffered more losses.

"I'll see what I can do from here. There's still patrols out that way?" Kyle said.

"Yes, sir."

Kyle looked for Captain Thomas. He'd left his station on the palisade to move closer to the action. Knowing better than to interrupt the battle chatter and worried Treetop would ignore a private tap, Kyle abandoned his post as well and headed over to him.

The captain was so engrossed by the display on the overhead monitor that Kyle spoke to him twice and finally shook his shoulder before getting his attention.

"What?!"

"Sorry. One of Miss Taleen's shuttles from the *Maris Stella* is taking fire out in the mine sector. The *Nod*."

Treetop relayed the information to Admiral Sullivan. "Yes, sir," he responded to whatever Sullivan said, and then returned to his station.

~ ~ ∞ ~ ~

Aisha Olcott struggled to level the *Nod*. Finally, accepting that the laser strike had damaged the ship's stabilizer, she gave up and switched to automatic, hoping the computer could do a better job. The shuttle continued to tumble out of control, distancing it from the enemy.

The processor read off a series of maneuvers as it implemented them—maneuvers Olcott thought exactly matched those she'd already tried. Evidently not. Slowly the little vessel responded to a repeated sequence of thruster discharges. The ship leveled but the thrusters would need to fire continuously to keep it that way, depleting its power supply in quick order.

Her passengers, surprisingly quiet up to then, issued a collective sigh.

"We're not out of the woods yet," Olcott said, never one to coddle.

~ ~ ∞ ~ ~

The *Mayzie* was on the *Blinkum's* tail. It emerged from the wormhole only two klicks behind her—just in time to see the shuttle's aft section disintegrate.

Austen! Austen is on that shuttle. The small amount of atmosphere loss indicated the airlock hatchway into the cabin might still be intact. As fast as those thoughts came to Nikko, he put them out of his mind to focus on the *Mayzie's* survival.

Before he could locate the cause of the *Blinkum's* damage, the *Mayzie* was peppered by shrapnel, which took out her main engine for good—the one they'd managed to get back online only long enough to make the crossing. The interior lights blinked off and then on again as the auxiliary engine kicked in. The auxiliary provided power for life support, but not much in the way of velocity. Nikko initiated an excruciatingly slow series of thruster blasts to shield the *Mayzie* on the null side of the wormhole, like they'd done in Diak space.

The *Blinkum* hung rudderless two klicks in front of them with four Diak gunships twenty klicks beyond that. He'd never outrun them. *And where is the Nod?*

As the *Mayzie* repositioned, the *Blinkum* fired on the Diak fleet, its laser burst going wide. Without maneuverability, the shuttle succeeded only in confirming to the Diak that she was out of commission.

From bad to worse. How did it go. . . out of the fryer into the burner? Nikko thought the idiom appropriate, though he had only a vague idea what a fryer or a burner was. Their only salvation was the *Maris Stella*. Usually the optimist, he doubted he'd ever see the ship again.

~ ~ ∞ ~ ~

The *Maris Stella's* port shields were still holding, but she'd lost all starboard shielding, and the last enemy salvo had disabled her starboard laser cannon as well. Travis dove toward the Diak ship, giving it everything he had, at once relieved that he and Sar Mode held communal control but irked to be at her mercy. Without weapons, the little scout ship's only defense was maneuverability. When the warship came into range, Sar Mode voiced the command to dampen its weapons' ability — or she could have been reciting the Diak Pledge of Allegiance for all he knew. Whatever language Sar Mode spoke, it lacked syllables and far exceeded his comprehension.

47 BATTLE WORN

With power devoted to maintaining stability, the *Nod* could only monitor the battle from fifty klicks out. The continuous thruster adjustments were depleting the shuttle's power, and soon they'd lose both thrusters *and* life support. If she cut power to the thrusters to extend life support, the final burst, without a counter thrust, would send them spiraling once more, away from any hope of assistance. As things stood, they had about thirty minutes before all systems failed. Staying in proximity to help — any help, even from the Diak, though unlikely — remained their single chance for survival.

Her passengers whispered among themselves but thankfully chose not to ask questions. After everything, they sensed the gravity of the situation and were uninterested in the minutia.

Frustrated with her inability to act, Olcott watched the battle on the command monitor. Her sister shuttle appeared as hapless as the *Nod*. Still in the line of fire, the *Blinkum* sat damaged and immobile. *Nod's* sensors showed life signs and indicated the vessel's weapons system were still operational — for all the good it did. The enemy ship would need to calculate the trajectory of the *Blinkum's* last laser blast, position itself directly in front of her cannon, and, without resistance, wait to be fired upon. Olcott wasn't optimistic that they'd be that cooperative.

The *Remarkable Mayzie*, also damaged, appeared to be making a run for it. . . slowly. Without checking sensors, Aisha could see that the salvage ship had lost her main engine. With neither Earth ship able to defend itself, the Diak were leisurely reforming for the kill. When they finished off the *Blinkum* and the *Mayzie*, they'd mop up and take out the *Nod*.

Come in Nod. *This is Commander Stephen Willis of the Earth Space Force responding to your Mayday. My patrol is fifteen minutes from your position. Report your situation.*

"Our situation is you're fifteen minutes too late, Commander."

As Aisha Olcott watched, the lead Diak ship launched a projectile that demolished the *Blinkum*.

~ ~ ∞ ~ ~

The *Maris Stella's* sensors no longer registered her shuttles, the *Nod* and the *Blinkum*, or the *Remarkable Mayzie*. The three ships had escaped through the wormhole to safety.

"What the hell is he doing?" Captain McDermott asked Turrey.

"No idea, sir. But it seems to be working."

The small Diak scout vessel piloted by Travis Barnes dove toward the enemy ship like a fly diving toward a flyswatter. Barnes' suicide strategy gave the *Maris Stella* — her starboard shields nonexistent — the time she needed to complete her thruster turn. With port shields now presented to the second Diak gunship, she made a run at the wormhole, returning fire as she went.

McDermott issued a shaky sigh of relief, and muttered, "That man was born to die a hero."

The ships computer announced, *Starboard shields down. Port shields at thirty percent.*

"Step on it, Turrey."

"Foot's through the deck now, sir."

Port shields at twenty percent.

"We're gonna make it!" Turrey yelled.

The ship rocked from a broadside strike. "Why would you say something like that, Turrey, you *idiot!*"

"I'm sorry, sir. I wasn't think —"

All shields down. Assessing nacelle damage. Main engine failure imminent.

Abruptly, the *Maris Stella* was engulfed in silence, her screens dark. They'd made it to the tunnel. From the salon, the roar of released emotions rose to a deafening level.

McDermott and Turrey looked at each other, startled by the sound.

"The passengers," McDermott said.

"*Right. . .* we have *passengers.* Permission to hurl now, sir?"

~ ~ ∞ ~ ~

Travis' dive silenced the gunship's lasers. But no way he trusted Sar Mode. He needed to get closer to it to render its laser cannons useless against him if they should come back online. Fire from the gunship on the opposite side of the armada quieted as well — but not from anything he'd done.

He knew nothing of the scout's capabilities and wondered how long the disrupter would suppress weapons fire. He got his answer when the gunship's lasers regained power and discharged once into empty space. Close-range gun turrets rose from its surface, tracking him.

"Sar Mode, come in. . . Sar Mode?"

Nothing. It appeared his ghost pilot was out of reach — hopefully through the wormhole. *Did everyone make it safely away?* He needed Sar Mode's help to access the scout's sensors. It was never lost on him that she might use the opportunity to rid herself of not only the gunship, but Travis, as well.

Snuggled into a shallow niche created by a protruding laser cannon, he'd moved dangerously close to the larger ship. The proximity alert should be sounding, but he suspected Sar Mode had disabled it. *What else has she disabled?* The only protection from gun turrets capable of revolving three-hundred-sixty degrees, was to position the scout so that any weapons fired at it might also damage the warship. They'd have to think twice before firing.

Now what? I can't wait here forever.

~ ~ ∞ ~ ~

With several hundred ships surrounding its perimeter, all firing on the station at the same time, Dark Landing suffered heavy damage.

Once again, the east armature anchoring the station to Spud appeared a prime target for the enemy. This time the arm was destroyed. Fortunately, with days to prepare, they suffered no casualties. The ESF evacuated all non-essential personnel and residents to Spud when the Diak ships first arrived. They would be safe unless the enemy boarded the facility. . . or took out the asteroid.

Kyle struggled to monitor the battle, the station damage reports, and the action in the outer mine sector. With no way to support the battle, he cut the chatter and focused on the other two arenas. They were receiving Maydays from four ships now, the *Maris Stella*, two of her shuttles, and the *Remarkable Mayzie*. *Remarkable* was an understatement.

An ESF unit was minutes from their position, with a second unit an hour out, when a transmission from the shuttle *Nod* advised that help would arrive too late, followed by the report that her sister shuttle, the *Blinkum*, had been destroyed.

~ ~ ∞ ~ ~

Drew found the *Maris Stella* shuttle bay empty — the Diak scout ship gone. Travis Barnes had joined the battle. He scanned the oversized bay looking for damage and headed to check the weapons and equipment room when the ship pitched violently from incoming fire. In the open, with nothing to hold onto, Drew hit the deck and rolled across its width, slamming against the emergency airlock hatch. Any telltale crack was lost to the blare of the ship's klaxon, but the resulting pain confirmed at least one broken rib. As he searched for something. . . anything. . . to grab onto, the ship steadied and the klaxon whoops quieted. He took a series of agonizing deep breaths. Confident the broken rib hadn't punctured a lung, he labored against the pain to stand upright, eyes closed in a grimace.

On his feet, he leaned back against the airlock hatch to catch his breath once more. At the sound of applause and screams of joy emanating from the salon, he opened his eyes. . . and unholstered his blaster.

~ ~ ∞ ~ ~

Sar Mode issued an order for the gunships to stand down. They ignored her and fired on the *Maris Stella* as she emerged from the wormhole. Without shields, the ship should have been an easy mark, but the Diak gunners, caught out of position, missed the target by a full klick.

Sar Mode accessed the *Maris Stella's* sensor data. It recorded only two other Earth ships. An expanding debris field publicized the *Blinkum's* fate. Crippled, the *Mayzie* made a valiant effort to elude the Diak. With the gunships occupied in dispatching the *Maris Stella*, the *Mayzie* might make it out of range, but that would buy her only minutes. The *Nod*, some distance away, appeared crippled as well — her thrusters firing in a continuous sequence. She wouldn't last much longer.

Her counterpoint controlled the gunships from the *Nod*. It played a dangerous game, risking its own life. Sar Mode burned to know the identity of the interloper and how long it had been scheming against her. She would find this one and destroy it utterly.

McDermott returned fire. *On my mark, three. . . two. . . one.* A miss.

The Diak unit withdrew to gain the advantage, each of the four ships on a separate course. Desperate to communicate with the gunships, Sar Mode transmitted her cease fire order across every available frequency.

"Ethel Grace?"

Nothing. She re-sent her transmission using older battle codes. Still no reaction.

The *Maris Stella* fired a continuous barrage. A direct hit reduced one of the enemy gunship's shields by fifty percent. But the Diak had attained firing attitude. The *Maris Stella's* and Sar Mode's life spans were measured in seconds.

"Ethel Grace?. . . Sar Mode?"

Jolted from her absorption at the sound of her name, Sar Mode looked at the human standing in front of her, his laser weapon pointed at her head.

"I have a message from Travis Barnes. *Fuck you!*" Drew Cutter fired his blaster.

~ ~ ∞ ~ ~

The gunship's laser had come disastrously close to destroying the *Nod and* the Chairman of the Council of Superiors. Luckily, the tactic worked well as a deception and removed the *Nod* from danger. It seemed rescue by Earth forces was minutes away. The Diak gunships would continue their attack until the moment of their arrival. He'd intended to destroy the other Earth vessels, leaving only the *Nod* and her passengers surviving, but that seemed unlikely now.

With a note of sorrow, he severed his connection to the two armada gunships left behind in Diak space. When the battle with the Known Universe defenders concluded, nothing of the once invincible Diak armada would endure.

The remaining hurdle was made harder by the existence of the *Maris Stella*. Sar Mode seemed no longer a threat. What happened to her he did not know, but she must have realized at the end that there was another Diak. Had she shared the information with the one named Travis or another? Somehow, he must overcome the scrutiny awaiting him at Dark Landing and find his way off. The damage and chaos he'd caused there—just short of destruction—would benefit his escape. *We will not die today.*

~ ~ ∞ ~ ~

The Diak gunships ceased fire. *Why?* Captain McDermott targeted the nearest ship. The *Maris Stella's* laser split it in two parts. They'd dropped their shields as well. *What the hell?* It seemed, at every turn, the Diak fought only to give up once they inflicted damage and achieved the clear advantage. McDermott was baffled. What made the difference?

As they targeted a second gunship, the cavalry arrived in the form of an ESF patrol unit. The patrol moved in and quickly destroyed the remaining Diak ships, none of which put up a fight.

Turrey turned to the captain. "Sir. . . *what the hell?*"

"Don' know, don' care. But, like my mom always said, where there's a pattern, there's a design."

Billy Grabe entered the bridge. "Cap'n, we have injured passengers, but nothin' too serious. But. . . Drew Cutter. . . terminated that ole lady hostage, Ethel Grace. Blew her freaking head right off. Seems Barnes left a message in the shuttle bay sayin' she was Sar Mode."

McDermott fell into his captain's chair too weary to react. "Have Whacker. . . ." Whacker was piloting the *Blinkum*. The captain steeled himself against the groundswell of loss that he'd been postponing until this moment. "Take Cutter into custody until we can sort it out." They'd lost three crew in all, and Travis Barnes. But they'd gotten the job done and made it home.

McDermott accepted a closed transmission from Sir James. "Congratulations, Captain. You've pulled off a miracle."

"I'm not certain I had anything to do with it, sir."

"Oh. . .? I hope to be at your debriefing in person. We'll chat then. By the way, where is Commander Barnes?"

"With all due respect, sir, you may need to commission a second series of statues. That guy was born to die."

"I'm saddened to hear that."

McDermott didn't think Sir James sounded at all *saddened*.

Sir James continued. "Willis' ESF unit will escort, or tow as necessary, your ships to Dark Landing. Inexplicably, they also prevailed against the Diak attack, though the station suffered extensive damage. As far as I know, all docking bays are out of commission. We hope one or two will be back online by the time you arrive. But it's possible you'll be inconvenienced a bit longer. Again, congratulations. I look forward to meeting you."

"Thank you, sir. Before you go, I want to report a situation."

"Yes?"

"Drew Cutter shot and killed one of the rescued hostages. He claims she was Sar Mode. Travis Barnes apparently left a message to that effect."

There was a long, uncomfortable silence.

"I see. . . well. . . that tidies things up, doesn't it?"

You would know, Sir. I'm betting. McDermott thought but didn't say aloud. So much for the mystery of the malfunctioning scanner. Of course, Sar Mode wasn't onboard yet when it went down the first time. But Travis Barnes was.

When the second patrol unit arrived to guard the wormhole, the first unit escorted the *Maris Stella* to Dark Landing, with the *Nod* and her passengers safely back onboard the mother ship, and the *Remarkable Mayzie* limping along at her side.

~ ~ ∞ ~ ~

The four ESF gunships, spread equidistance above and below one another in a semicircle in front of the Diak wormhole, settled in to guard the entrance and wait for reinforcements. Three uneventful hours passed while the pilots amused themselves sharing past adventures and retelling old jokes.

"Spender," the captain said, "you've told that joke a hundred times now. Is that the only one you know?"

"You guys still don't get it — the *Bindian* was sitting on the bar stool. *See?* How'd he get up there? That's what's so funny."

"No, Spender — it's not funny. You're the one that doesn't get. . . . Head's up!" A small, alien ship popped through the tunnel. The captain had seen that same craft not too long ago. "*Hold fire!*"

Their comms pinged. "Me again, *Travis Barnes* here. Still not armed. Please don't shoot. I'll be right with you — just sending a quick message to my mom."

48 REMAINDERS

"Here." Timmons corralled the four hostages assigned to him. "I'll escort you to med-lab. Everyone's scanned clean so far, so no worries." The security staffer smiled reassuringly as he herded them out of holding.

Along the marked route, residents cleaning up from the battle waved and cheered at Timmons' group. With wan smiles, the hostages waved back. Some looked in shock and others in mourning, except for the Bahdaneian, who stared forward with a stoic expression.

In the reception area at med-lab, Timmons turned them over to a nurse, then left after shaking each one's hand and wishing them good luck. He entered the conveyer just outside med-lab and studied the map on the back of the closed door.

"Number 42."

~ ~ ∞ ~ ~

"*Who* escorted them to med-lab?" Kyle asked.

"Timmons. He's off comm," Jonesy said.

Kyle turned to Captain Thomas. "That's not good, sir. There's no one more dependable than Timmons."

Jonesy nodded agreement.

Timmons had escorted the last group but failed to return to HQ. His comm went unanswered, and his quarters were empty.

"Who was in his group?" Captain Thomas asked.

Jonesy consulted his handheld, "A woman, thirty, with high blood pressure, two men, one fifty and one sixty-two, and one of the Bahdaneians — age undetermined. Our *Muck* agent, Victoria Windsor, arrived a couple hours ago and requested the two Bahdaneians be cleared for her debriefing. Do you need everyone's names and personal data?"

"Send it to me. And each was cleared without issue?"

Jonesy nodded. "Yep. And one of our guys just completed a physical roster check. Every hostage and crew member are accounted for."

"Send out a staff-only alert for Timmons and put together two search teams. I can pull from the ESF if you need more men."

Kyle and Jonesy left, and Captain Thomas initiated a priority tap to Admiral Sullivan. The admiral, in the security conference room on a feed with Sir James Hawking-Barstow, asked Captain Thomas to join him.

"They're all accounted for — everyone?" Sir James asked the captain when he arrived.

"Yes, sir. Only Timmons is missing."

"If a Diak took over his body, there should be a corresponding dead one, right? No stray corpses lying around?"

"None that we're aware of, sir. Teams are searching the station now. We. . . ." Captain Thomas tapped his comm to accept a transmission. "*Shit!* Excuse me — my apologies, sir. There *is* a dead body: A hostage, thought to be asleep in one of the cells. His name was checked off the roster."

Sir James paused in thought before responding to the news. "This must be confined to Dark Landing. As I understand it, no ships can dock there?"

Thomas glanced at Sullivan, who took the question. "No large ships, sir. One of the berths is accessible to shuttles. Where we can, we're assisting with the backlog of traffic that's been waiting in the void for our destruction or salvation. They're dropping and picking up passengers and cargo using shuttles. I'm ordering it stopped now." He tapped his comm.

While the admiral relayed his order, Captain Thomas sent one of the search teams to check the dock area and to see that the admiral's order was enforced.

When Sir James regained both their attentions, he said, "I want hourly updates until Timmons is found. And send in Commander Barnes. I'd like to congratulate him privately. The man is a living legend."

Captain Thomas summoned Travis. As the two ESF officers left the conference room, they were met at the hatch by Mitchell Jones, Security Nightshift Commander.

"We found Timmons body in Number 42. He was propped up at a table with a drink in front of him. There've been quite a few completed shuttle trips since he disappeared. Two of the vessels, a cargo and a passenger ship, have already departed."

The three men turned back to Sir James' image.

"Send me the registries for every ship there today," he commanded. "Secure the dock until I order otherwise. The Earth Defense Council is taking immediate jurisdiction. I want the information contained. From this point forward, no one is to discuss the matter, internally or otherwise. Use whatever threats or inducements will work. Sullivan, make a plausible excuse for Timmons' death for the record and his family."

~ ~ ∞ ~ ~

When the hatch sealed behind Travis, Sir James said, "You were correct, Barnes. There was at least one other Diak among the hostages. It's killed two men in the short time it's been there."

"I heard, sir. Word travels fast."

"We have to plug the gossip. There's absolutely no way to pursue the alien and also maintain confidentiality. That reality was one of the cards Sar Mode played."

"She was right—you can't keep something of this nature under wraps."

Sir James went on. "I have no choice but to extend my agreement with Sar Mode to this one, and pray it understands discretion."

"Curious though. Unless Sar Mode shared the information, how would this other one know what the terms *are*?"

The chairman ignored Travis' question. "In twelve hours, I'll advise Sullivan that the Diak has been captured and neutralized. I'm asking you to spread this information as inconspicuously as possible if you hear anything to the contrary from the men. If it does get out, it must get out as successfully resolved. Use your imagination — perhaps its remains were launched toward the nearest black hole. In a few years, if we're lucky, it'll be one more absurd space legend."

"I understand, sir."

"Thank you for your service, Commander. If all goes well, there should be no need for us to speak again. I wish you health, peace, and prosperity. *End transmission.*"

The feed ended abruptly.

You're welcome, sir. Same to you, sir. What the shit, *sir?*

Travis ordered the lights off and sat in the dark, mentally replaying the conversation. Was Sir James sincere? He planned to let this guy go and hope for the best? On the other hand, what else could he do? The Earth Defense Council Chairman was right: No organized search effort of this consequence could be kept secret. Word would get out. Someone would talk to the press. The public would demand an investigation. There'd be widespread panic. Of course, he could search on his own — maybe that's what Sir James expected of him.

Nah. When he and Letty were settled back on Earth, he'd suggest to her that all Taleen employees should be periodically scanned.

~ ~ ∞ ~ ~

Drew and Curtis sat in his office — his old-new office. They'd just concluded a meeting with the head of CoachStop Management. After accepting a fifteen percent salary reduction, they'd reinstated Drew as chief of security on Dark Landing. Curtis dodged immediate termination only because the station remained short-handed. But he knew they'd let him go as soon as they re-staffed. He saved CoachStop the trouble by submitting his resignation but agreed to continue as acting chief of administration for six months or until the position was filled, whichever came first. Drew and Curtis jointly recommended a subordinate doctor who'd been stationed on Dark Landing for several years as the new chief of medicine. The boss was taking their recommendation under consideration.

"It's rotten about Hargreaves," Drew said. He was sitting on the lounger in front of the desk. "I just met her, but she seemed a decent sort."

"I didn't know her that well myself. I pegged her as sneaky when we first met — got that right. But she proved herself on Mass Primary. She had guts."

The two men sat silent for several seconds.

"Soooo. . . " Drew finally said.

"*Soooo*. . . so what?"

"So, you're in my chair, asshole."

Curtis picked up a small horse statue and his handheld from the desktop and switched places with Drew.

Drew wriggled his rear into the chair seat, plopped his feet on the desk, laced his hands behind his head, and then issued a deep sigh of satisfaction. He looked at Curtis. "What's your long-range plans?"

"The Mine, of course."

"The nightclub? We never really talked about it much, but you think the co-op's going to lease you the facility? Even if they did, can you afford it?"

"No, but I have an idea."

"Oh?"

Before Curtis could explain his plan, Nikko appeared in the hatchway. "Mind if I join you?"

"Come on in," Drew said.

Nikko dragged a chair from against the bulkhead to the front of Drew's desk. "I just finished talking to my *Muck* handler. They'd like me to stay on a bit longer if that's not a problem. There's still the matter of drug traffic flowing through Dark Landing."

"No problem, as long as you share what you find with me," Drew said. "But I'd think all the shooting and with the military hanging out here put a serious dent in whoever was doing whatever in that regard."

Nikko shrugged and looked at Curtis. "You need to find a new assistant."

"Not me. I won't be working here much longer."

"The Mine?"

"Yep — gonna be a thing."

"That'll take a while."

"It will. But the ESF won't be leaving soon anyway."

"Don't suppose you want a partner. I might be interested when I wrap this other thing up. Fifty-fifty."

"Might consider it. Eighty-twenty."

"Not gonna happen." Nikko shook his head. "Fifty-fifty or nothing."

Curtis countered. "Maybe seventy-thirty. I'll have to think about it."

Drew interrupted their negotiation. "You guys want to take this outside? I need to get to work. Got to start the official report for CoachStop. Plus, my predecessor wasn't big on recordkeeping, and the override codes need changing."

~ ~ ∞ ~ ~

That evening, Drew and Letty sat together in a booth in Number 42 saying their final goodbyes. The subject of Xander Crawford never came up. The station's departure logs showed he'd left Dark Landing the morning after Drew rolled him off the *Maris Stella*.

"One more thing," Drew said. "I. . . ah, need a favor for a friend."

"Sure, what?"

"Think you could float Curtis a loan at a good rate?"

"The Mine! You want your *job* back."

"I do. I *got* my job back."

"Wow, congratulations. One condition."

"Anything."

"You take Toby for a month each year."

"Except that." Drew laughed. "Gods, *yes*." His heart swelled. He'd wanted to broach the subject with her earlier but held off. With Travis in the picture, he was afraid it'd shift their happy family dynamic too soon. He looked away for a few seconds to blink the moisture from his eyes. At some point in the middle of all that'd happened, he'd developed an honest affection toward the bugger.

Letty went on. "It'll be up to Toby—but he'll be thrilled. And Travis might have something to say about it, too."

"Of course." Drew turned and took her in his arms. "You know I'll always love you, no matter how stupid you are and how angry I get," he said. The generosity of her proposal shaded everything that went before. In moments like this, it was easy to forgive, and to ascribe actions and words to extraordinary circumstances.

"I know. Me too—you—but the opposite of what you said."

"*Thanks?* I think. One last kiss while it's still legal?"

Had he witnessed it, the kiss went a bit longer than Travis might have liked.

Drew'd had a private conversation with Travis earlier. He seemed genuinely shocked that Taleen Industries was in possession of antimatter weapons but *not* so shocked that Letty was prepared to use them. They both expressed fear of what the enforcers of the Amalgamation Decree of Intelligent Beings might do if they found out. Along with her engineers and scientists, Letty's life would be in danger. Travis vowed to watch over her and to let Drew know if he heard anything. Drew doubted, if that time came, they would be forewarned.

GLOSSARY

(For the new and returning readers, the entries below describe characters, organizations, and locations introduced in Book 1.)

BAHDANE - Along with Earth, Bahdane is one of the five Alliance planets. Bahdane has an Earth-like environment and is the only alien race which lives and works among Earthlings. Larger and bulkier than the average human, they are covered in short, glossy black fur, with an extended snout (similar to a seal), and have long, drooping ears which brush their shoulders. The ears are occasionally worn tied in a topknot on their heads. Bahdaneians make excellent administrators and have exceptional linguistic skills. Because of this, they are favored employees of the Multi-World Coalition for Travel and Trade.

BENNY (BENSON CAPONE) - Senior dock foreman on Dark Landing. Benny's been on the job for almost thirty years. Loyal and efficient but often caught between the conflicting objectives of the security and administration departments, he's also practiced at covering his ass and protecting his fast-approaching retirement and pension.

BIN – Bin, a hot, desert planet with gravity several times stronger than Earth's, is one of the five Alliance planets. Bin are squat, big-jointed aliens, with shiny exoskeletons, who move crab-like. Barely topping four feet, they can stand when threatened. Bin are a proud race, easily insulted.

CAMDU - A mountain planet with one-third Earth's gravity, and one of the five Alliance planets. Within their matriarchal society, Camdulings are intelligent and forthright. Physically, they are tall and willowy — males average ten feet, and females twelve to fifteen feet — with delicate features and deep azure blue skin. Similar to humans, they have two arms and two legs but boast a fifth appendage that retracts against their lower bodies when not in use, and serves as a third arm or leg, depending on the need.

CURTIS WALKER - Previously dayshift commander on Dark Landing, and acting chief of administration during the Diak threat, Curtis was promoted to chief of security when Drew Cutter left the station. Curtis's primary concern is *Curtis*, though flickers of something resembling empathy emerge in times of stress. Curtis's dream is to open a nightclub, *The Mine*, on Spud. Toward that goal, he's not above engaging in petty criminal activities.

DARK LANDING – A space station, Dark Landing caters to interplanetary trade and is a staging point for space science organizations. The last station in the trade relay, and as far as you can dock from any developed planet in the Known Universe, its proximity to multiple, stabilized wormholes makes it a transit hub for the occasional luxury passenger ship. But the station lacks accommodation and amenities to attract those ships or their passengers for stays longer than a day or two.

DOC (DR. TAMMY JAMESON) - Doc Jameson, an easy-going, competent professional, respected and liked by all, is chief of medical on Dark Landing. Upon learning of the Diak nanoids and their purpose, and in her eagerness to leave a legacy, she immediately grasps the nanoids' potential to render humans and aliens nearly immortal — *if* they can be controlled.

DREW (ANDREW VINCENT CUTTER) – On his third tour as chief of security on Dark Landing, he and Letty uncovered the nanoid contamination. Later, when the Diak threat was believed to be neutralized, Letty rebuffed his romantic advances. Allowing his insecurities to control his actions, Drew left the station to "find himself," and to overcome his fears and self-doubt. Drew reluctantly recommended his dayshift commander, Curtis Walker, as his replacement.

EDC (EARTH DEFENSE COUNCIL) - The EDC provides civilian oversight for Earth's military forces and intelligence gathering agencies. The council is headed by Sir James Hawking-Barstow.

ESF (EARTH SPACE FORCE) - Earth's military defense force. The ESF deteriorated over many years of peace and prosperity. Earth and the other Alliance planets are in the process of rebuilding their militaries, fearing that the Diak may one day return. A battalion commanded by Rear Admiral Jensen Sullivan, is temporarily stationed on Spud.

EARTH TECHNOLOGY OVERSIGHT COMMISSION (ETOC) - Headed by Secretary Anne Rostenkowski, the ETOC oversees and enforces the compliance of Earth technology regulations, along with the import/export of technology between Earth and aligned and nonaligned worlds.

ELEANOR FITZWILLIAM-BENNETT - Earth Governor, and sister of Martin Fitzwilliam, former chief of administration on Dark Landing, she conspired with the Diak to aid their plans for invading the Alliance for the promise of vast wealth and immortality. When the Diak threat was neutralized Governor Fitzwilliam-Bennett disappeared.

FAHDEEN - With Earth, one of the five Alliance planets. The Fahdeen are distantly related to the Bahdane and is the least friendly of the Alliance members. Except for its participation in the Multi-World Coalition for Travel and Trade, Fahdeen rarely interact directly with the other planets.

FITZ (MARTIN FITZWILLIAM) - Previously chief of administration on Dark Landing, Fitz conspired (with his sister, the Earth governor) to aid the Diak in preparing for invasion of the Aligned planets. Fitz was infected with Diak nanoids and eventually became the physical host for a Diak entity.

HOOKER MONKS - In preparation for invasion, the Diak introduced a nanoid virus to the Alliance planets. Initially transmitted by prostitutes through the exchange of bodily fluids, the virus soon entered the general populations. Three unlicensed prostitutes carrying the nanoids came to Dark Landing disguised as Praetorian Monks.

JONESY (MITCHELL JONES) - Once a lead security crew member, Jonesy was promoted to nightshift commander under Curtis Walker, Acting Chief of Security.

K.U. (KNOWN UNIVERSE) - That part of the greater universe which has been explored and mapped by aligned and non-aligned civilizations.

KYLE DRUBBER - Once the assistant nightshift commander, Kyle was promoted to a full commander status by Curtis Walker, the then acting chief of administration.

LETTY (KATHERINE LETECIA TALEEN) - Letty, orphaned as a toddler, is the sole heiress of Taleen Industries, the largest conglomerate in the K.U. At age twenty-four, she arrived on Dark Landing in search of her guardian and father figure, George Speller, who had been missing for several months. At the end of the Diak threat, she returned to Earth to take the reins as chairman of the board at Taleen Industries, a position previously filled by her now deceased guardian.

MARIGOLD - Dark Landing's shuttle. The shuttle and its occupants, piloted by Travis Barnes, accidentally crossed a wormhole (bridge) into Diak space.

MCTT or *MUCK* (MULTI-WORLD COALITION FOR TRAVEL & TRADE) - The MCTT was formed to regulate travel and trade throughout the K.U. Run by a fifteen-member board (three members from each Alliance planet) it is self-funded by fees and tariffs. MCTT also serves as the off-world police force for Alliance members when requested to do so and sometimes acts independent of Alliance authorization. As with any enforcement agency, MCTT is considered necessary, but not always trustworthy.

NIKKO BALOG - Involved with Curtis Walker in petty criminal activities, he left his position of compliance officer on the *Temperance* to work as Curtis's assistant on Dark Landing. Although there is some mystery about his origin, he is thought to be Earth Eastern European and speaks with a heavy Slavic accent.

PRESTON THE PIGEON - With no obvious explanation as to how the pigeon got past the station's environmental sensors, its appearance on Dark Landing coincided with a sequence of events leading to the discovery of the Diak threat. Preoccupied with more urgent concerns, Preston's presence went unchallenged. This allowed the station residents to become attached to the bird and to establish a local Audubon Society chapter for its protection.

SAR MODE - The appointed principal and commander of the Diak armada, she is charged with invading and colonizing new civilizations to accommodate the *Spread* of the Diak race and to provide fresh hosts for Diaks as their turning nears. Diaks are said to have turned when all the biological cells in the host bodies have been transmuted to nanoids, at which point the Diak must transfer to a new host or cease to exist.

SPUD - The large asteroid to which Dark Landing is attached by two, two-kilometer-long arms. The arms also serve as passages to Spud's underground installation (initially a mine and living quarters during the station's construction) which serves as a temporary bivouac for an Earth Space Force (ESF) battalion awaiting construction of the new Zeta Quadrant military base.

TSF (TALEEN SECURITY FORCE) - Described as "larger, better trained, and better armed than most planet militaries," the TSF is Taleen Industries' civilian security force. Consisting primarily of humans, it also employs native alien branches on each Alliance planet. Its members are trained in multiple disciplines and freely provide assistance throughout the Alliance for all level of emergencies. While providing these philanthropic services, TSF collects massive amounts of data which is catalogued by Taleen Industries and used to benefit its thousands of commercial enterprises.

TOBY (TOBIAS GOLDSTEEN-TALEEN) - Eight years old when his parents were killed in a Diak raid, he became one of several thousand refugees on Dark Landing, initially under the care of Drew Cutter. After the Diak threat was neutralized, Toby went to Earth with Letty Taleen, and she adopted the boy.

TRAVIS BARNES - A fleet commander with the Taleen Security Force (and ex-lover of Letty Taleen), Travis sacrificed himself to neutralize the Diak threat. A statue in his honor now stands in the middle of the Dark Landing bazaar.

WORMHOLE (BRIDGE, TUNNEL, DOOR) - Stabilized wormholes provide one-way shortcuts through space. While light-years measure real distance, travel distances are calculated in days and weeks, or hops. Wormholes appear in clusters and in greater numbers than believed centuries earlier. When one is located, there are often others at the opposite end to carry a ship, if not precisely in the reverse direction, then to another cluster with a wormhole headed the right way. As a result, travel times can vary significantly between going to a location and returning to the starting point. The Known Universe resembles a patchwork quilt with vast areas of space still unreachable in real time, and where wormhole access will never be discovered.

AUTHOR NOTE

Book reviews are crucial to all authors. I hope you enjoyed *Mass Primary*. Please take a moment to leave your honest review on its Amazon sales page. It can be as simple as one or two sentences. Perhaps there was something you particularly liked about the story: the action, the humor, a character, or an unexpected plot twist. I will be forever grateful.

Thank you for reading,
Robin Praytor